Praise for K. A. Mitchell's *Regularly Scheduled Life*

Rating: 5 Angels and a Recommended Read "K.A Mitchell has written a thought provoking, deeply emotional piece with Regularly Scheduled Life and I didn't want to go back to my own regularly scheduled life when it was over."

~ *Fallen Angel Reviews*

Rating: 5 Nymphs "A brilliant and well constructed romance that I found fascinating."

~ *Literary Nymphs*

Look for these titles by

K. A. Mitchell

Now Available:

Hot Ticket
Midsummer Night's Steam: Custom Ride
Diving in Deep
Collision Course

Print Anthology
Midsummer Night's Steam: Temperature's Rising

Regularly Scheduled Life

K. A. Mitchell

A Samhain Publishing, Ltd. publication.

Samhain Publishing, Ltd.
577 Mulberry Street, Suite 1520
Macon, GA 31201
www.samhainpublishing.com

Regularly Scheduled Life

Print ISBN: 978-1-60504-307-4
Digital ISBN: 1-60504-184-X

Editing by Sasha Knight
Cover by Anne Cain

First Samhain Publishing, Ltd. electronic publication: August 2008
First Samhain Publishing, Ltd. print publication: June 2009

Dedication

For Erin. It's all your fault.

Chapter One

"So, Sean runs like he's got a piano in his back pocket and he's already had a six pack before the game because the umps were late, but he's still trying to score from second."

Kyle listened to Tony's story while eyeing his own half-eaten pork Marsala. How many more bites could he manage before he'd be too full for that chocolate peanut butter pie? You couldn't come to Royal Mile and not have that pie. It was extra hard when the executive chef was sitting at your table, even if the chef's boyfriend got so enthusiastic with his story that he made the dishes jump.

Tony went on. "The ball gets to home when Sean's like a step from third, but does he go back? No. He goes for the plate. Takes out the catcher and gets tossed from the game. He's so pissed he goes over to the bench and kicks the shit out of it until he breaks his ankle. So that story about him being on crutches that weekend because of scoring the game-winning run is total—"

The hum hit Kyle's skin first. He didn't have to look to know who was there. Kyle's breath quickened and when he finally did look up, his heart stuttered like the clutch on his last car.

So fucking hot. A full-body rush every time he saw Sean. Light brown hair that was just long enough to need Kyle to brush it back, eyes that could shift from blue to grey with clothes or mood. Sean's eyes now reflected the royal blue of the shirt that clung to his broad shoulders, tucked in charcoal grey pants that showed off narrow hips and strong thighs.

"Dude." Tony flicked Kyle's hand where it had frozen on his wineglass. "What? Do I have something on my face?" Tony's eyes widened in a leer. "Want to lick it off?" As he leaned across the table, his boyfriend Jack cuffed him lightly on the back of the head.

Kyle's eyes must have flickered, or maybe his smile gave it away because Tony's amused leer vanished.

"Ah shit. He's right behind me, isn't he?"

"Yup." Sean came around the table. His hand slid across Kyle's shoulders as he retook his seat. "And why the hell you trying to fuck with my hero status in front of my boyfriend, dude?"

"Just proving a point," Tony said.

"Badly." Kyle rubbed his leg against Sean's under the table. "Sean told me about that years ago."

"Bullshit."

"He did. The bench was on the first baseline. Fresh green paint. He threw his glove first."

Sean put a hand on Kyle's thigh. The hum on Kyle's skin turned to a buzz, a low pulse of arousal, warming rather than urgent.

"So what point was Tony trying to prove?"

Jack nodded at the waitress who was serving, and she began to clear the dishes. After she took their dessert orders, Jack explained, "Tony bet me that the secret to a happy long-term relationship is—how did he put it—'a selective application of the truth'?"

"Otherwise known as lying." Kyle turned to look at Sean.

Sean's fingers teased along Kyle's inseam. They could take the chocolate peanut butter pie to go.

"So we're the example?" Sean began a long, slow stroke over the thigh.

"Six years tomorrow, dude. Isn't that why we're here?" Tony said.

"Ha. No lies. I win." Jack's smile was dangerous as he turned to face Tony. "Slap bet. You're going to pay sooner or later."

"Pick later and you can slap me with your dick." Tony ran his tongue over his lips.

The way Jack shifted in his chair suggested he liked the idea.

"What's a slap bet?" Sean asked.

"You lose you get slapped. It's from that TV show Tony loves." Jack rubbed the back of Tony's neck.

"An American classic, I'm sure." Kyle rolled his eyes.

"You know, man, there were some good comedies made after *Some Like It Hot.*" Tony leaned into Jack's caress.

"I liked *Airplane.*" Kyle finished off his wine.

Sean gave Kyle's thigh a squeeze. "Tony just watches because he always had a crush on Doogie Howser."

Tony looked down his nose. "Just goes to show you that even at thirteen I had highly accurate gaydar."

All four of them were still laughing when the waitress brought their coffee and desserts. As Sean offered a forkful of his caramel apple pie, Kyle felt like he was in an old Michelob commercial. Life really didn't get better than this.

ß

Sean closed his eyes and leaned back into his morning shower. After running his hand through his hair, he glanced at his fingers. No loose strands. Thirty-five years old and still not ready for Rogaine. He pictured his father and grandfather with a shudder.

The shower curtain jerked open. Kyle stepped in front of him, yawning.

Even after six years the sight of his lover hadn't stopped making Sean's stomach drop faster than the tallest roller coaster in Cedar Point. Kyle's black curls were a sexy bedheaded mess, and the rest of him—God, high cheekbones, full lips spread wide in a yawn. This late in October his dark brown tan had faded to bronze skin outlining hard muscles sprinkled with dark hair that v-ed from between his nipples to his thick cock.

Kyle blinked at him with sleepy dark eyes.

"Do you have to be at work early or something?" Sean asked.

"Nope."

"Then why are you up at five thirty?"

"It's our anniversary, *chulo*. I've got things planned." Kyle grabbed Sean's hips and turned him away from the spray before brushing a kiss across his lips.

"Oh?"

"Yep."

Sean's legs wobbled as Kyle dropped to his knees in front of him. "Okay then." Kyle's breath on his cock made Sean's voice thin. He braced a hand on the tiles and threaded the other through the thick curls he loved to touch.

Kyle ducked his head to suck on his balls, the hard, deep tugs Sean couldn't stand once he got really turned on. Kyle's morning stubble rasped across his dick as it slid along his cheek. In no time, Sean's cock had lengthened until the tip was rubbing against Kyle's ear.

"Kyle."

"Yes, *papi*?" Kyle mouthed the root, sucking and lapping as he made his way up to tongue the head.

Sean's knees got a little shakier. He'd only been awake for ten minutes. He might not be ready for Rogaine, but even at thirty he'd had trouble keeping his footing when on the receiving end of one of Kyle's blowjobs. He grabbed Kyle's head and pulled him forward as he sank against the back wall.

"Better?" Kyle looked up at him and winked.

God, he loved this man. He was about to tell him when Kyle's mouth screwed down around him and he forgot how to make words.

The suction started soft, mostly wet-hot licks of his tongue under the head until Sean's hand got frantic in his lover's thick hair. Kyle started going faster, taking him to the back of his throat and sucking hard before pulling off until his lips were tight around the crown. One hand jerked the base while his other fingers wandered to press on Sean's perineum. Sean didn't know how many times the same thought had run through his head, but every time Kyle went down on him was better than the last. Kyle used his mouth and lips and the lightest touch of his teeth, knew every single thing to do to make Sean shoot until there was a supernova behind his squeezed-shut eyelids.

When he managed to peel open his eyes, Kyle was standing under the spray, rinsing Sean's come off his face. "Don't be late for work."

"Now you worry about that?"

Kyle's teeth flashed white as he grinned and then leaned in to kiss him. "Dinner at Parillo's. More celebrating later."

Sean reached for Kyle's cock. "More celebrating now."

"It's almost six." Kyle's breath hitched.

"Must be losing your touch."

Kyle poked him in the stomach. "I'll take care of me. Don't be late." The sigh in his voice sealed the deal.

"Wanna watch you come." Sean reached back and soaped up his free hand. "Love to watch you come."

"Sean—"

Kyle didn't get much further than that. Sean pressed him into the side wall, soap-slick hand jacking Kyle fast. He listened to the harsh gasps, Kyle's deep voice going higher as he braced himself with his hands on Sean's shoulders.

And Sean knew just what would get him there even quicker. He lapped his neck, mouth slipping to the soft skin just under his ear, and bit down.

"Shit." Kyle's hips jerked, fucking into his fist.

A lick, another deep, sucking bite and Kyle's hips stuttered. Sean lifted his head to watch Kyle groan and shake as he coated Sean's hand with spunk.

"Bastard." Kyle squeezed his shoulders. "I do have to go to work today."

"It's a good thing your hair is long enough then." Sean laid another lick on the tiny bruise. "I love you."

"And I love you more than our California Closets. Reservation's at six thirty."

ß

First period study hall duty was definitely a perk of seniority. Last year Sean'd had eighth period study hall and the kids were usually animals by then, but first period, everyone who wasn't frantically trying to finish up homework was asleep. And any alternative was better than the first four years when he'd pulled lunch duty.

Two of the boys currently snoring in the back row were on his baseball team. In the spring, he could make sure they maintained the C they needed to stay on the team. He really didn't know where he was going to find another catcher if Neil Purcell got kicked off. Tommy Gainsley couldn't hit second with a cannon. But it was the end of football season now, and if Neil failed first quarter it was Coach Lashway's problem.

The bell rang, and Sean shook Neil awake before heading down the hall to his science classroom. Even with their celebration in the shower this morning, Sean had managed to get to work early enough to have all his labs set up for the day.

He turned into the science wing. The sound came from behind him. An echo bounced off the metal lockers, ringing in his ears. He knew it was only a tenth of a second, but it seemed to take a long time for his brain to register the sound.

A gunshot.

And then came the screams.

"Get everyone into the classrooms," he yelled. His eyes picked out a familiar face. "Marcus, grab everyone you can and lock my door."

His body ran toward the sound of the shot even as his mind tried to slam on the breaks. Running toward gunfire was incredibly stupid, but Sean couldn't seem to do anything about his legs. Two, three more shots. Not a frantic burst, but slow, steady, measured.

When he turned the corner again, it was easy to pick out the shooter. One figure stood among the bodies on the floor. *Sean,* his brain tried one last time, *you're an ass. What if you make it worse?*

He was already in the air when the shooter turned. Fire burst in his leg. Then they were down, the body under him struggling, and then another pair of hands, grabbing at the shoulders he was trying to pin down.

"Got it."

Sean looked up. John Olivera, the assistant principal, held a black pistol. Three other boys now helped sit on the kid he'd tackled. Sean took a deep breath, and acid flooded through his leg again.

"Nice takedown, Coach."

He turned his head to see Neil Purcell sitting on the kid's arm.

Pain rolled up his spine and into his head, and everything got a little fuzzy after that.

ß

Kyle turned up the radio to drown out the noise from the construction area behind him. The guys actually doing the work of pouring cement around the rebar knew way more than the suits in the trailers who were supposed to be supervising the work. The emergency call for the architect turned out to be not so much an emergency as a question the crew boss could have handled in his sleep.

His Camry bounced over a rut at the exit to the road as the

radio announcer began talking about breaking news in a serious voice. The first three words were enough to turn Kyle's blood to ice.

"McKinley High School remains in a lock down as police search the building. A single shooter was apprehended at approximately eight thirty this morning after wounding several students and teachers."

Kyle swung his car off onto the shoulder and turned the radio up louder.

"Unconfirmed reports place the death toll at two, one student and one staff member. According to news received from students on cell phones, a teacher was wounded as he attempted to disarm the shooter."

With his throat too thick for speech, he prayed silently. *Not Sean. Not Sean. Please, sweet Mary, not Sean. He wouldn't be that stupid.* Kyle's hands shook as he dug in his briefcase for his cell phone.

He was about to press Sean's number when he saw it. Two missed calls. He'd had it on at the site, but who could hear it ring over all that noise? Who would think there'd be any reason for an emergency phone call on a sunny morning in October?

Kyle pressed the call-back button.

"Mercy Medical Center."

In that second he was nothing. Had nothing. No brain, hands, feet, heart, stomach. Nothing. And then his heart started again with a painful thump. His stomach came back online with a gut-punch of nausea. *No. No. No.*

"My name is Kyle DiRusso. You called me earlier."

"Please hold."

Hold? Kyle hunched over the steering wheel, teeth clenched to hold back the bile rising in his throat, the phone crushed against his ear.

"Mr. DiRusso? I have you listed as an emergency contact for Sean Farnham. He was brought into the trauma center a few hours ago. He's in surgery but he asked that you be notified immediately."

He asked. Sean had asked. Which meant he wasn't dead. Had been conscious when he came in. Kyle made the sign of the cross with the phone in his hand before he even realized what he was doing and lifted the phone back to his ear.

"I'll be right there."

He snapped the phone shut, opened the car door and vomited up his Cheerios, orange juice and coffee.

By the time he got to the emergency-room doors, Kyle had passed a half-dozen news teams from the Cleveland and Youngstown stations. He was glad he'd forced himself to stop and dig through the glove compartment for copies of the healthcare proxy forms they'd both signed three years ago. He never really paid attention to politics so he had no idea if they were even still valid in Ohio, but he doubted he'd get any information otherwise.

Security gave him a long stare as he approached the nurse in the little glass booth and slid the paper across to her. "I'm Kyle DiRusso. Someone called me because Sean Farnham had been brought in. I'm—" What was he going to say? The reporters crept up behind him, but stayed back at least ten feet. The nurse's booth seemed to be part of a demilitarized zone between the press and the hospital.

Kyle resisted the urge to turn and see if the reporters were in earshot. He had no idea what Sean wanted. Most of the teachers at McKinley knew Sean was gay, but a school shooting was always national news.

"Yes, Mr. DiRusso. You can go through."

Kyle passed the swinging double doors.

"McKinley High?" A nurse approached him.

He nodded.

"We've set aside a special waiting room for you."

"Sean?"

"As soon as he's out of surgery one of the doctors will speak to you."

Kyle swallowed back another round of dry heaves.

He wondered if he looked as pale as the people waiting in the room. One woman alone staring blankly at her knees, a couple huddled together on the couch, the woman sobbing.

Did that mean two other people in surgery?

No one spoke, so he didn't offer his name. He just sat and waited.

Every fucking school in this country ought to have metal detectors. How could everybody keep letting this happen? What the hell was it going to take? Kyle peeled off his tie and shoved it in his briefcase. He still had the healthcare proxy in his hand and he put that away too.

His Italian-Hispanic upbringing told him he ought to be waiting in the hospital chapel, on his knees, but he wanted to be where they could find him immediately. He leveled his gaze on the crucifix across the wall. *Don't you let him die.* Then realizing God might not like taking orders, he amended it. *Please don't let him die.* Half-forgotten prayers overlapped each other in his head until they came to get him.

The surgeon called him out to speak to him alone. Kyle stared at the clean blue scrubs. Did they change after surgery so that you didn't have to look at the blood of someone you loved splattered like paint?

"He's going to be fine."

Kyle knew that wasn't the first thing the surgeon had said, but it was the first thing he could really understand. There was a lot more. Blood loss, infection, muscle and tendon damage, physical therapy, permanent disability. Kyle heard all those words and knew what they meant. But Sean was alive. Everything else they could work out.

"When can I see him?"

"He should be in a regular room in a few hours. The nurses' station will give you a pager."

Pager in hand, Kyle went outside to make some phone calls.

Kyle held Sean's hand as the doctor repeated what he'd told

Kyle earlier. Now that he could understand it better, it was even more horrible. Thinking about those two bullets ripping through, tearing inside Sean's skin into his muscles, almost severing the sartorious, lodging in his quadriceps. The graphic description left Kyle nauseous again.

"You were lucky the bullets missed the kneecap. If he'd been carrying a bigger gun, you might have lost the leg."

Kyle supposed the doctor's words were meant to be reassuring. Unfortunately, Kyle's imagination could supply its own pictures of "what if" without the doctor's help.

Dr. Watrobski finished up by explaining what pain medication was available once the shot Sean had been given wore off, and then added, "Mr. Farnham?"

The doctor had been calling him Sean, and he and Kyle both looked up at the odd tone in the surgeon's voice.

"Thank you. My daughter goes to McKinley. Just. Thank you."

Sean nodded, and then they were alone for the first time.

Kyle squeezed Sean's hand. "You fucking idiot."

"I know. I'm sorry."

Tears burned the back of Kyle's throat. All through the anger and fear he'd managed to hold on, but the relief, the heart-stopping simple fucking joy that Sean was still here with him was enough to drain the strength out of him. He put his head on Sean's chest, cheek finding heat through the thin gown. The smell was all wrong, laced with disinfectant and blood, but the warmth was enough. Proof of life.

"I didn't want to do it. I knew it was stupid. But it was like I was watching myself in a freaked-out dream and I couldn't stop it. The kids were screaming and...I just did it."

Kyle listened to the rhythmic beat of Sean's heart.

"It's not that serious. I can go home in a few days. God, did you call my parents?"

"Right after I talked to the doctor. They'll be here soon."

"Okay."

Kyle lifted his head, and his gaze caught the dark red

splatters on the side of the sheet, on the hospital gown. The sight of Sean's blood hit him like a bat to the back of his knees. He gripped the raised bar beside Sean's bed.

"Mr. Farnham? The police would like to speak with you." A nurse stood in front of the door.

"He's on morphine." Kyle straightened, but the two state police officers were already in the room.

"We just need to ask him a few questions."

"It's all right." Sean gave Kyle's hand a last squeeze and faced the police with his arms folded.

"What time did you hear the first shot?"

"Between first and second period. Eight-eighteen or nineteen." Sean's voice was calm.

"How many shots did you hear before you made contact with the shooter?"

"I'm not sure, three or four."

"Did you hear any gunfire after you had the shooter on the ground?"

"I don't think so."

"Can you identify the shooter?"

"I don't know his name, but I think I'd recognize him if I saw him again."

Kyle was pretty sure he was the only one who could hear the tremor in Sean's voice. Kyle wanted the policemen gone. "Can this wait? He just got out of surgery."

"And you are?" The shorter officer's tone suggested he'd have Kyle tossed from the room in a heartbeat.

Sean reached up and grabbed Kyle's hand. "This is Kyle DiRusso. My partner."

Sean's grip made it obvious they weren't law firm partners.

"We'll just be a few more minutes." The taller man took up the questioning, pushing back his hat and including Kyle in his eye contact. "When you approached the shooter, were you aware that there had been two fatalities in the administrative wing?"

Sean's hand tightened and the muscles of his shoulder tensed. "Who?"

"Frank Healey, the principal. And Kelsey Nash, a student."

"Jesus. She's in my fifth period." Sean's hand jerked in Kyle's.

"According to the reports we have, she was on her way to the nurse's office."

"Anyone else?"

"One of the victims didn't survive surgery. I'm afraid we can't release the name yet."

Kyle wondered which of his waiting room companions had been faced with that news. Another wave of relief rolled through him, followed hard by guilt. He fought against the urge to make the sign of the cross. He hardly ever thought about the religion that had been a constant presence in his childhood, but today the urgent call of ritual had his fingers and knees twitching. Nothing like the threat of death to bring on a sudden attack of piety. Both of his grandmothers would be incoherent with joy.

The police finished up with assertions that Sean would be required to make a more formal statement when his health permitted.

Kyle had just settled back on the chair, eyes scanning the IV tubing and the wires leading to the monitor behind when Gina and Peter Farnham came through the door.

He surrendered his seat to Sean's mother and stepped back as Sean's parents reassured themselves much the way Kyle had, his father taking Sean's hand while his mother rested her head against Sean's chest in a brief embrace.

After a repetition of the doctor's report, Peter shook Kyle's hand across Sean's bed, and Gina gave him a quick hug before their attention was back on their son.

"You saved a lot of lives today, son." Peter's voice was rough with swallowed tears. "Damned proud of you."

"Sean, you'll never believe it but the *Today* show called me. I guess the hospital wouldn't talk to them so somehow they found me, and they want to interview you tomorrow morning."

Kyle glanced over at the clock on the wall. It was just after six. He'd been in the hospital for only seven hours. It felt like half his life. "How can they—?"

"They want to set up a remote feed from here. Matt Lauer, sweetheart. He wants to interview you."

"I—" Sean looked up at Kyle and the confusion on his face made Kyle want to snap at the poor woman.

He clung to a cross-cut shred of patience. "Gina, he's had a lot of drugs in him today. I don't know if he's really able to—"

"Oh, I'll talk to them. We can set it all up. You won't even have to get out of bed, sweetheart."

Clearly nothing outranked the importance of being on the *Today* show.

"Okay, Mom," Sean managed around a yawn.

"Maybe we should let the boy sleep, Gina. He's had a hell of a day," Sean's father said.

Kyle dug in his pocket and started to pull their house key off his ring. "You can stay—"

"That's all right, Kyle. We're going to get a hotel. I'll call when we get everything settled with the *Today* people." She pronounced the name with the same reverence Kyle had given the Hail Mary he'd started murmuring in the waiting room. Everyone had a unique way of dealing with a crisis. Gina's appeared to be concentrating on the *Today* show.

Sean's parents were very sweet and usually didn't even make a ripple in their lives, but at that moment Kyle wished they lived a hell of a lot farther away than Erie, Pennsylvania.

Sean drifted off a few minutes after his parents left, his breathing even and slow. When Sean's hand relaxed and slipped from his grip, Kyle went down to the hospital's small chapel and quietly went to pieces.

Chapter Two

Pain gave Sean a vicious shove to push him out of sleep. He came awake, glaring at his knee. The throbbing radiated with each breath. Of his whole leg, he'd say maybe two of his toes didn't feel like his circulatory system was pumping lava instead of blood. Kyle wasn't here. As soon as Sean reached for the TV remote, he remembered why he didn't want to watch the news.

Kelsey Nash. He pictured her, second row, third seat, long dark brown hair, round cheeks, bright blue eyes, good with formulae, bad with equations. Gone. All of it. Erased. His hands fisted in the sheet. If he'd run faster, recognized the sound sooner...

Frank, Kelsey, someone else. A kid? A teacher? He tried to recreate the hall in his mind, see who might have been bleeding, but he'd only had his eye on that brown jacket, aim focused on the shoulders under the close-cropped hair.

His empty stomach gurgled. Three people were dead, and he was hungry. They'd kept him in recovery until he stopped puking from the anesthesia, and he'd apparently slept through dinner. What he needed was—

He looked up. Kyle was standing in the doorway, a Coke in one hand and a bag of Cheez Doodles in the other.

"You are a god among boyfriends." His voice rasped, but the doctor hadn't mentioned anything about his throat.

"Too bad I'm taken." Kyle wheeled the bedside table over so that it covered Sean's bed and put the can and the bag on it. "The nurse said you could eat whatever your stomach could tolerate, so..." He shrugged and sat in the chair. "It's not Parillo's, but happy anniversary."

"There are times when Cheez Doodles trump Parillo's." Sean tore open the bag.

"You could have probably had the whole vending machine brought in if I'd asked. You're the most popular patient in the hospital. It seems every nurse on the floor has a connection to McKinley. You're a hero."

Sean stuffed a few fat orange curls in his mouth and crunched. He really didn't want to think about it, but between the pain in his leg and the stink of hospital, the events of this morning were pretty hard to ignore. He popped open the can and washed down the Cheez Doodles. Watching Kyle over the rim of the can, he could see exhaustion in the narrow focus of his lover's eyes, the blink of his long dark lashes.

"You should go home to bed."

"Are you kidding? I'm not leaving you alone. They might send you home with something missing."

"Oh? What would you miss the most?" Teasing Kyle meant Sean didn't have to think about Frank or Kelsey or the still unnamed third victim.

Kyle's phone went off with its usual blare of Santana, and Kyle handed it to him without glancing at the screen. "It's your mom."

Kyle was right. His mother immediately burst into excited chatter about live feeds and media crews and hair and makeup. Shit. He'd forgotten all about the *Today* show. His mother's adoration of Matt Lauer was a little embarrassing at times. She'd caught him in a moment of weakness. Maybe some other nonlethal story would break overnight and he'd get pushed to the side for the birth of sextuplets.

After assuring his mother that he was fine, his leg was fine and everything was fine, he got another "proud of you" from his dad and passed back the phone to Kyle.

"I don't know how she got it all done in two hours, but a crew from the local affliate'll be here at four thirty. Maybe you should get us some razors." Sean rubbed his jaw.

"Us?"

"If I have to do this— What?"

"Sean, this is going to be national. If I— If we—"

Sean looked at him, waiting.

"Are you ready to come out to millions of strangers? What about your job?"

"Is it a problem for you?"

"No. But all your students...the parents."

"Will have to get over it."

If he was going to have to be on the *Today* show as some kind of—he inwardly rolled his eyes—hero, he was doing it as an out gay man. Let the crazies chew on that.

But if Kyle would be uncomfortable, he'd find another way to make sure he got heard. "I want you with me, but if you—"

"No. I'll do it. Just be ready for me to call you a fucking idiot on national television if they ask me what I think of what you did."

A nurse tried to chase Kyle home at ten, citing rules and starting to get insistent about immediate family, but when Sean said, "I want him to stay," she brought Kyle an extra pillow and blanket and closed the door. Sean felt like an ass for thinking it, but being a hero looked like it might have some benefits.

After a sleepless hour of unrelenting pain, he let Kyle talk him into another shot. "You're not going to turn into an addict in a day, you idiot."

It seemed like he'd barely been asleep for five minutes when the television crew arrived, followed immediately by his parents. The next few hours were a blur of blinding lights and people, more people than he believed could ever fit in such a small room. They insisted on moving his bed for better lighting and angles. In the midst of the chaos, people darted in to clip them to wires, to groom and brush.

Sean's mother had somehow managed to find McKinley

High Dragons sweatshirts in the middle of the night and had forced his father into one. After a brief consultation with the nurses, who were all fascinated by the process of filming inside the hospital, one of the crew sliced open the back of the sweatshirt his mother had brought for him and had him slip his arms into it.

Kyle politely but insistently refused the offer of a fourth sweatshirt, before pulling his tie out of his briefcase and knotting it under his chin. By the time seven o'clock rolled around, Sean thought his mother would pee on herself from excitement, and all he wanted was for everyone to leave so he could have another shot and go back to sleep.

The three-minute segment seemed to last an hour. By the time it ended, the lights burned Sean's eyes and he couldn't remember much of what he'd said. Everyone assured him it went well, and he thought Matt Lauer had laughed at something he'd said. One thing stuck with him, though. When Matt asked Kyle what he thought of Sean's actions, Sean almost lost it with nervous laughter, but Kyle just took his hand and said, "I think that everyone at the school was lucky Sean was there."

By eight thirty everyone was gone, and Sean and Kyle shared the cold, gluey oatmeal that was on his waiting breakfast tray. Kyle flipped open his phone and held it up for Sean to see.

"Twenty-six missed calls?"

Kyle turned it off and put it back on his hip, stifling a yawn so deep Sean could feel it vibrate his own jaw.

"You really should go home, man."

"Maybe for a little while after the doctor comes by." Kyle could only manage a quick smile. "I'll have your mom stand guard."

"Did you really mean it?"

Kyle tipped his chin, left brow raised in question.

"About me being there. That they were lucky. 'Cause you haven't said anything—" It was stupid to ask, and Kyle was just going to let him flounder and it pissed him the fuck off.

And then Kyle kissed him. "God, of course I meant it. You scared the shit out of me, but I am so proud of you." His lips twisted. "I'm the Proud Lover of McKinley High's Hero. I can get a bumper sticker."

"Fuck off." Sean kissed the laughter off Kyle's lips.

The kiss got a lot deeper than Sean sensed either of them had meant it to, but Kyle kept coming back for more, the stroke of his tongue in Sean's mouth sending a curl of want to his stomach that was almost enough to overpower the pain in his leg—with a little help from his new friend Demerol.

Finally Kyle rested his forehead against Sean's. "Wonder when we get to do that again."

"When the doctor comes, I'll ask him. But it's just my knee. I don't see why McKinley High's Hero can't get a blowjob."

"Of course, *you'll* have to be off your knees for awhile."

"There are plenty of other ways I can do you." Sean reached up to pull Kyle's head down, stretching the IV in his arm. "Ow. Fuck."

"It'll have to wait until we get you home anyway. I don't want to try Nurse Josie's patience."

To Kyle's profound embarrassment, Sean did ask Doctor Watrobski about limitations on sexual activity. Kyle's skin was dark enough to hide a blush, and Sean, damn him, didn't so much as pinken. After reminding Sean that he couldn't put weight on his leg for the next three days, the doctor okayed any non weight-bearing activity.

"As for anal intercourse..." the doctor went on and Kyle clasped his hands together in his lap to keep from hiding his face. The doctor looked at Sean and back at him, evidently trying to decide who did who. "...due to the damage to your sartorious muscle, ahh, nothing active or receptive until your physical therapist clears it."

The doctor switched Sean from the Demerol as needed to Tylenol with codeine and said they'd probably release him tomorrow.

"I can't believe you asked him."

"I'm sure Doctor Watrobski's had a blowjob, Kyle," Sean said with a shrug.

"Are you sure he's been fucked up the ass on the dining table too?"

"Last Saturday was your idea. I said we should go upstairs."

Kyle felt a whole different kind of heat flush under his skin as he remembered panting "Can't wait that long" in Sean's ear. He never could make it last long enough with Sean. When he was younger, he'd have laughed at anyone who told him there'd be one guy that would always get him that hot that fast, but all Sean had to do sometimes was look at him, intent and love in those changeable blue-grey eyes, and Kyle was rock hard without a touch on his dick. And if he kept thinking about it now, he was going to have trouble walking.

Remembering where they were and why worked better than an ice bath, and he plucked out his phone to call Sean's mother to come sit with him while Kyle went home to shower and change.

The hospital's physical therapist came in while Kyle waited for the Farnhams, fitted Sean with crutches and praise for saving her nephew's life. Under their watchful eyes, Sean made a trip into the bathroom on his own. Kyle's phone buzzed on his hip; he'd forgotten to turn it off.

He glanced at the unfamiliar number and shut it off again. Their answering machine at home was probably a smoking wreck. He rubbed the aching muscles at the back of his head and squeezed his eyes shut. All he wanted was to be able to erase yesterday so that everything could stay the same. When he opened them, Sean was still on crutches with a heavily bandaged knee and Kyle had more than thirty missed calls on his cell phone.

Kyle left Sean and his parents watching the Food Network

and talking about the *Today* show.

"Bring me back pizza," Sean begged as he left, making a face at the turkey and gravy congealing on his lunch tray.

Their house was the same as Kyle had left it yesterday morning. Walking through the door, he could almost forget what had happened. The kitchen still smelled like the coffee he'd left behind in the carafe. He rinsed it out and put their breakfast dishes in the dishwasher. Sean always did that, since he got home first—unless it was baseball season.

Kyle might have stood there clinging to the sink for an hour if the phone didn't ring.

After turning off the ringers and unplugging the answering machine, Kyle called his parents, brothers, sister, friends and secretary. Before he got in the shower, he packed a duffle of clothes for Sean to wear home, sweats and his McKinley baseball cap, toothbrushes and an electric razor. TV vans were still besieging the hospital, so he doubted he'd get Sean to the car without the press finding them. He stuffed in a book for himself and Sean's PSP in case they kept him longer.

He didn't realize how long he'd just been standing in the shower, mind blank, until the hot water ran out. Hurrying now, he dressed in jeans and a long-sleeved Henley, grabbed the duffel bag and shoved Sean's Penn State cap on over his wet hair.

Before picking up Sean's pizza, he stopped to get donuts for the nurses on the floor. When he saw that the television vans had migrated from the hospital to the donut shop parking lot, he decided to go through the drive-thru, feeling paranoid and stupid. It wasn't as if he was the one anyone was trying to talk to anyway.

He was lucky he'd put the healthcare proxy back in his wallet, since security stopped him twice on his way to Sean's floor. With flower arrangements towering over the nurses' station, he had to pass the box of donuts through a narrow opening between two giant vases. A nurse he didn't recognize accepted the box with a smile and told him he'd looked adorable on the *Today* show.

Sean's room had more arrangements than Kyle had seen in any florist shop, the smell so strong he couldn't even smell the pepperoni right under his nose.

"Holy—" He looked at Gina Farnham and substituted "crap" at the last second.

Sean's mother beamed. "They've been coming in every few minutes."

He's not dead, Kyle wanted to point out.

"Hey." Sean's soft greeting quieted the explosion that was building in Kyle's throat. "Thanks for the pizza, Kyle."

They both always cut back on endearments around their parents, as if a *baby* or *honey* would somehow cross the line of acceptance. Kyle slid the pizza onto the table, and Sean popped open the lid and stuffed a piece in his mouth.

"How's your leg?"

"Fine," Sean said around his mouthful, but the look in his eyes suggested that Tylenol with codeine wasn't quite doing the job the Demerol had. "Your work sent that one." Sean jerked his chin at a vase of spikey gladiolas in McKinley's colors of red and gold.

Quite a few teddy bears and what looked like about fifty balloons occupied the corner near the window.

Sean swallowed. "Someone's coming to take that stuff to pediatrics. Mom's got all the cards."

"This one's from the governor." Gina pointed to an elegant basket given a place of prominence on the nightstand.

Who will no doubt get right to work on legislation to approve gay marriage so I don't have to carry those healthcare proxy forms everywhere I go, Kyle thought wryly. He'd never even thought about marriage before, but he knew damned well that if Sean wasn't the nation's newest hero, the nurses never would have let him stay with Sean last night.

"Have you called your parents?" Gina asked.

"Yes. Dad said he was proud to know someone like Sean, and Mami said she'd pray for him."

Gina flinched. Kyle sometimes thought his Hispanic

Catholic heritage was almost as much of an imposition for Sean's parents as the fact that their son had brought home a man in the first place.

"Did they see the *Today* show?" Gina switched to her favorite topic.

"They thought it was wonderful." Actually Kyle's mother had asked why he wasn't wearing a school sweatshirt, adding her usual refrain of *why do you have to be so different and make things difficult for yourself?* Kyle watched Sean scoop up his third slice of pizza. "Jack and Tony said they'd come by later."

"Great," Sean mumbled as he chewed.

But Kyle could tell that what Sean needed was sleep—if the pain in his leg would let him get some. He wondered if there was a polite way to get Gina and Peter to leave him alone for awhile.

"You know, I think you should stay downstairs until you can put weight on your leg," Kyle said.

"Are you banishing me to the sofa?" Sean murmured.

"That's a good idea, Kyle. You don't want to set your recovery back. I'll make up the couch for you, sweetheart," Gina said.

"That would be great." Kyle handed her the key he'd had made on his way back to the hospital. "There're some sheets in the closet in the guest room."

"I'll freeze a couple of dishes for you both too." Gina was already at the door.

The first time Kyle had met her, he'd known immediately where Sean had gotten his take-no-prisoners determination from.

She called back sharply, "Peter?"

Sean's dad had been dozing in a second chair next to the window, a newspaper forgotten on his lap. He started and climbed to his feet.

"We'll be back after dinner to say good night. Call us if you need anything."

"Thanks, Mom." Sean caught Kyle's wrist in his greasy hand.

Kyle threw a couple of napkins at him. Sean wiped off his hands as they listened to the footsteps recede.

"Man, that was fucking brilliant. When did you get so smart?"

"Someone has to be, if you're going to run around getting shot."

Kyle used a napkin on his wrist and reclaimed the seat next to Sean. "I brought you clothes and your PSP. You need anything else?"

Sean grimaced. "I'd like a Coke. And to get back on the Demerol. My leg hurts like a bitch."

Kyle pushed to his feet. "I'll talk to the nurse when I go get your soda."

"I can talk to the nurses myself." Sean usually displayed much more patience than Kyle. The snap in his tone meant exhaustion or pain, or that he was cleaning the garage.

"So why haven't you?"

It wasn't fair to walk away when Sean couldn't follow him to argue some more, but exhaustion had also pushed the limits of Kyle's patience. He found a nurse on his way back from the vending machine.

"Here." He handed Sean the Coke. "The nurse said she'd call the doctor."

"I told you—"

"That your leg hurt. Sean, there were bullets in it yesterday." It didn't matter that Kyle wanted to pretend yesterday had never happened. It had. "They should at least make you comfortable enough to sleep." He leaned back against the chair and stared at the cooking show on the television.

Sean's pissy mood slid out on a sigh.

"You know." Kyle leaned over and feathered his fingers through Sean's light brown hair. He wanted the reassurance of Sean's breath against his palm, but settled for the familiar soft slide against his fingers. "If you hadn't asked the doctor about sex, he wouldn't have thought you were ready to come off the Demerol."

"You know, if you keep doing that, I might not kill you." Sean's eyes closed.

Chapter Three

Kyle blinked and came awake in the dark of the predawn hospital room. A quick glance told him Sean was still asleep. In this light he couldn't be sure, but Sean might be free of the fever that had kept him another two days.

Kyle's muscles protested as he pushed away from the chair, and he glared back at the so-called cushions. He'd sat on softer concrete. Sean's dad had offered to stay the fourth night, but Kyle hadn't needed to see the look Sean shot in his direction before he was already phrasing a refusal, claiming he'd become deeply attached to the orange-cushioned torture chamber. He stretched his back until it cracked and padded on his socked feet to the window.

Sean's room faced the parking lot. The TV vans were gone for the moment, probably setting up for Frank Healey's funeral later that morning.

"I want to go."

Kyle turned back to Sean. Since they'd talked about it yesterday, Kyle didn't worry that Sean had started reading his mind. The funeral would start at ten thirty. It would be close, but the doctor had been stopping by around nine. Gina had brought them both suits to change into in case Sean was released.

"I'll talk to the nurses when I go find us something to eat." Neither of them had developed a taste for the gluey oatmeal or watery eggs that arrived on the patients' trays. The hospital's cafeteria, on the other hand, had surprisingly good food.

"Did you get the stuff in to your boss?" Sean asked around a yawn.

Amid the piles of voice mail they'd listened to yesterday, Kyle's boss had told him to take all the time he needed, but if he could send in the preliminary work on the Circle Corporation's new mall it would be a big help.

"I did. Why don't you go back to sleep?"

"Can't."

Kyle tried to find a reason in Sean's clipped words and shadowed expression. Since Tuesday, Kyle'd had to learn to read new emotions in Sean's eyes. After that first night, Sean hadn't complained about his leg, though Kyle could tell the pain medication wasn't enough sometimes. And hearing that Nicole Gerbino, the girl who'd died in surgery, had been shot in the same hallway as Sean, had shown what grief and guilt looked like on Sean's face.

It was pointless to tell Sean he couldn't have done more to save her. He was convinced if he had run faster she would still be alive. Kyle stepped back toward the bed.

"I need to get out of here, Kyle. Promise them anything."

And there was something new again. Kyle'd never heard that kind of desperation from his lover before. Never had Sean looked to Kyle to fix things for him. Never had he seen Sean's eyes that dark with need.

The promise spilled out before Kyle could think. "I'll get you home today, Sean."

Sean shifted in the wheelchair and squinted at the sun. Kyle must have worked some kind of magic because Dr. Watrobski signed Sean's discharge papers at nine fifteen and he was shaved, dressed and wheeled to the front door by nine forty. The nurse chatted with him as Kyle went out to get his car. As far as Sean knew, his SUV was still at the school—along with his briefcase and cell. God, there was so much to do.

His parents' van pulled up behind Kyle's Camry. He hiked himself up on his crutches, right leg held straight by a full-length brace. Kyle was under his elbow as soon as he took the first step.

"I've been on crutches before, babe."

"I've seen it, but I swore to the doctor you wouldn't so much as brush your toes against the ground."

His mom appeared at his other side. "Wouldn't it be easier for you to get in our van? Kyle's car is so low to the ground."

Climbing up or climbing down were both going to be hard, and Sean would have to do one or the other no matter which vehicle he rode in. Bracketed between Kyle and his mom, Sean felt like the prize in a tug of war. He shot a look at his lover, but Kyle's face was carefully blank.

"If you think it would be easier, Sean, let's try the van." Kyle waited as Sean stretched across the back bench. With a quick wave and a "See you at the church," Kyle slid the side door shut.

Sean regretted his insistence on attending the funeral as soon as they bounced over the first speed bump in the hospital parking lot. The jolt of pain in his leg made him swallow hard and grip the pad on his crutch. He just wanted to grab another codeine and go home.

It wasn't as if he'd been close with Frank Healey. Teachers and principals were often at odds and he and Frank had gone a couple of rounds over a few students—Neil Purcell for one. But Frank was dead and Sean owed it to him—to everybody—to stand up at Frank's funeral since he was still lucky enough to be able to do it.

After a brief conversation with the cop doing traffic control in front of the church, his mom turned back to him. "Your father will pick us up when it's over."

The cop pulled open the side door and held his crutches while he hopped down.

Sean stared up at the stone steps leading into the church and took a tighter grip on his crutches. He'd lost sight of Kyle when the cop directed the Camry down a side street. Sawhorses and police held the press at bay, but Sean felt the cameras on him as he swung himself up on the first step. He wished Kyle were here. If he was going to stumble, he wanted to be able to lean on Kyle and not send his sixty-year-old mother tumbling down the steps of St. James Episcopal Church.

Just inside the door, the tip of his crutch slid out from under him and his foot hit the floor under half his weight. He caught himself before he fell farther, but he couldn't control the gasp of pain. His mother didn't turn, all sound swallowed by the organ music and the buzz of low-pitched conversation from the overflowing pews.

The buzz got louder, and Sean pasted a smile on his face as half the athletic department from McKinley surrounded him. He braced himself against the back slaps and managed to keep his foot off the floor, answering "Fine" to "How're you doing?" and "Don't know" to "When will you be back?"

"Where's Kyle?" Rhonda, the girls' basketball coach, asked with a smile.

A few of the other coaches looked away, the cross-country coach going so far as to turn and stare at the stained glass windows behind him. It wasn't as if Sean being gay had been a secret among the faculty. The science department all knew. But maybe it had been more of a secret than he'd thought, or knowing was different than guessing.

"He's parking the car," Sean said.

"I think the nearest parking spot is in Akron." Nick Lashway clapped him on the back again. "Here, Coach, take our seats."

Lashway jerked a thumb and his five assistants scrambled out of the third pew from the back. Sean's leg was burning enough to take charity from the football team, and with a murmured thanks, he eased into the pew.

When the service started, Sean missed the hum of conversation. The shock and grief made the air inside the church as thick as before a thunderstorm. He looked around at the stained glass and the kaleidoscope designs the sun made on the backs of the people in front of him. That's what Tuesday had done, left them shattered fragments of glass. Everyone's illusion of a peaceful Midwestern life broken against the reality of a world gone crazy.

Sean's left side tingled, leaving him too aware of the empty space beside him, Kyle's space.

He looked down to the front row and caught a glimpse of Frank's widow. She'd have to get used to that empty space. Her eyes were dry, fixed on the flower-draped coffin in front of the altar. It could have been him in there, and while Sean would like to think that his parents would have made room for Kyle in that front row, the fact that his mother was here and Kyle wasn't made his temples throb. There wasn't anything, not a damned thing that could have kept his parents from having Kyle barred from his funeral.

On his right, his mother shuddered. Sean took her hand, and she squeezed it hard.

"Mom."

"We almost lost you."

"But you didn't. I'm fine." Frank wasn't. Kelsey wasn't. Nicole wasn't. And maybe he should have been the one up there—if he'd moved faster and kept the kid from hitting Nicole. Her funeral wasn't until Monday. That was one he couldn't miss.

His mother shook again and grabbed his hand so tightly he knew the edges of her perfectly manicured nails would leave indentations. He covered her grip with his other hand, and she released him at last.

Despite his mother's urging, Sean stood through the recessional. If his leg didn't hurt so fucking much, he'd have started to complain about the pain in his arms, hands and shoulders from leaning on the goddamned crutches.

Mom stopped to talk with some of his coworkers while Sean made it out to the vestibule where he finally found Kyle. As soon as he saw Sean, his eyes widened and then narrowed. He stepped forward. "You look like shit and you don't smell much better. We're going home. Got it?"

"Yes, dear," he murmured in a meek falsetto. "Mom—"

"Knows where we live and I already talked to your dad." Kyle led him out a side door to a ramp.

Sean would have protested but the sight of the car, his ticket to codeine and the big recliner in the living room, changed his mind.

But the police shield did not extend to the side exit, and most of the reporters had chosen it as the backdrop for their cameras. One reporter changed his patter just as they reached the car. As Sean stretched his leg across the backseat, he heard the tail end of the report.

"...hero of the McKinley High shooting, recovering from multiple gunshot wounds."

Kyle shut the door on the rest of the speech. As soon as he'd climbed into the driver's seat he turned and faced Sean over the headrest. "'I read where you were shot five times in the tabloids.'"

"'It's not true.'" Sean picked up the quote from *The Thin Man*. "'He didn't come anywhere near my tabloids.'"

Kyle settled back into the seat and started the car. "Why do you always get to be William Powell?" But Sean could see Kyle's grin in the rearview mirror.

"Because you always get to be Cary Grant." The headache that had started during the funeral eased its grip.

"That's because you do a fabulous Katherine Hepburn."

Sean did his best Hepburn stuttering laugh as he watched the line of cars forming for the trip to the cemetery. "It would only be another hour."

Kyle's head snapped round. "What part of 'we're going home' didn't you understand?"

Sean shifted on the seat. Kyle usually went along with whatever Sean suggested. For him to be that commanding was completely out of character, and hot enough for Sean's body to feel something besides the throb of agony in his leg. The pain was still enough to keep sex purely in the realm of theory for now, but part of him wondered what it would take to get Kyle this stirred up again—hopefully not another gunshot wound.

"You're sexy when you're cranky."

Kyle snorted. "That's not what you usually say."

"What do I usually say?"

"Stop being a bitch and go to bed."

"Oh. That. Well, you're not being a bitch, you're being—different."

"Different how?" Kyle's eyes met his in the rearview mirror.

Sean hesitated. If he said he liked it, it was as if he was saying he didn't like the man he'd lived with for six years. And it certainly wasn't that. It just wasn't what he was used to from Kyle. "Bossier," he said at last.

"Thanks. Coming from you that's saying something."

"I'm bossy?"

"You know you are. I've been telling you that since we met."

"Yeah, yeah, and I'm lucky I'm so good in bed or you'd never put up with me." He wasn't going to be that for awhile. The tension crept back into the top of his spine. But Kyle wouldn't—he wasn't going to throw away six years because they wouldn't be fucking for a month.

"Well that and you're a good cook."

"It's good to be useful."

Kyle pulled into the driveway and shut off the car. Their house had never looked better. From the too many damned shutters Sean had repainted this summer to the clutter in the garage, he'd missed every inch of it. He leaned forward and slid his hand up through Kyle's hair.

"What?"

"Thanks for getting me the hell out of there."

Kyle didn't turn, his fingers still tight on the steering wheel. He pulled away from Sean's touch. "Welcome home, baby."

ß

According to the green numbers on the alarm clock, Kyle

had managed about twenty minutes of sleep before the panic jolted him awake again. Nothing unusual. That's how he'd spent every night since Sean had been shot. Dozing before waking and frantically looking for Sean, to get close enough to hear him breathe, to touch him.

But Sean slept downstairs in the recliner and Kyle was alone in their bed. He'd fallen asleep on the couch, but Sean had insisted Kyle go to bed for a good night's sleep. Kyle grabbed a T-shirt and slipped downstairs in the dark.

The TV was on, no sound, light showing Sean on the recliner with his head back, snoring softly. Kyle shouldn't risk waking him, but there was no way he could go back to sleep without a reassuring touch of warmth under his fingers. Just a light tap on the forearm resting across Sean's stomach had him shifting, pain drawing his slack mouth into a hard line.

Shit.

Kyle stepped back, but Sean never came fully awake. Kyle eased onto the sofa, knowing he'd sleep better down here.

Except he didn't. Sean was more restless than he'd been in the hospital, or maybe Kyle was just more worried since there weren't nurses a call button away.

What the hell was he going to do? He'd never had to take care of anyone like this before—if Sean would even let him. All he knew was they were damned lucky. Lucky he was able to watch Sean breathe, to hear that snore, that Sean Farnham was still here to be the best thing about Kyle's life.

A knot of emotions kept him too confused to sleep. Pride tangled with anger, fear with joy, and over everything, bone-deep exhaustion.

"Kyle."

Kyle sat up. "You need something?"

"I need you to go to bed." Sean's voice was soft, but Kyle could hear the hard edge pain put on his words.

Kyle pushed away from the couch, found his way to the dark kitchen and grabbed a fresh cold bottle of water from the fridge. After handing it to Sean, Kyle uncapped the pill bottle on the end table and shook one into his hand. He had to stare Sean down before he opened his hand to take the pill.

"Will you go to bed now?" Sean asked after he swallowed.

"I can't."

"Can't sleep?"

"Can't stay asleep."

"Want a pill?"

"No thanks." Even after everything, Sean was trying to make Kyle laugh.

Kyle wondered what it must have been like in that hall. The screams, the shots. Had it been like a blur or the almost silent slow-motion he remembered from the car accident that had left him with the scar above his left eyebrow?

And the bullets. Tearing and ripping through skin and muscle. Even now Kyle couldn't imagine how much that hurt. The only time he'd broken anything was when he fell out of bed at age four and broke his collarbone. He didn't remember much of it and he doubted those few stitches in his eyebrow really gave him any basis for comparison.

With as much stretch as the couch allowed, Kyle angled his head toward Sean.

"I can feel you looking at me. Makes it hard to sleep."

"Sorry." Kyle rolled onto his back.

"Hey. Do you think we could go pick up my car tomorrow?"

"Your car?"

"It's still at the school, right?"

Sean had talked about buying an SUV for years. When he bought the Durango in April, Sean had washed it every week for the first two months, still kept it polished and vacuumed.

"Yes, we can go get your baby. You know you can't drive, though."

"I know. I just don't want to leave it there."

"I'll call Jack, he can drop me off."

"My parents can help."

Sean's parents. Kyle knew they were just worried, that they

needed to see for themselves that Sean was all right, but Gina never did anything halfway. She was a little hard to take right now. "Sean."

"They're just worried."

"I know." And it shouldn't matter. Because Sean was home and he was alive.

ß

"You are not letting Tony drive my Durango."

"No, he can drive my car, and I'll drive the Durango." Kyle kept staring through the front window.

"Have you seen Tony's car? Why can't Jack do it?"

Kyle clenched his teeth and took his five hundredth deep breath since he'd gotten off the couch this morning. He wasn't sure if it was because he was exhausted or because Sean was in pain, but he definitely knew why there was a nationwide nursing shortage. Patients were a pain in the ass. "Because Tony offered and Jack has to work."

"Fine. Just don't let him drive my car."

"I won't." *And if he gets here soon enough I won't shove the keys up your ass,* he added to himself. He knew it was hard for Sean to have to sit there, to let people—let Kyle—do stuff for him, but he was going to fucking have to get used to it.

Tony's battered white Rabbit pulled up next to Kyle's Camry. He stepped back into the living room. "Do you need anything before I go?"

"I think I can manage to make it to the fridge and the bathroom."

"Your mom and dad are coming over in an hour. If you don't stop being so difficult, I'm going to leave you alone with them."

"Fine. I'll take a Coke."

Tony was already on the couch by the time Kyle got back with the can of Coke and intercepted Kyle's hand-off to Sean.

"I think the boy needs a beer."

"Not on top of the codeine he doesn't."

Tony put the can on the coffee table and held up his hands in surrender.

"Anything else?" Kyle tried to make his tone neutral.

"I'm fine." Sean's answer was just as careful.

"Okay. I'll be back as soon as I can."

Sean pulled the top on the can and smiled. "Take your time."

Kyle had never seen a faker smile in his life.

"Want me to drive?" Tony asked as they headed out the door.

Halloween was Monday, and the air was full of the smell of wet leaves and earth. Air free of the smell of hospitals, blood and tension.

Kyle wanted to stand there and breathe forever.

"Sure." He followed Tony to his car.

The Rabbit shuddered and bucked at every intersection, but the gelled tips of Tony's hair never quivered.

"So, how ya doin'?"

"Fine."

"Oh yeah, you're just bursting with fine."

"I'm not the one who got shot."

"No, you're not."

"So why are you asking me? Sean's going to be all right. Why wouldn't I be fine?"

"'Cause you look like you wanted to dump that soda on his head."

Kyle stared out the window at the lawns full of pumpkins and cornstalks.

"You make it sound like I'm pissed at him."

"Aren't you? Fuck, man, if Jack did something like that and got himself hurt, I'd want to kill him myself."

Kyle ran a hand through his hair. "Oh God, I am such a

piece of shit. He hasn't even been home a day."

"You're not a piece of shit. You were with him five days in the hospital. Give yourself a break. Give both of you a break."

"Like what?"

"Let him go to the fridge for his own fucking drink."

"Did he tell you that?"

"No. But you're not making things easier on either of you. Just back off. Trust him."

Tony hadn't lived through Tuesday. He hadn't heard the news on the radio, called the hospital and sat there with his whole fucking world on hold. But Tony had known Sean for twelve years.

"Just back off?"

"He's not stupid; he'll ask if he needs something."

Tony might have known Sean for twelve years, but Tony had never lived with Sean, didn't know how he never asked for anything for himself. That Sean was the one who made sure Kyle didn't eat his lunch out of a vending machine, that Sean was the one who dragged him to bed when he would have stayed up all night finishing another project. That Kyle was the one who always needed something. He couldn't tell Tony any of it, not when Tony already thought he was driving Sean nuts.

But if Kyle was making Sean crazy, shouldn't he just back off? Sean's first physical therapy appointment was on Monday. After that, they'd probably encourage him to move around more, even if he still couldn't put weight on his leg.

"I could go back over and sit with him. Give you a chance to run some errands, get to the store. I promise I won't let him OD on codeine."

Kyle should say no. It wasn't Tony's responsibility to stay with Sean, it was Kyle's. Even if he could stand to restock the fridge. They were out of juice and fat-free half and half.

"He's a big boy."

"And how would you know?"

"My, uhhh, lips are sealed." Tony looked over and waggled his eyebrows. "You know you want to say yes."

"Get a lot of dates like that?"

"Got Jack. Before that is ancient history."

Kyle had always wondered if Tony and Sean had slept together. He could have asked, but he'd decided a long time ago he was happier not knowing.

"You don't mind?"

"If I go home, I'll have to do laundry. I promised Jack there'd be clean shorts tomorrow."

Sean's Durango stood alone in the faculty parking lot. Kyle had never seen the lot that empty before—even on a Saturday or Sunday there was always someone around—and with school starting again Monday, he figured there would be lots of cleanup still going on.

He swung out of Tony's Rabbit and shut the door, blocking out all but the deep bass of the 80's music pouring from the stereo. Even over the bass, the scratch of leaves across the asphalt sounded eerily loud in the bright sunshine.

Kyle climbed into the Durango and sealed himself inside. The anniversary card he'd put on the steering wheel that morning was open on the passenger seat. He tugged the card free of the envelope, smiling at the naked hunk with a strategically placed balloon. He'd embellished the card's sexual suggestion with a handwritten addition, a suggestion they hadn't been able to carry out. His throat tightened again.

Sean wasn't dead. They'd get a chance to do that and more. The trip to Australia, a house at the beach, all of it.

The engine turned over and the stereo assaulted his ears with Sean's 80's arena rock. No wonder he and Tony got along so well, neither one of them would recognize the fact that new music had been recorded steadily over the last two decades.

He turned it down and waved at Tony, who flashed him a grin that stretched to his temples before slamming the Rabbit into reverse and squealing out of the lot.

Kyle's grin was just as big as he remembered that the Farnhams would probably beat Tony to the house. He was only sorry he'd miss Gina and Tony meeting.

Sean heard the front door open and dragged a smile to his lips. “Hey, babe.”

But Tony came in from the hall instead.

“Aw, sugar, it’s nice to see you, too.”

“Where’s Kyle?”

“Out. Getting groceries, I think.”

“Groceries?”

“Yeah, man, you know the things you eat?”

Kyle hated to go to the grocery store. On the rare occasions when he did, he came home with double the list at three times the cost.

“Is my car all right?”

“It’s fine. It missed you. Whatever. What’s with you? I thought drugs were supposed to make people mellow.”

“You would know.”

“We are not discussing my misspent youth.” Tony held up his hands in protest.

“Or the barbeque two years ago?”

“That was before Jack.” Tony dropped his ass onto the coffee table.

“You know we have furniture designed just for sitting.”

“Really? I hadn’t noticed. But nice try.” Tony leaned back on his hands, still sprawled on top of the *Sports Illustrated* magazines littering the coffee table.

“What?”

“Changing the subject.” Tony raised his foot as if he would kick one of Sean’s before smiling sheepishly and planting both feet on the floor.

“There was a subject?”

“You.”

“I’ve had an interesting week, but you know the whole story, which is nice because it gets kind of boring the tenth time I have to tell it.” Sean tried to change the channel by aiming the remote around Tony’s head.

“I’m talking about how fucking edgy you are.”

“Did Kyle say that?”

Tony laughed. “You two are like some freaky brain twins. No wonder you’re so annoyingly happy with each other. No. He didn’t say anything. But you’re acting like you can’t stand to have him in the same room and that ain’t like you, man.”

The truth was that Sean had never wanted Kyle more, and that thought terrified him more than another run down that hallway with the gunshots echoing around him. He didn’t even want Kyle to go back to work.

It wasn’t that Kyle was unreliable. He was the most dependable, loyal guy Sean knew, which was one of the reasons Sean loved him. No, it was just Sean and the stark terror inside him at how much he needed Kyle with him. He didn’t even want to think of going to Nicole Gerbino’s funeral tomorrow without Kyle next to him. Nicole Gerbino. Who wasn’t ever going to get older than fourteen. The girl he should have saved.

“Sean? Man, I guess those are good drugs.”

“Huh?”

“I said, ‘Do you want me to stay and run some interference for you when Kyle gets home?’”

“Not necessary. My parents are coming for dinner anyway.”

“I’m clearing off then. You know parents make me itchy.”

“Tony, you’re thirty-three fucking years old. It’s time to grow up.”

“You first, dude. Oh, that’s right.” Tony looked around, nodding at the furniture, the house, those fucking striped drapes that Sean still hated. “Well, I’m still opting for fun.” Tony winced as the doorbell rang. “Oh fuck.”

Sean grinned. “I don’t think you’ve ever met my parents.”

“I didn’t ever plan to,” Tony muttered.

But Tony’s opportunity for escape ended with Sean’s mom and dad coming in from the hall. Tony jumped off the coffee table like someone stuck dynamite up his ass.

“Hi, sweetheart.” Sean’s mother came over and kissed him, keeping her body an exaggerated distance from his leg. “I’ll get started on dinner right away."

"Mr. Farnham. Mrs. Farnham." Tony nodded a greeting, his gaze darting around as if he still thought he could find an escape route.

"Mom and Dad, this is my friend Tony."

"Oh, Tony, we've heard so much about you."

Tony looked like someone had stepped on his foot—in a drag queen's fuck-me heels. "That's nice."

Sean had heard more enthusiasm from his students when reviewing a lab on the boiling point of water.

"Where's Kyle?" his mother asked.

"He went out to pick up some things," Sean said, hating the accusation in his mother's words.

"We could have done that for you, sweetheart."

"Mind if I put the Penn State game on, son?"

"Go right ahead, Dad."

"Tony, why don't you help me in the kitchen? Sean tells me you're a chef."

Tony glanced at Sean as if expecting help, but his friend's discomfort was the most fun Sean had had since Tuesday, so he just stared back blankly.

"Actually," Tony began weakly, but he was already being dragged along in Mom's wake. "Um, Jack's the chef."

"Well, I'm sure you can still help carry a few things in from the car."

Dad turned up the game loud enough to make conversation pointless, and Sean took grateful advantage of the few minutes to close his eyes and let the familiar Saturday rhythm of whistles and play-by-play wash over his ears.

He didn't realize he'd fallen asleep until a hand landed on his shoulder. He glanced up at Kyle who leaned down to whisper in his ear. "Your mother is making a twenty-pound turkey."

"Oh God, I'm sorry, babe." The sooner his parents went home to Erie, the sooner he and Kyle could try to get things back to normal. At this rate, his mother would be here until Thanksgiving.

"Of course, it's almost worth it to see Tony in an apron, fisting a turkey," Kyle added in a dry murmur. "Too bad Jack's missing it."

Sean covered a bark of laughter with his hand.

His father was glued to the half-time recap. Not that he was ever much help with Mom. Kyle couldn't exactly say anything. It was going to be up to him.

His mother came out of the kitchen and stood at the entrance to the living room.

"Why didn't you tell me you were going to the grocery store, Kyle? I could have saved you the trip."

"I'm sorry, Gina. I'll find somewhere to put it all."

"I don't know how. There must be twenty bags. Did you really think you would need instant pea soup? Sean doesn't even like peas."

"We'll donate what we have left over to the food bank." Kyle's smile froze on his face.

"It's fine, Mom." Sean squeezed Kyle's hand where it gripped his shoulder, rubbed the tension out of his fingers, ending with a tap that promised he'd do something to fix it.

"I'll have everything out of your way in a minute, Gina. I'm so sorry to have made a mess."

In his own house.

A drill bit bored into the base of Sean's skull. He wished to hell he'd never woken up from his nap. Kyle tapped Sean's shoulder once in answer and was gone, following Mom into the kitchen. His father never looked away from the television.

Tony stayed for dinner, his face reflecting both fear and pride as Mom commented on how much help he'd been. Sean wasn't sure if Tony spent more time directing the man-you-owe-me looks at him or at Kyle.

"So, Dad, what's going on at work?"

"Not much this part of the season. Third quarter reports are all in."

His mother gave Kyle a sharp look. *No, Mom, Kyle did not put me up to trying to get rid of you.*

"I do have one account I need to get through before the end of the month, though," Dad continued after he'd shoveled in some mashed potatoes.

Thank you, Dad.

"But that's Monday," his mother protested.

"Is it, now?" His father's voice was mild. Sean crossed his fingers in his lap. His father never forgot what day it was. He knew damned well when the end of the month was. The man knew what time it was in Ghana. "Well, Gina, I hadn't thought of that."

I love you, Dad. His father rarely opposed his mother in anything but when he did, he was as intractable as granite.

"Peter."

"Now, I'm sure the boys can get by. I shaved every bit of the turkey off. There's enough in the fridge to last them two weeks."

Sean saw a tear sparkle at the corner of his mother's eye and almost interceded. But when he thought of the way his mother had made Kyle feel guilty for bringing groceries into their own house, Sean bit back the words. The drill bit started up again, stretching from the back of his head all the way through to his right temple.

"I'll be fine, Mom. Really."

"Oh, sweetheart, are you in pain again?"

For once, his leg was the least of his complaints.

"You never should have gotten up from your chair. We could have all eaten in the living room." The distress in his mother's voice kicked the drill in Sean's skull into overdrive.

"It's fine, Mom. The doctor says it's good for me to move around some."

"Why don't you both go sit with Sean, and I'll help Kyle clean up before I have to run to work." Tony's offer dropped into the middle of the tension.

Tony's looks had been prophetic. They'd both owe him for this. Sean had seen his mother's kitchen after Thanksgiving.

Chapter Four

When Kyle was eleven, his teenaged cousin had been killed in a drunk-driving accident. He never forgot that funeral. Not because it was his first. His beloved grandfather's had been six months before and that had been bad enough. Abuelito always talked to you as if you were someone special, someone important, and Abuelito never thought your ideas were silly. But Junito's funeral had been much worse than Abuelito's. His grandmother and aunt had flung themselves onto the coffin as Kyle's mother had tried to hold them back, and the church had been so thick with hysteria that it had made him shake. As they left the cemetery, his dad had taken Kyle and his brothers aside and explained that it was especially hard when children died, that children's funerals were often like this. Kyle had sworn then and there he was never going to another funeral for someone under eighteen. He'd been able to keep that vow until today.

Determined to avoid the problems they'd had at the principal's funeral, Kyle insisted they leave early. He mentioned that things would be easier if Sean applied for a handicapped permit while his leg healed, but one look from Sean told Kyle it would probably require an act of God to get Sean to even look into an application.

It was another beautiful fall morning, the sky such a perfect shade of blue Kyle could almost convince himself that they were headed out for something far more pleasant than a fourteen-year-old girl's funeral. A large group of teenagers stood around the front steps, their formal dress making them look younger and more awkward than their actual years. Kyle had never understood how Sean could stand to interact with that age. Who would want a daily reminder of the misery of adolescence?

As he and Sean approached the steps of the church, moving inside the police cordon that kept the cameras at bay, a big teenager broke away from his knot of friends and stepped forward to meet them. His suit jacket barely contained his wide shoulders, and he didn't seem to know what to do with his hands, alternatively twisting them behind his back and shoving them in his pockets.

"Coach?"

"Neil." Sean's smile was genuine. "How are you? You weren't hurt?"

"Nah, not at all. Thanks to you. You comin' back to school?"

"I'll be back as soon as I can."

"In time for the season?"

"I'm sure I can make it by March, Neil. It's nothing serious."

"Cool."

Neil's approach seemed to be some kind of signal to the rest of the students, because they started to drift over in small groups, girls blushing and giggling, boys making hesitant eye contact before their gaze shifted to the brace on Sean's leg.

Most of the boys avoided looking at Kyle, but he could feel some studying looks from the girls. He wondered if Sean had considered just what being an out teacher in Canton, Ohio would mean when he decided to announce it on the *Today* show.

"Didja hear Chris wasted his parents before—you know?" Neil asked.

"Yes, I did." Sean's tone managed to convey sympathy and patience. "It's too bad."

Kyle had heard him talk to students before, but the professional Sean was so different from his lover it was always a bit of a shock. And the fact that Sean could respond so calmly when Chris Bowman's name came up would never stop making Kyle want to shake Sean and remind him of what that disturbed little shit had done.

"Hope they never let that fu—freakin' bastard out."

Kyle was in complete agreement with Neil's assessment. Whatever Sean was going to add was lost in a roar from behind them.

"How dare you show your face here?"

Kyle looked around. A dark-suited man approached, face red and ugly with fury. Kyle searched the group of teenagers, trying to find the target for the man's rage.

"If it weren't for you, my baby would be alive." The screaming man continued toward them as the crowd separated. Kyle could see he was headed directly for Sean.

Kyle stepped in front of his lover as the man closed in on them.

"Get out of my way, you fucking faggot."

Heart pounding, muscles tensed, Kyle waited for the man's violence. The first lunge Kyle managed to counter with a shove of his own. The man's arm shot back for a punch and then he jerked back as if on a leash.

"Dude." Neil and one of the other boys had taken hold of the man's shoulders, restraining him.

The man made another try for Sean through Kyle, screaming again. "Fucking faggot. Got my daughter killed."

The boys pulled him farther back. Kyle saw the tears on the man's cheeks, but given that he was trying to beat the crap out of them, adrenalin stomped out any hint of sympathy.

"Mr. Gerbino." Sean's voice held only a trace of strain. "I did everything I could. I'm so sorry about Nicole."

"Don't you fucking say her name. If you hadn't tried to be a hero she'd be alive. You should have died. Not my baby. Perverting the school. And now my baby's gone. God should strike you dead."

Kyle was only dimly aware of the fringes of their circle, too intent on making sure that if the boys lost their grip, the man couldn't get to Sean.

It seemed like forever before a police officer stepped into the middle of the crisis.

"I want that faggot out of here. He's not coming into the church." The words were for the policeman, but Gerbino spat them at Sean.

The boys relaxed their hold, and Gerbino made another lunge for Sean. Neil grabbed Gerbino again as the furious man fought off the restraining arm of the cop.

"We'll handle this, sir."

"Get him the fuck out of here. I don't want to see his face."

"Sir, why don't you make your way inside and we'll take care of—"

"I want to see him gone."

More police surrounded Gerbino. Neil backed away and circled to Sean's side.

A policeman came up to them.

"I understand, officer. I'm sorry Mr. Gerbino's so upset. We'll leave." Sean's voice was perfectly calm.

Kyle put a hand on Sean's arm. He could feel the muscle vibrate through his suit coat. Sean was nowhere near as calm as his voice.

"We'll accompany you to your car, sir." Two policemen bracketed them.

That was the last fucking straw. The cops had done nothing to stop Gerbino's abuse, and now they were being escorted away as if they'd done something wrong? "You don't have to worry. We're leaving." Kyle spat the words out.

"For your protection, sir."

Kyle scanned the crowd. It seemed like a hundred people had gathered to watch the scene, complete with the ubiquitous cameras. He doubted Gerbino was the only bigot in Canton who had the opinion that Sean should have died in that hallway. As they turned away, the collective stare at their backs was palpable, a hundred tiny stones flung at them.

Kyle straightened his spine. "Thank you." He met the cop's blank gaze.

"Coach." Neil stuck out his hand, his smile as broad as his shoulders.

Sean shook it. "Thanks, Neil."

"No problem. Hurry back."

As soon as they were clear of the sawhorses, someone shoved a camera and mike in Sean's face.

"Do you have any comments?"

Instead of letting the cops brush the woman away, Sean stopped. "I share the community's grief over what happened at our school. Nicole's death was a horrible tragedy that I wish I could have prevented." Sean took a deep breath. "I regret that Mr. Gerbino's grief may have led him to rash decisions."

Now that the other camera crews could see that Sean had stopped to talk, there was a concerted movement toward them.

"We should go, Sean."

"Mr. DiRusso, do you have anything to add?"

Panic clogged Kyle's throat. Why did they care what he had to say? If he said what he wanted, he'd probably end up in jail. "Sean's a hero. He came here to offer his condolences but he's still recovering and needs to get off his feet." He hoped that was boring enough to keep him off the news.

The cops shifted their protection to the edge of the sidewalk, and Kyle and Sean made their way to the car.

After Kyle closed the backseat door, the cop who'd spoken to them earlier said, "We'll follow you home, sir."

Kyle was about to tell him it wasn't necessary, but his brain provided news clips from several well-publicized bashings that provoked an internal shudder and had him changing his mind.

"Thank you."

He swung into the seat and waited for the police car to join them.

"Christ, what a mess." Sean's voice was a lot less steady.

"Fucking lunatic," Kyle agreed.

"I'm just a convenient target since he can't get to the kid." Sean had yet to say Chris Bowman's name; it was always "the kid."

Lights flashed in the rearview mirror, and Kyle pulled away from the curb.

"What the fuck? Kyle, they're following us."

"Good. I want them to."

"What the hell for?"

"Maybe you didn't notice, but some guy just tried to kill you in front of the church."

"He wasn't going to kill me. He just lost his daughter and he needs someone to blame."

Kyle snorted. "Far be it from me to stand in the way of your aspirations of sainthood, but do you really think he's the only one who feels that way? There are enough gay martyrs. I don't want you on the list."

"Where the fuck is that coming from?"

God, they shouldn't be having this conversation in the car. Kyle needed Sean to see him. To know how serious he was about every word. He swallowed back a wave of bile. "From fear, Sean."

"Aw, come on. I had you to protect me, all butched out."

Kyle bit his tongue. "It's not funny, Sean."

"And it's not that serious. It's just a guy freaked out because his daughter's dead." Sean's voice got softer. "It's not like I didn't say the same thing myself."

"You can't blame yourself. Everyone knows that if it weren't for you a lot more people would be dead."

"Not everyone." Sean's laugh was shaky.

Kyle had never been happier to turn down their street, but as the car passed the quiet houses, dread tied his stomach in knots. What if they got there to find "faggot" spray-painted all over the siding? He heard his uncle's vicious whispers in his ear: *Pato! Maricon!* He pulled into the driveway and everything was the same. The house was fine, Sean was alive and eventually everything would get back to normal.

The cop in the passenger seat waved as the police car sped away.

ß

Sean deflected the rest of Kyle's attempts to talk about the scene in front of the church. And then his first physical therapy session drove it completely from his mind. He was shaking with exhaustion and pain when he rejoined Kyle in the waiting room. The concern on Kyle's face told Sean he looked as bad as he felt.

The pleasant, tiny woman he'd been assigned to seemed incapable of inflicting that kind of torture on a fellow human being, but she'd clearly lived a past life as a guard in a concentration camp. She cheerfully told him she didn't want him putting his full weight on his leg, but that he should start moving around the house, and definitely should get off the recliner and start climbing the stairs. At the moment, he just wanted to collapse into the chairs in the waiting room.

The pain had him snapping at Kyle when he tried to hold the door for him. "And we're taking the stairs, not the ramp."

"Okay, sorry."

Sean sighed. "Atilla's orders."

"Atilla?"

"My physical therapist. She's a sadist, a tiny hell-spawned sadist."

"I'm sorry, *chulo*."

"I can take a cab, you know."

"I can drive you. I'll just have to work through lunch and bring stuff home. They don't care as long as I make my deadlines."

"But I have to go every day."

Kyle shrugged. "I already talked to Mr. Young. It's fine."

Fine. They did a lot of *fine* lately. Even though it was the one thing Sean knew they weren't. They would be; he'd make them be.

Maybe his physical therapist had awakened a masochistic streak in him because he insisted on watching the news that night. The scene in front of the church was, of course, the lead story. They deleted the wrong f-word, and Sean was surprised at how calm he looked. At the time, he'd thought he was shaking with tension. He tried to catch a version on another channel but Kyle ripped the remote out of his hand.

"*Captain Blood*'s on Turner Classic Movies. I want to drool over Errol Flynn and you can tell me I'd look like him if I grew a mustache."

"So you want to fuck yourself?" Sean thought about grabbing the remote back, but decided he'd had enough torture for one day.

"'Any port in a storm, sugar.'" Kyle landed the kiss that completed the quoted line.

"Hey, I get to do the William Powell lines."

"I've got to get it where I can, then. C'mere."

Kyle slid down to the end of the couch, and Sean levered himself out of the recliner and stretched out with his head in Kyle's lap. With familiar fingers rubbing the ache out of the base of Sean's skull, he was asleep before the end of the first naval battle.

ß

Kyle knew he was dreaming. No matter how good in bed Sean was, he'd never managed to suck him off and fuck him at the same time, but Kyle didn't care if this was real because it just felt so damned good. Sean's hands were everywhere, cock deep inside him while the heat of Sean's mouth burned sweet on his dick, sucking faster, harder until— Fucking hell he was awake.

The cut-off orgasm pooled like lead in his balls, sending a

spike into his legs.

With a grimace he shifted onto his side and looked at Sean, or the back of Sean's head. It was Sean's first night back in their bed after four nights on the recliner. No wonder he'd starred in Kyle's dream.

Sean rolled onto his back and Kyle breathed in his lover's sleep-warm skin, unable to resist dropping a kiss on his shoulder.

Kyle stroked his cock until the pain of frustration melted back into pleasure. Holding his breath only made the slide of skin louder, and Sean shifted again with a sleepy grunt.

Clenching his teeth to hold in a groan, Kyle rolled away. Jerking off in bed next to Sean wasn't going to work. If Sean woke up, he'd feel like he had to do something about it, and Kyle didn't want him messing up his leg and making himself more uncomfortable.

Kyle clambered off the bed and shuffled into the bathroom, his dick slapping against his stomach despite the fact that it felt like it weighed fifty pounds. He jumped under the shower as soon as the spray was warm enough and reached for the soap and a memory that never failed to get him off in a hurry.

August two years ago—the August they'd gone to Rehoboth Beach.

Sun darkened the freckles across Sean's broad shoulders and the salt made his hair stand up in spikes as he turned over and winked up at Kyle from their beach blanket.

"Stop looking at me like that. I'm getting hard."

Kyle blinked and looked out at the sunlight on the waves.

"Too late." Sean rolled to his feet. "C'mon."

"It's not even noon."

"If you wanted to stay on the beach you shouldn't have looked at me like that. Christ. I'm not going to make it."

Their guesthouse was right off the beach, but it still seemed damned far away with Sean shooting looks over his shoulder every few feet. When they hit the street, Sean hauled him in for a deep hard kiss.

"Feel what you did to me? What are you going to do about it?" Sean's tongue stroked the side of Kyle's neck toward his ear, and Kyle was having trouble remembering how to walk.

A quick rinse under the outdoor shower and they hit the gate to the back stairs still tangled, Sean's tongue deep in Kyle's throat, his hands on Kyle's hips to grind them together.

Another thrust of Sean's tongue and that immediate need hit Kyle like a punch to the gut. Kyle pressed Sean into the whitewashed boards just under the stairs leading up to their room, body pounding with a don't-care-where urgency. He couldn't remember the last time they'd had sex outdoors, and while Sean always made Kyle hot enough to burn a hole through the mattress, Kyle had never seen his lover this needy, this desperate. Sliding his hands up Sean's wet chest, he dropped to his knees. He licked the line of hair under Sean's navel, thumbs flicking across Sean's nipples.

Sean rocked his hips, his cock bumping Kyle's chin. "C'mon. Suck me now."

Strong fingers tugged on Kyle's hair.

Breathing in the salt, sun and sweat on the skin next to his lips, Kyle pulled Sean's swim trunks down far enough to free his cock.

"Now," Sean urged, tugging Kyle's head forward.

Kyle licked his lips and wrapped them around the head, stroking with his tongue. Sean groaned and thrust farther into Kyle's mouth, pushing his way to the back of Kyle's throat. Kyle swallowed and tried to catch his breath as Sean pressed in again, fucking his mouth.

"Suck me, please, Kyle."

If he'd had breath—and hadn't had a mouth full of cock—Kyle would have joked, "Trying to, *chulo*," but he was glad he couldn't. He didn't want anything to break the spell of Sean like this, so desperate for him that they couldn't even make it back to the room.

He wanted to open his mouth, his throat, take Sean deeper than he'd ever done, suck him until he sucked Sean's spine out through the cock that filled his mouth. He had the rhythm now, a little sloppier than he wanted, but Sean was snapping his hips forward too fast for technique. Precome splashed salty slick against the roof of his mouth.

I got you, papi, he thought.

His hands gripped Sean's hips, not to slow Sean's thrusts but for balance. Kyle's fingers brushed the rough spot just above Sean's hip, a sand burn from a wipeout body surfing yesterday. Kyle shifted his hold.

"Want more, God. Gotta fuck you." Sean yanked on Kyle's hair hard enough to sting and pulled him off.

That would not be a problem at all. "Okay." Kyle rocked back and pushed to his feet, taking a few unsteady steps toward the stairs.

Sean grabbed him from behind, pushing him to his knees on the first stair tread. "Now."

Kyle's dick had been a hot spike trapped in the mesh of his swim trunks. With Sean yanking his trunks down over his ass as he pressed him forward onto the stairs, it felt like someone lit the tip on fire.

"Jesus, here?"

"Fuck yeah."

Sean had Kyle's trunks off one leg, enough to push Kyle's knees apart on the step. Kyle braced his forearms on another step. He tried not to think about the fact that anyone could come around to the back of the building—or just walk out on the porch of the house next door. Tried not to think about the absence of lube or the presence of sand. Sean's mouth found that spot under his ear. Kyle's back arched and his thoughts blurred, forgetting everything but the press of that body into his.

"Still not fucking around?" Since they stopped using condoms last year, they asked each other that every time as a joke, but the way Sean growled it now, like he'd tear him apart if Kyle said yes, sent another impossible pulse of blood to his dick.

"No."

"Good. Suck on my fingers, babe."

They really were going to do it here, quick and dirty like a couple of teenagers, a fact that scared Kyle as much as it turned him on.

He opened his mouth for two fingers, soaking them with all the spit he could manage.

"That's it, babe."

Kyle's blood pumped hot and thick, in his cock, in his ass, heat he could feel in his belly, his spine, the tips of his ears.

Sean yanked his fingers free, and Kyle braced himself with a tight grip around the stair tread under his fingers, his eyes staring at the ground between the open slats of the stairs, at the brown and white pebbles that filled the backyard.

Sean's teeth sank into the back of Kyle's neck just as those fingers slammed into his body. The first penetration always burned, and going hard and fast like this had Kyle clenching his teeth against a groan of protest. But Kyle was so turned on the sting turned sweet in a few thrusts, and he rocked back.

Sean's fingers left him as roughly as they'd gone in. Kyle glanced back over his shoulder, trying to see some trace of his usually playful lover in Sean's face. Sean eyes were alight with an intent and need that kicked Kyle's own hunger out of control.

Sean never looked away as he spit into his palm and slicked his cock, movements more slow and deliberate than anything he'd done since they left the beach.

Kyle was ready to start begging. "Do it."

"Gonna fuck you so hard."

"Yeah."

Sean wrapped an arm around Kyle's hips as he pressed inside. "Christ, you feel good. Hot and tight. Fucking burning my dick."

Sean's words hit Kyle's ear with harsh sound and tingling breaths, as Sean drove deep on a long, burning scrape.

Kyle knew there'd be no waiting for his body to adjust to

the fullness that stole his breath. He tightened his grip on the stairs as Sean's hands clamped his hips and fucked him, strong, hard and deep like he'd promised. The sand trapped between their bodies scraped and scratched as Sean rode him, no more words, just loud gasps and quick nips all over his neck and shoulders.

Sean's thrusts shifted, or maybe Kyle's body moved but that was it. He wasn't just taking it anymore, he was slamming back with equal force, the deep stroke of Sean's cock lighting him up from the inside like a fucking Christmas tree, until his body was full of pleasure so sweet his throat tightened on a sob.

"That's it. Fuck me back, babe." Sean pulled out and then slammed back in, the force driving Kyle's head against the stair.

Kyle cushioned his head with his forearm.

"Come for me, Kyle. C'mon. Can't wait."

Kyle didn't want to. He pried his hand free and brought it to his own cock. His strokes were dry and gritty with sand, but his body was past caring. He needed to hit that edge more than he needed air. So close, so fucking close.

Sean's breath told him how close he was. Sean got quieter the nearer he got to coming, choking breaths replacing openmouthed groans. Kyle sped up his hand on his dick, racing for that final shock of pleasure that would push him over.

A loud rush of breath in his ear and Sean's hips snapped, pushing him gut-deep as he flooded Kyle with heat.

Kyle groaned with frustration and jacked himself harder, but Sean kept fucking, pleasure increasing as his come smoothed the way.

Sean had his breath back. "Come, babe. Do it. Gonna fuck you till I'm hard again. Never gonna stop." His hand snaked around Kyle's hip and pressed down just above the root of his dick.

"Fuck." Kyle came so hard he thought he broke something. Long sharp pulses tore through him as he pumped over his hand, onto the pebbles under the stairs, again and again until he was dry and shaking.

Kyle watched his spunk slide down the tiled wall of the shower. Steadying himself with a hand against the wall, he waited to catch the breath that memory had ripped away. Sean'd had to help him up the stairs, and they didn't leave the room the rest of the day. Sean had felt guilty about pushing so hard, and Kyle had enjoyed the subsequent blowjob too much to protest. Just before they fell asleep he'd told him, told him how much he'd loved seeing Sean lose control like that. He had never been sure Sean had heard him.

Kyle ducked back under the shower to rinse and heard a crash.

"Shit." Sean's voice was muffled by the water filling Kyle's ears, but not completely.

Guilt churned in Kyle's stomach. Sean needed him now, more than he'd needed him that day, and all Kyle could think of doing was jumping in the shower to get off. He'd probably woken Sean up.

He spun off the water and grabbed a towel. Still dripping, he opened the door and crossed the hall.

Sean was back in bed, feigning sleep. Kyle couldn't find whatever had caused the crash. The passage between the bathroom and bed was clear. It must have been Sean crashing into the wall.

"Sean?" he whispered.

He dried off and approached their bed. The fall-back change in the clocks meant it was light enough out for Kyle to see Sean's face. Soft and relaxed. Sean had always been good at faking sleep.

"I know you're awake."

"Hmm?" He could even fake a sleep-scratchy voice.

"Did you need something?"

"Sleep would be good." All the pretense was gone from his voice.

"Okay. Do you want me to make you some breakfast?"

"I can handle it."

"What time's your PT appointment today?"

"Eleven thirty, but I said I could take a cab."

Kyle tried to summon a patient tone that wouldn't sound patronizing. "That's a waste of money we don't have with you not working. It's no problem for me to drive you."

"I'm going to get disability and— Fine. I'm too tired to argue." Sean rolled away toward the middle of the bed.

Kyle sat on Sean's side of the bed and reached for Sean's head. He pulled his hand back and bit his lip. "I'll bring you up something to eat."

"I told you I can get it myself."

"I don't particularly want to come home to the smell when you fall down the stairs and break your neck. So you can either drag your ass downstairs before I go to work, or you can stay up here until I come to get you at eleven." He gave up on a reasonable tone.

"Christ. I'll get up." Sean sat up and grabbed the pain pill and water bottle Kyle had left on the nightstand.

"How bad is it?"

"A lot better when I'm asleep."

"Sorry, *chulo*." Kyle ran his hand through Sean's hair, but Sean didn't lean into the caress like he usually did. "Worse than when you hit your thumb with the hammer in July?"

Sean glanced down at his still-blackened nail. "A lot worse."

"Worse than when you stepped on the toothpick and it went all the way through your foot?"

"Yes. Are you trying to make me sound like a klutz?"

"Worse than the first time you got fucked?" Kyle tried with a grin.

"Definitely."

"Ouch." Kyle rubbed the back of Sean's neck.

"Does it always have to be about sex for you?"

Shoving himself away from the bed, Kyle whipped off his towel and tossed it at the wall. "Right. Because I'm the one who asked the fucking surgeon in the hospital how soon we could have sex again."

He stalked into the closet and grabbed his clothes. *And I love you more than our California Closet.* He couldn't even stand to look at it right now.

He was hitching his belt by the time Sean said, "Kyle."

Kyle looked over at him and waited.

"Do you think you could make some coffee that doesn't suck?"

"I can try. Given my obsession with sex, I'll do my best not to jerk off in it." Kyle grabbed his shirt and tie to finish dressing somewhere—anywhere else.

Chapter Five

Sean tried to break his own house record for how quickly he could zip through five hundred channels of nothing. He had a stopwatch in the garage with the baseball gear, but for now he was using the clock on the cable box. According to those red numbers, Kyle had been gone for an hour.

His half-finished coffee mug sat in the sink. How Kyle could screw up something as simple as pouring water and measuring grounds was something that continued to amaze Sean. He had, however, claimed that Kyle's coffee was good, and managed to choke down a full mug—fortified with cream and sugar. Swallowing Kyle's coffee without making a face ought to have been enough to name him Boyfriend of the Year.

Yeah, the remark about Kyle's sex drive had been a shitty thing to say, although "Sorry you're stuck jerking off for the next few weeks" didn't sound much better. When Sean's bladder dragged him out of sleep this morning, he didn't expect to get an earful of Kyle in the shower. It wasn't like Sean had never heard Kyle jerk off before. But this time, instead of Kyle's moans turning Sean on, he'd been left feeling vaguely ashamed and dirty. Like he was spying on a stranger.

After the funeral yesterday, Sean really didn't need anything else to guilt over. But it didn't excuse his being an asshole, and he was going to apologize to Kyle as soon as he came to pick him up.

When the doorbell rang, Sean clicked the mute on the TV and began the slow process of getting up and to the door. Given what had happened yesterday, he probably shouldn't even answer it. The thought of facing Vince Gerbino again made him seriously consider sinking back in the chair. But the door was unlocked, and if Gerbino was coming in, Sean would rather face it on his feet. He hobbled out into the entrance hall and managed to get the door open without wobbling.

Instead of an angry father, a gorgeous guy stood on the step. His cinnamon brown hair was a shade too perfectly highlighted to be anything but out of a box, and his eyes were so green they had to be contacts, but however artificial Sean knew the man's looks were, he couldn't help staring. And the assurance in those eyes said the guy damned well knew it.

"Sean Farnham? It's great to meet you." The guy smiled, and Sean defied any guy with a working dick not to notice full lips that were just made for cocksucking.

Sean instinctively took the hand the man offered. "What can I do for you?"

"Actually, I'm hoping I can do something for you. I saw the news yesterday. That was a fucking mess."

Sean couldn't argue, but now that the initial effect of the guy's appearance was fading, Sean just wanted him gone. "Whatever you're selling—"

"You."

"Huh?"

"You. I want to sell you. Believe me, you could use the help. I'm sorry. Brandt Sobell. I work in public relations."

"Well, Mr. Sobell. I think I've had enough of any kind of relations with the public for a while so..." Sean shifted on his crutches and reached for the door.

"But the public hasn't had enough of you. Wouldn't you rather have some control over that relationship? They're going to keep after you. It's not going to go away."

Sean was afraid the man was right.

"You've got to be tired of standing there like that. Do you mind if I come in?"

"Will it cost me anything?"

"Not a cent, I promise."

Those bottle green eyes were wide with sincerity. From years of teaching teenagers, Sean knew damned well no one looked that guileless unless they were hiding something, but he still stepped aside.

Brandt Sobell laid his leather jacket over the back of the sofa and made himself at home on the cushions. The fact that Sean's brain was imagining what the outlines of that close-fitting green suede shirt hid just meant he was still alive. With eyes. And a libido buried somewhere under a layer of codeine and pain.

Sean settled back on the recliner, waiting. That was another trick he'd picked up from teaching. If you held someone's gaze silently, they'd start to say anything, guilty or not.

Brandt's quick smile said he knew that game himself.

"Look, Sean, I could waste our time telling you what a lovely house you and Kyle have and how impressed I was by your act of bravery, but I'm going to cut to the chase."

"Really?" Sean injected his tone with as much sarcasm as he could manage.

"Everyone wants a piece of you right now because you're a hero. Heroes make people feel good, hopeful. And lots of people are willing to pay for the privilege of meeting one, even if it's only through a magazine or on TV. With the right kind of management, you could live pretty comfortably even if you never set foot in a classroom again."

"I enjoy teaching, Mr. Sobell."

The guy stopped smiling, losing the dimples and adopting a serious expression better suited to one of the therapists they periodically hauled in front of the teachers to explain how educators weren't meeting the needs of today's over-stressed adolescents. PR guy sensed he'd lost ground and was now shifting tactics. Sean waited to hear what he'd come up with next.

"Did Kyle run into any trouble with the hospital?" Long

lashes framed that caring green gaze. The guy ought to be selling car insurance—on TV.

"Excuse me?"

"Without any legal claim or protection, did your partner find it hard to be at your side when you were wounded?"

Sean hadn't asked Kyle about that. There'd been that moment when he'd thought the night nurse would kick Kyle out, but that had been it. He wondered what Kyle might have had to put up with.

"You're in a position to change hearts and minds, Sean." The guy kept using his name to establish a connection. Sean wanted to tell him it was getting on his nerves. "School violence is a raw nerve. You saved children at the risk of your own life. Despite what happened yesterday, that's going to make a difference in how a lot of people think about gay men."

The guy wasn't saying anything Sean hadn't thought when he'd decided to introduce Kyle as his partner on the *Today* show. Still, no one did anything just for a cause.

"And what's in all this for you?" Sean asked.

"Here's what I'm offering. I handle the public for you, handle the press. I'm not just talking about the gay press, *The Advocate, Out.* I'm talking about the cover of *People*. Oprah. Places where everyone will hear what you've got to say. I'll make sure everyone knows that if it weren't for a fucking faggot, they'd be digging a lot more graves in Canton this week."

"And you'd do all this because of a concern for equal rights?"

"Oh, there's money in it. For you and for me. We'd do a contract, specify percentages. There's speaking fees, stipends, honorariums. And I'll be building contacts, a client base. I'm not going to bullshit you. There's a lot in it for me. In addition to it being my one chance to help a gay hero."

"One chance?"

"I don't know if you've noticed, Sean, but usually to get to be a gay hero, you have to die. I'm good with PR, but it's harder to get money out of a corpse. Though it can be done." The guy's eyes gleamed with avarice. "I'd rather work with the living, though. Much better looking."

Christ, was the guy coming on to him? Maybe that wasn't greed in his eyes.

Brandt Sobell leaned toward Sean. "The fact that you're easy on the eyes only makes my job easier."

The door opened. Whatever Sean had seen in Brandt's eyes vanished, leaving just the smiling salesman Sean had met at the door. Kyle was early.

"Hey, *chulo*, I thought if you wanted we could stop for some real coffee on the way," Kyle called from the doorway.

If Kyle was making a peace offering, it probably meant that he'd fucked up the coffee on purpose this morning, the bastard.

"Did Sherry and Alex get a new car? Because there's a Lexus—" Kyle came through the arch into the living room and stopped.

Brandt stood. "Kyle? Nice to meet you. Brandt Sobell."

Kyle took the offered hand. Sean wondered if his lover's dazed expression mirrored his own when faced with the guy's charm and looks. Maybe Brandt should be the one to carry the flag on Oprah. He could sell shoes to a snake.

After explaining why he was there, Brandt handed Sean a card.

"I'll just get out of your way and let Sean explain everything. It was great meeting you both."

Sean could see Kyle's gaze linger on those satiny lips. They were a little hard to ignore.

"Call me soon. Yesterday's news is a much harder sell." Brandt let himself out.

Kyle came over and took the card from Sean's fingers. "No."

"Just no?"

Kyle put the card on the end table. "Do you want to go out for coffee or not?"

"I've only had one codeine. I don't see how I could have slept through our discussing his offer."

"A lack of coffee?"

"Jesus Christ, Kyle. Stop being a fucking prick." At times like this he really appreciated being four inches taller than his lover, except at times like this when it took him half an hour to get out of his goddamned chair.

"Oh, I think you've got that title wrapped up. Did you forget that we needed a fucking police escort to get home yesterday?"

"Because you wanted one. Not everything turns out to be the disaster you think it's going to be. If I work with Brandt, I can control it." Sean managed to stand, but a lot of good that did him when Kyle was still half a room away.

"Brandt?"

"For Chrissake, Kyle, you're not jealous."

"Should I be?"

"He was only here ten minutes. Can we discuss this like adults, please?"

"Right now? Apparently not." Kyle turned back toward the hallway.

"Oh, don't pull that shit."

"What?"

"I've enjoyed chasing you through the past seven years of this relationship, but I'm just not up to it today."

"I can't talk about this now, Sean." Kyle faced him, but stayed in the archway.

"When's a good time for you? My schedule's free. Think you can pencil me in a week from tomorrow?"

"Goddammit." Kyle turned away again and then turned back. His hands clenched into fists, tightening and relaxing like he was working an imaginary stress ball. "If I stay here, I'm going to say something I'll regret."

"So say it. C'mon, Kyle. What the fuck can't you say to my face?"

They weren't quite there yet. Neither of them had completely lost their temper, but they were skating close to an edge they'd only been to once or twice.

Kyle dragged a fist across his forehead. "I don't want any of this. I don't want you hurt. I don't want to be afraid of getting bashed in front of St. Theresa's. I don't want to see another TV camera as long as I live. And I sure as hell"—Kyle flicked PR guy's card off the table—"don't want you getting help in making our lives more fucked up than they already are."

You couldn't live with a guy for six years and not see him pissed. Kyle could get pissed about a lot of things: traffic, being late for something—especially when it was Sean's fault—too many westerns airing on Turner Classic Movies, Sean throwing out Kyle's favorite ratty T-shirt.

But Kyle wasn't pissed. He was angry and he was scared. God knew Kyle could worry over anything, but Sean had never seen him this scared. Of all the fucking times for Kyle to have a meltdown, this was the worst. And all Sean wanted to do was fix it for him.

"Babe—"

Kyle stepped over the card on the floor and stood in front of Sean. "I wish to God this had never happened." Kyle put his hands behind Sean's neck.

"I know. Me too. But it did happen. And we've just got to get through it." Sean dropped one of the crutches and braced himself with a hand on Kyle's shoulder. "You don't want another scene like yesterday, right? This guy could help with that. Maybe could help with people like Gerbino. Give it a month, okay? A month and things will settle down. People will forget about me and we can go back to everything the way it was."

Balancing carefully, Sean moved his hand up to cover Kyle's cheek, thumb brushing his lips. "All right, babe?"

Kyle kissed the pad of Sean's thumb and then pulled him in until Sean was leaning on him. "Do I have a choice?"

He did, Sean knew. Kyle could go back to Cleveland, back to the life he'd had before Sean had convinced Kyle to move down to Canton with him. He could go all the way home to Philly, or move in with one of his three siblings or forty-seven cousins. Yeah, Kyle had a choice.

"God, I hope not." Sean breathed against Kyle's neck.

ß

The phone rang incessantly for the next few days. Kyle found himself wondering what would happen if he grabbed the handset from Sean and gave it two minutes on high in the microwave.

Nothing would change. *Brandt* had Sean's cell number.

Maybe Kyle was overreacting, but the guy made him a little nuts. Brandt had that slimy false charm Kyle associated with furniture and car salesmen. They were your best friend right up until they had your money in their pocket, and then you were on your own.

On Friday, *The Advocate* came to do a photo shoot and interview. The hero and his lover smiling from their couch in suburbia. On Monday, Sean was due in a studio in Cleveland for a photo shoot for *Out*.

Brandt was supplying transportation, had even offered to take Sean to PT, an offer Kyle couldn't refuse since he was supposed to be in meetings all day.

Brandt swore *People* was next.

On Sunday morning Kyle opened his eyes and waited for the daily dose of dread to hit him. Then he looked at his watch. Ten o'clock and the phone had yet to ring. Sean didn't have a PT appointment. Kyle didn't have to worry about him falling or trying to drive the Durango with his left leg. He rolled back over onto Sean's left side, draping a thigh over his good leg, and breathed in the scent of his neck. Sean pulled him closer, then let him go with a sigh.

"You're just waiting for me to make the coffee, aren't you?" Sean asked, a smile in his voice.

"Nope. I just want five minutes without having to share you."

Sean's free hand stroked down Kyle's chest and that was all

it took.

"Shit." Kyle rolled away. "Sorry."

"Sorry?"

The smell, Sean's body heat, morning, and then that touch all combined to get Kyle achingly hard. He wasn't going to give Sean another reason to make some comment about the fact that Kyle couldn't last a day without sex. He willed his erection to subside.

Sean trailed a hand down his spine. Which didn't help. At all.

"You're sorry?" Sean asked again. "Sorry I can get you hard like that? Why is that a problem?"

The hand on Kyle's spine moved over his ass. "Sean—"

"I can get you off, babe. C'mon back over here."

Those caressing fingers dipped lower, teased under his balls. Kyle pushed his ass back into that big, warm hand and took a deep breath. "What did you have in mind?"

"Roll on your stomach and find out."

A soft kiss on the back of his neck decided him and Kyle settled on his stomach with another sigh. Sean pressed against him, solid weight and hot skin. His tongue ran over the knobs at the top of Kyle's spine.

The doorbell rang.

"Fuck," Sean groaned and rolled away, taking all that tingling heat and pressure with him.

"Or not." Kyle clambered out of bed and crossed to the window. Tony's Rabbit was at the curb. "It's Jack and Tony." The doorbell rang again, long overlapping chimes from someone leaning on it. "You know they won't leave."

"And they have a fucking key."

Kyle struggled into a pair of sweats, easing the elastic over his half-hard cock. "I'll be back as soon as I'm done killing them. You don't mind if I bury the bodies in the backyard, right?"

"I hear it's great for the roses."

Kyle started downstairs to find Tony already in the hall.

"Hey. I thought maybe you needed some help."

"Not from you, thanks." If Kyle was interested in that kind of help from either of their best friends, it would have been Jack. He looked like a GQ cover model and if the adage about thumb size was true...

"Oh, what did we interrupt?"

"Nothing." The tent in his sweats made him a liar, but Kyle just didn't care. "What are you doing here?"

"It's the first Sunday of the month." Jack crowded in behind Tony.

"And?"

"Brunch. Standing date," Tony said.

"Since when?"

"Since we did it in September, and we hardly ever see you once school starts, and you said let's do it every month, and Sean said he'd cook, but we couldn't in October because Jack had to work."

As soon as Kyle made it down the rest of the stairs, Tony hauled him into his arms, punctuating his hug with a slow rub against Kyle's hard-on.

"Fuck you," Kyle muttered in his ear.

"You wish."

"Hey. How're you doing?" Jack gave him a more circumspect embrace.

"Obviously, we didn't expect Sean to cook, so Jack got us a table at The Pinnacle," Tony said.

"For what?" Sean was halfway down the stairs.

"Brunch. You've heard of it, right? Otherwise known as gay church?"

"And we're treating. I'm sure you guys could use a break." Jack still had an arm around Kyle's shoulders and gave him a squeeze.

"So, c'mon," Tony called up to Sean. "Do whatever you were going to do with your boy here, shower and be back down in five minutes."

Sean's outraged "Hey" echoed Kyle's "Excuse me?"

Jack reached around Kyle to cuff the back of Tony's head.

"Fine." Tony sighed and rolled his eyes. "Ten."

The Pinnacle was one of the few high-end restaurants in Canton. As the hostess led them to a table, Kyle saw two of his firm's partners sitting with their families. *Jesus, Mary and Joseph, please don't let Tony get us slung out of here.*

Maybe Jack had put in a word, since their table was well in the back and off to one side, almost hidden by a wall.

"Do you need anything to make you comfortable, sir?" the hostess asked with a smile for Sean.

"I can manage, thank you." Sean tucked one of his crutches between his legs to create an elevated rest for his still-braced knee. "I'm sure my friends will take care of me."

When they got up to go to the buffet, Sean pulled Kyle down by his shirtfront to murmur, "Nothing that ends in a vowel. No frittata, no quiche, no brioche."

"No saus*age*?" Kyle asked with a false French accent.

"Asshole." Sean swatted him away.

When Kyle got back with Sean's plate, there was a small crowd around the table. Being in the back hadn't done anything to keep people from finding them. Kyle renewed his grip on the plates. A month. Maybe six weeks. And then the occasional news story on the anniversary. It wasn't going to be like this forever, and Sean deserved all the credit. At least none of the people around their table looked ready to assault him.

"We just wanted you to know he doesn't speak for all the parents, Sean," a woman was saying as Kyle approached the table. "We feel lucky to have you in our school. God knows, you may have saved our boys' lives."

May have? Chris Bowman had three more clips in his coat pocket. Enough ammo to take out a third of the school. Two of the men in the crowd clapped Sean on the shoulder as they stepped away, revealing Sean's face at last. A little heat made the tops of his cheeks red, but his eyes were shining.

He deserved a moment of praise. Kyle knew that girl's father had upset Sean more than he would let on. If only Sean would see that the more publicity he got, the more the crazies would come out of the woodwork. Not everyone in Canton—or Ohio for that matter—was a well-dressed liberal who brunched at The Pinnacle.

Tony came up behind Kyle. "Adoring fans or crazy homophobes?"

"Adoring fans," Jack answered as they slid their plates onto the table. "And the ladies certainly find our boy adorable. I thought for a minute Mrs. Pendarsky—was it?—was going to end up in your lap."

Kyle took his seat across from Jack and started eating the ham off the frittata.

"So, Kyle, what's it like fucking a superhero?"

"Like I'd know." The mutter was out of his mouth before he had time to think about it. Sean's fork scraped across his plate, and Jack stared.

"Yeah, man, did his dick grow two inches?" Apparently, Tony had missed Kyle's inner bitch deciding to make an appearance.

"Is there a reason you'd think it needs to?" Kyle asked.

Under the table, Sean's hand landed on Kyle's thigh and squeezed.

Tony just smiled.

"Honey." Kyle raised Tony's evil grin by two dimples. "If it got any longer, gas pumps would be jealous."

Jack leaned sideways and kissed his lover. "Gotcha, sweetie."

Sean's fingers drifted up Kyle's inseam. His dick hadn't forgiven him for the interruption this morning. It wouldn't take much. Kyle dropped his own hand in his lap and grabbed Sean's wrist.

Tony turned sideways in his chair. "Jack, I believe there may be inappropriate behavior going on at this table. I don't know if I can handle having my view of my hero tarnished. We may have to leave."

"Shut the fuck up," Sean said, and Tony obediently fell silent, turning to gaze at Sean with wide adoring eyes.

Another couple was approaching the table, this time with a teenaged girl in tow. Kyle jerked his chin, and Tony turned around to look.

"Mr. Farnham, we just wanted to say..."

During the course of the brunch three more couples also just wanted to offer their thanks, and so did two of the waiters—one on behalf of a sister, the other on the behalf of a cousin. Even their ultra-conservative mayor stopped by to shake hands and wish Sean a speedy recovery.

Kyle thought maybe his smile was frozen on his face. He was pretty sure his dimples were going to be permanent.

He offered to bring the car to the door, but Sean insisted on walking. The morning had gotten colder, the sky gone iron grey with the threat of windy rain—or if the temperature kept dropping—lake-effect snow.

"Go warm up the car," Sean said. He'd decided a coat was too awkward to manage with his crutches.

Tony fell into step with Kyle as he headed for the car.

"You know." Tony scratched his ear. "Sometimes drugs can affect a guy's—"

It was on the tip of Kyle's tongue to say, *You'd sure know,* but his inner bitch had evidently gone off for a nap. "I thought you didn't hear that."

"Oh, dude. I definitely heard that."

"Well, his leg's really painful. And the PT takes a lot out of him."

Tony nodded. "So, why're you riding him about it?"

He didn't want to be. Didn't mean to be. And if Tony and Jack hadn't dragged them off to brunch, maybe he wouldn't have a reason to be.

"Look, Kyle."

Kyle did look. He couldn't remember the last time Tony had

called him by name. It was always *man* or *dude* or *Sean's boy.* And he didn't think he'd ever seen such a serious look in Tony's blue eyes.

"Don't read anything into this but that I've known the guy for a long time, but I'm sure he's not exactly getting a kick out of celibacy either. And if his leg hurts enough that he doesn't want his dick sucked, then maybe he should talk to the doctor again."

When they got home, Sean headed right for the stairs. "I'm really tired and I've got a headache. I'm going to take a nap."

It certainly didn't sound like Sean wanted his dick sucked anytime soon. "Okay." Kyle waited at the foot of the stairs until he didn't hear thumping anymore and went into his office. It was narrow solarium off the living room, with 1920's leaded glass on three sides, and about a hundred percent of the reason why Kyle had fallen in love with this house.

As soon as he sat at the drafting table, the phone rang. It was probably Brandt calling for Sean. Kyle considered letting the machine get it, but if Sean really did have a headache... Kyle picked up the extension in the office.

As soon as he heard his dad's voice on the phone, Kyle's heart went into overdrive. His father never called him. His mom called and then put his dad on for their thirty-second update of *How's the job? Everything okay?* Holy Mary, had something happened to his mom?

While Dad's casual "How's everything? How's Sean?" managed to convince Kyle that no one was dead or on life support, his stomach and throat still felt thick with worry. There had to be some reason his father called.

Never one for casual conversation, his father got to his point. "Has Sean been back to the school yet?"

"No. They want him to do at least another week or two of physical therapy before they'll clear him for work. Insurance stuff, I guess."

Dad treated Sean with roughly the same deference he accorded Kyle's sister's husband, but even with the shooting, it was a strange conversation to be having with his father.

"I was just thinking. A couple of guys I knew in the service, ones who were still in after Nam, every time they sounded General Quarters... I was just thinking, maybe Sean should go to the school once or twice...before he goes back full time. Might make things easier."

His father had called because he was worried about Sean suffering from post-traumatic stress. Great. First sex advice from Tony and now Dad showed more concern about Sean than Kyle had.

"That's a good idea, Dad." It was a great idea actually, though how he was going to bring it up without Sean insisting for the thousandth time he was fine was something Kyle hadn't worked out yet.

"All right." Kyle could almost hear the crisp nod of his father's close-cropped head. "You boys take care. Your mother wants to talk to you."

Chapter Six

"And keep doing the exercises at home this weekend."

Sean managed to salute his physical therapist while turning to wrestle with the door into the waiting room.

Kyle put down his magazine and got to his feet. "Hey."

Sean balanced with the crutches first under one side and then the other so he could shrug into his coat while Kyle waited quietly. Sean had told Kyle over and over that he could wait in the car, but he never did. Sean hated the fact that they wouldn't let him drive yet, so Kyle had to keep taking time from work to bring him here and pick him up. Had it only been three weeks of therapy? It felt like a year.

He was starting to wish that Kyle would complain, but Kyle was being a fucking saint about the whole thing. By now, Kyle knew better than to try to help him with his coat, or to get the door, or to suggest that he take the ramp instead of the stairs. The fight they'd had over Brandt felt like it was still simmering. Kyle had slapped on a veneer of polite attention to the publicity that was seeping into every other aspect of their lives. Sean wondered how long it would take for Kyle to snap.

"So, how much of a bitch was Theresa today?" Kyle asked after Sean had stowed his crutches in the backseat and eased into the front.

"She used her whole quotient up yesterday so I got to spend lots of time in the whirlpool."

At first, Sean kept thanking Kyle for picking him up, but Kyle always made a face that made Sean feel even worse than being dependent did.

"You want to go out and get something to eat?" Sean asked.

"Not unless you really want to. There're some of those cornbeef quesadillas from Juan O'Grady's left."

Sean knew damned well Kyle would normally never turn down a chance to go out to eat, but every time they went out, they could barely eat a mouthful between people coming over to their table to tell him how scared they'd been to hear the news and what a great guy Sean was. It might be great for the public perception of gays and it might be making Brandt some money in the future, but in the middle of a restaurant, the attention made Sean uncomfortable. He couldn't imagine what Kyle hid behind his polite smile. They were living off their freezer and takeout since neither of them could stomach the sight of turkey after the second week.

"Tired?" Kyle asked.

"Not really." After all that time in the whirlpool, Sean felt almost back to normal.

Sean stared through the windshield and then snuck a glance at Kyle's face, the features so familiar but so composed and distant. It had gotten worse since he got home from the photo shoot on Monday. Kyle was going all-out for the Oscar for Considerate Boyfriend in a Supporting Role, but Sean knew Kyle was holding something back. "Do you want to go to the football game?" Kyle turned the radio down as they waited at the light to cross Market Avenue.

"What?"

"The football game. McKinley's in the divisional playoffs."

"I know that." What Sean couldn't believe was that Kyle knew that. Kyle's attention to sports was limited to the men's swimming and diving events at the Olympics, and attending Tony's Super Bowl party. Though Sean suspected the Super Bowl party attendance had more to do with margaritas and chili than with an interest in the game. In six years of living with a stats-obsessed baseball coach, Kyle had just managed to grasp the difference between an ERA and an RBI.

"All these years you've never once gone to a game with me."

"I thought you might like to go."

The light changed. Sean watched the streets go by. Maybe Kyle had decided that since Sean was now as out as Elton John that going to a game together wouldn't cause problems for Sean with the kids or parents.

"Do you want to go?"

"Isn't that what I said?" Kyle turned right on Harrisburg Road.

Sean would have gone down Thirty-fifth Street. This was the long way. "No. You asked if I wanted to go."

"I want to go."

"To the football game."

Kyle's casual hand-in-lap steering shifted to a perfect ten and two on the wheel. If he weren't wearing the leather gloves Sean's mother had bought him last Christmas, Sean bet he'd be able to see white on Kyle's knuckles. But the polite façade never cracked.

"So, you're too tired?" At last they turned onto Willow Avenue.

"I'm fine. We'll go to the game."

Sean was still trying to figure out why they were going as they hung their coats up in the hall. He wasn't sure how much more of this he could take. He didn't want another fight, but he couldn't stand watching Kyle be so goddamned careful all the time.

"Do you want me to nuke up the quesadillas?" Kyle asked.

"No."

"You want to grab something on the way to the game?"

"No."

Kyle looked up at him, really looked at him. A quick dart of his tongue moistened his lips as he swallowed.

Sean leaned forward and traced his tongue along the thick bob as it rolled down Kyle's throat. Kyle put a hand up to rest on Sean's chest, not pushing him away, but not letting him closer. There was a question in Kyle's eyes, in the slant of his dark brows.

And right now there was no pain keeping Sean from pressing forward with his answer. He pushed Kyle into the coats lining the hall. The hand on Sean's chest fell away as Kyle tipped his head to meet Sean's kiss.

"So, you really liked the whirlpool, huh?" Kyle muttered against his mouth.

"Shut up." Sean dropped his crutches and grabbed the back of Kyle's head. Kyle's hands made a muffled sound as they slapped flat against the wool-covered wood.

As Kyle's lips opened on a moan, everything hit Sean at once, that long-missed smell, Kyle's taste, the wet slide of his tongue and fuck that healing sartorious muscle, because all Sean wanted to do was grind his cock into Kyle's belly.

Kyle's hands dug into Sean's hips, holding him steady as they kissed, and there was nothing careful or polite about the thrusting tongue in Sean's mouth, the tug of teeth at his lips when they pulled apart.

"Upstairs. Now," Sean grunted against Kyle's lips.

"Okay." But Kyle was kissing him again, cock hardening against Sean's hips as Kyle inhaled Sean's mouth. It took all Sean's concentration to keep his hips still.

Sean lifted his head and steadied himself with a hand on the door as Kyle bent and picked up his crutches, tucking them under Sean's arms.

"Race you." Kyle winked.

"You're on." Sean swung backward and pivoted on his good leg, blocking Kyle's access to the stairs with his crutch. "I win." He hitched himself up on the first step.

"Still have to make it to the bed."

"We'll see."

Managing the stairs on crutches was one thing. Managing the stairs on crutches with all his blood pounding into his hard-on was almost impossible. He paused to rest halfway up.

"Sean?" Kyle's voice held urgent concern, and suddenly

Sean knew how he was going to win.

"I'm okay," he said without a trace of the irritation he usually showed when Kyle tried to help him.

At the top of the stairs, Sean deliberately stumbled. As Kyle hurried up the last few steps to catch him, Sean tripped Kyle with a crutch and took off for the bedroom. Kyle cursed and chased him, but Sean was sprawled on the bed before Kyle caught him.

"You are such a competitive shithead." Kyle dropped onto the bed.

"Sore loser. Whose idea was it to race a cripple?"

"I just wanted—" Kyle stopped, but Sean could fill in the missing words *I just wanted everything to be normal again.* Kyle went on, "So we up here for a reason, or did you just want to try to trip me into falling down the stairs?"

"Oh, I got a reason. Interested?" Standing, Sean used one crutch for balance as he pulled his sweats and boxers off his legs.

Kyle's gaze focused on Sean's level of interest. "Did you get clearance to fuck?"

"I have to wait until my appointment with the orthopedic doctor next week." Sean tugged his shirt over his head and sat back on the bed, swinging his legs out straight.

"You asked her?"

"Of course. Theresa's a lesbian. She thinks it's cute how desperate I am to get back to pounding your ass."

Kyle's slow smile made every inch of Sean's skin grow hot and tight. "Did you tell her how often you're up on your knees begging to get done?"

"And mess with her perfectly good stereotypes? You know the taller guy always tops." Sean lifted his head to watch Kyle yank off his tie and unbutton his shirt. "Did losing the race take the wind out of your sails?"

Kyle unbuckled his belt and unzipped so that his pants fell around his hips. The dark, flushed head of his cock was just visible at the waistband of his briefs.

"Guess not. Come on up here and let me blow you."

"I'm not gonna argue with that."

Kyle shoved off the rest of his clothing and climbed on the bed. They'd been touching, of course, they *were* sleeping in the same bed, but it felt a lot longer than a month since Sean had had all of Kyle's skin against his own, since Sean'd had that perfect weight on his chest.

"Missed you, babe." Sean threaded his fingers through the soft black curls.

"Yeah, me too." Kyle kissed him, slow and deep and much more carefully, his weight balanced off Sean's legs.

"You don't have to do that. It doesn't hurt all the time anymore." And he needed Kyle to stop thinking about his leg and the shooting and being so goddamned worried all the time. That was the whole point of this, well, that and a good long come.

"But I don't want to..."

"Fine. Just climb up here then." Christ. Sex with Kyle was never this fucking complicated. Even when they'd first started fucking, when Kyle had told Sean he was lucky he was a great lay since he was annoyingly bossy, everything had just worked.

Kyle didn't actually sigh, but almost made a sound that suggested it was a fucking imposition to get his dick sucked, which made Sean want to forget the whole thing.

Moving up to straddle Sean's chest, Kyle stared down with those dark almond-shaped eyes. "I'm sorry."

"For what?"

"For screwing this up."

Sean ran his hands down Kyle's sides to cup his ass. "It's not screwed up. It's just a little slow to launch. We're out of practice." He fisted Kyle's dick. "C'mere, babe. I want to taste you."

Kyle made one of his tight, high moans and rocked his hips forward into Sean's grip. Sean twisted his hand, and Kyle's lashes dropped against his cheeks.

"Can't reach you there," Sean said.

Kyle swung off and turned around so he straddled Sean's face, leaning down to lay a long lick up the length of Sean's dick.

Sean arched his neck until he could get his lips around the head and suck, his hand working the shaft. Kyle's groan vibrated against the root of Sean's cock. He wanted to drive Kyle out of his mind, make him desperate, do something that would break down this awkward distance between them.

Sean took Kyle deeper, hand and mouth working him in a quick bob, but Kyle's hips never bucked that thick cock into his throat, and Kyle never missed a beat as he tongued Sean's dick, licking into the slit, soaking him with spit until he was gliding in Kyle's fist. Sean let Kyle's dick slide free and dragged him closer, rolling his balls into his mouth. Kyle's hand stuttered, his tongue slowed, and Sean pulled Kyle lower until Sean could lick up the crease of Kyle's ass.

The shudder rolled down from Kyle's shoulders, twisting his body as he arched off Sean's dick. Sean worked his thumbs down into the crease, pulling Kyle wide open for his tongue.

"Fuck," Kyle gasped.

Sean rubbed the soft skin, spreading his spit, pressing lightly on the opening.

"Stop fucking teasing me."

"Not teasing."

"You can't."

"I can."

Kyle pulled all the way off him, sitting back on his heels. "What?"

Sean dug in his nightstand drawer, tossing lube and a heavy velvet pouch onto the bed.

"Is that Tony's housewarming present?"

"Yep." Sean used his arms to lever himself until he was sitting up against the headboard, his legs out straight in front of him.

"You're kidding." Kyle loosened the drawstrings and pulled out the solid glass dildo.

"You want to get fucked, don't you?"

Kyle ran his hand over the dildo. As sex toys went, it was pretty, clear glass, with a bulb at the top, an *s* curve on a shaft dotted with blue bumps. The flared base had a small handle attached. Tony had claimed it was art suitable for display. Sean wouldn't go that far, but it would definitely be a conversation starter if they left it out. Kyle's fingers traced those bumps, and Sean knew Kyle was gauging how they would feel on him, in him.

"What the hell." Kyle shrugged.

Sean smiled and picked up the lube. "Sit on my lap, and don't fucking worry about my leg. If it hurts, trust me, I'll tell you."

He held the dildo between his thighs and spread lube around the bulb at the head. Kyle straddled Sean so he had three dicks in his lap—his own, Kyle's and the slippery length of glass.

"Couldn't we just—" Kyle's words cut off as Sean rubbed a thumb around his hole.

"Are you actually suggesting I disregard medical advice?"

"No-uh." His voice broke as Sean's thumb popped into his body.

Kyle's cock rubbed up against Sean's as he shifted on Sean's lap. The weight on his thighs stretched and burned Sean's healing muscles, but the pain wasn't enough to diminish the pulse of blood to his cock. And definitely not enough pain to stop, especially when Kyle's back arched and his muscle clamped around the base of Sean's thumb. God, he wanted that smooth heat around his dick, but right now he wanted to watch Kyle's face when those hard glass knobs teased over his rim, when the curve of the shaft drove the head against his prostate.

"You're so tight, babe."

"Long time." Kyle put his hands on Sean's shoulders.

Still too fucking gentle, Kyle's hands just resting there when he should have been squeezing, pleading, demanding. Sean urged Kyle up on his knees before wiping a hand in the sheets to get a grip on the base of the slippery glass.

When the tip stretched him open, Kyle's breath made that hitching sound Sean knew so well, the sound that always made Sean's hips want to slam forward, pump him hard and deep into Kyle's body. Sean put a hand on Kyle's hips and dragged him down.

Kyle jerked up, his hands hard on Sean's shoulders in warning.

Sean looked up. "If you tell me that's bigger than I am, I'm going to be insulted."

"No, but—" Kyle shifted. "It's different."

Sean held the dildo steady. "Want me to stop?"

"No." But his gasps were short and tight. "You know, no matter what you'd like to think, you're not quite as hard as glass."

Sean snorted and pulled Kyle's hips down while he pushed up with the dildo. It slipped and Kyle's ass slammed down on his fist, the dildo in almost to the base.

"Fucking hell." Kyle's teeth were clenched.

"It's slippery. And I can't exactly feel what I'm doing."

"I can. Shit."

"Should I—"

"Don't fucking move it."

"Okay."

He brought his free hand up to the back of Kyle's neck and tugged his head down for a kiss.

"Sean." Kyle was still gritting his teeth.

"It'll be good in a minute, babe. You know it." Sean licked up the side of his neck.

"Well, it's not you in there so you can wait the fucking minute."

Sean traced his tongue along the space behind Kyle's ear. Kyle was panting now, quick and loud, his breath moving the hair around Sean's ear. Sean bit him just as he shifted his hand, turning the glass inside Kyle.

"Oh fuck. Do it."

Kyle bucked up and when he came back down there was no resistance as Sean fucked the dildo into him. He twisted it, and Kyle's fingers clamped on his shoulders.

Sean stroked his hand down Kyle's back. "How's it feel?"

"I can feel the bumps. Oh fuck yeah. It's—that. Yeah. So good. God."

Kyle rode him then, nothing but a few muttered *fucks* and *goods* as his hands flexed on Sean's shoulders, smooth lean body twisting and bucking as Sean moved his hand on the base as much as he could.

Sean leaned in to kiss Kyle's neck, his jaw, any part of him he could reach, lapping at the sweat dotting the brown skin. His goddamned sartorious muscle gave a scream of protest as he rocked up to meet Kyle's next downward push.

He didn't realize he'd grunted until Kyle froze.

"Is your leg all right?"

"It's fine." He reached up to his shoulder and pulled one of Kyle's hands free, dropping it between them. "C'mon, babe. Get us both off."

Kyle tried to get them both in his fist while Sean steadied him with a hand at the base of his spine.

"Harder," Kyle panted.

Sean's hand was cramping but he could manage a little twisting. Kyle moaned, his hand working an uneven rhythm as he tried to jack them together.

"Let go of me, babe. Just go."

Kyle gave it another awkward try and then Sean's cock bounced free against his stomach, the slap of skin a burst of good pain.

"It's okay. Just go."

Watching Kyle lose himself in his body, the way he surrendered and fell into pleasure, always kicked Sean's own body into overdrive. Kyle's knuckles brushed the head of Sean's dick as he worked himself, making tiny pulses of almost-there tingles tug at Sean's balls. Giving this to Kyle, even without being inside him, was almost like falling with him.

Kyle's moans got higher, and Sean looked down to watch him shoot. He twisted the glass, fucked him all the way through his release, waiting until Kyle's hand slowed and he was just pressing on his softened dick. One last spurt landed on the head of Sean's cock, making him jerk.

Kyle swung off him and had barely sucked Sean's cock clean when the orgasm slammed into Sean's body, hard and fast, nitro in his balls, pouring through his cock, heat and pleasure all liquid inside him, and he couldn't stop coming, though he must have poured a gallon down Kyle's throat, spilling over his chin. Kyle softened his mouth to licks, letting Sean ease down, but he'd come so hard and so long nothing could stop Sean's crash landing into his body.

He jerked away from Kyle's mouth and his leg gave another scream of protest.

Kyle rolled onto his back, head angled toward Sean's feet, eyes even with the thick pink scar. Kyle's eyes always looked soft after he came, the angles of his face smoothing out with relaxation. As Kyle stared at the lines crossing Sean's flesh, he could see the tension rush back into Kyle's face.

"It's okay. I'm fine," Sean said quickly.

"I know."

Are we? But what Sean couldn't make himself ask aloud went unanswered.

Kyle's heart was still pounding as he rolled off the bed and took the dildo into the bathroom to wash it. His body was a lot happier than his head. But then their bodies weren't exactly the problem. Sean's leg was healing and he'd be back to himself in no time. Kyle just wished everything else could be fixed with a little physical therapy.

His ass clenched as his soapy hand bumped down the knobby shaft. Their physical therapy had definitely been a lot more fun than what Sean described with Theresa. Leave it to Sean to figure out a way around the doctor's restrictions, a way that got Kyle off so hard he was still high from it. But that was the problem. It hadn't been sex with Sean; it had been about sex *for* Kyle. And it wasn't because they'd used a dildo. Sean had done everything but get off the bed and watch him, he'd been so intent on making it work for Kyle.

And Kyle hadn't wanted to do a thing to stop it. How did everything get so fucked up?

He dried the toy and his hands and made a face at himself in the mirror. He'd gotten exactly what he'd been wanting, Sean focused on him instead of everything else that had happened, and now he was complaining about it? *Thanks for the ability to guilt out over everything, Mami.*

When he got back to the bedroom, Sean was trying to grab his crutches off the floor while keeping his leg on the bed.

Kyle stuffed the dildo back into its bag. "What time should we leave for the game?"

"Half an hour if we want to get a seat." The fresh pain made Sean's eyes a pale grey.

Guilt made a double knot in Kyle's stomach.

Kyle stood Sean's crutches up next to the bed. "I'll heat up the quesadillas while you shower."

Sean looked like he was going to say something, maybe ask again why Kyle insisted on going to the football game, but Sean's mouth just tightened in what Kyle recognized as his my-leg-hurts-like-a-bitch-and-I-don't-want-to-talk-about-it face. Kyle started to apologize, then leaned in and kissed Sean until his mouth was soft.

There was still one thing that Kyle was sure wasn't fucked up. "I love you."

"I love you more than my PSP."

Chapter Seven

Sean breathed in the familiar smell of cleat-ripped grass and pointed to a spot in the bleachers a few rows up from the field. Even an hour before kickoff the stands were almost full, but people made room for them as Sean hauled himself up the few steps. The guy in front of them jokingly offered his shoulder as a footrest until his words sank in, and he coughed and turned away to study the empty field.

Sean's own gaze kept straining across the island of light on the field to the school buildings beyond, their outline indistinct in the black November night.

"Did you want to go over to your classroom?" Kyle asked.

"No." The sharpness in his voice startled them both. Sean forced a laugh. "I don't want to know what kind of shape it's in after weeks with a sub."

"But isn't there anything you need from it?" Kyle was oddly persistent.

"The department chair brought over all my stuff when she stopped by on Halloween. It's not like I won't be back soon." He tapped his crutch against the metal under their feet. "And I don't have my keys anyway."

"Okay."

The drilling pain started up on the left side of Sean's head again. He couldn't remember ever getting headaches like this before. Pain throbbed in time with his pulse, in time with the drum cadence as the band ran through some warm-ups.

The opposing team ran onto the field for their stretches.

"My God, teenagers have gotten big," Kyle murmured.

"It's the pads."

"Do they have a chance to win?"

"A fair one. Anything can happen in the playoffs, though."

The home team came out through rows of cheerleaders. Something was off about the uniforms. Sean stared. Black armbands. Even the red sweaters of the cheerleaders bore the thin black stripe. He turned around. The band too.

As the band launched into McKinley's fight song, the sharp horns and boom of the bass drum intensified the throb in Sean's head. It was the only explanation for why the field seemed to be at the far end of a foggy tunnel, why suddenly the black armbands stood out on such a dark night.

"Sean?"

He blinked. And it was all back. Just a cold late-autumn night, and a pain in his head that made him nauseous.

"I'm fine."

"Worn out?" Kyle lifted one of his slanted eyebrows. It gave him a sexy, devilish look that Sean had never been able to copy.

Sean leaned close enough to whisper, "I'm not the one who had the hard ride."

Kyle looked away, but Sean could see his throat work around a swallow. Kyle turned back to murmur, "You never told me the football coach was so hot."

Sean picked out Lashway walking through the rows of kids in a short-sleeved red polo and khaki shorts, a red baseball cap on his shaved head. "If you like the gym rat type."

"I like those biceps. How's he look without the shirt?"

Lashway looked like any other buff guy Sean had seen, but Sean had always liked a lean hard body—like Kyle's. Sean shrugged.

"Jealous?" Kyle's voice held more life than it had all week, and the throbbing in Sean's head eased a bit. Even if his leg still ached, this afternoon had been worth it.

Sean held up his pinky and nodded at Lashway.

Kyle's gaze shifted back to the field. "Liar. And do I even want to know how you know this?"

Sean shrugged again. "We were both coming out of the showers one day. He runs a spring practice."

"I can't believe it."

Sean's headache receded even more when the game started. The piercing whistles of the officials and the blare of the announcer didn't echo through his skull the way simple conversation had been doing before. For the entire first quarter neither defense broke, and the teams stayed between the thirty-yard lines.

Kyle stood at the start of the second quarter. "Want some popcorn?" He nodded at the concession stand.

"Whatever you want."

Kyle climbed down, looking somehow out of place. His navy fleece pullover and jeans weren't any different from the clothes on the rest of the fans. Maybe it was the way he just headed directly for the building off to the side, never bothering to look back at the field despite the groans or cheers from the crowd.

With their first possession of the second quarter, the opposing Panthers from North Akron broke a run from scrimmage that would have been a touchdown if Marcus Williams hadn't horse-collared the kid on the six-yard line. Marcus was smart and fast, but Jamal, the regular free safety, probably would have taken the kid down on the thirty—if he weren't still recovering from a gunshot wound to the spleen.

The two plays and one McKinley offsides later, the Panthers punched through the touchdown. In silence that settled on the home stands, Sean could hear his cellphone ring.

After Brandt's usual "Hey there," an expression that left Sean firmly convinced the PR guy was hiding a Kentucky twang under his carefully bland speech, Brandt said, "I've got some news, but I couldn't reach you at home."

"I'm at a football game."

"That's great. I'm glad you're getting out. I'll check in with you later."

Kyle came back with two Cokes and a bag of popcorn. He glanced up at the scoreboard. "Things aren't so good, huh?"

"Nope."

Despite missing the previous extra point, North Akron's kicker managed a twenty-eight yard field goal from the right hash mark to put McKinley down 9-0 at the half. The band marched out and the cheerleaders performed. Conversations in the stands centered on faith in Lashway's ability to analyze the defense and come up with a second-half strategy, but Sean could hear a loss of hope seeping through their assurances. Despite the potential end to the season, as the band shifted formation to perform the alma mater, Sean could honestly say he was enjoying himself and his popcorn.

He watched Kyle lick salt from his fingers, and at that moment Sean's leg didn't hurt badly enough to veto a repeat of this afternoon. Thumb between his teeth, Kyle paused and gave him a quick wink. If Akron scored again, they were leaving.

The band's marching cadence rolled to an end, and the announcer asked somberly if all in attendance would rise for a moment of silence to honor those who had died at McKinley on Tuesday, October twenty-fifth. Frank Healey, Kelsey Nash, Nicole Gerbino. As the announcer read the names, each syllable sent a jolt of energy to that power drill that had just been waiting to start on Sean's temple again.

After people sat back down, the announcer continued, "All of us here would also like to take a moment to honor the hero who saved so many on that day. He has taken some time from his recovery to cheer on the Dragons. Coach Sean Farnham."

Everyone turned and looked at him expectantly, as if Sean were going to suddenly levitate from his seat and fly around the stadium. He dragged himself up again, spotting Brandt down on the track that looped the field. Brandt's wave urged him to come down on the track next to the drum major.

Fixing a smile on his lips, Sean waved back, waved behind him and then sat back down. He wasn't getting out of the bleachers in the middle of the half-time show.

As the applause diminished, the band started the alma

mater.

"You called him?" Kyle asked.

"No." Did Kyle have to be so loud about it? Maybe no one could hear him since everyone was mumbling through the lyrics. "He called me. I said I was at the game."

Brandt came bounding up the steps.

"Hey there. I thought maybe you'd come down and say a few words. Hi, Kyle."

The game was about the kids, about everyone trying to get on with their lives. They didn't need him making a speech. Sean shook his head.

"So, look, I've got some great news." Brandt had been crouched in the aisle but as people climbing up and down knocked him against Sean's leg, Brandt stepped over it and into their row, squeezing himself between Sean and Kyle with a quick "I'll just be a second" in Kyle's direction.

Brandt had on a Red Dragons windbreaker and a baseball hat. He must have stopped at the booster club booth before he made his way to the press box. He didn't miss a trick. With that stuff on, he could have been any of the fathers or graduates lining the field. Sean hadn't been able to figure out Brandt's age. He fell in a grey area from twenty-five to forty, young-looking but mature-acting, with an ability to talk about music, sports or movies without dating himself.

The fans stood with a roar as the Dragons ran back onto the field.

"This isn't the place I guess," Brandt yelled in his ear. "I wanted to tell you in person so I drove down. Would you mind if I met you guys over at the house after the game?"

"Uh, Kyle?" Sean leaned forward until he could see his lover's face.

"I don't mind." That veneer of polite indifference was firmly in place again, but Sean knew Kyle minded.

"All right then." Brandt clapped Sean's shoulder as he stood. "You're going to love this." He took off down the stairs.

"I doubt that," Kyle said to his retreating back.

"Kyle..."

"Sorry."

McKinley ran the kickoff back to North Akron's twenty. Audible conversation became impossible.

"Later," Sean said.

Tommy Gainsley took a screen pass down to the ten.

"Fine," Kyle mouthed back.

On the funereally silent drive home, Kyle considered and rejected a dozen ways to bring up the fact that he'd rather be eaten by fire ants while forced to fuck some vapid female pop diva than let Brandt into their house, into their lives. Sean might see the whole promotion thing as something for the greater good, but no matter what, Sean couldn't save the whole goddamned world. Kyle just wished Sean would be as interested in saving them.

The car wasn't the place for this conversation, though. They needed the house to scream in.

Of course, Brandt was already there when Kyle turned into the driveway, the silver Lexus at the curb unmistakable even in this upwardly mobile stretch of town. Brandt hurried up behind Sean as he was unlocking the door. "Here, let me help with that."

To Kyle's amazement, Sean didn't snap that he was fine and could unlock the goddamned door without help, thank you very much. He just handed off the keys and leaned on his crutches. Brandt barely waited until the three of them were seated in the living room.

"How does fifteen grand sound?" Brandt opened his arms wide, like he was describing an imaginary fishing triumph.

"Less your percentage," Sean said dryly. Maybe he wasn't as taken in as Kyle thought. "Exactly what would I be getting ten grand for?"

"Oprah. They really want you. I told them how hard it was for you to travel and that you'd be missing out on your physical therapy—"

"Which is all true," Kyle put in. Brandt made it sound like he'd made that up.

"And they offered a stipend. But the best is that Oprah's giving McKinley one hundred thousand, ten of it earmarked for the baseball team in your honor, and another ten for the science labs. It's all going to be announced on the show, so you'll have to look surprised. They faxed over a contract this afternoon."

Perfectly calculated to ensure there was no way Sean would turn them down. Even without the special allotment for his baseball team, Sean would never deny the school that money, especially when he was always complaining about the way the equipment was more of a hazard than letting sixteen-year-olds near corrosive chemicals in the first place.

"Wow," Sean said.

"Yeah," Brandt agreed. "I've got a fax machine in the car. I'll get it right back to them before they change their minds." He was already at the door.

Sean turned to face Kyle. "I know you haven't been happy about any of this, but that's a really nice offer."

"It is. I don't know how you could possibly turn it down."

"You still want me to?"

Kyle did. And he felt like the most selfish bastard in the world, but there was so much else about this Sean wasn't thinking about. About how much harder it was going to be to go back to normal the longer this dragged on. About how many other sick bigots who considered the existence of a fag a threat to their masculinity would now know Sean's name, his face. Would have it forced down their throats that Sean was a hero.

"It's your call."

Brandt came back with a portable four-in-one. "It should only take about half an hour to get everything finalized. I know it's kind of late," Brandt added after Kyle looked at his watch. "So can I make myself more of a nuisance and ask if you'd mind if I crashed here tonight?"

Both Sean and Brandt looked at Kyle as if he was only one

who would think that was a problem.

"It's no trouble at all. We've got extra bedrooms." Kyle smiled. Was it possible to strain your face muscles from constantly faking a smile? His cheeks, lips and jaw felt like he'd been giving a marathon blowjob.

"Great."

"Can't he get a hotel with the five grand he's making off you?" Kyle said as they got ready for bed.

"Why did you tell him he could stay?"

"Because I wasn't about to play the bitchy wife. If you don't want him here, you say something."

"I don't care. But it's obvious you do."

"Could we not just now?" Kyle held up a hand. "I feel the Italian coming out and I'm going to get loud."

"You're the one who brought it up." Sean's heavy shift in the bed sent his crutches crashing to the floor.

"I did. And again, I'm sorry. Just forget about it." Kyle wondered if he was going to have to start apologizing for breathing soon. He went back around the bed and stacked Sean's crutches up against the nightstand.

Sean flipped through channels on the TV as Kyle eased back in on his side. Since Sean had the sound off, a muted click and the shifting light were the only indication each time he hit the button, the action slow, deliberate, and completely unlike his usual zip through his favorites. Kyle watched the wall.

With a click and a buzz, the television went off. "What do you want, Kyle? You want him out of the house? You want me to back out of the contract?"

"No," Kyle said to the wall. For once, knowing what he wanted was easy. He just couldn't have it. He wanted everything back to the way it was before.

"So what the fuck is it?"

"Did you stop for a minute to think what this contract would mean?"

"Besides money for the school and for us?"

Kyle rolled onto his back. "Besides that."

The tight breath that escaped Sean's lips as he shifted to face Kyle made it obvious that today had been too much for his leg. After a minute, Sean laughed. "God, you think what, that this going to be the, what was it, the *Jenny Jones Show*? I'm not confessing some secret gay crush on a straight guy."

"No, your face is just going to be synonymous with the latest cry for gay rights."

"So what? You want to be scared all your life?"

Not scared. Safe. But the scorn in Sean's voice made Kyle's answer impossible. "And what about after this?"

"We'll talk about it."

Which meant Sean would have such perfectly good reasons for doing the next PR thing that Kyle would have to be a complete shit to want him to turn it down.

Sean made another gasp as Kyle pulled the blankets up around their shoulders.

"Do you want me to go get you a pill?"

"I'll be fine as soon as I get to sleep. C'mere." Sean pulled at Kyle's shoulders.

"What?"

"I can get to sleep faster if you're touching me."

It wasn't for Sean, it was for Kyle and he knew it, but he settled against Sean's side, dragging a hand through his hair. Sean's hand spread hot and protective across the base of Kyle's spine. He rode the touch and the warmth and the rhythm of Sean's breaths into the temporary security of sleep.

ß

Kyle heard Sean get up at seven-fucking-thirty—on a Saturday. The weight of the blankets tried to drag Kyle right back down into that comfortable place where he didn't have to think. But as he lay there, he heard voices and remembered.

Brandt was there. If Kyle didn't get up, Brandt would probably have Sean signed up for an around-the-world publicity tour.

Dragging on a T-shirt and the jeans he'd worn to the game last night, Kyle made his way down the stairs. Brandt and Sean's laughter spilled out of the kitchen along with the rich scent of better-than-average coffee. With his leg stretched out on the other stool, Sean sat at the breakfast bar watching Brandt fold an omelet out of the pan. Sean's classic rock station pumped a hair band's screech into the middle of it all.

"Oh God, Brandt, give him some coffee. It's the middle of the night for Kyle." Sean reached for Kyle's wrist as he took a bite of the omelet Brandt had placed in front of him. "Sorry we woke you, babe."

Brandt handed him a mug and cracked some more eggs into the pan. The carton was almost empty. Another trip to the grocery store.

Kyle wrapped his hand around the mug and squinted at Sean's plate. "Why is there brown sugar on your omelet?"

Brandt flashed a smile from the stove. "My last boyfriend was Ukrainian. We had eggs on pasta, eggs on sandwiches. He used to make these all the time. Said they were like blintzes. There's cream cheese inside."

Cream cheese and sugar. On eggs. At seven thirty. Kyle held onto his mug and controlled a shudder.

"They're great. Try some." Sean lifted a forkful in Kyle's direction.

His stomach lurched. "I think I'll just have cereal."

"Because that would be different. What would you do if they stopped making Cheerios?"

Kyle usually didn't mind Sean teasing about Kyle's OCD, even with Tony and Jack, but Brandt was a stranger. Kyle felt like the outsider in his own kitchen.

To hide his embarrassment, he took a burning gulp of coffee. Brandt made good coffee, damn it. Better than Sean's. The sneaky bastard must have some secret supply of beans that he used to drag unsuspecting clients deeper under his spell.

Brandt tipped the pan with a skill that bordered on insolence and then reached into their refrigerator like he owned the damned thing and came out with strawberry jam. "They're even better with this." He crossed to put the jar down in front of Sean.

"Thanks." Sean opened the lid and scraped some jam onto the sugar, cream cheese and eggs on his plate. For a guy who'd been all fussy about the brunch at The Pinnacle, Sean was pretty fucking adventurous this morning. If Brandt suggested it, Sean probably would have sprinkled ground glass over his omelet. Kyle turned away and reached for the cabinet that held the Cheerios.

After pouring out a bowlful, he could see that unless he wanted to make Sean move his leg, the only way to the milk was to slide between Brandt and the bar. Brandt was just turning to slide the omelet out onto a plate, and they almost bumped into each other. Kyle's skin prickled. There was no doubt the man's body chemistry went way beyond just being a tall, good-looking guy. And it just made Kyle dislike him more.

Their hips touched as Kyle stepped around him to get to the fridge. How could the guy take up that much space? He was tall, but not big.

Brandt put his omelet on the bar directly opposite Sean and leaned in to eat.

Kyle could stand at the end of the island next to the sink or stomp off to the dining room. He leaned against the counter and scooped up some Cheerios.

Sean slid his glass of orange juice in front of Kyle. "That's the last of it."

"I'll go to the store today."

"This is really good, Brandt. I've never had anything like it."

That's because no sane person would try the disgusting mess. Kyle dug up another spoonful.

"I'm glad you liked it. I confess to an ulterior motive."

Just one?

"Since they're shooting the show on Tuesday, I thought maybe we should spend some time talking about what you're going to say, prep for the questions you're likely to get."

"So you want to stay here." Sean didn't look up from his omelet.

"If that's okay with you guys. I could always get a hotel, if you'd rather."

Kyle waited. Sean didn't have to look up at Kyle to know what he wanted. He'd already made his opinion perfectly clear.

"For the weekend?"

"Well, just tonight. I'll be back down to pick you up for the flight on Monday."

"We've got lots of room," Sean said.

"Kyle?" Brandt asked.

Kyle had to swallow a half-chewed mouthful. If they weren't already not having sex, Kyle would have told Sean to fuck himself because it was the only action he was going to get. "It's fine," he managed to say at last. "I've got a lot of work to catch up on today anyway."

"Great. I got the proofs from the *Out* photo shoot. They're incredible. Wait till you see what they're using for the cover."

Kyle had a feeling he wasn't going to be very happy about that either.

Chapter Eight

Kyle hated mornings, but Sean always thought Kyle looked adorable, chewing on his cereal with the tiniest stubble on his jaw, his hair looking like he'd just been fucked into next week. Sean wanted Kyle to stand behind him like he sometimes did, lean over him and slurp cereal in Sean's ear as they leafed through the paper. Yesterday had woken up a craving for the kind of touching they'd always done, pulling each other onto a lap or stopping for a long wet kiss and grope in the middle of the kitchen, but he'd had to ask just to get Kyle to hold him last night.

What did Kyle want him to do? Telling Brandt he couldn't stay would just have been rude. It's not like the guy had asked to move in. Sean had point-blank asked Kyle what he wanted last night, and he hadn't said anything. Sean couldn't read his fucking mind.

He scraped up a last bit of jam and cream cheese and pushed away his empty plate.

"Do you want another one?" Brandt asked. "There're enough eggs if Kyle's just having cereal."

"Thanks. I'm good."

Kyle put down his half-finished bowl. "I'll clean up."

"I'll help. I made the mess after all."

"No. You guys go ahead and get started on strategizing."

Sean put his hand on the countertop next to Kyle's cereal bowl, but Kyle didn't take him up on the invitation, he just crossed to the sink and dumped out his milk.

Brandt followed Sean down the hall into the living room. As much as Sean loved his recliner, he was beginning to hate the sight of it. He hesitated in the doorway.

"I could spread the proofs on the dining table. That way Kyle can see them when he's done," Brandt offered.

Sean stepped back into the dining room. After dragging over an extra chair for Sean's leg, Brandt grabbed his case and put it on top of the table.

"I love the layout. I printed these yesterday." As he scooted in close on Sean's left, Brandt handed over a folder full of glossy photo-stock pages.

Sean had been looking at himself in the mirror for thirty-five years and knew what he looked like. He was confident enough to label himself cute, but he wasn't exactly model material. He was now.

He didn't know how it had happened even though he'd been right there. He'd stood in front of that black background; he'd let them brush and comb and spray and dust him. It was one of the last shots, when the photographer had told him to unbutton his shirt. They must have done something on the computer because while the face and body were perfectly familiar, he wasn't sure he'd ever been able to look that sexy. Just below the yellow label of "Hero" across his hips, the photo provided enough definition of the crotch of his jeans that everyone who walked by the magazine would know he dressed left.

"Whoa."

"Yeah."

Sean looked through the rest. In one his brace was visible, but other than that, you couldn't tell that this was a man who had trouble standing up long enough to take a piss.

He pulled the cover shot out again. "Kyle. You've got to see this."

Kyle held his mug to the side as he came around on Sean's right side and stared over his shoulder. And stared.

Sean looked up at Kyle's face. For once, Sean couldn't even

find a clue to what Kyle was thinking.

"Don't recognize him?" Brandt said with a laugh.

Kyle looked at Brandt. "Oh that's my boyfriend. *Eso es.* Now everyone's going to know how hot you are." Kyle swatted Sean on the shoulders and then leaned down to look at the picture again. "Damn, *es mi papi chulo,*" Kyle purred, deep and low in his throat.

Warmth curled in Sean's stomach, shooting into his thighs. This was just what he'd needed all morning.

Kyle dropped a kiss on the top of Sean's head. "Back in a bit."

"Where are you going?"

"Groceries." Kyle's sigh ruffled his hair.

"I'll make you a list."

"That's all right. I can handle it."

After Sean heard Kyle leave, Brandt said, "Sounds like that's not his favorite job."

"Grocery shopping? He hates it. Before"—Sean pointed at his leg—"if it had to do with food, I did it. Clothes, he did it. Inside maintenance, Kyle. Outside maintenance, me."

"Sounds nice and neat."

"It was. It's saved us a ton of money since Kyle learned a lot about plumbing from his dad." Sean considered a frustrated Kyle at the grocery store coming home with another twenty bags. "Maybe we could hire someone. Insurance can pay for that, right?"

"To run errands?" Brandt's tone suggested that was ridiculous. "I don't know. You could ask."

Hiring someone to run errands because Kyle didn't like grocery shopping did seem kind of petty. It wasn't going to kill Kyle to do it for a few weeks. Sean used his hands to lift his ankle off the hard wooden seat.

"Do you need to move? Let's see what kind of positions will work best on the couch."

Sean snorted as he thought of the number of positions he

and Kyle had managed on that particular item of furniture. The recliner too.

"Shit. I meant for the show." Brandt laughed. "Not those kind of positions. I think your boyfriend would kill me."

Would he? Sean had expected Kyle to be jealous when he saw those pictures. Instead, he'd seemed pleased with them. As pleased as he was about anything lately.

"How long have you been together?"

Sean settled himself with his thigh stretched out on the cushions and his calf supported by his crutch. "We've been living together for six years, dated for almost a year before that." It had been Kyle's jealousy that tipped the scale.

"You might want to try a little more enthusiasm on that. Less broody."

"Sorry. I didn't realize we'd started."

"Aside from questions about the shooting like 'Were you scared?' or 'What were you thinking?' a lot of questions will probably be about your relationship with Kyle."

Sean hadn't considered that. "Oh."

"Well, they aren't going to be asking about your favorite movies or co-stars."

"Okay."

Brandt leaned in, forearms resting on his knees. "So how did you meet your partner?"

"We actually met a long time ago, in college. It was just a—I probably shouldn't say hook up, huh?"

"Probably not." Brandt had a nice smile. He'd probably make a good talk show host himself with that earnest concern on his face. "So?"

"We met through some friends in college." A party. One look at Kyle and that was it. Sean knew what he wanted. "But he was a freshman and I was a senior. Kyle wasn't ready for a relationship." Sean remembered everything. *Kyle slipping out of bed and grabbing his pants. "That was great. Where's the nearest coffee place?"*

"We hooked up a couple of times." Because the sex was just

that good. Even Kyle admitted that.

"Try dated there," Brandt suggested.

"We dated a little before I graduated. I didn't see Kyle again until I was visiting some friends in Cleveland..." *spending a vacation week hitting bars and going to parties* "...and when I did... I just..." There hadn't been a heavenly choir or anything, but when he saw Kyle again, those curls, those eyes, the way he stood with his hands tucked in his back pockets, just him.

"You knew," Brandt finished.

"Yeah. Everything about him just said *that's the guy.*"

"Was it like that for Kyle?"

"I don't think so. At least, it took me long enough to convince him. It wasn't until Kyle heard about this other guy I'd been seeing—and even after he admitted he didn't want to share me—it still took some convincing to get him to move down to Canton."

Brandt leaned back against the cushions. "I think we'll gloss over that part. Stick to how you just knew it was him. Don't bring up how hard it was to convince him."

"It wasn't like that." *Or maybe it was.* "Kyle was just used to always living in a city. I think he thought I was trying to drag him off to a farm."

"And since then?"

Sean smiled. "Our friends call us disgustingly happy."

"Are you?"

We were. "Absolutely."

Brandt could arch one brow, just like Kyle.

"I love him. I can't imagine life without Kyle as my lover."

"Let's try to stick to partner. Makes people think less about sex."

"Like those pictures in *Out*?"

It was the first time Sean thought he'd heard Brandt's real laugh. Not the one just for show. "How we market you to the gay media is different from the mainstream. And you are damned hot in those pictures." Brandt shot him a look from under his lashes. “Not that you’re regularly repulsive.”

“That’s a hell of a compliment. Not regularly repulsive. I should get a tattoo.”

“I’ll hire a skywriter.” Brandt winked.

The heat was back in Sean’s stomach, shifting lower. Sean tried to think of something else besides the warmth of Brandt’s laugh, what it did to his eyes, and what the attention and interest in those dark green eyes did to Sean. Brandt was a hell of a sexy guy, and it had been awhile since anyone but Tony flirted with him. Nothing would happen. But it felt damned good.

“Exactly where were you planning on getting the tattoo?” Brandt asked, leaning forward again.

When the doorbell rang, Brandt pushed up from the couch. “Let me.”

Sean struggled to his feet anyway, grateful for the distraction. If it wouldn’t make for an awkward explanation, he’d ask Kyle who the Patron Saint of Timely Interruptions was.

As Sean hobbled to the door, he heard a male voice say, “Sean Farnham?”

“No. Who are you?” Brandt demanded.

Sean reached the hall. Some guy in a suit and dress coat tried to push past Brandt who stood with an arm blocking the door.

“Can I help you?” Sean asked.

“Sean Farnham?”

“Yes?”

The man reached under Brandt’s arm to slap an envelope into Sean’s chest. “For you.”

“Don’t—” Brandt started.

Sean’s hand closed around the envelope. The guy turned and left. Sean had seen TV. He knew what had just happened. He’d been served with legal papers.

“Asshole.” Brandt shut the door with enough force to rattle the glass.

As soon as Kyle had dropped the last of ten grocery bags on the kitchen floor, Sean handed off the paper, watching Kyle's face as he scanned it quickly.

"Sued? For twenty million dollars?"

"Yep. The school district and me personally. Reckless behavior leading to wrongful death." Balancing on his good leg, Sean leaned down and extracted a carton of ice cream from one of the bags. Chocolate banana? He didn't even know that was a flavor. He handed the carton to Kyle.

Kyle started to put the blue-backed paper in the freezer, shook his head and slammed the paper and the ice cream down on the counter. "I think we've got more important things to worry about than whether the ice cream melts."

Brandt came around the bar from the other side and picked up the carton. Shoving it into the freezer, he said, "The Gerbinos aren't the only ones who will sue. Even parents whose children are fine will probably sue the school district for some of the insurance money. But I don't think anyone else will sue Sean personally."

"I guess it's a good thing Brandt got me that ten grand. Now I can afford a lawyer."

"Sure. Thanks, Brandt." Kyle leaned back against the counter.

"Kyle," Sean said. Why was Kyle taking it out on Brandt?

Kyle shot Sean an exasperated look that Sean had a little trouble seeing since something was making his right eye all blurry. He would have ignored the look anyway. Kyle was being a serious prick.

Brandt put the carton of eggs he'd been holding in the fridge and silently turned back to the bag he'd been emptying.

Sean propped an elbow on the counter and ground a palm into his eye. "I called Bob, the union guy, and he said the union lawyer would probably handle things. He said the Good Samaritan laws will probably protect me."

"I still think we should get a lawyer."

"That's not a bad idea," Brandt said.

Now Kyle was glaring at Brandt. For agreeing with him?

"Most of it will probably be settled out of court." Brandt wasn't deterred by Kyle's stare. "The school's insurance company will bargain the amount down to something they can live with. Do you have personal liability insurance?"

"Why, do you sell it?" Kyle snapped.

"Christ, Kyle. What is wrong with you? Brandt's not the one suing us."

Brandt thunked the orange juice on the counter and left the kitchen.

"Say something," Sean demanded.

Kyle just stood there.

"Why are you being so fucking rude?"

"I knew something like this was going to happen," Kyle said at last.

"For someone who didn't want to get cast as the bitchy wife, you're really nailing the performance. Brandt has nothing to do with the Gerbinos suing me."

"No. He's just kept you in the public eye. That has nothing to do with this."

"Do you know how much a lawyer will cost? If it weren't for Brandt, we wouldn't have that money."

Kyle put the orange juice away.

"Babe, listen. It's going to be all right. We probably won't even need the lawyer. The union will handle it. That's why I pay those dues."

Kyle turned back to face him. "What if it isn't? What if they just keep coming after you?"

"What if everything works out fine? Try thinking about that for a change."

"I can't."

Sean was done swallowing his words. "You know what, Kyle? I know it's hard to believe, but for once, this might not be all about you."

Kyle grabbed his wallet and car keys from the counter and stuffed them back in his jeans. "If I'm so goddamned difficult to have around, I don't know why you even want me here. As soon as the magazine hits the stands I'm sure there'll be guys lined up around the block for a chance to fuck you."

It was like Sean's feet were nailed in the batter's box and Kyle just kept throwing ninety-mile-an-hour fastballs at his head. "Where the fuck is that coming from? Have I ever given you a reason you couldn't trust me?" And nothing had happened with Brandt—would happen with Brandt. Sean wasn't going to feel guilty for flirting.

"No." Kyle had enough sense to sound embarrassed. "But God, do you think I want every guy who buys *Out* to be jerking off over my boyfriend?"

Kyle turned away. Sean could see Kyle was ready to walk off again, and that reflex might have saved them a lot of screaming matches over the years. Sean knew it was Kyle's way of controlling his hot temper, knew that he was afraid he'd inherited the kind of temper that had had his father kicking in a door and putting holes in the drywall. Kyle had to withdraw and think and pick at things, and he always came back more reasonable, and then things were better than ever.

But Sean couldn't seem to let him go this time.

"Don't you walk out now, Kyle."

"You want me to stay so we can make each other feel worse?"

Sean didn't know what made Kyle think that they couldn't survive a knock-down, drag-out fight. His parents had actually kept the battered door as a souvenir. "I want you to stay so we can figure this out. Tell me what's really wrong so I can fix it."

"That's not going to work this time."

"What?"

Kyle swallowed hard, lips curving in a sad smile. "You can't give me what I want. Even if you could, you wouldn't."

"What the hell is that supposed to mean?"

Kyle stepped closer, close enough to touch, but kept his

hands in his pockets. "Sean, let's move. Sell the house. Everyone's always looking for science teachers and I can telecommute until I find something."

"So you want me to walk away from the fight too?"

"God, what fight? There is no fight. This is not *Casablanca*. You aren't Victor Laszlo fighting Nazis."

"You know what I mean."

Kyle's throat was working continuously, and Sean wanted to reassure him, help him fight off the tight pressure of tears.

"No, I don't. What I know is that this is changing you—changing us. And as long as we stay here—"

That was it. Kyle had lost his mind. "I'm the same guy I've always been, Kyle. You're the one who seems to have a problem."

"Then fine. I'm going to go work on my problem. You just get ready for Oprah. And Brandt can put away the groceries since he's so fond of our kitchen."

Kyle went out the back door. He didn't slam it. Didn't yell. He was just gone.

Sean's right eye was so blurry he thought he was crying. Then the blinding pain hit and it was all he could do not to cry.

Kyle had driven three blocks before he realized he had nowhere to go. That was one of the things that sucked about not being in a city. You couldn't just take a walk and find something open, some place to grab a coffee or a drink—even on a Saturday.

He drove around the block to the park and pulled in behind the pavilion. Two dogs tore past him and he stopped to watch as they raced each other for a ball, the smaller one returning in a triumphant trot to place it at the feet of a woman sitting on a bench. She didn't look up from the book she was reading and the larger dog grabbed the ball in his teeth. With a snap of his shaggy head, the dog tossed the ball away again, and they were off.

Kyle walked through the picnic pavilion. The acoustics in

here sucked, and the way the roof was sheeted they'd be getting leaks soon. Even with sun, it was like a dank cave. Which suited his mood just fine. He sat at one of the picnic tables.

Why couldn't Sean see they weren't ever going to get back to their old life if he didn't stop letting Brandt push Sean into the public eye? Didn't he want to go back to everything the way it was? There'd be reminders enough. Sean's physical therapist said he'd probably need a cane for at least a year, if not for the rest of his life. Why did everyone think Kyle was being unreasonable for wanting their old lives back?

He shifted on the uneven wood slats, and his phone dug into his hip. Not that he had anyone to call. All his friends in Canton were Sean's friends. He'd kept in touch with some of the people he'd hung out with in Cleveland, mostly through emails, but none of them would understand.

He wanted someone to talk to. Mostly he wanted Sean to talk to but that didn't seem to be working. He opened his phone, flipped through the phonebook, and called his older sister Sophie. Girls were supposed to be good at relationship stuff.

"Kyle? Is everything all right? How's Sean?"

"He's fine. Soph—"

"Ricky—put Eddie down. Now. No! Not on the stairs." Her voice softened. "Sorry, Kyle."

"Soph, do you ever—"

"Ricky, that's hot. Hot! I swear to God if I'd known what I was getting into I'd never have let Domenic talk me into having kids. Ricky! Here, D.J., talk to Uncle Kyle for a minute."

His sister's oldest son took the phone with a breathy "Hi" followed by a deep silence. Kyle could hear chaos in the background.

"Hey, D.J., what's going on?"

"Ricky's trying to climb the stove and Eddie's puking on the carpet. Bye, Uncle Kyle."

There was a click in his ear.

Even though she was five years older, he'd always felt

closer to Sophie than anyone else in his family. He suspected Sophie's influence had a lot to do with his parents not having him declared legally dead when he came out. Sophie had bucked family expectations by going to college and having a career before settling down to make babies. Now, three boys under six kept Sophie a little too busy for relationship advice. He'd bet she'd love to be back at her job dealing with cranky tourists all day.

After about ten minutes, she called him back. "I'm sorry, Kyle. It's been raining for days and the kids are driving me nuts."

"Where's Dom?"

"At the store. He needs a part to fix the toilet. Ricky flushed every toothbrush and Eddie's favorite stuffed animal."

"Sorry, sis."

"What did you need?"

"Nothing. I'll let you get back before Ricky sets the house on fire."

"Holy Mother of God, don't give him any ideas. He already started a gas leak last month."

"Really?" It was the first conversation Kyle had had in weeks that didn't revolve around the shooting. And he was always fascinated by Ricky stories. His brothers were convinced Ricky was the next *Omen* child.

"Didn't Mami tell you? Dom left a hammer out where Ricky could get it and he smacked open a pipe in the cellar."

"Holy crap."

"I swear to God, I'm going to be on the news one day. Promise you'll come visit me in prison."

"I will. You made it out to Canton." *Which may be worse*, Kyle added to himself.

"Kyle, what's going on?"

He'd called her for help and now he didn't want to talk about it. "Nothing. Go get Ricky before he puts Eddie in the dryer."

"I'm chasing him around on the portable. It's fine."

"It's just... Things are hard. Everything's different now and all we do is fight and it's like he's not even the same guy."

"Kyle Matthew Francis DiRusso. You're lucky I'm not there to smack you one. Your husband just got out of the hospital. You should be grateful he's alive. Of course, it's hard. You thought everything would be easy forever?"

"I— You remember my confirmation name?"

"Shut up. If I know you, you're off hiding somewhere. Go home to your man and tell him you love him and you're sorry you're a total asshole."

He heard a shocked gasp and "Mommy said—"

"Domenic Junior, if you tell your father I said that word there will be Brussels sprouts for dinner for a week." In the same tone she'd used on her son she added, "Marriage isn't for wimps, Kyle."

"Thanks, sis."

"Of course, if you don't love him—"

Not love Sean? Kyle could hate Sean and still love him. It was Sean. His best friend. His lover.

"I do."

"So go home. Or come down from the attic or wherever it is you're hiding hoping he'll come find you."

Sophie was right—and Kyle'd known what she would say anyway. It's what anyone would say who wasn't living through it. And he was going to go home. Just as soon as he was ready to deal with Brandt's smirk, with Brandt knowing that Sean would do whatever Brandt told him to and Kyle couldn't do a thing to stop it.

Kyle left the pavilion and watched the dogs again, listening to the way their feet tore through the grass and leaves as they raced for that ball, nothing and no one on their minds in that second. Why couldn't he be like that—just forget about all the little things and know that as long as Sean had made it through alive, everything else would work out?

The bigger dog trotted back with the ball and dropped it at Kyle's feet. Kyle glanced over at the woman reading her book.

The dogs both looked at him and then at the ball as if to say, “Duh, man, do we have to explain this to you? Just throw the damned ball.”

Kyle picked up the slimy remains of a tennis ball and threw it far into the trees. The dogs sprinted away, crunching leaves and jangling collars. He wiped his hand on his jeans and headed back to the car.

As he was opening the door, his phone rang. Thinking it was Sophie again, he pressed the answer button without looking.

“Dude, what’s up?”

Tony. Fucking fabulous. Sean had probably called Tony to tell him what a prick Kyle was. He readied himself for the same lecture his sister had delivered—minus his confirmation name, of course. Francis. That was all his Aunt Loretta’s fault.

“Hi, Tony.”

“Seriously, man, what’s up with Sean?”

“Why don’t you ask him?”

“What the fuck? ’Cause I’m asking you.”

“What do you mean?”

“He didn’t answer the phone at your house and he didn’t answer his cell, and then when I tried the house again I get some guy who tells me that Sean went to bed. At two o’clock on a Saturday?”

“I don’t know.”

“What do you mean you don’t know? Who’s that guy at your house? Man, he sounded hot.”

Kyle considered beating his head against the car’s doorframe. “He’s a publicist.”

“Yeah? Well, I think you’d better get home and see what he’s publicizing because he was sounding all kinds of territorial about your boyfriend, dude.”

“Thanks, Tony.”

“Whatever.” Tony paused and then said quickly, “Kyle, you know I love you too, right?”

Actually Kyle didn't. He knew Tony put up with him because Kyle was important to Sean, but that was it.

"Thanks, Tony."

"So call me back. And definitely call me if you need help hiding the body."

If anything was going on with Brandt and Sean, Kyle thought he might need help with two bodies, but he didn't mention that to Tony. Kyle sped home.

Brandt intercepted Kyle in the hall as soon as he'd dropped his keys on the table.

"Where's Sean?"

"In bed."

Kyle stepped around Brandt to get to the stairs.

"Kyle."

"Don't." He was doing his best but if Brandt touched him, all bets were off.

"He's got a migraine. If he's asleep, don't wake him up."

"Sean doesn't get migraines."

"He does now. I thought I was going to have to take him to the hospital. He couldn't see and he threw up."

God, and Kyle had been playing with dogs in the park. Brandt had been the one to help Sean to bed, to help him when he was probably scared he was going blind, and it was all Kyle's fault.

"How is he now?"

"Better. Dark and quiet help."

"I know." Abuelito got migraines. He'd liked to have Kyle squeeze his hand while he lay in a dark room, and sometimes he'd have Kyle whisper a rosary with him.

"It could be the codeine, it could be post-traumatic stress. But you sure as hell aren't helping."

If Brandt weren't totally right, that would have been the moment when Kyle punched him. "And you are?"

"The publicity isn't going to go away whether I help him with it or not." Brandt's eyes were wide, and Kyle couldn't help believing that the guy was telling the truth. "Sean's a great guy. If you love him as much as he loves you, it's about time you get your head out of your ass."

Jesus, Mary and Joseph, wasn't there anyone who wasn't going to give him shit today? Well-deserved shit, but God, he got the message.

Kyle took off his shoes before padding upstairs. Their bedroom door was open a crack. He peeked in.

Sean had a bag of ice on his head and a pillow over his eyes. As Kyle pushed the door open, Sean moved the pillow. "Hey, babe," he whispered.

"Hey. How's the head?"

"Better. Christ, that was bad." But he was still whispering.

"Bad enough to make you forget about the leg for a bit?"

"Oh, yeah. Kind of girly, huh? A migraine?"

"No. Not really. My grandfather got them." Kyle sat on the edge of the bed and took Sean's hand. "He said it was better if I squeezed like this." He dug his thumb into the web between Sean's thumb and index finger.

"It is." Relief and amazement came loud and clear on that whisper.

"Sean, I'm sorry I freaked out on you—on Brandt."

"You just worry too much. Trust me, babe. We're going to be fine." He let out a deep breath. "Better than fine if you can keep doing that."

Kyle kept the pressure on Sean's hand while climbing the rest of the way onto the bed and getting his other hand in Sean's hair to gently massage his scalp.

"I love you," Sean murmured.

"And I love you more than Turner Classic Movies."

"That's a good one."

"Damned right."

Maybe everything could be as simple as Sophie and the dogs in the park made it seem. Alive was good. Everything else was bullshit. After six perfect years, he couldn't handle a month of bullshit?

"I'm going to stop freaking out. Brandt can fucking move in if he wants. As long as I get you. As long as you keep telling me—"

Sean made a soft, snorting gasp.

Kyle's body relaxed, even as shame made him shut his eyes. Not that Sean could see the lies in them now that he was asleep. Kyle was a complete shit and Sophie should be there to smack some sense into him. But he was still glad Sean hadn't heard those promises.

Chapter Nine

Even though Sean hadn't heard them, Kyle worked hard at keeping those promises. When Brandt dropped Sean off Tuesday night after they got back from Oprah and Chicago, Kyle gave Brandt a smile and asked if Sean'd had a migraine. When Sean insisted that he didn't want Kyle going in with him to his follow-up appointment with the orthopedic surgeon, Kyle went back to work and waited for Sean to call him, trusting that he wouldn't just decide to find his own way home.

After Sean called, Kyle waited outside the Morrison Bone and Joint Center in the patient drop-off area. They were leaving in an hour for Thanksgiving with Gina and Peter in Erie. As part of his non-freak-out promise, Kyle tried not to worry about whether Sean's leg would get too stiff on the three-hour drive.

Sean had a huge grin when he walked to the car. Walked. With a cane. Kyle tipped his head back. He'd forgotten how good it was just to see Sean walking on his own again. Even with a brace.

"Look at you."

"Yup. Can you go back in for the crutches? They left them in the vestibule for me."

"Sure."

When he got back, Sean was in the driver's seat. "Clearance to drive."

Clearance didn't necessarily mean he had to try it today. Kyle bit his cheek. He'd been doing that a lot since he made those promises. He'd built up a nice ridge on the right side.

"Great." He slipped into the passenger side, shifting the cane to rest against the passenger door where it wouldn't be in Sean's way.

"I still have to do PT every day for at least another month, but I got clearance to go back to work in another week. And," Sean added with a dramatic pause, "clearance to fuck your brains out."

"And me you?"

"Yep. Just wait till—"

"Did you forget where we're sleeping tonight?"

"Oh fuck. I did. But we can—"

"Told you to pack last night."

"Shit. You know my mom will freak if we're late."

"Uh-huh."

Sean backed out of the space. "Damn. What time is it?"

"Almost four."

Sean drove easily, smoothly, no hesitation on the gas or brake, and Kyle breathed a little more easily.

"You know, I could call my mom and tell her my appointment got pushed back to a later time."

Traffic was going to be a nightmare no matter when they left. And Sean's leg apparently wasn't giving him much pain. Sean reached over and put his hand on Kyle's thigh, fingers brushing his inseam.

"I could run upstairs and pack for you," Kyle offered.

Sean's fingers moved higher. "Don't forget the lube."

"We are not fucking at your parents' house."

"We'll see. We did before."

"They were out. God."

Sean's hand stopped inching and landed full on Kyle's dick. He shifted under the seatbelt and arched toward the pressure.

"Sean, these pants have to be drycleaned."

"Do you really care?"

"No." At that moment, Kyle didn't care if he had to throw

them out.

Sean's fingers outlined Kyle's cock through the wool, a brush of cool lining against heated skin at the slit in his briefs.

Traffic was already bad just cutting through downtown. Sean zipped down a side street to avoid a light. "We're taking my Durango. Because if we get stuck in traffic like this, we'll be tall enough for a little road head."

"Good," Kyle panted. "Then I'm driving."

"Think so?" Sean squeezed the head of Kyle's dick.

His ass came right up off the seat. "Will you hurry up?"

"What, you want me to get you off now?"

"Don't be an asshole, just drive."

Sean put both hands back on the wheel. "Eight more blocks."

And then sometimes it was good they didn't live in a city. Kyle put his hand on his dick and pressed to ease a little of that too-hard-too-fast ache.

When they pulled into the driveway, Sean said, "I'll call my mom, you go pack."

"You can actually talk to your mom and then—"

"Babe, I need you so bad I could do it in front of my mom."

Kyle had his keys out first and hit the stairs as soon as he opened the door.

"Fuck packing, just grab the lube," Sean called after him.

But it only took a few seconds to shove jeans, socks, boxers and a shirt into a bag. The anticipation revved his heart rate as he grabbed the bottle of lube from the drawer.

"Hurry up or I'll be on the phone when you get down here," Sean called.

"And I'll suck you when you're on the phone."

"Christ. I'm dialing now."

Kyle hobbled down the stairs to find Sean completely naked on the couch with the phone in his hand.

"I know, Mom. We'll be there as soon as we can. Yes, we'll call if it gets past ten."

Kyle wouldn't put it past Sean to fake it, so he bent his ear down to the receiver. Gina was definitely on the other end. Kyle knelt at Sean's waist and licked the head of his half-hard dick.

"Yes, Mom." The words were a little quicker. "We'll be careful."

Kyle lifted Sean's dick and stretched his jaw to take Sean's balls into his mouth.

Sean's sudden intake of breath prompted Gina to be loud enough for Kyle to hear. "What happened?"

"I just slipped. I'll be more careful. Gotta go to the doctor's now, Mom." The words were spilling out of his mouth as fast as an auctioneer.

Kyle let the sac slip quietly from his mouth and lapped his way back up Sean's now rigid cock.

"Bye, Mom. Love you too."

A loud beep and then Sean threw the phone onto the recliner. "You're an evil bastard."

"I thought you were in a hurry." Kyle sucked harder, making a loud smack as he came off the head.

"I'm going to fuck you so hard you'll feel me all the way to Erie."

It had been long enough that Kyle probably would anyway. He put the bottle of lube on Sean's chest and blinked up at him, batting his lashes. "Be gentle with me."

"C'mere and kiss me, asshole."

Kyle licked his way up Sean's chest, pausing to give a teasing suck to each nipple.

"Later, babe." Sean shifted on his side so that he was stretched out against the back of the couch. Kyle managed to get most of himself onto what was left of the seat, as much on his stomach as he could. "Oh no." Sean grabbed a hip and pulled Kyle onto his side so that his back pressed into Sean's chest. "Just like this so I can watch you."

Sean dropped kisses on Kyle's shoulder and neck before reaching an arm under his head to drag him into a long kiss.

"Not that I didn't appreciate the welcome-home-from-

Chicago blowjob and the are-you-sure-your-head's-better hand job, but I know you've missed fucking, huh?"

It was easy for Sean to talk. He didn't have two lube-slick fingers in his ass, scissoring, stretching, fucking him open.

"Yes," Kyle managed to gasp. Not that he minded the way Sean talked when he fucked him, loved the filthy promises almost as much as he loved the moment when Sean lost coherence and just kept murmuring *fuck* in Kyle's ear until even that was impossible to manage.

Three fingers now, a hard quick twist and thrust, Sean's mouth on Kyle's neck under his jaw nipping just hard enough to make it feel so good.

"Can't wait, babe. Tell me, please."

"Now."

Pulling Kyle back with a hand on his hip, Sean pushed inside, not too fast—just steady and deep and so perfect Kyle could feel him everywhere, pleasure pounding down his spine and through his legs, building in his hips. He arched back to get all of him, and Sean started to thrust.

"Feel good on me. Hot and tight. Missed being in you."

Kyle had missed it too, but as long as Sean kept fucking him so deep Kyle couldn't form a sentence. He braced himself with a hand on the armrest and hiked his leg over Sean's hips. Kyle's dick was aching for a touch but he'd go off too soon because it had been too long and he had to wait until Sean was close enough to follow him over, wait until Sean was reduced to stuttering breaths.

The phone started ringing, and Sean stopped. Kyle got control of his larynx. "You're not actually thinking of answering it are you?"

"No." Sean slammed deep, and heat rippled up into Kyle's stomach.

"Go—od."

But when the answering machine clicked on, Sean stopped again.

"Hey there. It's Brandt. I just heard. They've moved the

airdate to Friday, so be sure to set your DVR."

Kyle was almost pissed enough to roll off the couch, but he remembered his promise—and then Sean started fucking again, hips moving in a swivel that had Kyle's eyes rolling up in his head.

Sean grabbed Kyle's hair and twisted him back into another kiss, messy and wet while his slick hand went to work on Kyle's dick. The *Oh God, papi* in his head might have become *you bastard*, but it didn't change the fact that Sean was still the best fuck Kyle'd ever had, that Sean knew when to back off to make it that much sweeter when he sent Kyle over the edge.

"Look at me." Sean gave another yank on Kyle's hair.

His eyelids weighed a ton each, but he managed to force them up. Sean's eyes were green-blue-grey all at once, intense focus under sandy lashes. That look, just for him, and Kyle forgot about the phone. "Fuck me."

Sean pumped harder, and Kyle's neck slid over the armrest. With them both on their backs, Sean pinned Kyle tight with a grip over his arm and under his head and the other forearm pushing down his hips.

Sean's cock felt like it was fucking straight through Kyle's body, right into the base of Kyle's own dick, each speed-of-sound thrust a hot splash of so-fucking-good-I'm-going-to-die everywhere inside. Sean's hand needed to move off the shaft of Kyle's dick, get to that spot under the head, get his thumb on that spot, but Kyle couldn't tell him, couldn't even pry a hand loose to get there himself because he couldn't remember how to make his muscles move.

Sean had been whispering *good* and *fuck* and *yeah*, but now the words turned to harsh groans. Moving his hand up Kyle's cock with blurring friction over the crown, thumb running right up the underside, and that was the jolt that finished him. Sparkling heat streaking through his dick and he bucked and came, shooting over and over. Sean started to move away, to pull out and Kyle arched his ass back. "No. Come in me. I want to feel it."

Sean's deep strokes weren't as easy to take after coming so

hard, but Kyle could hear the change in breathing that meant Sean was close. Kyle tightened his ass around Sean and heard him grunt. Longer, deeper, almost all the way out and in and then the stutter before the last deep push, Sean's breath a tight whisper in Kyle's ear as he flooded him with warmth.

Sweat and come glued them together. Drops of sweat rolled from the nape of Kyle's neck, off the ends of his hair into his eyes. The salesman had explained a lot about the stain-resistant qualities of the couch. He wondered if the labs had tested for this.

"Gotta shower." Sean's voice rumbled against Kyle's back.

"Yeah."

"Now, I mean. We'll have to save the afterglow for another time."

"Right."

But with the spray beating down on them, Kyle sagged against Sean with a sigh. "What hit me?"

"'The last martini.'" Sean picked up *The Thin Man* dialogue.

"I was being serious."

"I'll make you some coffee."

"Stop being so arrogantly pleased with yourself."

"I just don't know if I've ever fucked you this close to unconscious before. Usually, you're all full of energy after."

It was on the tip of Kyle's tongue to say *people change*, but he didn't want either one of them to change. Everything had been so perfect before, why should anything change? He dragged Sean down for a kiss and didn't say anything at all.

Kyle knew that Sean was enjoying the freedom of being able to drive again too much to accept that his leg was killing him, so when they stopped near Ashtabula to off-load the coffee they'd drunk, Kyle opened the driver's side door ahead of Sean.

"I'm bored," he explained, pretending he couldn't see the lines of pain around Sean's mouth in the lights over the parking lot.

"Fine. But don't think I promised you road head."

"You have such a lovely way with words, darling."

"What's that one from?" Sean tapped his cane on the floor between his feet.

"Me. Book of Kyle."

"Chapter and verse?"

"Blasphemer." Kyle steered them back onto the road leading to the interstate. As he checked the side mirror, Sean winked at him. He might as well have dragged his hand up Kyle's inseam. Heat flashed through him and he forced his attention back on the holiday traffic. He should have packed the lube.

Chapter Ten

Every year Kyle waited for Sean's room to change, for Gina to put away the baseball trophies on the dresser, or to give away the clothes still hanging in the closet, but Sean's room still looked like Kyle imagined it had the day Sean left for college. Considering the fact that the first thing Gina had done when they arrived was show them her scrapbook of Sean's press clippings, Kyle shouldn't have been surprised. What had surprised him was Gina kissing his cheek in greeting.

"Your mom does know you left home eighteen years ago, right?" Kyle pulled off his jeans and shirt, tossing Sean the extra T-shirt he'd brought for him to sleep in.

"Seventeen," Sean corrected, his sensitivity about his age prompting a laugh from Kyle. "She used to tell me she wanted me to know that I could always come home." Sean put a hand on his chest and intoned, "No matter what, sweetheart." He pulled off his own shirt and sweats and sat on the bed. "She already has a guest room. So I guess she never felt the need to fix up this one."

"Thank God she doesn't make me sleep in the guest room."

"I wouldn't come home if my parents did that and they know it. Besides. That's your dad's territory."

They did end up in twins in separate rooms at Kyle's parents' house. "There's no other way to do it. We're all kind of scattered around the house because the family's so big. Sophie and Dom end up in bunk beds." And getting a hotel would break his mother's heart.

"But Ben and Karen don't."

"Privilege of being the oldest, I guess. I didn't mean to start a fight over it."

Sean caught his wrist. "Kyle, this isn't a fight."

Then why did it feel like one? He never remembered feeling like this before, like every conversation was going to turn into some kind of argument.

As Sean used his grip on Kyle's wrist to pull him closer to the bed, Sean teased the inside of Kyle's wrist with a calloused thumb.

"What?" Sean looked up.

The bedside lamplight hit him from behind, and it wasn't fucking fair that it made him look so gorgeous that Kyle's heart and dick both jumped. Sean's thumb pressed again on his pulse. The backlighting did more for him than Myrna Loy and Jean Harlow put together, glowing on his light brown hair and shading his eyes dark blue. God, Kyle loved him. Why didn't it feel like that was enough?

Kyle shook his head.

Sean tugged hard enough on his wrist so that Kyle fell onto the bed on top of Sean.

"No." But Kyle smiled.

"No what?"

"No, we can't. Not here."

Sean rolled Kyle under him and pinned one arm over his head to mouth his neck and ear. "Please, babe."

"Sean. I can't." Just a lick on his jaw, and Kyle could barely keep the groans from spilling from his throat.

"Can't what?"

Sean knew damned well what, but he was going to make Kyle say it. And fuck if it didn't turn Kyle on almost as much. "Can't be quiet with your dick in my ass."

Sean grinned and kissed him, sending a dizzying rush of blood to Kyle's dick. His hips started giving in, rolling up into Sean's. He lifted his head from Kyle's mouth and propped himself up on one arm, weight still across Kyle's chest.

"You know, I got my cherry popped in this room."

"Really?" In all the years they'd been together, they'd never discussed their first times.

"Yeah. My parents were out of town over night. I took my fake ID down to Erie's one gay bar, picked up a guy, brought him back here and got nailed." Sean scanned the room as if remembering and his eyes didn't look happy.

"How was it?"

"He tried to be nice, but he was a little too big and a little too drunk to make it easy. Sucked me off after. Took a while, though." Sean gave a rueful smile.

"How old were you?" Kyle ran his hand through Sean's hair.

"Seventeen. What about you?"

"Sixteen. Working summer camp. Doing inventory in the boat house. I kept hoping I'd get paired with Jesse. Just always got a feeling around him. One minute I was counting lifejackets and the next he pushed me down on my knees. I finally figured out why making out with girls hadn't been much of a charge."

"He fucked you there?"

"No, I blew him. We didn't fuck until almost the end of the summer."

"And then the tearful parting on the beach, *Grease* style?"

"God no. He was a total closet case. Fucked a girl all summer too. And I thought I told you never to mention that movie in my presence."

"Sorry. Guess he was pretty good, though."

"Why?"

Sean ground his hips against Kyle's. "You're hard."

"That's all you, *papi chulo*. I haven't thought about Jesse in years."

"Good." Sean's voice was almost a growl.

"Oh?" Kyle couldn't believe Sean could be jealous over a guy from fifteen years ago. Sean never seemed to get jealous over anyone. "It's funny. We've never talked about that stuff before."

"I've always been more interested in having sex with you rather than talking about it with you. And the thought makes me jealous."

"Jealous?"

"Yeah. I really don't want to know about other guys you've fucked or Christ, were fucking before you moved in."

Kyle rolled them over again. "You never said anything."

Sean shrugged as much as he could with Kyle pushing him into the mattress. "Wasn't going to change anything, was it?"

Kyle didn't have an answer for that. He'd always thought he was the jealous one. Even now the thought of Brandt made him grind his teeth. But Sean being jealous was kind of hot. Kyle sat back on his heels between Sean's legs and tugged at his boxers.

"I thought we couldn't." But Sean lifted his hips.

Kyle backed off the bed so he could yank the boxers all the way off, then tossed away his own briefs. "We know I can't be quiet, but you can." He tried not to stare at the scar, at least not when Sean could notice, but sometimes Kyle couldn't help it. The sight of it brought a flush of anger every time.

Sean pursed his lips in consideration. "Hmmm."

Kyle decided to hurry Sean's decision with a hand on his dick. Sean made a soft, satisfied sigh and rolled his hips to meet Kyle's quick, hard strokes. A suck on his finger to get it spit-slick and he was rubbing beneath Sean's balls, tracing the thick vein that led to his hole.

"Think so?" Sean's breath came faster.

"Know so." Kyle teased around the entrance, rubbing and pressing.

When Sean started trying to grind down onto his finger, Kyle pulled his hand back and got two more fingers wet in his mouth.

"Told you we should have brought lube." Sean's whisper was hoarse.

"Don't you wish I'd listened?" Kyle pressed just the tip of

his finger inside Sean's ass.

"You never do."

Kyle jammed his finger forward. Sean arched off the bed with a hiss.

"Leg still okay?"

"Stop worrying about it. Check my bag."

"What?" Kyle worked in a second finger.

"Lube. In. My. Bag." Sean gasped the words between Kyle's thrusts.

"Quite a Boy Scout, aren't you?"

Sean twisted and reached into a drawer next to the bed. After digging around for a few seconds, he tossed a scrap of cloth at Kyle. A yellow and blue striped Scout tie.

"No shit." Kyle grinned and pulled his fingers free.

Sean grunted and then groaned as Kyle wrapped the tie around the base of Sean's cock.

"I've heard some interesting things about the Scouts. Sure you didn't have fun at camp like I did?" Kyle asked.

"Nope. Quit in junior high. Kyle." The words seemed to be caught in Sean's throat.

"Yes?"

"That's tight."

"I know." Kyle grinned. With a stretch, he could just reach the side pocket of Sean's bag without moving from the bed. Fishing around, his fingers closed on a small plastic pillow. He pulled it out. "Tingling sensations?" Kyle read. "My dick's not sensation enough for you?"

"I just grabbed a couple packs last time I went to see Tony at the bar."

"May cause burning? Fucking hell, *chulo*. This may be over before it starts."

"Where's your sense of adventure?"

Kyle tugged on the tie around Sean's dick.

"Oh yeah," Sean whispered.

Kyle snapped off the tab and spread some of the minty-smelling lube on his fingers. "Well, at least things will smell fresh. You first." He slipped a finger in.

Sean jumped. "Fuck."

Kyle raised an eyebrow. "Is that a stop?"

"No. Just. Oh shit." The last whispered word dragged out for ten seconds.

Kyle slipped in a second finger. Sean's muscles quivered and pulsed. As Kyle twisted his fingers deeper into the slick soft heat, Sean panted, "Fuck, fuck, fuck."

"You're supposed to be the quiet one," Kyle murmured.

He twisted his wrist again, and Sean arched hard enough that the bed shifted.

Kyle quirked an eyebrow again.

"Christ. Fuck me." Even in a whisper, Sean's voice held a command that was hard to ignore.

Kyle pulled off his T-shirt and wedged it between the headboard and the wall. Then he cautiously tested the lube against the head of his dick. He could just see himself streaking to the bathroom, yelping loudly enough to wake Gina and Peter.

A quick burn and then a cold tingle flashed over his skin. It didn't make him want to run to wash it off; it made him want to bury his dick inside Sean. Hard. Fast. Now. Kyle squeezed out the rest of the tiny envelope's contents and sent shocks of cold and hot running up and down his cock.

"It's gonna be over fast with this shit," Kyle warned, lifting that scarred leg to rest straight up against his chest. No matter what Sean said, bending his knee for even a quick fuck would be too much strain.

"C'mon."

Kyle pressed forward. Sean clamped down hard, squeezing Kyle's cock. He shifted side to side, pushing to get that heat around his lube-cooled dick. "Fuck, you're tight. Relax, *chulo*."

Sean's eyes narrowed to slits. He let out a long deep breath. Tingling heat on Kyle's cock, tight quiver of velvet smooth muscles, he was going to lose his fucking mind. He grabbed Sean's hips and worked in deeper.

"Yeah. Like that," Sean grunted.

Every fucking inch was so good, better than the last as Kyle pushed his way in, until he was cradled deep inside, all that heat and pressure. He couldn't even feel the cool burn of the lube anymore, just Sean's body pulsing around him. Kyle flexed his hips to pull out, and the air set off the lube again. "Holy shit, Sean." All Kyle's muscles shook as he buried himself deep.

He held Sean's leg and started working in long, slow strokes, fiery chill as he came out and then the soothing heat of Sean tight around him. He went deeper and deeper, slamming hard enough for his balls to slap against Sean's ass.

"Yeah, fuck me."

Kyle was doing just that, intent on dragging it out as long as he could before he lost control and fucked hard until they both exploded, when the blare of Def Leppard sounded in his ear.

Sean's phone. Sean's motherfucking phone.

It could only be Brandt. Was the bastard wired to their dicks?

"Gonna get that?" Kyle slammed forward hard enough to force the breath from Sean's lungs.

"Asshole." Sean slapped a hand around on the nightstand.

The phone blared again. "Pour some sugar on me." Those had to be the stupidest lyrics ever written.

"I'm not the one who. Left. It. On." Kyle punctuated each word with a hard thrust. "Maybe you want to wait until your parents come in and get it."

Sean finally got the phone in his hands.

"Go right ahead. Have a chat."

"Bitch." Sean pressed a button and the phone chimed as it turned off.

"I'm not the one with a dick up his ass."

"Kyle."

"Or a Boy Scout scarf around his dick."

Sean tightened his ass around Kyle's cock hard enough to

force a whispered groan from Kyle's throat. "Do that again, and we'll wake up your parents."

"Are you going to stop being a pissy bitch and fuck me?"

"Uh-huh." Kyle ran a hand down Sean's chest before grabbing his hips. "I'm going to fuck you until you beg to come." *Until you forget that asshole's name. Until I'm the only thing you can think about. Until everything's the way it's supposed to be again.*

He started slow again for a few strokes before hanging on and working his hips in tight swivels that made Sean's breath come in quick pants. Sean's muscles milked Kyle's cock, pulse pounding pleasure in every stroke, everywhere from the sweet pressure on the head to the grip and slide on his shaft. He never wanted to stop, wanted to stay inside Sean forever, to watch him fight the weight of his eyelids, watch those lashes brush his freckled cheeks in the lamplight. Sean's mouth was still tight with anger, but as Kyle wrapped his fingers around Sean's wrist he looked up at him and smiled.

Kyle grinned and brought his sticky hand to Sean's dick.

"I really do...am going to kill you." Sean panted for breath. "After I come."

But a chill that had nothing to do with the minty lube shook Kyle. Had Sean actually started to say *I really do hate you*?

He wouldn't have meant it. Kyle could have said the same thing if he were suffering a constricting band around the base of his cock while having his ass pounded and burning lube on the head of his dick.

"Please." Sean's raspy plea made Kyle almost as desperate.

Kyle felt the tremble in the leg muscles against his chest, around his hip. He loosened the tie around Sean's cock, and Sean made a whining growl in his throat and pushed Kyle's hand away. Kyle could almost forget the need boiling in his own balls as he watched Sean jerk himself over the edge. This deep inside him Kyle swore he could feel Sean's orgasm everywhere, his dick pumping a flood of warmth against Kyle's stomach, as the look on Sean's face brought a flush of heat inside too.

Sean stopped bucking and lay there panting. Kyle eased out and finished himself with a few strokes, spraying Sean's chest as the electric shocks bowed his spine and rushed out of his dick. Kyle gently lowered Sean's leg and leaned forward to kiss him as the last shudders left them both. Sean's mouth was soft and wet, their heartbeats thumping down to normal together. Sean had been right. They'd needed this.

When Kyle finally rolled off, Sean grabbed the scarf and wiped them down. "I think I can finally throw this out now."

"Maybe you should save it for another twenty-five years. It's a good thing we've got a big attic."

"You know, not only did we have sex at my parents' house, we had kinky sex at my parents' house."

Kyle elbowed Sean in the ribs. "Isn't there some kind of no-taunting rule in baseball?"

"In football and wrestling. Baseball players are too classy to taunt."

"Yeah, it's real classy to spit and grab your balls on TV."

"Fuck classy. I think I just heard my dad go into the bathroom."

"When?"

"Right about when you came."

"Shit." Kyle brought his spearminted hands up over his face. "I'm just going to lock myself in here till we leave."

"I think you should clean that stuff off first. Then you can go into seclusion without your dick falling off."

"It is starting to itch. I'll go get us a washcloth—or did you want to shower?"

"That they would hear for sure. I'll go."

Life was a lot easier with a cane instead of crutches. Sean could handle both the doorknob and the washcloths and towels he'd gotten in the bathroom. As soon as he turned the knob, the smell of mint hit him right away, memory pumping blood to his dick. It'd be pretty funny if he started springing wood whenever someone chewed gum. Kyle jumped about a foot when he came in.

"Just me, babe." He peered around Kyle's shoulder. Kyle was sitting on the edge of the bed with his back to the door, staring at Sean's phone.

"Go ahead and listen if you want. He was probably just calling to make sure I got the message about the air date for the Oprah show." And Brandt certainly wouldn't be flirting in a voice mail, would he? Half the time Sean wasn't sure that he wasn't reading too much into Brandt's charm.

"I wasn't—no. Shit, this stuff is getting itchy." Kyle turned with a smile as if he hadn't just been about to spit out a huge lie about not caring who had called Sean's cell at quarter to midnight.

Sean handed Kyle the washcloth he'd brought. "I brought a spare in case you can't control yourself again."

"Yeah, I'm like that."

Sean looked at the phone. It was stupid not to play the message, even though he knew it would piss Kyle off. And then it pissed him off that it would piss Kyle off, and Sean just grabbed the phone and checked his voice mail.

"Hey there. I don't know if you got my other message, but the…" Brandt repeated the rest of the message he'd left before and then added, "They sent me a clip and it looked great. You looked great. Not at all repulsive."

Maybe it was good Kyle hadn't listened. Sean held out the phone. "Want to hear it?"

"I said no."

Sean was pretty sure Kyle wanted to add something more to that, but he didn't. Just hung the washcloth off a knob on the dresser.

"Need the light for anything else?" Sean asked.

"Just let me get something to sleep in." Kyle pulled his discarded T-shirt over his head.

Kyle was right. Sleeping naked at Sean's parents' house was probably not the smartest thing, even if Sean had been looking forward to pressing against Kyle's warm skin all night.

His old bed was just a double, and they'd have to sleep closer than they did at home.

Sean pushed himself back off the bed and found his boxers. As he bent down for them, his leg muscles burned in protest. He clenched his teeth to keep in a wince.

"Sean?"

"I'm fine."

"Okay."

Kyle sat on the edge of the bed as Sean clicked off the light and sat on the other side, rubbing his thigh. It eased the ache a little. Kyle stretched out on the bed, close enough that the heat of his body radiated to Sean's back. He let go of his sore thigh.

Tomorrow he'd take a nice hot shower and the muscles would be better. He hadn't taken a codeine in more than a week. It was just stiffness, like when he healed from any other injury, like a sprained ankle, or the separated shoulder from a collision at home plate his senior year. He'd be fine. He swung his legs up onto the bed. Kyle rolled a little closer. Sean tangled his fingers in those sweat-damp black curls and pulled Kyle in for a kiss.

The slow tangle of tongues sent a flicker of heat to Sean's gut, a tingling rush like that minty lube was still on him. Even after coming so hard, Sean's hips rocked into Kyle's.

"Didn't you just turn thirty-six?" Kyle whispered against his lips.

"Thirty-five. And I'm making up for lost time."

Kyle's hand moved down between them, fingers wrapping around Sean's cock to pull it through the slit in his boxers.

Blood flooded Sean's dick, turning a bit of interest into full-on hard and aching. Kyle's slow fisting grip made Sean's hips jerk. On the plus side, his leg didn't hurt anymore.

Kyle started to wiggle lower under the sheet. And that was a whole lot more on the plus side. Just the thought of that mouth on Sean's cock forced him to choke back a moan.

"Might want to chew on a pillow, *papi*." Kyle pulled the sheet back and angled his head over Sean's lap.

It should have taken longer. No matter how much Kyle knew about sucking him, Sean shouldn't have been right up under the edge of a come from just a couple of swipes of Kyle's tongue and a deep wet bob.

Sean grabbed a pillow and stuffed it into his mouth. Kyle knew how to make it last, and he knew how to make it quick. He was going for the lightning round. His hand worked the shaft while his lips tightened under the crown, tongue a relentless flicking counterpoint to the hard suck and Sean had no time for a warning because it was there, the sweet hot burst that sent him bucking into Kyle's mouth.

He licked and stroked Sean's softening cock, just enough pressure to pull every last twitch of pleasure out of him, just soft enough to keep him on the good side of sore. It was nice. Then the bastard wiped his mouth on Sean's T-shirt.

"Leg better?" Kyle asked as he scooted up until they were face to face.

Sean would have sworn Kyle couldn't have noticed him rubbing his thigh in the dark. "Yeah."

"Aren't you a lucky bastard? Blowjobs are therapeutic."

"Hmm. When you put it that way, I think my leg might hurt again in the morning."

Kyle shifted around on Sean's pillow. "Seriously, if massage helps—"

It did, but asking Kyle to play therapist just felt wrong. He'd already become dependent enough on Kyle. He was looking forward to being able to do things on his own again. "I like the other therapy better. You got anything that needs massaging?" Sean's legs and arms were so heavy he doubted he could do more than offer a body to grind against, but he had to make the offer.

"I'm good. Some of us are feeling our age."

Sean dragged a hand up to cup Kyle's face, thumb just brushing the corner of his swollen lips. Sean wanted to explain about Brandt, remind Kyle that all the publicity stuff would be over soon, but he didn't speak. Things had been better—Kyle had seemed happier this week. If he brought it up again, it would just fuck things up.

"Love you," Kyle muttered against Sean's thumb.

"Love you more."

Kyle smiled, waiting for Sean to finish their game. For a moment, he couldn't think of anything. Because it had just hit him. He did love Kyle more. He'd always known that, never expected it to change, but right now that knowledge seemed to coil through his guts like fear. He was always going to be the one who loved more. Why did it scare him all of a sudden?

"More than Aerosmith," Sean finished at last.

"Yeah? Well, when you love me more than Def Leppard will you change that fucking ring tone?"

ß

By ten a.m. Sean had started to wonder if Kyle really was going into seclusion. Sean had left him still asleep at eight and gone down to help his mom in the kitchen. His cousin was coming with her two uselessly obnoxious tweens, and she'd be no help at all—even when she wasn't screaming at the girls. His aunt would help, but she and Mom could both stand a break now and then. He loved to cook anyway.

Sean dropped the last peeled potato in the pot of water and gave the stuffing another quick stir. "This should be ready now," he told his mom. "Want me to stuff?"

"Thank you, sweetheart."

Kyle appeared in the kitchen doorway, hair wet from his shower, shaved and in the sweater and tie he'd brought to wear to dinner, but his eyes were still bleary.

"Saved you some coffee." Sean pointed to the counter.

"Thanks." Even Kyle's voice was scratchy.

Mom was dotting the sweet potatoes with marshmallows, so Sean washed his hands and brought Kyle a mug.

"You okay?"

"Kept waking up. And," Kyle added in a whisper, "I had to wait until your dad was out of the living room so I could sneak by."

"Oh, babe." Sean tried not to laugh. "You do realize he'll be at dinner."

"I can put it off longer this way. Let me do some dishes." Kyle poured out a mug of coffee and took a swallow right away.

"He's not going to say anything." The idea of his father even acknowledging that Sean had sex was impossible to contemplate.

"But he'll look at me. Maybe he didn't hear anything."

"Maybe he did and he's going to demand that you marry me."

Kyle sputtered into the mug.

"There's some Cheerios in that cabinet. And then Mom and I promise to let you do the dishes." Sean went back to stuffing the turkey.

"That's sweet of you, Kyle, but you can just sit with Peter if you'd rather."

"Really, Gina, I'd love to help."

"Chicken," Sean said softly.

"What, sweetheart?"

"Hey, Mom, have you ever heard of a turducken?"

As Sean explained the word to his mother, he watched Kyle tuck himself into a corner and lean against the counter to revive himself with coffee, orange juice and a bowl of Cheerios. So what if Sean did love Kyle more? Kyle loved him, and he needed him, was the best time Sean had ever had, in or out of bed. They'd get through this. Kyle already seemed less tense. Last night was the first night Kyle'd had trouble sleeping in weeks.

Sean's phone vibrated against his hip. It was the third time since he'd gotten up this morning. Kyle caught him looking down at it.

"He'll just keep calling until you talk to him," Kyle said, carrying his bowl to the sink.

"I know."

"Talk to who?" his mom asked.

"Sean has someone who's handling publicity for him."

"Oh, that nice man you told me about who's doing it for free."

"Not for free," Sean added quickly. "But I should call him back."

"Of course, you can use our phone."

"No this is fine, I'll just—" If he stayed in the kitchen, the presence of Kyle and his mother would insure that the conversation was brief and businesslike. But tension was already radiating off Kyle and Sean didn't feel like dealing with it. "I'll go into the den."

He washed up and went through the dining room and into the den. There was nothing besides a little harmless flirting going on with Brandt, and Sean deserved some fun. Brandt was easy to talk to, no pressure, no strain.

"Hey, Sean, I just wanted to make sure you got my messages. I'd hate to have you miss the show."

"No, it's fine." Sean stepped toward the door before he realized closing it would probably be a bad idea.

"How's the family?"

Sean laughed and lowered his voice. "Kyle's hiding because he thinks my father heard us having sex last night. Other than that, it's fine."

"Must have been some good stuff." Brandt chuckled. "I've got another moneymaker for you. Money and a good cause. Yesterday, I heard from the Human Rights Campaign. They want you as a spokesman, do a couple of print ads, maybe a couple of satellite radio spots, a spot on Logo. I told them we'd get back to them. After they see you on Oprah, they're going to be really eager to talk."

"But isn't that a charity?"

"It's a political group with a huge fundraising base. They're going to pay someone to do the spots. Might as well be you. Again, you'll be taking time from your job, from your PT, probably having to travel. You deserve compensation for that."

"And you deserve a percentage."

"You know me too well." Brandt's laughter was just as warm over the phone. "Hey, I don't want to keep you from doing the family thing."

"Actually, I'm mostly doing the cooking thing. But I should rescue Kyle."

"Doesn't he get along with your folks?"

"Oh yeah, they get along great. He's just—" Kyle didn't really need Sean to protect him. "Avoiding my dad."

"What *were* you boys up to last night?"

Kyle deep inside, Sean needing to come so badly he was going to tear off the scarf even if his dick came with it.

"Catching up," Sean said.

"If that's what you want to call it. I managed to skip the home-for-Thanksgiving thing this year. Work's an excuse everyone can relate to. So, what time do you guys eat?"

"Why? Are you planning to mysteriously appear?"

"I'm thinking that would be a bad plan."

"One fifteen sharp. God help the turkey if it's not done. Or my dad if it's not carved and steaming on the table."

"Remind me to send your mom some flowers or something."

"For what?"

"For letting me drag away her helper. I'd hate to be responsible for the turkey being late."

Sean laughed. "I think you're already in her good graces. You got me on Oprah. Mom's a talk show nut." He heard the clank of dishware and peered around the corner to see Kyle setting the table. Was he frowning? Because the conversation was taking so long or because Mom was making him set the table? "My aunt and uncle and cousin will be here soon. I'd better go and shore up the defenses."

"All right. I'll talk to you after you've seen the show. Oh—"

Sean heard the doorbell and his father going to let his aunt and her family in. "I really should go."

"Talk to you later. Tell your mom I'm rooting for her. Victory over the bird."

Sean laughed again. "I will." As he hung up, he saw his mom go by on her way into the living room. He slipped across the hall to join Kyle at the table. Wrapping his arms around Kyle's waist, Sean looked over Kyle's shoulder at their reflections on the gleaming china. Despite the blur, Sean knew Kyle was still frowning.

Kyle pulled himself free and walked over to the buffet, returning with the box of silver.

Sean moved to stand right behind him again. "Can't wait until we get home tonight, babe. Wanna fuck in every room in the house."

Without turning, Kyle laid out a place setting. "What's going on? Did you raid your father's medicine cabinet for Viagra?"

"Ugh." Sean shuddered. "Please don't go there." He tried to grab Kyle again, but he'd moved on to the next place setting. "I've just been thinking about yesterday, last night. Missed you."

"We've seen each other more the past month than we ever have before."

Sean leaned his cane against the dining table and hobbled toward the kitchen, dragging Kyle with him.

"Sitting together in the hospital doesn't count." Sean backed Kyle into the corner where he'd eaten his breakfast. "Watching you worry and freak out doesn't count." He shifted to lean into Kyle. "This counts."

"You're hard." Kyle sounded suspicious.

"Yeah. C'mon and kiss me before those evil brats come running in here shrieking."

"There's a reason preadolescent girls feature prominently in horror mov—"

Sean cut off the last syllable of the film lecture with a hard kiss, then backed off to let his tongue stroke slow and sure in Kyle's mouth. Sean leaned back until their lips were just sliding against each other as they shared a breath. Kyle tried to get closer again, but Sean stepped away as he heard shrill voices and running feet heading their way.

Heather chased Hannah around the kitchen table, waving Sean's cane. After two laps, they were gone, his cousin Sheila's equally annoying screech ringing through the house: "Put that down."

"So what was the reason?" Sean asked.

"Hm?" Kyle looked confused. Sean hoped the kiss was the reason.

"About the preadolescent girls?"

"Oh. I forgot." Kyle's smile was quick, and then he went back to whatever he'd been thinking that made him so quiet. "Do you want me to go retrieve your cane?"

"From the hell spawn? That's true love, babe."

"No, my nephew Ricky is hell spawn. Those girls just have an over-developed sense of entitlement."

"They're spoiled."

"You think?" Kyle headed for the door as Sean sank onto a kitchen chair. His leg was killing him. Kyle turned back. "Um? Which one's Heather and which one's Hannah?"

"I don't actually remember either."

As silence descended over dinner, Sean decided he almost preferred the earlier chaos with the girls, or even holidays with Kyle's family. Usually, there were so many people crammed into Kyle's parents' house at Christmas that he and Kyle's brothers ate their dinner on the stairs because there wasn't a seat or even a square foot of floor that wasn't full of relatives or crawling children.

Sean eyed the twins who were wearing identical glazed looks. They said *please* and *thank you* instead of *ew* and *that's gross.* Something must be brewing. Whatever drug Sheila had slipped the girls had to wear off soon.

After the first round of grazing was over, his mother turned to her sister. "Carol, maybe you could come back over tomorrow to watch Sean on Oprah with us." His mother nodded at him.

"Mom, remember I told you we're driving back to Canton tonight? Kyle has to work tomorrow because he missed so much time while I was hurt."

"Oh." But neither his mother's smile nor intentions were deterred. "Well then, Kyle can drive back tonight and your father and I can bring you home on Saturday."

Under the table, Sean ran a soothing hand over the tense muscles in Kyle's thigh.

"No thanks, Mom." The muscles under his hand relaxed. He rubbed over Kyle's Dockers again, and Kyle's leg inched closer.

"Really, sweetheart, it's no trouble. And I'm sure Kyle doesn't mind."

"I don't want him to drive back alone, Mom." If Kyle hadn't slept well, there was no way Sean was letting Kyle drive home alone with the added hazard of a tryptophan-induced stupor. All that didn't matter, because Sean was going home with Kyle tonight. To their house. Where they could have sex without worrying about time or who might hear. "And I need to start to get ready to get back to work. And—" This would be the clincher for Mom and her scrapbook. "The guy doing my PR has something new lined up that I need to talk to him about."

As soon as he said it, he realized the mistake. It wasn't just a clincher for Mom, it was the clincher for Kyle. His leg jerked away from Sean's hand, and Kyle's conversational style became as catatonic as the twins.

Again Kyle offered to wash the dishes and Sheila said she'd help. Sean stood in the doorway to the living room. Mom beckoned with her scrapbook, opened now for Aunt Carol. Dad had left the recliner vacant for Sean, and all he wanted was to sink down on that leather and get the strain off his thigh. He'd pushed his leg too far today. Two trips up and down the stairs, all that standing to cook, all on top of hours of driving—and fucking. Though the fucking was worth it. Instead of giving into those leather cushions with a sigh that probably would have been obscene, Sean leaned on his cane and limped out to the kitchen.

Kyle and Sheila's laughter trailed off as he came in.

"Hey, Sheila, I think the girls are online in Dad's den."

"Shit." She tossed him her dish towel and hurried out.

Kyle tipped another plate through the stream of water before handing it to Sean. "Are they really online?"

"No. But they're probably up to something. They're never quiet this long."

Kyle did another two plates before asking, "Does Brandt really have something else lined up?"

Sean decided he'd better be sure to have the dish in his hands before he answered. "Yes. Spokesman for HRC."

"That's a pretty big deal. You'd be like Martina Navratilova. Only not as butch."

"Fuck off."

Kyle didn't seem too upset about it.

Sean took the turkey platter from him. "So is it all right?"

Kyle started on the rest of the serving bowls. "I'm not going to tell you what to do." He scrubbed hard at the glass in the sink. "Fucking marshmallows."

"But you'd like to?"

"No. I—just want you to think about it. Think it through before you decide."

"It would help if you'd tell me what you want."

Kyle opened the cabinet under the sink and rummaged around. "Right now I want something stronger than the dishrag to get off the burnt-on marshmallows."

"Here." Sean leaned over the sink and pulled the scrub pad from behind a ceramic turkey.

"Thanks."

"Kyle."

Kyle scrubbed for a minute and then started rinsing the glass. "I already told you what I wanted."

"To move? Sell the house?" Sean couldn't believe they were actually talking about this again. "You love that house."

"I do."

"You really think that would change things or fix things or whatever it is you think it's going to do?"

"I don't know."

"You want to completely screw with our entire life and you don't know, but you want *me* to think things through?"

Kyle subjected the almost licked-clean mashed potato bowl to as vigorous an attack as the one the sweet potato dish had received, but his voice was soft. "I want to start over."

"You know what, Kyle? We can't." Sean tossed his towel onto the table and limped away. "I'm going to pack."

Chapter Eleven

Gina Farnham made an absolutely amazing apple pie. In truth, her pies were so amazing they were better than the ones Kyle's Italian grandmother made, and that was saying something—the kind of something Kyle would never say out loud for fear of suffering a curse. This year though, both the pumpkin and the apple were tasteless and dry. The fault wasn't the cook's but her son's. He washed down the half-eaten slices with bitter black coffee, ignoring the tantalizing offer of whipped cream.

Dessert was painful enough to get through, but for fun, it beat the ensuing three-hour drive home like a blowjob beat a root canal. At first, Sean had the football game on the radio as Kyle drove, but when they lost that station, there was nothing but silence from Ashtabula on.

Kyle was tired of feeling angry at Sean for being thick-headed about what the publicity could do—was doing—to their lives, so he decided to think of other things to be mad at him for. With each exit they passed, he added another item to his growing list. Cheerful and talky in the morning. A pig about his socks. Wore his sideburns too long. As they neared Cleveland, there were a lot of exits so he had to think fast. Stubborn, arrogant, baseball, football, whatever ball, 80's music, know-it-all—

"Kyle? Are we going to Cleveland for something? Feeling a need for a tour around your old neighborhood?"

"What?"

"You're going to miss our exit."

Bossy, Kyle added silently and started to move right across the lanes.

For awhile that afternoon, he'd hoped Sean was eager to get home tonight because he intended to try to make up for lost time by fucking in every room in the house. Considering Sean's lame attempt at sarcasm was the first thing either of them had said for more than a hundred miles, Kyle seriously doubted that either of them was going to be in the mood. Not that conversation was necessary for sex, but Kyle didn't have the energy to stuff his anger down far enough to even look at Sean right now.

Kyle took both their bags from the back of the Durango while Sean carried in the leftovers. Kyle hoped there was a slice of Gina's apple pie tucked in there. They still weren't talking when Sean thumped his way into the kitchen to put everything away. Kyle thought about waiting for him, but when Sean started finding extra ways to occupy himself in the kitchen, Kyle went upstairs alone. He'd finished in the bathroom by the time he heard Sean on the stairs. With a glance at the bags he'd thrown on the bed, Kyle decided to unpack tomorrow. He tossed the bags into the closet and stripped to the skin before climbing in on his side of the bed. Sean still wasn't out of the bathroom.

Sean came in and turned off the light. His weight sank onto the bed and the covers shifted and whispered. Kyle lay on his back and stared at the ceiling. And then it was morning and his alarm was beeping in his ear.

Sean woke with Kyle's alarm. As Kyle slipped from the bed, Sean rolled onto his side, burying his face in the pillow that smelled like Kyle. The scent pumped more blood to Sean's morning erection, even while warmth and familiarity tried to lure him back to sleep. He peeled open one eye to look at Kyle's alarm clock. Seven forty-five.

Kyle was cutting it close. No time to join him in the shower—if he even wanted Sean to bother. He hated feeling like this. When he and Kyle weren't talking it fucked up every single part of the day. Sean could apologize, but it wasn't as if he'd done anything wrong. Kyle was pissed about Sean doing more publicity. Sorry wasn't going to work when he intended to go right on doing it. The only thing he would have taken back was springing it on Kyle over Thanksgiving dinner—with Sean's parents as an audience.

And Sean could admit to feeling a little guilty about flirting with Brandt, something he hoped Kyle didn't have a clue about. But it wasn't as if Sean was having phone sex with the guy. They just had fun talking.

Kyle came back into their bedroom to dress. Naked, damp, warm. Sean watched, barely controlling the urge to stroke his hard-on as Kyle bent over to pull on a black pair of briefs, bringing his ass into Sean's view. By the time Kyle was knotting his tie—Jesus, he looked hot in that cranberry shirt—Sean wished he'd figured out something to say to make things better.

Pausing in the doorway, Kyle asked the same question he'd asked almost every morning for the last six weeks, "What time's your PT?"

"I can drive myself today, remember?"

"Oh. Right." Kyle left.

If Sean got up and went downstairs, he could talk to Kyle over his coffee and Cheerios, maybe find something that would get him smiling and laughing. The front door slammed shut, and Sean flopped back against the pillows with a wince. Kyle had to be seriously pissed-off to skip breakfast.

Sean leaned over and grabbed his cane. Hobbling to the bathroom on his sleep-stiff leg was more challenging than usual, given the unusual stubbornness of his morning wood. The fact that the smell of Kyle's aftershave filled the bathroom didn't help either.

Leaning his cane against the toilet, Sean balanced against the tiled wall as he hopped into the shower. With a resigned glance at his dick, Sean slicked his hand with Kyle's liquid soap and started jerking off. The soap was the same woodsy scent as his aftershave, and Sean could imagine Kyle here with him, their bodies wet and slippery against each other, tongues tangled as their hands worked their dicks together.

Halfway through, an unwanted question popped into his head, putting a hitch in the rhythm of his strokes. What was Brandt like in bed? Smiles and charm? Pleas and submission? Rough and demanding? How would his hand move on Sean's cock? Sean squeezed his eyes shut. That didn't help, since all the images were on the inside. His grip tightened, and he sped up his strokes as he thumbed the head. He took a deep breath and when he came, the scene playing on his closed lids was Kyle's mouth around his cock, Kyle's warm brown eyes looking up at him. Satisfaction and relief held him boneless against the wall for a long time.

ß

Mom had sent them home with plenty of leftovers, but Sean decided to go grocery shopping after PT. He'd make something nice for Kyle that wouldn't remind him of Thanksgiving and the whole publicity thing. Kyle had said he wanted to start over. They couldn't, but maybe they could find a way through this that didn't leave them snapping at each other all the time.

Theresa had worked him hard at PT, but given him lots of time in the whirlpool, so he felt good enough to put his cane in the cart and use it as a walker. He had no intention of ever using one of those motorized chairs, he could walk, thanks. Even if he was a bit slow.

A display of tomatillos caught his eye, and he remembered how much Kyle loved *mole verde*. He was scooping pumpkin seeds in the bulk aisle when his phone vibrated against his hip. He glanced at the display before answering. Brandt. His cock twitched in his sweats and he let the call go to voice mail.

After two more aisles, he listened to the message. It was a simple "Call me back."

Sean added a can of chilies to the cart and decided he'd be safer with a text. *Can't talk right now.*

As soon as he'd sent it, the phone buzzed. *Everything ok?*

Fine.

Not feeling regularly repulsive?

Sean laughed in spite of himself. *I'm gorgeous. Have you seen this month's* Out*?*

Mom flip out at the turkey?

No, Kyle flipped out over the HRC spokesman thing. But texting all that would really be crossing the line into disloyalty. And not taking the call hadn't kept him from starting this again with Brandt. He realized he was still in the international foods aisle.

Gotta go. Call you later.

As he turned down the next aisle, he ran smack into Vince Gerbino. Sean's mind raced, trying to think of something to say, but the man's face turned red and he dropped the basket he was carrying and walked down the aisle. Sean leaned against the peanut butter shelf for a minute. Every time he started to feel better, Nicole was there to remind him of what he didn't do. Couldn't fix.

It was better when he checked out. He'd taught both the front-end manager and the girl who rang up his groceries. They both asked about his leg, and talked about how lucky it was that he'd acted so quickly. Then the girl started asking about Oprah. Sean said all the generic things about how nice she was and what the studio looked like, but what stood out in his mind was the woman in the audience who said that she felt bad about the way she kept making fun of her gay nephew for not being a real man and that she was going to apologize to him. Sean had said, "I think you just did."

That's what he was doing it for. Not for the smiles and the warm recognition in the grocery store, but for the chance to change people's minds. To make up for what he couldn't go back and fix. He just had to convince Kyle of that.

ß

Kyle was the last one to leave the office. He didn't think

he'd heard anyone else around after three. The Friday after Thanksgiving never ranked high for productivity, but Kyle had a lot to catch up on. And he didn't want to think about what was waiting at home.

Sean didn't get mad often, but when he did, he stayed that way for awhile. Kyle wouldn't have been surprised if the Durango wasn't in the driveway, but it was.

He took a deep breath and opened the door. The mouth-watering smell hit him first. Spice. Food. Home.

"Hey, babe. Dining room or kitchen?" Sean called.

"Kitchen's fine." Kyle came into find Sean pulling enchiladas out of the oven. Green sauce, stuffed with beef, black beans, rice and cheese. All of Kyle's favorites. The thickness in his throat disappeared.

Kyle pulled off his tie and slipped his arms around Sean's waist. "God, that smells good."

Sean laid his hands over Kyle's for a minute and then squeezed and pulled away. "Eh, canned beans and microwaved rice." But he was smiling.

Kyle smiled back at him. Sean leaned forward to press their grins together, and Kyle could take a deep breath again.

Kyle got some plates and forks and they settled at the bar to eat. Sean might have claimed that it was all canned, but that *mole verde* was from scratch. He loved the way Sean made up.

"How was PT?"

"Long. But there was whirlpool."

"Oh?"

"Oh yeah." Sean leaned over and kissed him.

Kyle couldn't finish his dinner fast enough. He carried his plate to the sink, and Sean stopped him with a hand on Kyle's hip. "Clean up can wait."

Kyle let his smile hike his eyebrows up.

Sean pushed him against the counter, leaning in to lick a line up Kyle's throat. "Uh-huh. Do you remember our first night together?"

Kyle definitely did. And then his stomach sank under more than the weight of the two enchiladas he'd inhaled. *Oh, papi, that's not the kind of starting over I meant.* But he nodded.

"What was your favorite position?"

All of them. Kyle considered what would put the least strain on Sean's leg. "When you had me on your lap while you were sitting in your desk chair."

"Wasn't that the second time?"

"Third time, first night."

"Oh, right. It was actually in the morning." Sean led the way out into the dining room. "You were looking for your pants. Trying to sneak out while I was in the bathroom."

"I had a phobia about awkward mornings after." Kyle dragged Sean against the wall and kissed him. "But you know what really got me? The way you talked. Told me everything you were going to do and how good it would feel. I'd never had someone talk to me like that. God, that was hot."

"Was?" Sean tilted his head as he leaned against the wall, smiling with spit-wet lips.

"Still is."

"Okay then." Sean grabbed Kyle's shirt and pulled him in so their lips were almost touching. Brushing his lips along Kyle's jaw, Sean whispered, gravelly and deep. "Gonna fuck you, Kyle. Gonna drag you down, make you sit on my cock, gonna slam up so deep you'll fucking taste me."

By the time Sean finished that obscene litany, Kyle's dick was hot and tight. He leaned in for another taste of Sean's mouth, sharing the spices from supper, the tingle and heat as their tongues rubbed together.

Sean pushed him back with a hand on his chest. "Didn't need foreplay that time. I just grabbed you and you swung onto my lap. I barely had time to get a rubber on before you sank onto my cock."

"You'd already fucked me twice. God, I walked funny for a week."

"So is that why you wouldn't return my calls?" Sean slipped

his hand down Kyle's chest until Sean could palm Kyle's dick, rubbing hard through the wool of his slacks. Kyle arched into that hand, a groan vibrating his throat. He almost grabbed Sean for balance and then remembered his leg and just smacked the wall instead.

"Doesn't feel like you need much foreplay." Sean tightened his fingers around Kyle's cock. "Feel just as hard as you did then."

"I'd woken up that way."

"Me too. Woke up that way this morning too. Didn't get much better as I watched you dress."

That wasn't the way Kyle remembered things going this morning. But it was easier to let Sean rewrite history. To let him use history to try to get them back where Kyle wanted them to be.

"Oh?"

"Wanted you bad. Thought about fucking you all day." Sean tipped his head at the dining table.

As Kyle stepped back, Sean turned Kyle, bending him over the polished cherry surface. Sean's hands slipped around Kyle's waist to work at his belt buckle, button, the zipper, and then Sean was sliding the pants off his hips and ass.

"Kick 'em off," Sean said, moving away.

The pulse of blood in the tip of Kyle's cock bordered on painful. He rubbed against the cool smooth wood of the table before he finished pulling off his clothes.

"Don't get started without me." The sound of Sean's uneven step went in the direction of the kitchen.

Kyle unbuttoned his shirt. "Do you want some help?"

"I'm good." Sean turned the stereo on loud, one of Kyle's favorite R&B CD's already cued up.

Even as the beat of slow sensuous bass made Kyle's hips sway, doubts snaked through his brain. Sean was doing what he always did: making Kyle happy. And Kyle was doing what he always did: letting him. And this wouldn't solve anything. Not dinner or make-up sex or going back to that first night. Sex wasn't the problem, so it couldn't be the answer, but then Sean was back and his hand pressed Kyle forward onto the table again. Sean dragged his tongue up Kyle's spine and it might not fix anything but damn, when they had this, what the hell else mattered?

Sean's mouth was wet and hot under Kyle's ear, fingers slick gliding along the crease of his ass.

"That's not that tingling shit again, is it?" Kyle's voice sounded thick.

"No." Two hands on Kyle's ass now, pulling and stretching before those fingers went back to teasing him. "It's that twenty-bucks-a-two-ounce bottle you like so much."

"Uh—ok—ay." The last syllable rose as Sean slid a finger inside, quick burn and then so good pumping through him in time with the beat, the fuck of Sean's finger—fingers—curling and twisting.

Sean pulled his hand free and sat in a chair.

"Wouldn't this be easier in your recliner?"

Sean hooked another chair with his ankle and dragged it closer. "Shut up and sit on my dick." His lips curved in a half smile as he snapped the bottle open and poured more thick liquid over his fingers, stroking it over his cock until it shone, bright cherry red crown breaking through the fist.

Kyle's mouth watered, but as much as he loved the silky way that lube felt, it tasted like shit. "I meant for your leg."

"My leg is great. I sat around most of the day. C'mon."

Kyle didn't need more urging. He swung his leg over Sean's, balancing with his knee on the extra chair. Sean's cock glided over Kyle's entrance, the tip barely pressing inside, but Sean held Kyle's hips, keeping him from sinking down all the way, and Kyle's balance was too precarious to fight him.

"Still not fucking around?" Sean asked with a smile.

"No. You?"

Kyle didn't have time to process the tiny flicker of Sean's eyelids as he gasped, "No," because Sean was already arching up and pulling Kyle down, and then he pretty much forgot about it, because eight and a half inches of thick cock in his ass made it really hard to think about anything else.

Sean helped Kyle push his hips up and down until he was riding Sean's cock, meeting his thrusts. Kyle pulled himself all the way up and off so Sean could have all that perfect tight pressure on the head of his dick as Kyle sank back down.

Needing more traction, he shifted until his foot was on the chair instead of his knee, the stretch pulling him so wide open that Sean went deeper and they both groaned.

"So good inside you. Fuck yourself on my dick, babe."

Kyle held onto Sean's shoulders as Sean wrapped his arms around Kyle's hips and they worked each other faster, Sean's thighs slapping Kyle's ass.

Somehow Sean managed to get his mouth on Kyle's shoulder, sucking a deep bite that spiked the pleasure pounding through Kyle's body.

"Didn't. Do. That. First. Time."

"I didn't know how much you'd like it. What gets you hotter, babe, the bite or knowing you're wearing my mark on you the next day?"

"Both," Kyle gasped. Not that he wanted any visible hickeys, but having Sean's mark on him under his clothes made heat pool in his gut every time he thought about it.

Sean went for the same spot again, harder, sucking deeper, until it was almost too much and then everything was too much, too good, and Kyle had to grab his cock and stroke it or he was going to lose his mind.

"Couldn't manage that the first time." Sean lapped at the hollow of Kyle's throat. "I had to jerk you off."

"You'd fucked all the coordination out of me."

"And I'm not now? Damn, you're even using complete sentences." Sean grabbed Kyle's hips and fucked up hard and fast until every nagging thought and doubt went off in some corner of Kyle's brain and there was only now. This. The smell of them together, sweat and sex, and the sound of bodies sliding and slapping together. The smooth feel of Sean's hair as

Kyle grabbed it to hang on.

"Gotta fuck you harder, babe."

"Yeah." But before Kyle could move or protest, Sean lifted them both up and put Kyle's back across the two chairs, holding his hips and pushing his legs over his head. Kyle reached back to grab the legs of the chair under him as Sean slammed forward.

"Make that sound again. I can feel it from inside you." Sean stared down into his face.

Kyle closed his eyes. "Then do that again. That."

A dip and roll and Sean's strokes lengthened. "Yeah. Feels so good on my cock."

Kyle reached for his dick again.

"Don't come yet. Need to fuck you more," Sean begged, and when he shook his head to get his sweat-sticky hair out of his beautiful eyes, Kyle nodded and reached back for the chair leg. "God, I'll get you off so good, babe. Promise."

With Kyle this close it wouldn't take much, and he loved it when Sean did this to him, brought him to the brink and backed off, shifted his thrusts every time they were on the edge. He knew when Sean let him go nothing ever felt better because the orgasm lasted until he couldn't stop shaking.

Another long stroke, all the way out and in, and then fast and hard again, Sean reaching for Kyle's dick, sure and smooth and God, he was going to go, but Sean's grip relaxed. Kyle groaned in frustration but he was glad, because as long as this went on there was no *why* or *what if*, just Sean over him and in him, stretching the pleasure out as long as they could take it.

"Ah, fuck," Sean growled. His hand went fast and tight on Kyle's dick, a twist on the head, and the first shot felt so good nothing could be better, but then it was, more and more, his balls tight against him as he spilled over Sean's fingers, pumping again and again. Sean's hand pressed him hard against an aftershock before he released Kyle's dick to grab at his thighs, snapping forward.

Kyle rubbed the last pulses of pleasure out of his cock as

he watched Sean come, head back and mouth open on a whispered moan. Kyle's heart pounded so hard it hurt, a fist against his breastbone, pulse trying to explode out of him.

Sean lowered Kyle's legs and took a long deep breath. "That first time was good, babe, but I think we're just getting better."

"Yeah."

Sean hung onto the chair back as he leaned in to kiss Kyle, slow and soft.

"You should get off your leg. Especially if you're starting work next week."

"Who's bossy now?" Sean smiled against his lips.

"Prize still goes to the guy who told me to shut up and sit on his dick."

"Could have told me to fuck myself."

"Where's the fun in that for me? Damn. My back is killing me." And Kyle's heart still hadn't slowed down.

"You're ruining the afterglow."

"If you wanted afterglow, we should have done it in bed."

"You picked the chair." Sean helped Kyle to sit up.

"I don't know, I thought maybe it'd be easier for the guy with the bullet holes in his leg."

Sean made a face.

"I'll take care of the kitchen," Kyle offered. "You put your leg up."

"My leg doesn't hurt." Sean's eyelids flickered again. He always did that when he felt guilty about something.

A memory teased the back of Kyle's brain.

"Did you see Brandt today?"

"No. I don't even know where he is." Sean shrugged. His gaze remained steady.

"Isn't he based in Cleveland?"

"I think so. That's the area code for his cell. You know, since you've got some kind of problem with him, maybe you should call around some of your friends. See if anyone up there knows him."

Kyle couldn't believe he hadn't thought of that before. "Maybe I will."

Sean picked up his cane and then leaned in and kissed Kyle again. "God that was good, babe."

It was. So good his heart still slammed painfully in his chest while blood roared in his ears. So good Kyle could almost forget about the way Sean's face took on a different smile when he talked to Brandt on the phone. So good it didn't matter that Sean wouldn't even think about moving some place where the shooting wouldn't be the first thing on everyone's mind.

"Kyle. You tired? You want me to clean up?"

The sight of Sean naked and leaning on a cane jarred his brain. Maybe for Sean it didn't matter because it would always be the first thing on his mind no matter where they were. "No. I'll do it."

Chapter Twelve

Sean looked up at the steel-grey clouds. Every kid in Canton would be hoping to extend their weekend with a snow day tomorrow.

"I don't get why you want to come with me," Sean said with a glance at Kyle in the passenger seat. Kyle had never shown that much interest in Sean's school before. "There's really nothing all that interesting about my classroom. Especially on a Sunday."

"Hmmm. Maybe I just want to act out a fantasy."

"Huh?"

"Doesn't everyone have a hot teacher/naughty schoolboy fantasy?"

"I haven't heard yours."

Kyle flushed and shifted. "It's probably not much different."

"Than?"

"Your basic. Desks, discipline, a ruler."

"Discipline and a ruler, huh?" Sean had never had any idea Kyle went for stuff like that. Seven years and he still hadn't completely figured Kyle out. Sean would think Kyle was kidding if he didn't look so hot and bothered. "I've already had you over every desk in the house."

"Not my drafting table."

"Yep. Remember the night last summer you insisted that Tony was a lightweight and just because he'd been tending bar for twelve years didn't mean you couldn't outdrink him?"

Kyle groaned. "I remember the hangover."

"The two of you had quite a time with Jim Beam. The drafting board was all your idea. Kind of a loud one too." Kyle had been yelling by the time he came, clenching tight and hot around Sean's cock.

Kyle made another embarrassed groan. "Just tell me they weren't still there."

"Jack dragged Tony out when you took off your shirt. You were, uh, kissing Tony at the time. I think you were trying to prove who was drunker." He didn't worry about Kyle cheating on him—especially not with Tony—but watching Kyle kiss another guy had had him slamming Kyle over the nearest surface as soon as the door closed. The memory sent a pulse of blood to Sean's cock. He tried to ignore it but his brain was providing him with all new images. "A ruler? Who gets to be Teacher?"

"Forget it."

"Oh, I don't think so, babe. But not today. Your hot-for-teacher game will have to wait until we're somewhere without security cameras." Sean pulled into the parking lot. New signs warned: *Anyone on school property is subject to a search at any time.* Cameras turned every other lamppost into a Cyclops. Sean fished his work keys from the compartment in the center console. "Did you remember your wallet?"

"Of course."

"When I called and said I was coming in, they said everyone had to carry ID. And we'll have to go in the front door. Even though there's another door that's right next to my classroom." He was talking too quickly. Almost as if he were nervous. It was just that being there without the usual background noise of six hundred students intent on discussing everything and anything that didn't have to do with academics made it feel abnormally quiet.

A security guard met them at the door. Although he recognized Sean and called him by name, he still escorted them to the front desk where they were required to produce identification and sign in. The extra security measures might be making some parents happy, but the ache in Sean's thigh and the cane in his hand reminded him that for some of them it was a little too late.

There was no way to completely secure a school. Even if they forced everyone to enter through a single door, added metal detectors and random searches, a determined nutcase could easily find a way in. It wasn't security that needed the upgrade, it was people.

As he signed the paper on the counter in front of the secretary's desk, he looked beyond it to the administration offices. He'd never heard exactly where Frank Healey had been shot, never wanted to read any detailed accounts of that day—his own memory was enough, thanks. He looked down. Brown carpet with black flecks. New. So new a trace of that new carpet smell was still strong enough to break through all the other smells of a school.

He kept glancing down at the carpet as he led Kyle toward the science wing. He didn't know why. It wasn't as if he was going to find a chalk outline or a...stain.

The lockers in the hall weren't new, but they were freshly painted with shiny red enamel. He found himself checking for bullet holes, but those had been repaired. Carefully. New carpet again. He almost expected to hear the echoes of the screams and the gunfire, but there was nothing. Just an empty hallway full of new carpet smell.

Kyle hadn't said a word since they got out of the car. As Sean led the way around the corner to his room, Kyle hung back.

"That's it?" Kyle's eyes were fixed on the space behind them, as if he, too, were trying to find the stains and bullet holes.

"Yeah. About there." Sean pointed down the hall.

He remembered a trip to Gettysburg when he was fourteen. He'd seen the statues and the pictures and the diagrams. Fifty thousand men might have spilled their blood there, but a hundred and twenty years later there was just a lot of grass.

He supposed he'd always known that no matter how

horrific the violence, life had to go on as soon as it was over. He'd just never experienced it personally. He took a deep breath and led Kyle over to the spot where, as near as he could remember, he'd tackled Chris Bowman. He hadn't really expected a commemorative plaque, but frustration at not being able to pinpoint such a life-altering moment forced a quick sigh.

"Okay?" Kyle asked, lifting his gaze from the carpet.

"Yeah." Sean was, which was kind of surprising, even to him. He ran his hands along the lockers. Gettysburg was grass, and this was just a hall.

"What was it like?" Kyle's voice was soft.

Sean hesitated. He'd talked about it on national television. Why was it so hard to talk about it with Kyle? Sean realized that since that first day in the hospital, he'd never tried to describe that day to Kyle. They talked about the publicity, about his leg, but not about the actual incident. And it was still hard to tell Kyle what he'd really been feeling. That he'd been terrified that he was going to make it worse. He hadn't told anyone that. Hated even admitting it to Kyle.

"It was weird. It was loud and quiet at the same time. And it happened in jumpy cuts. Like an action movie. And the whole time"—he looked directly at Kyle—"the whole time I kept wondering what if this makes it worse? What if I get all these kids killed?"

Kyle reached for his face and then stopped, hand hovering before he lowered it with a smile. "But you didn't. You saved them."

Sean stared at the carpet so hard the black flecks seemed to separate from the brown and hover above it. "Not Nicole."

Kyle shook his head. "You saved them. No one could have done more. No one did."

Sean turned and went back to his classroom. No matter how many times he'd tried to tell himself that Nicole might have already been dead, it didn't help.

His room was in good shape. At first glance nothing seemed to be missing, and when he checked the grade book, it looked like the sub had been taking good notes. The department chair had promised she'd keep an eye on things.

"So what do we need to do?" asked Kyle.

Sean sat on the stool behind the large lab table that doubled as his desk and started checking through the kids' most recent labs. "It's not as bad as I thought it would be. I need to check the supplies for the next couple of labs, and take these papers home to look over."

He swung his briefcase onto the table and shoved the stack of papers inside. The same kind of surprise that he'd felt in the hall left him confused. He'd expected to be plagued with memories as soon as he set foot in the school but instead, nothing. Just routine. Just his regular classroom, desks, lab tables, sinks, burners.

He flipped through the plan book. The kids were only a week behind. The sub had done a great job. He pushed away from the stool and made his way to a cabinet.

"What do you need?" Kyle asked again.

He knew why Kyle had wanted to come along; it was the same reason Sean was secretly glad Kyle had insisted. But now that Sean was here, and everything was the same and he obviously wasn't going to start acting like someone with a bad case of post-traumatic stress, he wished Kyle had stayed home. Sean could have spent hours looking through stuff, like he did at the end of summer, just to get ready for the day-to-day instruction. He wanted that normalcy back.

He unlocked his supply cabinet. Shit. The stuff for the next lab was on the top shelf.

A stepladder stood between the cabinet and the wall, but he knew damned well Kyle wouldn't let him use it. Normally, he would just stretch up to reach stuff, but between his leg and the hydrochloric acid, he decided he wasn't going to risk it. As he scanned the shelf, Kyle came to stand next to him.

"I need to move some stuff down to a lower shelf."

Kyle dragged over a chair and climbed up. He patted the top of Sean's head. "How's it feel now, Mr. I'm Four Inches

Taller."

"Shut up. You know you love having to look up to me."

Kyle peered down. "Wait, is that a bald spot?"

Sean dropped the cane as both of his hands came up to check the back of his head.

Kyle started laughing.

"Asshole."

"I don't think that's appropriate language for the classroom, Mr. Farnham."

"I'll make those decisions, Mr. DiRusso." He wished he had a ruler to slap in his hand. How serious had Kyle been about that fantasy? Sean leaned down to pick up his cane. When he straightened up, Kyle's denim-clad ass was right in his face. Wow. Those jeans really fit.

"Did you just want to put me on a pedestal, or am I actually looking for something?"

Sean told him what bottles to move, and wished there was something he could think of that he needed way at the back of the shelf just so he could watch Kyle's ass tip up as he leaned in.

Sean was no longer particularly interested in spending time digging through the room. Now that the chemicals were within reach, he could just come in early on Wednesday to set things up. They didn't really need to be here much longer. They could be home, making up for lost time.

"Anything else?" Kyle peered down again.

"Nope."

Kyle dusted his hands off on his jeans. "Were you staring at my ass?"

"Yup."

"Good."

Sean held onto the chair back as Kyle stepped down, toward him, into him, until Sean had to drop the cane again and wrap his hand around Kyle's waist before they both lost their balance. His head didn't hurt; his leg didn't hurt. For the first time since the shooting, he actually felt like himself, like it had all happened to someone else. Even better, *they* felt right.

At that moment he didn't feel like Kyle was cataloguing all the ways the shooting had changed their lives, that Sean needed to try to figure out exactly what the fuck Kyle expected him to do. There was just them. Fitting together the way they always had, electricity tingling—sparking—between them, Kyle's smile warming Sean from the inside out.

In three days, he'd start back to work. What Kyle had been saying made sense. Sean wanted to fall back into that routine, into their regular lives. He wouldn't say he hadn't enjoyed his fifteen minutes of fame—and trying to change the world for the better—but he was done with it.

When Kyle picked up Sean's briefcase, Sean didn't protest, just relocked the cabinet and the classroom door and turned back down the hall to the main lobby. It was always going to be *that* hallway. Carpet and paint couldn't change it; nothing could. But he could learn how to walk down it and think about something else. About who he was going to start at second base this season, about whether he could get through everything in time for the state exams in June, about what he was going to make Kyle for dinner and exactly how many different ways they could fuck until they passed out.

"We have any other stops to make?" Kyle asked as they went back outside.

"Not that I can think of." The grey sky had grown darker. "It's going to snow, though. Might be the last chance to pick up anything if it gets bad."

"I've got you and Turner Classic, *papi chulo*. I'm all set."

Sean climbed into the driver's seat and stowed his cane behind him. Not being able to drive had been the worst part of those weeks. That more than anything had left him feeling completely dependent on Kyle. He'd been angry about it, he realized now, and taking that frustration out on Kyle was the reason Kyle had been so unlike himself. Things were going to be better now.

"I'm going up to shower off whatever weird chemicals I got

on me," Kyle said when they got in the house. He stopped on the stairs and turned, hips tilted and eyebrow arched. "Want to join me?"

Sean definitely did. Exactly how long had Kyle had those jeans and why hadn't Sean noticed them before? But there was something he had to do first.

"I've got something to take care of. I'll be up in a few."

Kyle shrugged and went upstairs. Sean headed for the phone in the kitchen.

Kyle stood in the shower long after rinsing. Using up the hot water was petty, but Sean had said he'd be right up. Sean had been quiet once they got in the school—completely unlike himself. He usually said whatever was on his mind, and from watching him, Kyle knew there were a hundred things he hadn't said. Sean hadn't gotten a migraine, and there'd been nothing like the dramatic flashbacks people with post-traumatic stress got in movies. He was just quiet. Grief? That was reasonable. Expected. Trying to puzzle it out kept Kyle so distracted he jumped when Sean pulled the curtain back.

"Hey." Sean grinned.

"I'll be right out."

"Stay." Sean climbed in. Kyle shifted around so Sean could get under the spray. When Kyle designed the house they'd always talked about, he was putting in one of those huge showers with the multi-level sprays and an industrial-sized water heater. They should have done that instead of the kitchen addition.

Sean's hair turned dark, almost black as it got wet, and Kyle watched the water pour over his shoulders, across his pecs, his nipples.

"I called Brandt," Sean said.

Kyle stopped himself from leaning in to taste the water on Sean's skin, and handed off the soap. "Oh?"

"Yeah. I told him I wasn't going to do the thing for the Human Rights Campaign."

Kyle's ears were ringing, his heartbeat as thick and loud as if he were running for his life. Sean wrapped a hand around the back of Kyle's neck, and Kyle tipped back his head to look at Sean's face, at his eyes, their color brighter with his hair gone dark from the water. Those grey-blue eyes, wide open like the winter sky.

"I told him I was done," Sean said. "Brandt's gonna have to find another gay hero."

Kyle didn't know who moved, just that they were kissing, kissing like they'd gone without for months. They started slow, almost too soft. Not that there wasn't heat. God, there was heat. A rush of warmth pumping from his stomach, flooding his thighs, his balls, his cock.

Holding Sean's face between his hands, Kyle licked deeper into his mouth, kissed him until they were grabbing each other for support, kissed them back to everything being perfect. Sean's hand was in Kyle's hair, combing through it, tingling his scalp as the water ran down them both.

Sean had listened. Had realized what was happening to them. Kyle had been dragging around this huge weight all by himself, and Sean lifted it away. Kyle couldn't get close enough, couldn't tell him with that kiss how fucking happy he'd just made him. He broke away from Sean's mouth and lapped a trail down over his shoulder, stopping to suck on his nipple until his fingers tugged hard on Kyle's hair.

"Yeah," Kyle murmured against Sean's chest before licking down lower. Kyle dropped to his knees.

Sean's cock was already hard, lifting up toward his belly. Kyle guided it into his mouth and felt it thicken even more. God, he loved this. The taste, the weight on his tongue, the pressure against his throat as he sucked Sean down. Sean moved his hand from the back of Kyle's neck to his cheek, rubbing the hollow made by the suction, pressing Kyle's cheek in against Sean's cock.

Water ran up Kyle's nose and he had to pull off to catch his breath. He stared up at Sean, at the want and love and happiness on Sean's face. The same emotions made Kyle's throat so tight he had to bury his face in the groove of Sean's thigh. Mouthing his way along the skin to his hipbone, Kyle fisted Sean's cock and stroked him slowly until the tight band around his chest eased enough that he could breathe.

When Kyle moved his mouth back over Sean's cock, Sean bucked up, pushing between Kyle's lips. He held Sean's hips and shoved him back against the tiles. A loud groan broke from Sean's lips, and he stopped trying to fuck into Kyle's throat.

He rewarded Sean with a deep kiss on the head, sucking pressure and flicking tongue, working a hand in a steady stroke from root to lips. Kyle flattened his tongue over the slit, tasted come and groaned, knowing damned well what that vibration always did to Sean. Kyle sometimes tried to hum the whole way through, but he always got too distracted by how much he loved sucking Sean off, hearing the sounds from his throat get louder and then quieter the closer he got to coming. Kyle loved the way Sean's hands got desperate in Kyle's hair, the way Sean cradled the back of Kyle's neck, the tremble in Sean's thighs, the thick weight of cock in his mouth. Kyle opened his jaw and took Sean deeper, moving a hand to gently play with Sean's balls, to press and rub the silky spot behind them.

"Fuck." Sean's hips made an aborted jerk and his hands landed heavily on Kyle's head.

The cock in Kyle's mouth swelled, and Sean's balls drew up closer to his body. Kyle backed off.

Sean's voice deepened to a growl. "Fuck you."

"Later," Kyle whispered and rubbed his smiling lips across the head of Sean's cock, sliding on spit and precome.

Sean urged Kyle forward with a tight grip in his hair. "If you don't get me off soon, the hot water will run out and you won't have anything fun to suck on."

"That would be tragic." Kyle slid back down over Sean's cock, as deep as he could go, groaning and swallowing around the head.

Sean's hips were almost vibrating with the strain Kyle knew came from holding back that need to fuck all the way back into his throat. He sped up to a quick bob, Sean's strangled gasps driving Kyle's hand down to grip his own cock.

"Don't come yet," Sean panted.

Kyle rubbed his hand on his thigh and reached back for Sean's ass, pulling him closer with the rhythm of his mouth, tilting his head and neck to get every inch he could manage.

"Christ. Kyle—" With the whispered whine of his name, Sean shot so deep in Kyle's throat he couldn't even taste it.

The extra slick of come and the jerk of Sean's hips let Kyle finally manage to get all the way down without gagging. He groaned again, and Sean yanked on Kyle's hair so hard his eyes stung. His tongue worked the vein throbbing on the underside of Sean's cock as he bucked through his orgasm, licking and sucking until Sean pulled Kyle off with a sharp gasp.

Kyle sat back on his hips and licked his swollen lips, still feeling Sean's cock pulsing deep in his throat.

Sean tipped Kyle's head up and stared down into his eyes. "That's a hell of a thank you."

Smiling, Kyle swatted Sean's ass. Even that little curve of his lips hurt, and his throat was too raw for speech. But damn, that had been worth it. From the trembling he could still feel in the hips under his hands and the finger tipping up his chin, Sean would agree.

The water shifted from just warm to freezing.

"Shit." Sean jumped and turned to spin off the taps.

Kyle climbed out. Sean followed a little more slowly, leaning one hand against the wall above the towel rack for a minute.

Sean tossed a towel onto Kyle's head and rubbed it through his hair. Kyle jerked the towel away, but before he could finish drying himself off, Sean had him pressed back against the wall.

Sean brought one hand up to rub gently over Kyle's lips and then down over his chin and throat. "All these years and you still have surprises for me." Sean kissed him lightly.

Pride flushed under Kyle's skin. He'd thought Sean had been too lost in coming to notice that Kyle had finally worked his way down that last inch.

Sean linked his fingers behind Kyle's neck. "If you want to

climb in bed, I'll show you how I say you're welcome."

Chapter Thirteen

Sean knew Kyle had been upset about the publicity. He'd made that pretty damned clear. But Sean hadn't realized how much it would mean to Kyle if Sean dropped it. And he wasn't just talking about a spine-melting blowjob. Though that one had definitely ranked in his top...one.

But Kyle's face, the way he'd looked at Sean—when was the last time he'd seen Kyle look at him like that? Like Sean was his whole world. Christ, he'd missed that look. And it used to be so easy to put it there.

Sean went into the bedroom. Kyle had ripped off the covers and was sprawled on the chocolate brown sheet, his hand drifting almost lazily over his flushed, hard cock.

"Plan on helping me out sometime, or did you just want to watch?"

"Not today. Roll over."

Kyle turned face down as soon as the words left Sean's mouth. He limped to the bed and eased down until he covered Kyle with the length of his body. Kyle stretched his arms out over his head and Sean pressed his own on top, interlacing their fingers. He kissed the damp skin of Kyle's neck, and then licked the top of his spine.

It had only taken about three minutes from their first kiss to know that a mouth on one particular spot under Kyle's ear could get him squirming in nothing flat. That wasn't much of a surprise—Sean had a weakness for neck kisses himself—but it wasn't until they got back together that Sean had figured out that Kyle's back was one big erogenous zone. Only contact with his ass or cock got him hotter.

Using the point of his tongue against the knobs of Kyle's spine had him bucking his hips into the mattress.

"Wanna do that until you beg, and then rim you until you come. Then I wanna fuck you stupid."

Kyle tipped his ass up against Sean's cock.

"I'll take that as a yes." Sean urged Kyle up further on the bed, pushed him until they were diagonal, and Sean could keep most of his leg on the bed. Smiling down at the wide-shouldered stretch of warm bronze skin, Sean began to map the muscles with his mouth and hand.

He remembered his anatomy class, naming the muscles in his head as he got Kyle panting. Thumbs stroked along the lower edge of firm delts while Sean's tongue traced the long lines of Kyle's trapezius. Kyle claimed years of torture from his brothers and sister had left him immune to tickling, so the brush of fingers at the edge of his ribs brought a groan instead of a flinch. Kyle's lats were so beautifully defined Sean could feel the ridges under his tongue. Kyle wasn't ticklish but he was sensitive to the lightest touch, rolling up into the stroke of Sean's tongue, fingers tightening on the mattress.

As soon as he reached the dip above Kyle's ass, Sean started at the top again. He hadn't done more than leave tiny bites across the top of Kyle's shoulders when Kyle grabbed at the mattress, popping off the bottom sheet.

Sean bit back a laugh before licking down Kyle's spine, using his thumbs to trace the point where the trapezius connected with Kyle's skull. Kyle moaned and pushed his ass up again. Sean brought his hands down to Kyle's thighs while he tongued the sweet dimples at the top of Kyle's ass.

Even though Kyle's voice was muffled by the pillow he had his face in, Sean could hear every word. "If you stop again, I won't blow you until Christmas."

"Hmm." Sean stroked his hands across the curve of Kyle's ass, and murmured right into Kyle's skin. "It's December third now. What's another three weeks?"

"Next Christmas, then."

"You'd never last. You love sucking me off."

"Keep right on believing that."

Sean flicked the tip of his tongue at the top of the crease and then made a nice inverted triangle from dimple to crease to dimple.

"I swear to God, Sean..." Kyle tried to wiggle his ass up into Sean's mouth.

Sean dug his fingers deep into Kyle's ass cheeks, pulling him wide open.

"C'mon." Kyle ground the word out through clenched teeth.

"Knew you'd beg."

Sean licked long and slow, sweeping along the crack. When Kyle bucked again, Sean used his weight to keep Kyle flat against the mattress. It had been too long since they'd had this kind of slow teasing sex. Every time since the shooting had been over too fast, both of them so starved they hit the edge of desperation with the first touch.

Sean lapped wet circles around Kyle's hole before lowering his mouth to kiss and suck. Kyle's groans, his taste, the fight in the muscles of his legs, all of it was pumping life back to Sean's cock. He moaned and pulled Kyle closer. As Sean dipped the tip of his tongue in and wriggled, Kyle made a sound that Sean was going to tease him about for weeks—a strangled squeak.

He wanted to hear it again and drove his tongue in deeper. Kyle twisted around underneath him. Sean lifted his head to watch Kyle try to work an arm between his body and the mattress.

"No." Sean's voice was so hoarse it even startled him. "Keep both hands up there or I'll tie them."

It was an empty threat. Their one-piece headboard had nothing to tie Kyle's hands to, but Kyle slapped his hands flat on the mattress. He tried again to grind his hips against the sheet, but Sean kept Kyle pinned flat, interspersing quick thrusts of his tongue with a rub and stretch of his thumbs.

"You. Fucking. Bastard." Kyle's voice held almost as much

frustration as arousal.

Sean smiled against the wet skin. Kyle wouldn't be able to get any friction on his cock until Sean allowed it. He could keep Kyle on the edge forever. Until his whole body shook. Until he was hoarse from begging and cursing. Until Kyle needed Sean more than he needed another breath.

Moving up to suck a bite near the top of Kyle's ass, Sean fucked Kyle with two spit-slick fingers, turning his wrist so that his knuckles rubbed all the right nerves.

"Fuck me. Please."

"No."

"Control freak."

"You love it." Sean twisted his wrist again, pressing the balls of his fingers on that swollen gland.

"Goddammit. Let me come."

"Say please." Sean dipped his head to put a matching bite on Kyle's other cheek.

"Asshole. Please let me come."

"No." Sean pulled his fingers out and went back to slow tongue circles and pressure from his lips.

Kyle rocked as much as he could, a constant stream of *fuck*'s rolling past his lips. Sean lifted his weight just enough to let Kyle rut against the mattress, enough to let him work up closer to that edge while Sean groaned a vibration deep against Kyle's wet skin.

Pulling Kyle onto his side, Sean dove for the drawer that held the lube. "Don't finish without me, 'cause I'm gonna fuck you anyway."

Kyle's hand stopped moving on his dick. "Then. Hurry. Up." A whine softened Kyle's demand.

Sean slicked his cock, stroking until the skin was almost too tight before curling up behind Kyle. Brushing up against Kyle's hole, Sean waited, feeling the pulse and twitch of the muscle.

"Sean, please."

Kyle needed him, wanted him. It wasn't just the teasing game they'd been playing. Kyle's voice was rough with desperation.

Sean could just drive straight in. If he caught Kyle at the moment when he wasn't relaxed and ready, he'd flinch and groan and soften anyway after a minute, and he'd love every second of the stretch and burn. There were times when they both wanted it that way. So fast they couldn't catch their breaths, so rough and frantic they tore at each other until there were bruises. But that wasn't how he wanted it now. He wanted Kyle opening around him so that they eased together on a sigh, rocked slow and deep until they couldn't stand it anymore and pounded their way to the end. That plaintive note in Kyle's voice made Sean want to protect Kyle from everything, even the sweet sting of a hard fuck.

The way Sean should have protected Kyle from the fallout of the shooting. But "I'm sorry" wasn't a conversation Sean was having right now, he'd apologize using his body. The ring of muscle against the head of his dick pulsed and opened around him. He slid forward just an inch and waited again.

Kyle panted as he reached back to grip Sean's thigh, trying to drag him forward. Sean felt Kyle soften again and sank all the way home, heat and the smooth thrum of muscles milking every inch of Sean's cock. Kyle released a breath that went on forever and pushed back until Sean's balls were tight against Kyle's ass.

Even when they went slow like this, Kyle was tight, always the perfect heat and pressure on Sean's dick. Sean moved a hand to play across Kyle's chest as he started rocking them, Kyle keeping pace, meeting every thrust.

As Sean's thumb brushed a nipple, Kyle twisted his neck and Sean met the kiss halfway, their mouths sloppy and full of *good-so-good-love-you* groans. When Kyle pulled away and caught his breath, Sean watched him. Watched Kyle's thick, dark lashes hide the warmth in his eyes as Sean arched his body against the curve of Kyle's. His mouth opened as his head tilted up for a harder kiss, his muscles tightening around

Sean's cock, pulling him deep with every stroke.

When Sean lifted his head this time, he saw a slow spiral of fat fluffy snowflakes piling an insulating layer against their window. He slowed even more, matching the drift of the snow. Kyle's back rippled as he clamped down on Sean, no words, just the urging of his body.

Sean lifted Kyle's leg up and behind his own, so that he could reach between Kyle's legs, slide two fingers under his balls and down to where Sean's cock stretched him wide. He rubbed around himself, pressed on Kyle's hypersensitive skin, and Kyle made a sound like he'd swallowed a scream. Kyle's heel pressed hard against his good thigh as he tried for the leverage to fuck himself harder.

"Yeah, babe." Sean dragged Kyle's hand away from its grip on his thigh and put it on Kyle's cock.

Sean flexed his hips faster, deeper, his fingers going back to press along the satiny skin from Kyle's balls down Sean's cock, feeling his own thrusts against his fingers as he drove into Kyle's body. Sucking a quick bite on Kyle's shoulder, he watched as Kyle's hand moved from long strokes on the shaft to quick jerks on the head. Sean let his body rush up to that edge with him, his brain fuzzing white like the snow on the window as he heard the first of Kyle's I'm-coming choked-off groans. The pulse of Kyle's muscles around Sean's cock finished him as he drove Kyle onto his belly, pumped twice more and shot deep inside him.

It took a couple of fits and starts, but eventually Sean's brain seemed to work out how to move his muscles, and he responded to Kyle's huffed breath by shifting some weight off him, easing from Kyle's body at the same time.

"I think you fucked with the plan," Kyle said into the pillow.

"I said I'd fuck you stupid. How do you get the area of a triangle?"

"*Pi r* squared."

"Wrong. Do I have to get my ruler, Mr. DiRusso?"

Kyle pressed up on his forearms and turned to look at him.

"You're not letting go of that anytime soon, are you?"

"Should I?"

"I'll let you know." Kyle collapsed back against the pillow. "Until then, what's for dinner?"

Sean smacked that up-tilted ass.

Kyle laughed and rolled onto his side, facing Sean. His gaze was steady now, no laughter in his eyes. "Are you sure?"

Sean didn't have to ask about what. "Yeah, I am. I want our life back."

Kyle kept staring at him, as if he wasn't sure he could believe him. "What about changing people's minds, like that lady on Oprah?"

"I did my bit. I'm not saying I didn't like it or it wasn't important." Sean reached up and brushed a curl out of Kyle's eyes. "But it's not worth what it was doing to us."

Kyle blinked hard. And then he smiled and Sean knew he'd never made a better decision in his life. He watched Kyle's throat work for a few seconds, then Kyle said, "Thanks."

Sean leaned in for a long, slow kiss. His thumb found a trace of moisture at the corner of Kyle's eye. Swallowing back the lump in his own throat, Sean joked, "Okay, but if you want another example of 'you're welcome' you're going to have to wait."

ß

Sean was even more nervous his first day back than he'd been his first day teaching. He'd over-prepared, worked out a response to every possible question about the shooting or his personal life, but class after class the most off-topic question was "When do we have to have our physicals for baseball season?"

Maybe it was because he had every second of the class period planned out, but he suspected the kids were just as eager to not have to think about the shooting. A snowball settled into his stomach when he looked down at his seating chart and saw the whited-out space that had once held Kelsey Nash's name. Her seat had remained empty, a mute reminder that things still wouldn't ever be exactly the same.

Besides, the kids had had seven weeks to decide what they thought about having a gay chemistry teacher. In their lives, two months might as well have been two years.

Exhaustion had him leaning hard on his cane by the end of the day, but that was his only complaint. No migraines, no flashbacks, no whispers from students or teachers. It could have been a lot worse, he decided as he levered himself up into the Durango with a push from his cane. His next PT appointment wasn't until tomorrow. He ordered pizza so that the delivery would coincide with Kyle coming home and could barely stay awake long enough to eat a slice.

The next day was the same, same lab for the alternate periods. He fielded his first personal question from tall, shaggy-headed soccer forward Ian Reynolds who stopped by his desk on the way out to ask if his leg still hurt.

"Sometimes," Sean answered, but the kid was already nodding and hurrying out the door.

Samantha Thomas lingered at the end of sixth period lab. "Mr. Farnham?"

Since she already had his undivided attention, Sean sensed she was stalling for time. The fact that she was flicking the ends of the hair hanging over her shoulder told him he was in for something a little more personal than did his leg still hurt.

"Yes, Sam?"

She blushed and he thought she might give up and run out, but he should have known from her tenacity over why the heavy metals had to be off on the bottom of the standard periodic table of elements that she wouldn't quit until she had an answer.

"How long have you and your partner been together?"

Sean was ready with "I'd rather talk about a problem with chemistry" or "I'm not going to discuss my personal life" but she hadn't interrupted class, and he knew that straight teachers talked about their families all the time.

What the hell. "Six years."

"Wow. That's cool. I—I just wanted to say—well, I think it's cute."

And with that, she gave into her blushes and ran out, almost bumping into the first group of seventh period students on their way in.

Cute he could live with.

The twelve hours of sleep the night before gave Sean enough energy to throw together a salad to go with the leftover pizza, even after an hour of PT with Theresa, Attila's less nice sister.

He told Kyle about Samantha over dinner and they both agreed that *cute* was a hell of an improvement over *fucking faggot.*

"We'll see how things go during baseball season. Male coaches don't have a time-honored stereotyped tradition like lesbian softball coaches and gym teachers."

"The kids love you, Sean."

"It's not the kids who worry me."

Maybe that worry was what woke him with a start at one thirty. Sean didn't know what he'd dreamed, he just knew he didn't want to go back into that nightmare. He got up to piss, to force himself fully awake. Kyle greeted him with a grunt when Sean got back into bed, pulling him into a warm bundle of arms and body and blankets.

Half an hour later he was sweating and alone with a pounding heart. Kyle had transferred his affection to a pillow. It didn't matter. No more sleep. He didn't even want to know what kind of fucked-up dreams had jarred him awake. He wasn't going to give his brain another chance to parade them through his head.

Now that he was up, the sweat made him cold, and he pulled on a T-shirt and a pair of sweats before heading downstairs. He checked his email, watched about five seconds of three infomercials and went into the kitchen. Not bothering with the lights, he opened the fridge and studied the contents.

"My dad always used to say he was going to tape a picture to the door."

Kyle's voice floating out of the dark was the least adrenalin-producing moment of the night. Sean didn't even jump. He kept staring at the pickles and mayonnaise and tomatoes wondering which would be better, a sandwich or a beer, and would he dream if he slept on the recliner.

"Hey." Kyle slipped up behind him, running warm hands underneath his shirt. "You're freezing."

Sean leaned back against him.

"Were you hungry?"

Sean shook his head. Kyle stroked his hands over Sean's abs, just hard enough not to tickle. When Kyle moved up and over his nipples, Sean turned his head back for a kiss.

"Can't sleep?"

"Go back to bed, babe."

"Aw. I was counting on a game of cards."

Sean laughed. "I played so much solitaire these last weeks the sight of a deck makes me twitch."

"Want to fuck?"

Sean shut the fridge and turned in Kyle's arms. "Oddly enough, I don't think so."

"Sounds serious. How about a medicinal blowjob?"

"Maybe later."

Kyle's brow arched. "Do you want to stay home tonight?"

"And miss harassing Tony at work? No, I want to go."

"Want to tell me what's wrong?"

Sean didn't know what was wrong so there wasn't anything to tell. He just knew he wasn't going back to sleep. "Can I renegotiate that blowjob?"

"Absolutely."

Sean must have dozed a bit on the recliner after Kyle blew

the fuck out of him. Kyle defied any guy to have the energy to fight off sleep after that level of effort.

But an hour later, Sean was flipping through all five hundred channels for the fifth time in two minutes. Kyle shifted on the couch and said, "This reminds me of when you came home from the hospital."

"You kept staring at me when I trying to sleep. It was annoying."

"Huh." Kyle bit his lip, embarrassed, but what had happened after their trip to the school on Sunday had made it okay to talk about the shooting. For them to say what they were thinking. Kyle hadn't realized how much they'd both avoided talking about it directly. Sean even seemed able to say the shooter's name now, had taken an interest in the sentencing scheduled for next week. "I needed to be sure you were still alive."

"Kyle. God, I'm sorry." Sean stopped surfing and reached out to run a hand through Kyle's hair.

Sean hadn't said what had driven him downstairs, but Kyle could tell Sean had been having nightmares. God knew Kyle'd had enough of them during those first few weeks, and he wasn't the one who'd been shot.

"Do you think it's Chris Bowman's sentencing?"

"I don't know."

Kyle heard the dismissal in that answer. And he could understand it. Talking about a nightmare sometimes made it worse. He hoped this wasn't going to start a whole cycle of tiptoeing around mentions of the shooting.

"Is that western still on Turner Classic?"

Sean tapped the remote. "Yep. Weather Channel or ESPN?"

"AMC?"

"You're pretty desperate, aren't you?" But Sean entered the number for American Movie Classics.

When some wretched cop movie from the eighties popped up, Kyle sighed. "ESPN. At least the anchors are usually hot."

Kyle fought another yawn as the cute guy on the left made

some kind of remark to the stud next to him that might have been funny if Kyle understood what the BCS had to do with college football's apocalypse. The last thing he remembered was the sound of Sean's laugh.

The creak of the recliner woke Kyle up. Cutie and stud still obsessed over the BCS. Or maybe it was the same story. Kyle squinted at the cable box. It was either three fifty-five or five thirty-three. He couldn't seem to get his brain to make the numbers make sense, but he was reasonably sure it was still the dark part of Friday morning which meant that no one had to be awake right now.

Sean stood. "I'm going to make breakfast."

"What are you making?" Kyle asked around a yawn that made his eyes water. The red numbers on the cable clock wavered again. "You've got time to lay the eggs yourself."

"You'll find out in another few hours. Go back to sleep."

He shouldn't. He should get up and keep Sean company, but his body wouldn't cooperate.

Sean called Kyle out to the kitchen around six, handing him a cup of coffee as soon as he shuffled in. Kyle sank onto one of the stools and stared at the baked French toast with almonds, something Sean said was shirred eggs, but looked like a crustless quiche, and so much bacon Kyle was surprised PETA wasn't picketing their house.

He snatched up a piece of bacon. "Admit it. You switched to the Food Channel after I fell asleep."

Sean shrugged and yawned.

"Are you sure you still want to go out tonight? Maybe Jack can meet us if we switch it to tomorrow."

"He works the whole weekend. I'll be fine."

"I'll be home by five, or do you want to meet at the bar?" Kyle decided he liked shirred eggs. He was afraid to ask how much cream and butter were in them.

This time Sean held the yawn behind clenched teeth. "I'll wait for you here."

If Kyle thought there was any chance Sean would call in

sick his first week back, Kyle would have suggested it. Instead he said, "Maybe you should pack an energy drink for lunch."

ß

Kyle knew Sean had missed driving, so he kept his mouth shut about what a pain parking the Durango could be downtown. Even when they had to walk an extra block.

Sean rubbed a hand along Kyle's neck as he walked with his hands tucked in his pockets. "I'm way too tired to drink. You're going to have to keep Tony happy."

"Thanks in advance for my hangover."

"I'll make it up to you."

They headed down the side street. To celebrate Sean's first week back at work, Tony had offered to treat at the bar where he worked. Of course, Tony always treated when they met him at the bar, but they hadn't been out since the shooting. The small storefront with an all-black interior couldn't have been more different than Jack's wood-paneled burgundy trimmed restaurant. But then, neither could Jack and Tony.

Kyle braced himself for a wave of smoke, but it wasn't six yet, and the bar wasn't too crowded.

A bellow greeted them as they cleared the door. "There's the hero!"

Tony was his usual subtle self. From a distance, someone—someone who'd never met him—might mistake Tony's blond crew cut and clear blue eyes for Midwestern farmboy innocence. But closer inspection revealed a tattoo on his neck and as soon as he opened his mouth, he left innocence standing on a corner by the bus stop on the seedy side of Cleveland.

Tony leaned over to kiss Sean as they came up to the bar. "Need help *getting it up* there, son?"

"I think I can manage getting up on my own." Sean lifted himself onto the barstool.

"Where's my kiss?" Kyle asked Tony.

"I thought maybe you'd need a few shots of Jim Beam again first."

Did everyone remember that night better than Kyle did?

"Yuengling," Sean said.

Tony pulled a draft for Sean and set a shot in front of Kyle.

Kyle looked from the shot to Sean with a narrowed gaze.

"What'd he do now?" Tony asked.

"I'm completely innocent," Sean asserted. "But if you two go at it again, I'm putting it on YouTube." He waved his phone. "With a mushy soundtrack."

"Your boy was just trying to prove that I was too drunk to get it up." Tony's evil grin lit his eyes. "He was wrong, wasn't he?" He looked expectantly at Kyle.

"I don't remember anything significant."

"Bitch." Tony grinned again and gave Kyle a sloppy kiss before he moved down the bar to fill a couple of orders.

"Are you two at it again?"

Kyle turned in surprise to find Jack behind them.

"Hey. I thought you had to work." Sean slipped off his stool to give Jack a hug.

"I couldn't miss the big night out."

Jack pulled Kyle off his stool and into a bear hug. "How are you doing, Kyle?"

"Great." Actually he was. He couldn't remember the last time he'd felt so relaxed and he hadn't even knocked back the shot yet. Despite Sean's nightmares, Kyle knew things were getting better. For the first time since Brandt showed up, Kyle felt like he and Sean were on the same side.

Jack winked. "Just a warning, though, if you and Tony start making out again, Sean and I are going to leave you to it, and I've got to warn you, he bites."

"You love it." Tony had come back in time to hear Jack's last words and leaned over to kiss his lover.

"Kyle loves it too. Maybe we should leave you guys alone."

Kyle glared at Sean and got a beery kiss.

"Hmm. What other kinks does your boy have?"

Kyle tugged Sean in close and murmured in his ear, "No blowjobs until next Christmas, I swear."

Sean pulled away. "I'll never tell." He smirked at Tony.

"So, Sean, tell us about Oprah. Was it first class all the way?"

Kyle tossed back the shot and chased it with a swallow of Sean's beer. The warmth of the whiskey blended with the warmth of their friends' company. Tony winked and set another shot in front of him. Kyle knocked it back without even thinking. More than buzzed, more than happy—safe was the word for it. He hadn't felt safe like this since he'd heard the report of the shooting on the radio.

Drawing a small crowd, Sean made them laugh with his imitations of Oprah's many handlers. Kyle felt a flush of warm pride as Sean recounted the story about the woman who felt bad for mocking her nephew. Now that it was over, he could definitely see why Sean had wanted to do something. If seeing Sean kept people like Kyle's uncle from spitting out insults every time he saw a man he considered less than totally straight, it was worth it—for a while. Now that they had their lives back, Kyle could admit that it hadn't been completely bad.

He was pretty sure that was only the fourth shot, but he still seemed to be the last one to stop laughing.

Everyone stared at the TV. He wasn't so buzzed he couldn't read the ticker across the bottom, "Shooting at gay student club in California high school." In seconds the live coverage started. Someone had recorded the whole thing on a cell phone camera.

Most of the visual was blurs, but the sounds were clear enough. Shots. Screams. Breaking glass. He wanted to cover his ears. He wanted to cover Sean's ears. He thought of reaching for him, but Sean was so far away and Kyle's arms wouldn't work.

And then over the chaos: "Where's that faggot teacher now? Why doesn't he save you?"

Kyle pushed off the stool and wrapped himself around Sean's back as if he could shield him when everyone in the bar turned their stares from the television to them.

"Turn it the fuck off," he shouted at Tony.

"No." Sean's voice was hoarse. His body was hard under Kyle's, not trembling, just rigid, refusing any comfort Kyle could offer. He might as well have tried to embrace a boulder.

The newscaster recounted the whole story. At three fifteen, the twenty-year-old brother of one of the Gay-Straight Alliance student members had walked into Santa Rosa High School, asked for directions to the club meeting, pushed open the door and then opened fire with an automatic pistol. Students dove behind desks, and several managed to escape by breaking windows. Two students were dead, eight wounded. The shooter turned the gun on himself after making a full round of the room. The newscaster flipped her hair and remarked, "Ironically, the brother of the shooter missed the meeting because he was getting extra help from a math teacher."

Tony put a shot down in front of both of them. "Jack will drive you guys home."

"No thanks." Sean pushed the drink away.

The reporter went on with background about Santa Rosa, California and the high school. Being slightly drunk hadn't made hearing the news any easier, but Kyle swallowed his shot and the one Tony had put down for Sean. Kyle blinked hard at the television, and the image of Santa Rosa High School felt like it had been etched on his eyelids with acid.

It was nothing like the open plan of Sean's school. Santa Rosa's building looked like something out of a gothic thriller. It wasn't exactly Manderley from Hitchcock's *Rebecca*, but it wouldn't have been out of place on a Hollywood backlot with its ivy, arches and aged brick. He wondered when it had been designed, if it had always been used as a school. If he could keep concentrating on all those small details, he wouldn't have to think about why the whole country now knew exactly what another high school building looked like.

As Kyle put the empty shot glass down on the bar, Sean turned inside the arm Kyle still had wrapped around Sean's waist.

"That helping?" he asked.

"Nope." And Kyle knew he was supposed to be comforting Sean. That all of this was much worse for him, that he was the one living that all over again, but all Kyle wanted was for Sean to pull him tight against that solid chest, rest his head on Kyle's and promise that this would all be over in the morning.

"I've got to get out of here," Sean muttered.

"Okay."

When Kyle stepped back, he wasn't sure which of them was going to be more unsteady on the walk back to the car.

Def Leppard blared from Sean's hip. Kyle knew who it was. Sean glanced at the display as he flipped it open and his first word confirmed it.

"Brandt? Yeah, I saw it."

Sean turned away from Kyle as he spoke on the phone. Kyle watched the TV, which was now running something on the Mideast. School shootings were getting too commonplace for exclusive airtime Kyle noted, disgust rolling up his throat in thick waves. He wanted another shot, not that it would help, but after a few more, he might not care. He'd recognized Sean's question about the last shot for the warning it had been and shook his head when Tony lifted the bottle and arched his brows. He had a feeling that even six more shots wouldn't be enough to keep him from caring about the conversation that was taking place just close enough for eavesdropping.

Would it be better or worse if Sean moved away far enough so that Kyle couldn't hear him? Better or worse to hear the actual decision in Sean's voice or to have him turn to Kyle after it was over and tell him that it was all starting again.

Either way, Sean turned to face Kyle as he answered Brandt. "Yes, of course, I'm going to do it now."

The cold air sobered Kyle on the walk back to the car. After the first block, a thin snow hit them in the face, snow with just enough sleet in it to sting. Trying to keep the nasty stuff out of his face kept Kyle from filling up the silence between them with bitter reminders that Sean had promised this was over. But

Sean hadn't actually promised, just said that he was done with it. If he'd made a promise, maybe Kyle could have convinced him to keep it. But he hadn't. Kyle's head throbbed.

Sean slowly climbed up into the car. Kyle took the cane when Sean held it out.

"Brandt's on his way down, he called from the car."

Kyle bit hard on his tongue to keep from pointing out that Brandt had been pretty damned sure of Sean's answer.

"He's going to meet us at the house."

How nice. Given the intact state of his brain-mouth filter, Kyle would have to ask Tony how much the bar watered their whiskey. But then Sean had to ask him a question.

"Is that going to be a problem?"

Just say it's fine, Kyle. He glanced at Sean's profile, bright from the reflection of their headlights on the snow-wet street. Sean was what mattered; the nightmares he'd had last night would probably be much worse tonight. He returned Kyle's glance, and he realized he'd taken too long to answer.

Sean pulled into a Dunkin' Donuts parking lot and put the Durango in park. He stared out through the windshield at the snow for a few minutes.

Kyle still didn't know what to say. It was too late for a *no, that's fine.* He was just afraid that if he opened his mouth, all kinds of terrible things were going to come out. Sean let out a long breath and turned to face him.

The tension in Kyle's gut burned off the last of the alcohol. His head felt surprisingly clear as he tightened his grip on Sean's cane. Before the shooting, Kyle could count on one hand the number of times they'd even raised their voices at each other. Now, it took barely a second to get ready for a fight. And then Sean's face took on a look of patient understanding and all that adrenalin had nowhere to go except to make Kyle madder. It was probably the same look Sean gave students who were still getting the wrong answer no matter how many times he explained the equation.

"I know I said I wasn't going to do any more publicity. So

you're probably pissed off at that."

Fuck him for being so reasonable. It was impossible to argue when Sean was completely right.

Sean went on. "But after today, I just keep thinking that if I'd done more, if I'd been able to reach more people, it might not have happened. That's why I'm going to try working with Brandt again."

Kyle looked out at the snow-streaked night. How many miles was it back to their house? Three? It was probably close to thirty outside. He could walk. Screw his brain-mouth filter. He couldn't keep his mouth shut anymore. He turned his body to face Sean.

"Aren't you just the voice of reason?"

"Someone has to be, if you're going to act like an asshole."

"Right again." Knowing he was being an asshole didn't make it any easier to control his temper.

"Could you maybe tell me exactly what the fuck it is you don't want me to do? Help people? Try to stop violence? Erase a little homophobia?"

"You can't save the whole goddamned world, Sean." He stabbed the floorboard with the cane.

"I never said I was trying to."

The hurt in Sean's eyes softened Kyle's voice. "You couldn't have saved those kids in California."

"Now who's being too fucking reasonable?"

Kyle flinched but didn't look away, and Sean went on.

"How do you know? Maybe people would have been more alert if they'd been thinking about the danger. Maybe someone would have sent the guy to administration instead of right to the meeting."

"He would have found another way, someone else to give him directions." Crazy people always seemed to find a way in this world. All you could do sometimes was keep your head down.

"Not if he was caught. I can't believe you actually are telling me there's nothing that can be done about hate crimes."

"You know that's not what I mean." Since when did Sean make everything about politics?

"Well I sure as fuck would love to know what you mean, Kyle, because you're not telling me shit. Am I just supposed to guess what would make you happy? What I need to do to keep you from making us miserable all the time?"

Sean's attack startled Kyle into dropping the cane. He couldn't ever remember Sean being such a bastard. "I'm making us miserable?" Kyle hated the way his voice broke, but every one of his internal organs kept trying to find space in his throat.

"Fine. It's all my fault." Sean tipped his head back.

"I didn't say that."

"So whose fault is it?" Sean paused and then drew in a sharp breath. "Brandt's?"

Kyle bit his lip.

Sean made a quick snort of bitter laughter. "That's what this is all about? You're jealous of Brandt?"

"Should I be?" Because the way Brandt looked at Sean, the way Sean seemed to smile more when he was around didn't feel ridiculous to Kyle.

"Maybe I should be. You're the one who looks at him like he's a chocolate cannoli."

And that just made Kyle hate the guy even more. This at least was something concrete to fight about. And it had a solution. Not that Kyle was going to win. Not when Sean was looking at him like that with his eyes soft and intent.

"There's nothing to be jealous about." Sean reached out and cupped the side of Kyle's face. "I promised you, we both promised when we stopped using condoms and you know I'd never take a chance with your life."

Kyle lowered his gaze. "I know." But there was a lot of room in the way they'd outlined their expectations of fidelity all those years ago. Kissing and a hand job hadn't felt like cheating when they first moved in together, but it sure as hell did now.

And if the hand on his boyfriend's cock was Brandt's, it would feel a whole fucking lot like cheating. Because of the way

Sean was different around Brandt, the way Sean seemed to share things with Brandt that he didn't with Kyle anymore, the way his voice was so full of smiles and flirting when he talked to Brandt on the phone.

"So you don't think he's hot?" Kyle studied Sean's face.

"Do you want me to lie?"

Kyle couldn't resist answering Sean's smile.

"You know he is. But you're still the only guy I want to fuck." Sean leaned over until their foreheads touched. "I love you, babe."

"I love you more than chocolate cannolis."

Sean kissed him quickly and straightened in his seat. "I will refrain from commenting on which of us is more fun to suck cream from and ask if I can buy you a cup of coffee, you lush."

"I had four shots."

"Six. In about twenty minutes." Sean backed out of the parking space and headed for the drive-thru.

The vans from three network affiliates were waiting for them—well, waiting for Sean—when they pulled up to the house. Kyle knew he shouldn't have let Sean tease him about cream filling and tempt him into a good mood with a chocolate éclair. The pastry sat like a bar of iron in his stomach.

The lights on the vans turned in their direction. They couldn't even get into their driveway. All this must be a big hit with their neighbors.

At least the reporters waited for Sean to get out of the car. He limped toward the crews, and Kyle followed behind. Sean stopped in the driveway.

"Whoever's blocking the driveway gets to go last." But he flashed his smile and the offending van backed down the street.

Kyle watched from outside the circle of lights. No one was interested in his opinion on the Santa Rosa shootings, and it seemed only local stations were barely interested in Sean's opinion. They'd only sent their younger field reporters, no one

Kyle recognized. Of course, it was too late to make the early news.

Sean was good at this. No denying that. Cameras flattered him, and maybe being a teacher was what made him look completely at ease answering their questions. Even those questions designed to provoke him, like the one that made Kyle think that he might punch out the pert little reporter who asked it: "Do you feel your public appearances after the shooting might have inspired the Santa Rosa shooter to act?"

"I can't say what inspires hate and violence in people. I'd rather concentrate on helping the victims and their families. On making sure that violence doesn't keep happening in our schools."

Yeah, Sean's answer was much better than the punch Kyle was contemplating. In fact, Sean was so well-spoken and polite he bored the reporters into leaving. Sean let Kyle move the car into the driveway and finally they were safe in their house, hanging up their coats in the hall.

Sometime between coffee, an éclair, kissing chocolate icing from Sean's lips and the ordeal with the TV reporters, Kyle had managed to forget Brandt was coming. But there he was, at the door, before they'd even sat down.

"I saw the vans leaving your street. I assume they were here for you?" Brandt came into the living room. "Hi, Kyle."

"They were here for me all right." Sean didn't sit in his recliner but next to Kyle on the couch, which made Kyle happy enough to mentally promise him a bedtime blowjob until Sean patted Kyle's leg, making him feel he was a delusional child. Imagination didn't account for the warmth of Sean's smile at Brandt.

Brandt perched on the edge of the recliner, leaning forward on his knees. "I was hoping to get here before they did. Sorry about that. So what did they ask?"

"I can't believe the things they said." Since Kyle couldn't seem to get rid of Brandt, the bastard should know Kyle wasn't going anywhere. "One of them actually suggested Sean was responsible for the shooting today."

"I thought they might."

"Sean was perfect, though." Kyle patted Sean's thigh. Maybe he'd like feeling patronized.

"He's a natural." Brandt held Kyle's gaze with his dark green eyes. "Have you watched him on Oprah?"

Kyle hadn't. He wanted to check his watch to see exactly how long it had taken Brandt to make him feel like an ass.

"Not yet."

"Oh you should. He's so smooth, you'd think he'd been doing this his whole life. But you know, Sean, that question is going to keep coming up. Are you ready for this?"

"For what?" Kyle asked.

Brandt answered as if Sean had spoken. "If you want to keep going, I think we should go on the offensive. Not wait for them to come to us. We'll get you out there even more. Let everyone see what a gay hero looks like. Remind them that while cowards hide behind words and guns, you faced death to save lives."

As much as Kyle hated that Brandt was back in their lives, he still admired that speech. The guy was missing out on a career not working for politicians. Fuck, he'd be a perfect candidate.

"Like what?" Sean asked.

"More than HRC or spots for GLAAD. We'll do Ellen, the rest of the talk shows, public appearances, work on talking points so you can stay on message. First we need to decide what we can get the most mileage out of."

Mileage? Someone was targeting gay kids in Sean's name and this asshole was talking about getting mileage out of it? Kyle knew what mileage meant. Money. How could Sean not toss this guy out of the house? What if Kyle did it? Just stood up and told Brandt to get the fuck out. That if Sean wanted to go on trying to change this violent world, he'd be doing it without the help of someone with dollar signs in his eyes.

Maybe for once Kyle could just show some fucking guts.

Before he could make up his mind, Sean rubbed the back

of Kyle's neck and said firmly, "The only thing I'm interested in is in making sure other kids don't go through that."

"You know as well as I do that you have to play their game if you're going to have a chance of winning. And if that means manipulating the message—"

"Telling people what they want to hear, even if it means lying?" Kyle asked.

"If it gets them to listen," Brandt said, smile still in place. "Look. I'm sure if we boil it all down, we all three want the same thing."

Kyle seriously doubted Brandt shared Kyle's desire that Brandt be infected with a venereal disease that made his dick fall off, but he didn't say anything.

"We all want a world where everyone can be safe and happy. Where kids don't have to worry that their sexual orientation is going to get them shot or beaten up if they dare to tell anyone about it."

Why did everyone have to be so reasonable tonight? Why couldn't Brandt just talk about how much money he wanted to make instead of making it about something no one could argue with?

Sean nodded. "I'm afraid you're going to have to work around my schedule, though. I can't miss much more time. I still want to teach."

"We'll work something out."

There weren't any other arguments left.

Chapter Fourteen

With a last good night, Brandt closed the guest room door, and Sean made his way down the hall to their bedroom. He wasn't exactly sure what kind of reception he was going to get. He couldn't blame Kyle for being mad about changing his mind. At least Kyle had stuck around for the discussion, actually made himself a part of it for a change. So maybe Kyle wouldn't try to make Sean feel guilty by looking up at him with those soft dark eyes.

The lights were out, and Kyle was a lump huddled on his side of the bed.

Sean controlled a sigh and stripped off his clothes. Tonight, he'd wished he could bury himself in heat and pleasure. Forget about everything but how good it felt to be inside Kyle.

Sean pulled the covers back and climbed in. As he settled back against the pillow, Kyle rolled over to face him.

"Hey." Kyle's voice was soft.

"Hey."

"How's your leg?"

"No worse than it usually is at the end of the day."

"Good." Kyle's teeth flashed in the dark, and he kissed Sean, mouth hard and wet.

Just as Sean opened his lips to respond, Kyle started licking down his neck, right along his breastbone. Sean's cock took serious interest in the direction Kyle's mouth was taking. He barely had time to think that things weren't going the way he'd expected before Kyle gulped Sean's cock to the back of his throat and two fingers started a slow rub over his prostate that had him arching up off the mattress.

"Shit."

Kyle growled—Jesus, Sean didn't think he'd ever heard Kyle make a sound like that—but he growled around Sean's dick. Between the vibration and the pressure of Kyle's throat, Sean saw sparks behind his tightly closed lids. He sank back into the mattress, but Kyle didn't let up and Sean arched again, pleasure pumping through his body with every pulse of that soft throat, every stroke of those fingers.

When Kyle pulled off, Sean seriously wondered if he was going to cry, but then Kyle was mouthing his balls, softly at first and then harder than he could stand. The fingers inside him eased him through the intensity, let him last a little longer until he had to shove at Kyle's head.

"Can't. Oh fuck, Kyle, too much."

Kyle lifted his head, and nuzzled at Sean's thigh, stubble rasping his balls, the skin of his groin. He laid a long lick on the underside of Sean's cock, flicking his tongue under the head in time with a quick fuck of his fingers. Then Kyle stopped everything—the bastard—and rested his chin on Sean's stomach, cheek rubbing against Sean's cock.

Sean's eyes had adjusted to the dark enough to read the expression on Kyle's face. Smug and happy, grin wide and one brow arched. Sean released his holy-fuck-so-good grip on the sheets and ran his fingers through Kyle's hair. Kyle's grin grew wider and he moved to mouth Sean's hip, sucking a painful bite on top of the bone.

"Hey," Sean protested.

"What?"

"Watch the teeth."

Kyle's tongue poked out between his teeth and he wiggled it. Sean reached down, intending to haul Kyle up and flip him, but Kyle grabbed his hips and used his weight to pin Sean's legs to the mattress.

Sean's cock twitched against his belly. Kyle was almost never this aggressive. Whatever had gotten into him, Sean liked it. And then he knew. Kyle was trying to drive Sean out of his mind so that Brandt would know about it. Kyle was marking his territory.

Sean smiled. Sex beat the hell out of getting peed on.

He actually wished he usually got loud. Kyle'd love it if he could make Sean moan enough to be heard in the guest room, but Sean knew if he tried to force it, it would be laughable. But there were other sounds that traveled.

"Fuck me." He used his regular voice, deep and loud in the silence of their room.

"Maybe in a bit." Kyle's mouth took him in again, fingers curling inside Sean's body so that his knuckles were pressing up in a way that made Sean's whole body shake.

He didn't have to fake that groan. "Fuck me, babe, please."

Kyle pulled off, and Sean rolled onto his stomach before lifting himself up on his knees.

"Is your leg going to be all right like that?"

"It's fine."

Kyle laid over him, testing the weight, and Sean said, "It's still fine." Sean turned his head to find Kyle's lips. "Want it hard, babe."

Kyle's groan definitely must have made it to the guest room.

Sean smiled. "Didja come?"

"Almost." Kyle laughed.

His body was still throbbing, and it seemed to take Kyle forever to lube his dick.

"C'mon."

Kyle pushed Sean's legs wider to make up for the difference in their heights, and then stopped again.

"It's all right. Please, babe."

Kyle took his time pressing in until Sean arched and rocked back, slamming them together.

In two strokes they had the headboard thumping against the wall, a rhythm as fast and hard as Sean's heartbeat. Kyle shifted, found the perfect thrust and Sean let him know, as loud as he could without feeling like an idiot. "There. Fucking there."

Kyle drove deeper, and Sean tightened his muscles around him. The rough sound Kyle made had Sean smiling into the pillow, and then Kyle fucked him right up to the edge, until he was going to shoot just from Kyle's cock inside him.

The electricity built in his balls, pulsed from his ass to his cock. Every time Kyle stroked across his prostate, the pulse got hotter. He had to come now, his dick so hard it ached. Kyle was gasping as he hugged Sean's back, mouth wet and hot on Sean's shoulder.

"Ready?" Kyle growled the word into Sean's skin, more sensation rippling down his back.

"Yeah. Now." He dragged the words out of his gut.

He felt Kyle's smile against his shoulder and then Kyle dragged Sean's hand to his cock, so they jacked him together. His balls drew up even tighter, waiting. One last hard thrust and a thumb on his slit and it tore out of him, long bursts draining him, until he was nothing but twitching muscles. Kyle groaned and pumped warmth inside him. Just as Kyle's weight started to press down, he rolled off and landed on his back.

Sean was still trying to remember how to breathe without gasping when Kyle slipped out of bed and came back with a towel.

"Want to change the sheets?"

"Can you do it if I don't move?" Sean said into the pillow. "We need a bed for fucking and a bed for sleeping."

"We have one. But someone's in it." Kyle pushed Sean onto his side and cleaned him up.

"Oh right." Like Kyle would let him forget that. Forget that this had been about showing off for Brandt.

"C'mon. Roll this way. We'll sleep close." Kyle pulled him against his chest, resting his chin on Sean's head.

It wasn't light yet when Sean woke up with his cock throbbing. He couldn't remember any sex dreams, though he suspected it had a lot to do with Kyle pressing his own dick into Sean's stomach, rubbing and rocking them. So maybe this wasn't all about Brandt. Maybe Kyle understood that Sean needed this, needed it so he didn't hear those words echoing in his head: *Where's your faggot teacher now?* So he didn't have to wonder if there were two new graves because of him.

Sean rolled Kyle onto his back. That earlier aggression must have melted away, because Kyle's legs dropped open around Sean's hips. Kyle's mouth was soft on Sean's neck, whispering, "Fuck me. Just lube, I'm ready."

Sean wanted to go slow. Wanted it to take hours, take them till dawn so that he wouldn't have to worry about falling asleep again. But Kyle's body was so warm and tight, as soon as Sean pressed in he couldn't wait. He grabbed Kyle's hip for leverage and thrust in, deep and hard. Kyle hiked his legs up higher, his hands digging into the sheet for something to hold onto. Sean kept slamming them forward, not caring what sounds the headboard might make.

He fell asleep still inside him, their bodies stuck together with come and sweat. But he woke with his heart pounding when it was just light. He swallowed back the terror and tried to peel them apart without waking Kyle.

Kyle made something that sounded like an unhappy puppy whimper when Sean finally managed to untangle himself and roll off the bed. His thigh ached and it took him a few seconds to stand. Kyle made that sound again, and patted the sheets, looking for Sean.

Sean's heart tightened at the sight. He wanted nothing more than to give into him, to crawl back into that warmth and fall back asleep, but waking up in stark panic wasn't worth it. "Go back to sleep, babe." Ignoring the pain in his thigh, he leaned in and ran his hands through Kyle's messy curls. "I'll make breakfast."

Kyle made a happier sound and turned his face into the

pillow.

It was already seven, so he wasn't surprised to find Brandt in the kitchen reading the paper and sipping coffee.

"Sleep well?" Sean poured himself a cup of coffee.

"Great." Brandt's smile crinkled the corners of his eyes. "There was this odd pounding that woke me up, though."

Sean smiled back. "Can't imagine what."

"I can." Brandt licked his lips. "Can he walk?"

Sean busied himself with the waffle mix. He was pretty sure they had frozen strawberries. If he didn't flirt back, it didn't count right? He should say something. Because if Kyle came down and they were flirting when he did… Sean winced as he stretched to grab the waffle iron from the top shelf.

"Here. Let me get it." Brandt was right next to him. The guy was taller than Sean remembered. Brandt pulled down the waffle iron and set it on the counter. "Is your leg all right?"

"It's a little stiff."

"Stiff, huh?"

Brandt had stepped away after getting the waffle iron, but Sean could still feel him there, the awareness, the interest.

"Brandt, look. I think maybe—"

"I got it." Brandt held his hands up in surrender. "I'll behave. Sorry."

Sean's relief was mingled with disappointment and resentment. Nothing had been going on, but after two nights of almost no sleep he didn't have the energy to deal with Kyle freaking out.

Kyle came downstairs just as Sean was sliding the first waffle onto a plate. Sean looked up and bit his lip, not knowing whether to laugh or roll his eyes. It was about thirteen degrees outside, and Kyle was dressed in a skin-tight wifebeater that showed off not only the gorgeous definition in his shoulders and back, but the giant hickey Sean had sucked onto his collarbone this morning.

Kyle came over and kissed Sean's neck, reaching around to grab Sean's mug and take a gulp from it.

"Aren't you cold?" Sean started another waffle.

"Nope."

If he thought about it, Kyle staking a claim this obviously was more flattering than irritating. But as Sean fought off another yawn, he hoped that was as far as things were going to go. He was too exhausted to spend the day reassuring Kyle.

Kyle handed off the waffle to Brandt while he got himself some orange juice. Sean let out a little of the breath he was holding. Brandt grabbed the remote from the breakfast bar and clicked on the television. Flicking through quickly, he settled on Headline News. The Santa Rosa shooting came up again at ten after the hour.

Kyle set his orange juice down with considerable force. "Don't you think he's heard that enough?"

Where's your faggot teacher now? The shooter's words came over the crack of gunfire.

Brandt waited until that part of the tape stopped. "And he's going to hear it again. And again. If you're going to do this, Sean, they're going to play this tape over and over. You're going to hear it in your sleep."

Like Sean didn't already.

A shot of McKinley High came up, followed by Sean's face and the anchor making the connection for the rest of the country.

Sean's head started to throb, but he thought about two dead kids at a Gay-Straight Alliance meeting and he said, "I can do this."

Kyle met his gaze over the top of Brandt's head. Those soft sad eyes were a perfect match for the unhappy puppy whimper Kyle had made when Sean climbed out of bed this morning. But this wasn't about Kyle. Or them. Sean turned away and lifted the waffle out of the iron.

ẞ

Brandt made sure Sean didn't miss any classes—even if it meant leaving after school to fly to New York or Chicago, finally making it back to Canton around one thirty in the morning. His leg ached almost constantly, but PT didn't often fit in his schedule. Kyle didn't complain, even when Brandt stayed the night, even when most of their interaction consisted of Sean telling him where he'd be for the next couple of days. Most nights Sean was too exhausted to dream. Nights when he woke in a sweating panic, Kyle tried to wrap himself around Sean for comfort, but it only made him feel like he was smothered, suffocated like in his dream. Sex helped sometimes, and Kyle offered, but he usually ended up trying to stay awake.

One night after terror yanked him out of sleep for the third time, he got up to change his sweat-soaked shirt and shorts.

Kyle didn't make a sound, but Sean knew the minute he woke up, could feel those dark eyes watching him.

"I think I'll just stay up. I need to finish my progress reports."

"Sean." The hesitation in Kyle's voice told Sean he wasn't going to like what Kyle had to say. "Maybe you should talk to someone."

"A therapist? Why? It's not like I don't talk about it, and I don't need to pay someone to listen to me. Besides, it's not like I remember the dreams. What exactly would I talk about?"

Kyle took a breath, like he was going to continue pressing, but the breath cut off. So they were back to that. To Kyle treating Sean like he was fragile, being the so-fucking-considerate boyfriend, tiptoeing around.

Sean pulled up a pair of sweats and tugged a long-sleeved shirt over his head. The sweat drying on his skin left him covered in goose pimples.

"Come back to bed."

Sleep and warmth and Kyle's breath in his ear—but sooner or later Sean would be wide awake with a racing heart. His gut twisted and his balls hiked up. Shaking his head, he said, "I really should have finished the reports yesterday. I'll make you breakfast."

ß

The week of Chris Bowman's sentencing must have been a slow news week, because Larry King called.

As they waited for their flight at La Guardia, Brandt said, "Jane Seymour hurt her back skiing in Aspen."

"Oh?" It wasn't as if Sean was particularly interested in grading the pile of labs in his lap, but Brandt didn't usually drop random bits of celebrity gossip into the conversation.

"So, I'm looking at the replacement for Grand Marshal at Walt Disney World's Christmas Parade."

"When?" Sean met Brandt's gaze. The numbers had been getting a little blurry anyway.

"Christmas."

The word hit his stomach like the load of fish the DiRussos served on Christmas Eve. "But when Christmas?"

"Christmas Day. Why? And you're doing Ellen on the twenty-eighth. I know you have a break from school."

Christmas was a command performance at Kyle's parents. No one missed it. Ever. Not even for Mickey Mouse.

"Sean, this is a big deal. They've really gone out on a limb for you. It's exactly the kind of family-friendly venue we need."

"I know." And Kyle would love it. Love the chance at a couple days of Florida sun instead of day after day of lake-effect snow and sleet. If it weren't on Christmas. "Can I borrow your laptop for a minute?"

ß

Sean made time for both Kyle and PT on Saturday. Considering what he had to tell Kyle, he wasn't sure which would end up being more painful.

When Sean came back from the kitchen with two beers,

Kyle was still sprawled on the couch where Sean had pinned him, jeans open, dick still wet from Sean's mouth.

"Here." He handed Kyle one of the bottles and pulled an envelope out of his briefcase before sitting on the coffee table to face him.

"What?" Kyle sat up.

"Why?"

"You're playing with the bottle cap."

Sean dropped the cap on the table and picked up the envelope. He handed it to Kyle.

Kyle eyed the envelope as if it had teeth, but as soon as he'd opened it and started scanning the computer printout, his dimples flashed.

"Oh, *chulo*, I never thought we could get a flight this late. I was so worried about your leg and driving seven hours to Philly. Now, I won't even have to miss work."

"Um."

"What?"

"Read it again."

Kyle's smile was gone. "One ticket. And you'll be...?"

"In Disney World. Grand Marshal for the Christmas parade."

Kyle laughed, dry and tight. "You and Brandt? Disney World for Christmas? Sounds great. Wish I could be there."

Sean tried to rub the ache away from behind his right eyebrow. "I knew you wouldn't come, even if I'd asked."

"That's not the point." Kyle's voice was even, but he lurched to his feet, knee knocking against the coffee table, sending Sean's beer wobbling over the edge where it foamed over the carpet. "Fuck." Kyle grabbed at the bottle to right it and headed across the hall to the kitchen.

Kyle was yanking the paper towel roll from the holder as Sean came into the kitchen.

"Just leave it, Kyle." Sean's voice was soft, coaxing. He reached for the roll in Kyle's hands, but Kyle brushed past him and back to the living room.

This was it. He wasn't chasing him any farther. "Jesus, Kyle, what the hell?"

Kyle was already on his knees, soaking up the spilled beer, towel after towel. He didn't turn.

Ignoring the protest in his overused thigh muscles, Sean knelt next to him. "If I had asked, would you have come with me?"

Kyle balled up the paper towels and threw them against the table leg. "You know I wouldn't have."

"Then what's the big deal?"

"You know what?" Kyle sank back on his heels. "You don't get to be all fucking reasonable and make me look like an asshole this time. You know goddamned well why this bothers me and you still act like it's nothing."

"Maybe it is nothing and you are acting like an asshole."

"Is that the kind of PR talk you're learning from Brandt? It's going to go over great in Disney World."

"Kyle, it's one year. And you know how important this is. What's more Christmasy than trying to make the world a better place?"

"God, are you running for Miss America? If I wanted to listen to your PR bullshit I'd watch you on TV."

"Like you would."

"Sean, this isn't some interview where you get to make flip answers. You know how important this is to me."

"So why do I feel like I'm being interrogated?"

Kyle pushed off the floor and stood. "Asking you to act like you give a shit about me is an interrogation?"

"Walking away? There's a shocker." Sean levered himself up on the sticky coffee table.

"Why? Did you want to call me something else besides an overreacting asshole?"

"I want you to tell me what you want me to do to fix this." Sean was almost shouting.

"You won't. And I can't." Kyle's voice was almost a whisper, a tiny hiccup in it as he paused to swallow. "So maybe we should just..."

"Should what?"

"Nothing."

The beer soaking into his socks left Sean's feet cold and wet. He wanted to grab Kyle and make him stay here and finish this. Because maybe if Kyle would say what he was really thinking they could fix it. And if words couldn't, he knew that their bodies could.

He put his hand on Kyle's shoulder but Kyle shrugged it off.

"Kyle."

"Forget it."

"Forget what?"

"Whatever you want." Kyle went into his office and turned on the computer.

ß

The ringing of his phone startled Kyle from his study of the blueprints. It was after one and he couldn't remember the last time he'd looked away from the monitor. A text at quarter after one was probably an advertisement for a new service plan, but he fished it out of his briefcase and flipped it open.

Come to bed.

His chest tightened. As long as he'd been busy with the plans for the Circle Corporation's latest expansion, he hadn't had to think about that fight. About what he'd almost said—about what he'd wanted to say. His neck ached from all those hours on the computer, and he rolled it around on his shoulders as he made his way upstairs.

Kyle didn't realize how cold he was until he'd pulled off his jeans and sweater and started shivering. After hours in wet socks, his feet were so cold they hurt. All that glass that made the solarium warm and inviting in the daytime left it cold and black at night.

Sean pulled the covers back for him, and Kyle crawled in. Sean was warm, so fucking warm, and his arms went around Kyle as their legs tangled together. Sean kissed his forehead as Kyle pressed in against his chest.

Kyle's throat ached. He couldn't lose this. Didn't want to think about crawling into an empty bed without Sean's warmth to greet him. He turned to press his lips against Sean's skin. Sean pulled him tight, but no matter how close Kyle got, the ache in his throat spread to his shoulders and neck. Finally, Sean's fingers found their way into Kyle's hair and the tension went out of him in a shudder. But he just lay there, counting Sean's breaths for hours.

Chapter Fifteen

As Kyle came through the security checkpoint at the Philadelphia airport, he saw his youngest brother Nate, arm draped around a beautiful girl whose head barely came up to Nate's armpit. It must be something serious if Nate was going to expose the girl to the family at Christmas. Kyle forced a smile to his lips and stepped forward to meet them.

Nate slapped him on the back in a hard hug and then turned to the girl next to him. "Kyle, this is Elise."

Kyle controlled a smirk when Nate's eyes glazed over as he said her name. Baby brother had fallen hard.

Elise offered him a hug and a peck on the cheek. She seemed so delicate Kyle wondered how quickly his mom would scare her off. Though if Sophie liked her, Elise would be safe enough. Come to think of it, all the women in his family were tiny, but that didn't make them any less formidable.

"So where's Sean?" Nate asked as they made their way out to the car.

Why hadn't his mother told everyone? Was he going to have to explain it a million times? "In Disney World. Some publicity thing." Kyle glanced over at Elise. She had a sappy look that echoed the one on his brother's face. They were both doomed. "From the shooting."

"Oh yeah? Why didn't you go with him?"

"And miss Christmas? Mami, Nonna and Abuela would have had coronaries. And then Dad would have killed me."

Nate shrugged. "They'd get over it."

Easy for you to say. Their baby could get away with it. But not the fag in the middle. Kyle shook his head. His mother considered it an insult that he missed birthdays. Missing Christmas was high treason. Family was holy, and Mami was its patron saint.

"Mami's so busy fighting with Nonna over the calamari, I don't think she'd even notice," Nate added as they got to the car.

"Do you think they pick a dish to fight over every year?"

"The Feast of Seven Fishes provides a lot of opportunity."

Nonna came out of the kitchen as they came in the front door, wrapping Kyle in a hug before he even took off his coat. She seemed to be shrinking away to nothing; he had to almost kneel to meet her.

"There's my boy."

He'd always suspected he was his nonna's favorite. His sister Sophie had spared him having to tell her he was gay, since Kyle didn't know how he'd ever have gotten the words out. Not long after that, Nonna had cornered him and instead of the lecture about the Church and God he'd expected, she surprised him with, "They say it's not right that you love other boys, but I can't see what's so wrong with it. You love who you love, *ragazzo*."

Now as she squeezed him, Kyle marveled at the strength in those birdlike bones.

"So where's your tall young man?"

Kyle might be Nonna's favorite, but she never could remember Sean's name.

"He couldn't make it this year. He had to go away on business."

"Why didn't you go with him?"

Kyle shut his eyes and prayed for patience. "Because then I wouldn't have seen you, Nonna."

"Ah, you. Always the smooth talker." She gave him another kiss and held his cheeks for a moment. "You look too sad, *ragazzo*. You should have went with your young man. Come and seen Nonna a different time, huh?"

"I'm fine, Nonna."

"Bah." She pushed at his face. "And now I will see what other nonsense your mami is up to in the kitchen."

His family already filled the house. Kyle steered around toddlers and running children to greet both of his great aunts, who asked about Sean and the shooting. His father's brothers gave him thin smiles. They didn't show the open hostility of his mother's brother, but he wondered if his uncles all thought that he was contagious, as if too much friendliness with a gay man would infect them. He almost turned to mutter something to Sean before he realized he wasn't there.

He'd been through this alone before. He'd only had the comfort of Sean at his back for five years; he could remember how to get through this by himself. Though if one more person asked why he didn't go to Florida with Sean he was going to go insane.

Twenty-six adults made a sit-down dinner impossible, so Kyle and his brothers took up their places on the staircase. Ben at the top, his wife off making sure that their kids didn't finish off one of the pastry trays when no one was looking. Kyle left a space for Sean before he remembered he wasn't there. After that, it would have been awkward to move, since Nate had already taken his own spot, Elise squeezed in next to him. Kyle picked at the tangle of squid tentacles and capellini on his plate, wondering where Sean was eating Christmas Eve dinner. Things between them had gone back to normal that morning after the fight. Or as normal as things were between them lately.

He chewed on a tentacle clump and listened to Nate explain family relationships to Elise.

"Which one is the demon spawn?" Elise whispered.

"That's my sister's kid, Ricky."

At that moment the three-year-old came flying through the living room in screaming, sobbing hysteria. Sophie came out of the kitchen, and Ricky slammed into her thighs, clutching on for dear life.

"What's wrong, honey?" she asked.

"Somebody probably showed him a crucifix," Nate suggested.

Sophie cuffed the back of Nate's head with a blow that echoed up the stairs.

"Ow." Ben and Kyle echoed Nate's outraged cry of pain.

Elise was smart enough to take Sophie's side, and the two women took Ricky into the back hall to calm him down or re-up his sugar level. Elise might make it, Kyle decided.

"So," Nate said, rubbing his head. "Can I have the PlayStation if you guys get divorced?"

Nate's laugh died away as soon as he'd said it, and Kyle could feel his older brother's eyes boring into his back. Divorce. According to Nonna, DiRussos never divorced. They threw dishes, dented walls, fought, screamed and swore, but they didn't divorce. Sean had been around since Nate was in high school.

"We're not married," Kyle said.

Nate turned around to face him. "Whatever. You know what I mean."

Kyle couldn't meet his baby brother's eyes. "He's just in Florida."

ẞ

The Ortizes came over on Christmas Day, filling the floor with kids playing with toys and games. Sean always crawled on the floor and played with them, usually manipulating Kyle into joining him by murmuring an obscene bet in his ear. Kyle wondered how many people had ever paid for a loss at Hungry Hungry Hippos with a week's worth of blowjobs. Kyle had gotten really good at cheating.

Just before dinner, his mother commandeered him into hauling down the serving platters while she warmed the *pasteles* her cousins had sent from Aguadilla. He jammed his thumb against the cabinet. After considering his mother's always astounding reach, he substituted a *crap* for the *fuck* that had been about to escape his lips.

"What now?"

"Nothing, Mami."

"Why did you come, Kyle?"

He almost dropped the platter. "Mami—"

"You know I don't mean you're not welcome here, but Sweet Mary if you were going to drag us all into misery with you, why didn't you just go with him, hmm?"

"But Christmas..."

"Will come again next year. You have to do what's right for you—and your..." She waved her hand. "Your father says what Sean is doing is good. So he should do it. And you..." She grabbed his chin. "I always told you holidays, you should be with your family, and that's what he is."

His mother hadn't spelled Sean's name right on anything in five years, and now he was family? Kyle wondered when that had happened. He started to speak, but his mother shook him like he was still five years old.

"Sometimes, if you're apart too much, especially on holidays..." There was a sudden flash of emotion in his mother's eyes. Dad had spent more than a few Christmases on a destroyer when Kyle was a kid. He tried to pull away. He didn't want to know this about his parents.

His mother held on, forcing him to meet her eyes. "Your sister says there's a man traveling with him?"

Sophie and her big fat mouth.

"So." His mother nodded like that settled things. "You have to do what's right for you. And your family. This will always be your home. I just don't like to see you so sad. You always take the hard way, *mi amor.* Always. I don't know why." She released his chin and patted his cheek. "Now, stop making the babies cry with that face and go eat."

Kyle took a deep breath, inhaling the familiar sweet and spicy smells coming from the oven. "Thanks, Mami." He hugged her.

"It doesn't always have to be so hard, you know. Go drink some *coquito*."

ß

Snow in Chicago mysteriously delayed Kyle's flight from Philadelphia to Cleveland for four hours. It was after ten when he walked down the terminal in Cleveland. He checked Sean's flight, on time, due in forty-five minutes. Maybe Mami was right. Things didn't have to be hard. He could wait for Sean, and they could drive back together while Brandt disappeared to wherever Brandt went when he wasn't fucking up their lives.

Kyle opened the spy novel Nate had given him and tried to make himself comfortable on one of those blue chairs. The press against his tailbone reminded him of the chair he'd lived in for that week Sean spent in the hospital.

Sean's flight got in early. Kyle's seat gave him a view of the whole terminal, so it was easy to identify the crowd off the plane from Orlando from their shorts, Disney T-shirts, stuffed animals and princess costumes. After the initial rush to baggage claim had passed, the crowd thinned and then stopped. Kyle was reaching down to check his phone to see if Sean had missed the flight when he heard his lover's laugh.

Sean and Brandt walked down the center of the terminal, Sean's gait smooth, the cane almost imperceptible. He laughed again as Brandt gestured with his hands to punctuate whatever story he was telling. Sean's eyes were fixed on Brandt as they walked right past Kyle.

He almost let them go. But as he watched Brandt put his hand on Sean's shoulder to steer him toward the escalator, he decided that he wasn't going to make things easier for that bastard.

Kyle stood. "Sean."

Sean turned back, losing his balance, and Brandt steadied him with a firmer hand on his back.

"Kyle. I thought you were already home."

Was it guilt or surprise that put the strain in Sean's voice?

Sean crossed the few feet back and wrapped his arms around Kyle. Every inch of their bodies touched, and Kyle could feel Sean's heartbeat, quick and hard against him. Kyle breathed in Sean's skin, a scent more familiar, more home than *pasteles* on Christmas Day. Mami was right. This was family. He wanted to climb inside Sean's skin right there. Fuck security and luggage and Brandt. Kyle's fingers stroked the back of Sean's neck as he leaned away.

"So?"

Kyle blinked up at Sean. "Oh. My flight was late so I decided to wait for you. I figured we could drive home together and save Brandt the trip." Kyle smiled at Brandt over Sean's shoulder.

"Oh, babe, I'm sorry. We brought the Durango up. We're flying out again to L.A. tomorrow, anyway."

We. The word used to only apply to them, to Sean and Kyle, and now it got used a lot for Sean and Brandt. Kyle nodded. *So much for things not being hard, Mami.*

"So, how was the family?"

"Great. They all asked about you. I think they like you better." Kyle fell into step next to Sean as they made their way to baggage claim.

"That's because I know how to do the dishes."

"I know how to do the dishes."

"Yes, but you actually have to do them for it to count."

Sean kissed him as they separated in the garage, a soft slow rub of his lips across Kyle's. "Race you home."

"What do I get if I win?"

"Laid. Of course, you get that if you lose too."

Of course, Sean beat Kyle home. Sean would easily admit that he'd always been a little too competitive, but no one got laid. Kyle had taken a long look at him under the lights of the kitchen and dragged him off to bed. To sleep.

When Sean slid off his jeans and sat on the bed, he stared at his leg as if he could see the lines of fire running with his pulse. He ran his fingers around the scars. Kyle knelt in front of him and started to rub at his thigh, fingers kneading and easing the ache. Sean pushed his hand away.

"It hurts too much," he said, but even to him it sounded like the lie it was. He hated the idea of turning his lover into a physical therapist. Brandt had asked him why once, and Sean had joked saying that if Kyle was going to rub anything, Sean would rather Kyle aim a bit higher. But that wasn't it. It just felt wrong. Like asking Kyle to wipe his ass or something. He wasn't going to be someone Kyle had to take care of.

Sean shut his eyes when Kyle rolled to his feet, unwilling to see that look on his face, the patronizing one Sean had seen far too often lately. Kyle went into the bathroom and came back with ibuprofen and a cup of water. He slapped the pills into Sean's hand.

Sean thought about getting up and taking them right back into the bathroom, but his leg hurt too much for a grand gesture. Getting him a couple of pills wasn't the same as rubbing his leg. He gulped them down and swung his legs up on the bed.

Kyle went around to his own side and slid under the covers, moving toward Sean. He wanted to lie back against Kyle's chest, but he rolled onto his stomach, away from Kyle. He didn't even know why, just that everything Kyle had done—waiting for him at the airport, urging him to bed, getting him the pills—pissed Sean off. He had a mother, thank you. And he was getting sick of the way the two of them kept edging around things. That he had to worry about how Kyle was going to react to everything and wonder if the next day was going to be the one where Kyle stopped being so patient and just snapped. He wanted it over so he could stop dreading it. Though what *it* would actually mean he hadn't thought through yet.

Kyle ignored Sean's body language and plastered himself to Sean's back. "I love you." The words were a puff of breath in

Sean's ear.

Sean's throat strangled his answer.

ß

Sean had been exhausted, but he couldn't believe how late he slept the next morning. By the time he pried his eyes open, it was almost nine, and Kyle had probably already left for work. The leg still hurt, even after some of the stretches Sean had learned in PT. When he finally made it downstairs, he found Kyle talking to Brandt in the dining room, Brandt's laptop in front of Kyle, a pile of contracts on the table.

"Sean's been getting so much fan mail, I had to hire a service," Brandt said as Sean approached.

"And who pays for that?"

"I do," Sean said. "It's not like Brandt's keeping things from me."

Kyle turned. "I didn't say he was. I just wanted to know more about what's going on. Find out if you'd earned enough to take me to Australia yet." Kyle's light tone couldn't hide the tension in his body.

Sean backed off and tried a smile. "Not yet."

"Almost, though." Kyle glanced back at the spreadsheet on the laptop. "Who knew being shot would turn such a profit?"

Kyle's words echoed in Sean's ears. Brandt stared at the contracts, trying to make himself invisible. Sean limped into the kitchen. Maybe after he'd had some coffee, Kyle would seem like less of an asshole.

Kyle followed him.

"Aren't you going to be late for work?" Sean kept his back to him as he poured out a mug of coffee.

"I'm going in at ten. It's a slow week."

Sean added too much sugar to his coffee, but Kyle was standing between him and the fridge and he couldn't get to the half and half—at least not without facing Kyle.

"Sean, I wasn't hassling him."

Sean turned. "So what's got you so defensive?"

"I'm not. I was just interested in how things were going."

"That's a first."

Kyle yanked open the refrigerator, took out the fat-free half and half and put it in front of Sean. "Could we not do this? You're going to be gone when I get home—"

"So we'll reschedule for Thursday? Put it in your planner. One forty-five, fight with Sean. Round two."

"Sean—"

"Putting it off doesn't change anything, Kyle. We've got to have this conversation."

"What conversation?"

Sean held his gaze for a long time, until the silence spreading between them bounced off the walls and slammed back, severing the connection as Kyle looked away. Before he did, Sean caught the trace of fear in Kyle's eyes and he wanted to take it all back. Hold him and promise him that everything was fine.

And then Kyle proved again that Sean would never completely figure him out. Kyle stepped forward, twisted Sean's T-shirt in his fist and yanked him down for a hard kiss. Sean managed to slide his mug onto the counter before the coffee splashed over Kyle's suit, grabbed onto his shoulders and met the thrust of his tongue as it swept Sean's mouth. Heat rolled down Sean's spine, getting him hard faster than he thought possible.

Kyle lifted his head and spun Sean until he was facing the counter, hand sliding up under Sean's T-shirt, thumb flicking across his nipples before stroking down to his waist. Sean splayed his hands on the counter and leaned against Kyle. His hand drifted over Sean's stomach muscles, making them twitch and jerk and roll toward his spine in order to give those warm fingers room to slide underneath the elastic on Sean's sweats.

Following the line of Sean's groin down to cup his balls, Kyle's hand tucked them up tight against Sean's body. He rocked into the touch, letting his neck drop onto Kyle's shoulder. He jacked Sean slow and steady, not enough of that dry friction to burn, just a steady stroke of pleasure that had Sean rocking his hips. After shoving the sweats down over Sean's ass, Kyle unzipped his own pants, wool and knuckles rough against Sean's skin.

He wondered where Kyle thought this was going, since he was too short to fuck Sean against the counter like this. Then he didn't care where it was going because Kyle's hand tightened around the base of Sean's cock and squeezed its way up, milking precome and thumbing it out of his slit. Kyle smoothed a drop around and under the head with a twist that pulled Sean up onto his toes.

Kyle pressed into the slit again and took his hand away for a minute, leaving Sean hanging, listening to the thick wet sound of Kyle's hand on his own cock. Kicking Sean's legs together, Kyle wrapped an arm around Sean's waist. With his hand back on Sean's cock, Kyle jammed his dick between Sean's thighs, the head pressing up behind Sean's balls as Kyle thrust.

He settled into a rhythm that had him jerking Sean's cock down into his body at the same time Kyle's dick jabbed into the tight skin behind Sean's balls, a friction and pressure that was almost like getting fucked. Kyle pulled him backward, forcing Sean off balance, taking most of his weight, breath hot and sticky in Sean's ear.

And that was it. Just the sound of breathing and the slap of skin over the morning news coming from the TV. This wasn't about showing off for Brandt. Sean could hear Kyle holding his gasps and moans in behind his clenched teeth. Sean wanted something besides the almost atonal recitation of news, sports and weather, wanted to hear Kyle begging, demanding, wanted to spit out filthy promises of exactly what he was going to do when Kyle got home, but by then Sean would be in L.A., and he couldn't seem to say anything anyway.

The friction started to burn, balanced by that quick slam of pressure between his cock and balls, a splash of pleasure from inside pulsing down his cock. With another tight gasp, Kyle pinned Sean's legs closer together. Kyle's thumb pressed into the slit again, smoothing the slick drops down, before he jerked Sean backwards and fucked harder between his thighs. The hot breath on his neck turned into a scrape of teeth. Another slam forward and Sean's hands skidded across the counter, sending the mug flying to shatter on the floor.

Kyle grunted and drove harder, twisting his wrist, flicking the head of Sean's cock. A quick catch in Kyle's breath just before he shuddered, and he bathed Sean's balls in quick bursts of warmth. The sensation sent Sean over the edge, and he fell forward onto the counter as the last spasm robbed him of what was left of his balance.

Kyle kissed the back of his neck and then stepped away, leaving Sean panting and hanging onto the counter, like he was some trick Kyle had jerked off in a bathroom.

"I'm going to run upstairs and change. What time do you get in on Thursday?"

"The flight info's on the fridge."

"Okay."

Sean bent to pick up the pieces of his mug, listening to Kyle's feet pound up the stairs.

Chapter Sixteen

Despite Sean's insistence on having that conversation in December, when Kyle packed for a business trip to Cleveland the first week of February they still hadn't talked about anything besides schedules, meals, laundry and bills. This must be what it would be like to have a roommate who occasionally grabbed you and fucked you blind. Maybe they should have had that conversation in December, whatever the fallout.

The sex was still them, better than good, still that nuclear fusion every time Sean touched him. Whatever it was about their bodies wasn't affected by the fact that they were living like people forced to share a house for reality TV.

"Same hotel?" Sean asked from the bedroom doorway.

"Yeah. Meetings tomorrow and Friday. Conference Saturday."

Every other year Sean had come up to Cleveland with him so they could go out, but he had to give some speech to a group in New York on Saturday.

"Tony called again. They want us to come over on Sunday."

"It's the Super Bowl, isn't it?"

"Yeah. Five o'clock?"

"Fine with me." This was the longest conversation they'd had in a week. "Is Brandt going?"

"Do you want me to ask him?"

"If you want." Kyle shrugged and slung his bag over his

shoulder.

Sean caught his arm as he tried to edge through the doorway. "Kyle."

He met Sean's eyes and that hum hit Kyle's skin and fuck if he didn't still love him, didn't still pray that every morning when he woke up things would be different, that Sean would say, "I love you, babe. Let's sell the house and move to Delaware and I'll never use the words *hero*, *Brandt* or *PR* in your presence again."

Sean leaned down and kissed him, scraping stubble across Kyle's shaved cheek as he pulled him into a hug. "See you Sunday."

ß

Tequila and Coke made a better combination than Kyle thought. Tequila never gave him a hangover, but with two important meetings with the partners and new clients tomorrow, he was pacing himself. His pacing was off though, since the lights had a few extra rings around them when Kyle turned around to lean on the bar and watch the dancing.

"Kyle?"

Tall, model-pretty and smiling at him. Kyle wasn't sure if he was lucky or doomed. With a quick smile he answered his old friend and ex...whatever. "Daniel. Hey."

Daniel leaned in for a quick kiss, and shit, he smelled good. Way better than anyone in a sweaty, smoky club should. Kyle straightened from his lean on the bar.

"Did you move back to Cleveland? Where's...?"

"Sean. No. We still have the house in Canton."

Daniel had been their lawyer for the purchase of the house, had made sure that the inheritance and tenancy would hold up no matter what kind of restrictions the state might place on unmarried couples.

"He around?" Daniel asked.

Kyle sucked down some more tequila. "Around the country. He's giving a speech in New York on Saturday."

Daniel's brow furrowed. "I thought he was a gym teacher or something."

"Or something," Kyle agreed.

Daniel blinked and then his eyes widened. "Fuck me, he's that teacher."

Kyle nodded and finished his drink.

Daniel's lips pursed in a low whistle. He and Kyle had never been lovers, more like fuck buddies, but they'd had a lot of fun when Kyle lived in Cleveland. Daniel looked like Benjamin Bratt with darker skin, even without the enhancement of tequila and spinning disco lights. But the best thing about Daniel was his ability to cut through bullshit.

He hooked a finger through Kyle's belt loop. "Wanna dance?"

And unlike Sean, Daniel loved to dance. Kyle followed Daniel's pull through the crowd.

They didn't touch at first, just moved between the other sweating bodies. Kyle missed this living in Canton. The beat vibrating the floor under his feet, up through his bones until he felt it in his blood, became a part of all the other men moving together.

When Daniel put a hand on his back to guide him, Kyle let the beat move him closer, until their hips touched. Daniel smiled, a flash of white in the strobing colors and put his other hand on Kyle's shoulder.

Kyle knew he should feel something. Nerves, guilt, maybe even a little triumph, but his chest just felt empty, even as his dick responded to the press of Daniel's thigh between his legs. As Daniel pushed Kyle's hair off his forehead, he glanced up into that beautiful face, ran a hand over those gym-hard pecs. Kyle had been fighting anger for so long he'd become numb. But now, God, he just wanted to feel something. He put his hands on Daniel's shoulders and their hips ground against each other. Daniel was going to kiss him, and Kyle was going to let him.

When Kyle licked his lips, Daniel laughed and kept dancing. The music echoed the pulse of blood in Kyle's cock as one song blended into another. When Daniel's hand shifted to Kyle's ass, he tipped his head up. This time when Daniel smiled, Kyle felt warmth curl his gut.

He pulled Daniel's head down. Daniel still wore that grin when he kissed him, and Kyle wondered which of them was drunker. He breathed in the smell of sweet oil from Daniel's hair, and ran his thumbs along Daniel's jaw. Daniel cupped Kyle's ass until they were plastered together, and Kyle was pretty sure what they were doing couldn't be called dancing anymore.

The flick of Daniel's tongue against Kyle's lips did everything it should to his body. Mouth open, he arched up, grinding his cock against Daniel, then suddenly it was all wrong. Wrong taste, wrong angle, just wrong. Kissing might not be on the list of what constituted cheating, but Kyle knew it was about to go a lot farther than that, and he'd only let it get this far because of how distant he and Sean had been.

Daniel's mouth teased across Kyle's jaw to his ear. "Hey, Kyle? Do you still suck cock like my favorite wet dream?"

Kyle huffed a quick laugh. "Sorry, Daniel. I didn't really plan to stay out this late. I've got an eight o'clock tomorrow on new zoning codes for parking lots, and that's coma-inducing even with sleep."

Daniel kissed the skin below Kyle's ear and then nipped it. Was there a list of his kinks somewhere on a bathroom wall?

Kyle pulled back, trying to ignore the caress of fingers on his spine.

Daniel grinned again and shrugged. "It hasn't been that long, and I've got a pretty good memory. What are you doing tomorrow?" Sometimes Daniel had been able to read his mind.

"Like I said, meetings and—"

"Tomorrow night. There's a really good DJ at Skylight."

"Sounds good. Where do you want to meet?"

"Where are you staying?"

ß

The meetings went so well, the partners invited Kyle to join them when they took the clients to dinner. Dinner dragged on through drinks in the bar, so Kyle used a bathroom break to send Daniel an apologetic text. When he flipped open his phone, he saw that Sean had sent a text of his own. *Earlier flight tomorrow. See you Sunday.* As Kyle slid the phone back into its case, it vibrated again. *Miss you, babe.*

Daniel must not have gotten Kyle's text because when Kyle showed up an hour late, Daniel sat on a couch in the hotel lobby, Blackberry in hand.

"I got your message. But I figured if parking lots are as boring as contract law you'd still like to go dancing." If it was possible, Daniel smelled and looked better than he had last night.

A few hours of escape into nothing but a beat pounding through him sounded great, as long as Daniel knew that dancing was the only escape Kyle was looking for. "Want to come up while I change?"

After Kyle keyed open the door, he tossed his briefcase and coat in the small closet.

Daniel had already dressed to go out. On his toned hard body, the black leather jacket and faded ass-hugging jeans were overkill. Daniel would have been sexy in a muumuu. Just dancing. Right. Kyle tried not to stare as he stripped off his tie.

"Mind if I shower? I smell like old men's cigars."

Daniel moved closer and sniffed. "You do."

Kyle almost stumbled as he stepped back. "Look, Daniel. I'd get it if you want to say forget about going out tonight, but I—"

Daniel sat on the bed, legs sprawled wide and an open grin on his face. "But you're not *that* pissed at him?"

Mind reader. Smart, sexy fucking mind reader. Kyle shut his eyes.

"Right. Not that you're not still—"

"Astoundingly hot?"

"And arrogant."

Daniel shrugged and sat up. "Hands off. I get it. It's not like I haven't been a rebound fuck before. The offer still stands if you change your mind."

Kyle shook his head.

"Fine. Go shower. But if you lick your lips and look up at me through your eyelashes again, don't blame me for what happens."

Kyle brought a shirt and briefs into the bathroom so he'd be at least somewhat dressed when he came out. Instead of leering at him though, Daniel simply sat on the bed with a bemused expression.

"What?"

"I'm sorry. I think I just seriously fucked things up."

Kyle waited.

"Sean called."

Kyle's heart thumped like it was doubling for Moby's drum machine. "Shit. What did he say?"

"Let's see. Hello. Is this Kyle DiRusso's room? Who are you? Well, where is he? Do you think you could manage to tell him that Sean called?"

"You sound like a court reporter."

"Actually, they use even less inflection. But it was verbatim."

"I should call him back." Kyle ran a hand through his wet hair and started looking for his cell phone. By the time he'd remembered it was still on his pants in the bathroom, Daniel stood at the door. Kyle hadn't even had to tell him their plans were canceled.

Daniel put a hand on the knob and then turned back. "Is he worth it?"

Kyle thought about the best six years of his life, of having that bone-deep security of knowing there wasn't anything Sean wouldn't do for him, and weighed it against the misery of the last couple of months. "Yeah. He's worth it."

"Get to it then. Good luck."

Daniel shut the door softly behind him.

Sean didn't answer his cell, and Kyle hung up when it went to voice mail. Maybe Sean was on the plane. Maybe he was already home. Maybe he just wasn't answering.

Kyle tried the house and got the machine. He called Sean's cell again, hoping he wasn't going to have to try to explain this in a message with no way of knowing how Sean was taking it.

Kyle breathed a silent prayer of thanks when Sean finally answered. "Yeah."

"Yeah?" Kyle forced a quick laugh. "Hell of a way to answer the phone."

Silence. Long silence. Kyle counted six breaths before Sean finally said, "So?"

"You called me." If Kyle launched into an explanation, it would be as if he were guilty of something. And he wasn't.

"I called your room. Daniel answered."

"You remember him, right?"

"Yeah. I remember he tried to get a hand in your pants every time you saw him."

"Well, he didn't."

More breaths. And then Brandt's voice, "Hey, you ready?"

Sean's voice faded a bit as he answered Brandt. "Yeah." And then back on the phone. "I've got to go. See you Sunday." Sean clicked off.

Maybe Kyle would have been better off with a message. Then he wouldn't be considering flinging the phone into the wall.

He could call Daniel, or go out alone. But he waited, wet hair dripping onto his neck, hand clutching his not-broken-into-pieces cell phone, hoping Sean would call him when he was done with whatever the fuck he was doing with Brandt that was so important he couldn't talk for two minutes.

ß

On Sunday morning Sean jerked awake from another nightmare. His heart kept pounding as he fought off sleep and disorientation. Considering he'd slept in more hotel rooms in the past three months than he had in the rest of his life put together, he ought to be used to waking up and not knowing where he was. What made this disorientation worse was that he knew where he was. He was home. He'd fallen asleep on the recliner. But the sound of snoring from somewhere near him wasn't Kyle.

Sean forced himself to sit up despite the throbbing in his leg. The sound of the chair clicking back into place changed the tone of Brandt's snores, but didn't wake him. At last, Sean's head cleared enough to make sense of the situation. With his leg hurting more than usual, he hadn't wanted to climb the stairs last night. But even more, he hadn't wanted to sleep in *their* bed while Kyle was off in some hotel room with a guy he used to fuck regularly.

Sean wasn't overreacting. Kyle had sounded guilty as hell on the phone.

Even a tiny shift brought a wave of pain. This wasn't the usual ache of overworked muscles. Hot needles jabbed everywhere from his knee, all around his quadriceps and hamstring up into his groin. Nightmare, check. Leg throbbing, check. All he needed now was a fucking migraine to make the morning complete.

He glanced at his watch. Ten after nine. He never used to sleep this late. Brandt made another snorting gasp on the couch. Odd, since the guy hadn't snored any of the times they'd shared a hotel room. Sean eyed the empty bottles littering the coffee table. But then again, they'd never been as drunk as they were last night.

Sean had asked Brandt to stick around for Tony's party—which he could admit was petty, but Kyle knew damned well how Sean felt about Daniel. Brandt traveled with a couple of his favorite TV shows and movies on flash drives, and they'd watched some sitcom Sean had never seen—since Kyle wouldn't watch comedy made after 1960. Sean couldn't remember the last time he'd laughed like that.

If his leg didn't hurt so much, now he'd be laughing at Brandt's hippopotamus snorts. The guy's good looks and easy charm made him border on annoying perfection. The window-rattling volume of his snores when he fell asleep drunk was a welcome flaw.

Sooner or later, Sean would have to wake him. They were going to have to go out to buy some more beer since he'd promised Tony he'd bring some. And who knew when Kyle would decide to stop partying in Cleveland and haul his ass home.

But right now, his leg did hurt, too much to even think of getting up for coffee or a piss. He squeezed his eyes shut and tried to ignore it.

"Does that work?" The snoring had stopped.

Sean opened his eyes. "Not as well as a blowjob." The words were out of his mouth before he realized who he'd said them to.

Brandt studied Sean for a long time. "Are you asking?"

Though it might serve Kyle right—out fucking around in Cleveland—Sean and Brandt had become good friends in the last few months, and if something happened between them, it wouldn't just be a random blowjob. Sean broke the stare.

"Okay then. I'm going to shower."

Sean tried not to notice the outline of Brandt's cock in his jeans as he rolled off the couch.

"Omelets?" Brandt asked.

Sean shook his head. "I'll get something."

But by the time he'd scrambled some eggs, his leg was screaming at him, and he was almost too nauseous to eat.

Brandt came into the kitchen. "Sean, c'mon. Go sit down."

Sean let Brandt herd him to the sofa. His heart and dick jumped a bit when Brandt knelt at his feet, but all Brandt did was reach out and start rubbing the muscle of Sean's thigh. A massage to help him when his leg got really tired wasn't anything Brandt hadn't done before. But this time with Brandt looking up at Sean, hair ungelled, laying long and wet on his head, lashes still spiked from his shower, this time with Brandt curving those full lips in a smile, this time with what Sean had said about blowjobs and pain relief hanging in the air between them. This time was different.

Sean tried to think of something to say. "I blame it on New York. Everything is upstairs or down. What the fuck happened to elevators?"

Brandt laughed even as his fingers dug in, hurting at first and then soothing, rubbing away the burn. "Well, you're in for a rest. There's just the GLAAD awards next week and that's all I've been able to line up."

"I could use a break. I start coaching in a few weeks."

"Well then I won't feel too bad about it. This might be it, unless you want to take a harder political stance or go into inspiration speeches. I haven't had any new calls since January."

"I hope I haven't fucked things up for you."

Brandt shrugged and stopped rubbing. "It happens with everything eventually. People move on to the next hot topic." Brandt's wide green eyes under those water dark lashes, those eyes staring up from between Sean's legs. Christ, he was only human. Brandt's fingers moved gently now. "Unless there's something more you want to do?"

Sean could hear more than a question about PR in Brandt's voice. His hands were whispering up Sean's thigh. Sean bit his lip and reached down to pull them away. "No." He smiled. "Thanks."

Brand shrugged again, but sat back on his heels.

"So, what will you do next?" Sean asked.

"I've had a couple of things going. And I'm always on the lookout for the next big thing. You've earned me a nice pile of change and a lot of contacts, Mr. Sean Farnham, Gay Hero."

Brandt winked.

It wasn't as if Sean had forgotten Kyle was due home anytime. He and Brandt weren't doing anything wrong, which was probably why neither of them moved despite the sounds of Kyle coming in through the back door. They certainly had time.

Kyle crossed the hall from the kitchen. "Hey, *papi chulo*, why didn't you eat—" Kyle stopped. In the silence that followed, Sean heard his lover swallow.

Kyle spoke again. "Guess you were too busy. By the way, Brandt, you'll probably need another shower. He shoots like a fire hose if it's the first of the day."

Anger tightened Sean's hands to fists. "What the fuck, Kyle? Guilty conscience from your weekend of fun?"

Kyle turned and walked back out through the kitchen, slamming the door as he went.

Brandt climbed to his feet. "I guess I should go."

"And miss the party?"

ß

Yeah, Sean could have called Kyle, could have gone after him, but fuck if he was going to chase him over this. If Kyle wanted to think that Sean would screw around with Brandt in the middle of their living room, that was his problem. Though he was a little surprised that Kyle hadn't called or come back by the time Sean and Brandt left for Tony's party. Kyle rarely stayed mad for long.

Over a year ago, Tony had moved into Jack's mcmansion in the shiny new development off of route sixty-two. Immediately, Tony doubled the guest list for his Super Bowl party. He had to work Christmas and New Years to get the day off, but he claimed he loved a national event that was all about food and men. The truth was, Tony actually loved football, though he'd deny it if asked, claiming that he only liked the tight pants.

Sean parked right behind Tony's battered Rabbit, so out of

place in this cul-de-sac of perfectly maintained homes and three car garages.

"Want me to get the case?" Brandt asked.

Sean knew it was stupid even as he refused and handed off his cane before hoisting the beer onto his shoulder on his left side.

Tony surprised Sean by meeting them at the front door, since usually by this time he was busy with last-minute details involving the creative use of as many phallic-shaped foods as possible. He blocked the door for a second and then stepped aside.

"Who the fuck is this?"

Brandt smiled. "You must be Tony."

"Dude. Smart and pretty. Your mom must be so proud. Excuse us a sec." Tony dragged Sean into the living room.

Since the game wasn't on yet and the food was all in the dining room, they had the place to themselves.

"For Christsake, Tony, man, could I at least put the beer somewhere first?"

"How about up your ass? Where's Kyle?"

Sean shrugged. "Off somewhere being an asshole." Was Tony forgetting that he was *Sean*'s friend?

Tony stared at him. "Shit. You really don't know where the fuck he is, do you?"

Like it was some kind of crime? Like Kyle was a child in need of supervision?

"He walked out this morning. You've got his number. If you care so much, you call him."

Carrying that case into the kitchen without limping cost Sean more pain and effort than he would ever admit. But he wasn't going to ask his friend for help.

Chapter Seventeen

Kyle wouldn't admit to anyone that he'd been watching his cell phone, though he had opened it a dozen times to be sure it had reception and to adjust the ring volume. When his hand moved to pick up the handset on the landline to call himself to double-check, he forced himself to hang up, put away his cell and turn on the TV. Dark green wallpaper made the motel room shrink in on him and reminded him of Brandt's eyes. And with that thought, Kyle was up and pacing again.

How did he get here—in the fucking Comfort Inn—when he had a bed and sofa and a life in a house a few miles away. He should have just shown up at Tony's like nothing happened. Except he couldn't. Couldn't talk to Sean if Brandt was going to be there. Couldn't keep from throwing things if Sean kept insisting he was fine.

Kyle looked out at the rain-wet parking lot. The dirty snow was as ugly as the wallpaper, but it suited his mood.

Maybe he had overreacted. Even if nothing had happened with Daniel, he still felt guilty about what had almost happened. Sean had a right to be asking why Daniel had answered the phone. And maybe there was something to Sean's accusation of a guilty conscience. But the sight of Brandt kneeling between Sean's legs had ripped through Kyle's guts.

Sean knew how he felt about Brandt. Knew he was coming home in a few minutes. Whatever had or hadn't happened didn't matter as much as Sean not caring what Kyle saw. That Sean had deliberately fed Kyle's intestines to the shredder.

Sean didn't even care enough to find out where Kyle was, to even call.

When his cell rang, he didn't even check the number, just grabbed it.

"Dude. Where the fuck are you?"

Tony. Not Sean. Kyle's heart joined his guts in the shredder too. His too-vivid imagination provided all kinds of horrible reasons why Tony might be calling. Sean had been in an accident. Sean had decided he never wanted to talk to him again.

Sean had made Tony call to tell Kyle to pack his shit and move out.

"Is he all right?"

"He's fine. Are you all right?"

Kyle took a deep breath. "Yeah. I'm fine." He wondered if Tony might have any Xanax. But then he realized why he couldn't go over and pick one up.

"And where are you fine?"

"The Comfort Inn by the Hall of Fame."

"How very Super Bowl of you. I need you here, dude. Need the snark at the announcers and the commercials and the melodramatic sideline reporting."

"And to tell you how good your chili is."

"That too. You know, Kyle, dude, I don't want to get in the middle of this."

"So don't."

Tony ignored him. "You could make it for the second half. Sean looks like he's about ready to kill something."

"Is Brandt there?"

"Yeah. And he looks like he's going to be getting lucky tonight."

When Sophie was pregnant, she'd dumped a can of anchovies on Mami's *plantanos*. Kyle's stomach felt pretty much the same way now as it did when he'd watched her eat it.

He must have made some kind of sound because Tony said

quickly, "Dude, no, not like that. Brandt can take his pick here. Charlie hasn't left his side and Julian's curled up at his feet and Gavin keeps trying to get him drunk. Kyle, Sean didn't—"

"Ask him."

"What the fuck is with you two?"

"Why the fuck do you even care?"

Tony whistled a long breath into the phone. "Okay then. I just called because I was worried, man. But the way you two are acting you deserve to be miserable little shits." He hung up.

Kyle was a miserable shit for taking it out on Tony, but seriously, did he think being a bartender gave him credentials as a marriage counselor?

Maybe Sean told Tony to call with the story about Brandt being hit on by other guys to hide the fact that Sean was upstairs fucking Brandt in one of the guest rooms. Maybe it was some weird junior high game where Sean had Tony call to find out if Kyle wanted to talk to him. Or maybe he should put a lid on his paranoia and remember that he had to be completely brilliant if he was going to impress his bosses at the nine thirty follow-up meeting about the bids they were putting in for Unibank.

ß

As he drove home, Kyle decided sleepless nights at too-small Comfort Inns were good for his career. Two hours of hard-won sleep made Kyle brilliant enough that Mr. Young offered him the job heading up the design team for Circle Corp's westward expansion. They wanted an architect on site—in Detroit. He'd be out there at least six weeks coordinating the surveyors and initial groundbreaking. He'd been given two weeks to decide, and he had to be in Detroit by March first. With everything so fucked up between him and Sean, there couldn't be a worse time to disappear for six weeks.

Kyle would apologize for Daniel. Apologize for walking out yesterday and then...and then beg Sean to see what the fuck was happening.

For the first time since they'd bought the house, Kyle dreaded going home.

The Durango was in the driveway, but no Lexus. Kyle let out a deep breath and came in through the front door.

Sean was on the couch. "So, you remembered you still live here?"

"Do I?" Kyle tried to remind himself that he was going to apologize, but if Sean was going to start attacking, he wasn't going to bother.

"That's up to you," Sean said in a monotone.

"That's certainly encouraging."

Sean looked directly at him for the first time. "I'm not the one with a fuck buddy in my hotel room."

"Oh yeah, because Brandt was looking for a missing contact lens?"

Sean kicked his cane under the coffee table. "He was rubbing my leg, you know the one with the fucking bullet wounds in it?"

"The one you won't let me rub? That one? Yeah, I know it. I didn't realize you had someone else for that."

"Is that what this is all about? You don't trust me?" Sean pushed his way up off the couch.

Sean could always make everything Kyle's fault. Somehow even if he'd walked in on Brandt blowing him, it would have been Kyle's fault. He fought for control of his temper. "You say he was massaging your leg, I believe you. So why is it okay when he does it and not me?"

"You sound like a two-year-old who doesn't want to share his toy."

Kyle turned and started to walk toward the solarium, past Sean and his stupid argument. He always turned to insults when he was losing.

Sean grabbed his arm and pushed him into one of the pillars separating the solarium from the rest of the room. "Not this time. We're finishing this now. Did you fuck Daniel?"

Kyle glared right back. "No."

"Well, I didn't fuck Brandt, so what the hell is your problem?"

Anger Kyle knew. But Sean had never filled him with disgust. He tried to shake off Sean's grip. The familiar hand made his skin crawl. "My problem?"

Sean let go of his arm and slapped the pillar. "Jesus Christ, Kyle, what the fuck will ever be enough for you?"

Kyle looked away. Because if he had to look at that sanctimonious expression on Sean's face, he might just punch him. The job in Detroit was looking pretty fucking good right now. "Maybe I should—"

"What. Leave? You've been threatening to walk out since the day of the shooting."

Sanctimonious and delusional. "That's not true."

"Isn't it? Tell me you haven't been thinking about it. And you know what, I'm tired of waiting for it. Go."

"You're throwing me out of our house?" Kyle hated the way his voice broke.

"Babe, I'm not throwing you out. I'm just opening the door. I've done everything I can to make you happy and it isn't enough. Never will be enough."

"Oh right. You're the one who left a good job in Cleveland to move to some little burg to be with the guy you love?"

Sean shook his head. "Like you'll ever let me forget it. Go the fuck back to Cleveland. To Daniel. I'm sure he'd love the chance to put up with all your insecure bullshit. I'm way past done."

"You know what, Sean, the next time you want to talk about insecurities, try looking in the mirror at the guy who had to turn saving kids' lives into some kind of national crusade to keep his name in the headlines."

Those beautiful grey-blue eyes narrowed, color hard and flat. "Think what you want as long as you get this: you can leave or I can leave. But this is over."

Kyle bit the inside of his cheek so hard he tasted blood, but fuck if he would cry in front of that bastard. "Do I at least get to pack?" But if he stayed to pack, he might lose it. Cry, beg, smack the fucking arrogance right out of the guy he thought he knew. "You know, fuck it. I'll come over tomorrow morning after you leave for school. Have a nice life."

ß

Kyle didn't break anything. Didn't punch out any walls. And while he didn't do more than doze that night at the Comfort Inn, he still managed to get up and make it to the house in the time to get clothes and go to work. If he just had to think about where to run the plumbing and the size of the loading docks and the number of exit doors, he'd be fine. If the Comfort Inn didn't run out of Cheerios at their buffet breakfast, he'd be fine. He could settle back into a routine as long as he didn't stop to wonder what happened now. With the house, with his stuff, with the way it felt like half his chest was missing.

The receptionist called him at eleven thirty. "Mr. DiRusso, your lunch appointment is here."

He didn't have a lunch appointment.

Sean. The wave of relief knocked him back into the chair for a second.

But when he got to the receptionist's desk, Tony was there waiting, wearing unripped jeans and a hesitant smile so very far removed from his usual toothy grin that Kyle hardly recognized him. "Can I buy you some lunch?"

Kyle was going to refuse. He didn't want to talk about it, didn't want to have to explain this to their—Sean's friends. To listen to what he should have done.

As he hesitated, Tony said, "Please?"

Kyle went back into his office for his coat. "I'll be back in an hour, Kate."

An icy wind full of hard little bits of snow nearly knocked him off his feet, but he decided to walk. There was a sandwich place three blocks down, across from city hall. Tony kept pace with him.

They walked in silence for awhile, Tony's hands in the pockets of his worn leather coat. As they waited for a light, Tony bumped him with his shoulder.

"What?" Kyle asked.

"So I called last night. No one answered."

Kyle started across the street. Tony caught up to him in one stride. "I drove over after work and the lights were still on. Your car wasn't there."

"'Cause it was at the fucking Comfort Inn."

They kept walking. Another block and Tony exploded, "He's been through a lot, Kyle. How could you do this to him?"

Kyle stopped. He knew somehow this would be his fault. "Do what?" An old woman in a fur hat larger than her head smiled as she passed between them.

"Leave him."

"I didn't."

"Dude."

"He. Threw. Me. Out." Kyle started walking again, past the sandwich shop, past city hall, into one of those cement parks that were supposed to be modern and artistic, but were actually depressing with grey stone and sharp metallic structures. He dropped onto a stone bench and let the cold fill him up. Let it erase that spark of anger, that stupid hope he'd had that Tony could somehow help, could get through to Sean when Kyle couldn't.

Tony sat next to him on the bench, perched gingerly on the edge. "Dude. S'fucking freezing."

Kyle shrugged and settled back, ice on his spine, perfectly numbing.

"You fuck around?"

"No."

"Did he?"

"No."

"You total his Durango?"

Even now, Tony could almost make him laugh.

Tony gave a small grunt and shivered. Kyle's fingers burned inside his leather gloves, but at least it gave him something else to think about.

"Can I tell you something?"

Kyle shrugged.

"This is all about me."

Kyle turned to look at Tony, brow arched in question.

"You've got to fix things, for me."

"How do you figure that?"

"You guys, you're like perfect. Always, from the time you moved here. Both of you so fucking happy sometimes it made me sick."

A pigeon landed in front of them, pecked around hopefully and took off with a disdainful glance.

"And jealous," Tony added. A few more pigeons circled them and fluttered when Tony waved an arm. "Then you introduced me to Jack. And fuck, he's—" He waved his arm again and if it was possible to curse while cooing, the pigeons did as they headed skyward. "He lets me be an asshole, you know, and he loves me anyway. And he's funny, and sexy as hell and..."

Kyle wondered where the hell Tony was going with this. He watched him and waited.

"So, I know how happy you guys were and Christ, Kyle, if you and Sean can't make it work, what the fuck chance do I have?" Tony looked away, across the slate stones that made up the courtyard.

Kyle didn't have an answer for that. The cold burned through the wool of his coat, numbed his toes.

Tony bumped his shoulder. "So, can we go eat somewhere before my nuts freeze off?"

ß

Sean came home on Wednesday through the kitchen and

tossed his stuff on the stairs before starting dinner. It took him three minutes before he realized he didn't have any reason to make dinner. Kyle wasn't coming home in an hour. Or two. Sean shut the fridge door and sat at the counter. At least now he knew why it was a good thing they'd never finished a fight. Six years of what he thought was perfect couldn't handle one problem. And the fact that Kyle hadn't called or tried to see him only meant that Sean was right. Kyle would have left him sooner or later. All Sean did was make it easier on him. Like he always did.

And it hurt, more than he thought it could since he'd never expected to be without him, always believed that Kyle was the one he'd be with for the rest of his life. It was kind of like wondering what life would be like without an arm. He should have been ready for it, since he'd almost had to figure out how to live without a leg. And he would. But he couldn't stop wondering if maybe there was a chance, that maybe Kyle would call him and they'd find some way to work this out.

Sean knew he'd screwed up too, that they were both wrong, and both right. Maybe if Kyle had shown some sign that he wanted to hold on harder, that he didn't have one foot out the door already, Sean wouldn't have wanted to push him the rest of the way out.

He got up and went through the living room to the solarium. Seeing Kyle's drafting table still there gave him an odd sense of comfort. He ran a hand across the smooth white surface. He could call Kyle—if only to find out where he was—but Sean wasn't ready. Wasn't ready for this to be permanent. His hand curled hard over the edge of the table. Sitting in the house alone wasn't going to work. There was a wrestling match at the high school tonight, and Neil Purcell was undefeated.

He went back into the kitchen for his coat and cane and headed over to the school.

The gym noises spilled into the hallway, whistles and calls from the crowd. As he paid his admission and nodded at security, a groan echoed through the gym. Stepping into the gym, he could see that the jayvee match was still going on. The groan had been a McKinley wrestler going to his back.

The sharp slap of the referee's hand on the mat signaled the pin. Sean turned from the match to contemplate the climb into the stands. Anything close to the mat was already gone. He stepped away from the door and rested for a minute on the bottom bleacher, leaning on his cane.

"Hey, Coach." Neil was already in his warm up.

Sean stood to face him. "Nice season you're having."

"Yeah." Neil lowered his eyes. "Coach Peterson says I've got to think about one match at a time."

"That's good advice. You know, I didn't get your forms yet for baseball. They have to be in by the fifteenth."

The kid blushed and looked like he wished all one hundred eighty-nine pounds of him would sink through the floor. "Yeah, about that. Um—"

Sean tried to keep his expression open and encouraging, but Neil had always carried himself with more confidence than most of the other seventeen year olds he worked with. To see him blush and stammer was weird.

"My dad, he, uh, won't sign the permission slip because, you know..." Neil swallowed and looked over at the ongoing match.

Sean did know. And he couldn't say he was surprised, even though he'd never met Neil's parents since they didn't show up to any games. He supposed he could offer to talk to Mr. Purcell, but given the boy's acute state of embarrassment, he let it go. At least he knew why Neil had been uncharacteristically silent when he passed him on his way out of study hall the past week.

"Sorry to hear that." He kept the disappointment off his face.

"Me too. I wish— He's going to pay for me to go to a summer camp for wrestling, though. But..." Neil shrugged.

"Don't worry about it, Neil. Who've you got tonight?"

Neil was relieved enough to jump onto the change of subject that in ten seconds Sean knew all about avoiding throws and using legs and a dozen things that made minimal sense to someone with a passing interest. But when Neil turned to jog back toward the locker room, at least he was smiling.

Sean climbed up a few rows and leaned against the gym wall. His hand was already reaching for his cell phone to call Kyle before he remembered why he couldn't. Kyle would have had Sean laughing in two minutes with a rant about idiotic parents and their terror over the corruption of their innocent adolescents. Adolescents who were exposed to sexual images from birth. And Sean wouldn't feel like he'd somehow let Neil down, that it was Sean's fault Neil would miss out on the season because Sean had decided to come out.

But after what Kyle had said to him when he left, Sean wasn't sure Kyle wouldn't tell him it was exactly what Sean deserved for his *national crusade to keep his name in the headlines*.

He placed his hand over on his thigh and tried to rub away the ache through the layer of denim. The jayvee match ended with a crowd-pleasing throw and pin for the home team, but Sean had to force himself to clap.

ß

On Friday, Sean went in to school early, only to be ambushed by the new principal who called Sean into his office as soon as Sean went through security.

Don Baker had been promoted from one of the elementary schools to take over after Frank's death. He was the kind of soft-spoken, too-much-into-respect-for-everyone's-feelings kind of administrator Sean hated. He couldn't trust someone who was always trying to see all sides. Sean liked the division clean and neat. Administration was out to screw the teachers; the teachers fought for every inch they could get. Sean didn't know how to handle a guy like Baker. He didn't sit at his desk, but at a table where the only other seat was next to him, like a couple at a restaurant.

"How are things going, Sean?"

Sean would swear the guy had his degree in social work instead of educational administration, but he sat down and dragged up a smile. “Fine. What can I do for you, Don?” If he could make the guy get to the point, Sean could get out of here and ignore whatever the point was.

Baker looked like he was in pain—or maybe the guy had chronic constipation. “I’ve got this note from the district’s central administration. They say they haven’t received proof of your three counseling sessions.”

Sean had really been hoping that would go away. He read the notice when it came, insurance carrier, grief counseling, all parties closely involved, etc. and stuffed it in the back of a file.

“I’ve been trying really hard to get things back on track for the state exams.”

“I understand, Sean.”

Of course he did. Sean barely managed to keep a neutral expression on his face.

“But the school board laid this all out, and they and the insurance companies are pretty adamant about having everything documented.”

“Okay.”

“Sean.” The guy actually put his hand on Sean’s elbow. Sean fought the urge to shake it off. “I’m afraid that the board insists that if you don’t send in some paperwork regarding these sessions, you may be suspended.”

Sean turned enough so that the guy’s hand had to slide off his arm. He was fucking good at his job. “Is there something wrong about the way I’m running my classroom? Have there been complaints?”

“No, nothing like that, but with the lawsuits, the district just wants to make sure that everything looks great on paper, you know?”

“So what’s the deadline?”

“End of March.”

“I’ll take care of it.”

Baker burst into a wide smile. It probably delighted the

first-graders, but it made Sean feel like he had spiders under his skin. No adult should act like Mr. Rogers, especially around other adults.

"I'm so glad to hear that, Sean." Baker handed off a small directory. "There's the listing for the ones that the insurance carrier approves. I'm sure you can find someone in there and send us the dates of the appointments."

"Will do, Don."

At least he wouldn't have to pay for the bullshit.

ß

Tony showed up Saturday morning. Sean let him in and went back to the couch to stare at his laptop's screen of stats from last season. Maybe there was a kid on the modified team he could put at the plate to replace Neil.

Tony made himself at home, strolling into the kitchen and coming back with two beers. Sean shot him a quick glance and went back to his stats. Tony wandered off again, coming back from the dining room with a bottle of Crown Royal.

"It's nine a.m," Sean said when Tony placed the bottle next to the beers on the coffee table.

"I know. I'm the one who got home from work five hours ago."

Sean snorted and grabbed a beer. After letting Sean drink and scroll for a few minutes, Tony finally said, "So."

Sean had known sooner or later Tony would come around to find out what was going on. But he still didn't really know what he was going to say.

What he finally came up with was "I'm fine."

"Yeah. That's why you're holding a beer and eyeing the whiskey at nine on a Saturday morning."

Suddenly, he was just as mad at Tony as he was at Kyle. Where the fuck did everyone get off telling him he had some kind of problem? "I told you, I'm—"

"You're pretty fucking far from fine. Dude, I've known you for twelve years. I knew you were in love with Kyle before you did. You wanna tell me what happened?"

"Why the hell do you care?"

"Oh, I don't know. Maybe because I give a shit?"

Sean decided that whiskey wasn't such a bad idea and uncapped the bottle. After one fiery swallow, he thought a second would be an even better idea. Then he passed the bottle to Tony.

Tony put it back on the table so Sean grabbed it again. If he got drunk fast enough, he wouldn't be able to answer. And God knew it was easy to distract Tony. He lifted the bottle to his mouth again.

"Jesus, Sean, do you even know where he is?"

"I called him."

"And?"

"I asked if he needed anything. He said he was fine. Staying with friends."

"Where?"

The conversation hadn't gone that far. Sean had spent the whole thirty-second phone call hoping he wouldn't ask Kyle if he wanted to come home, and then wishing he could just give in and ask. But Kyle had only said, "I can't talk right now." And wasn't that exactly why Sean had called him at work, when he knew Kyle couldn't really talk?

"What friends does Kyle have in Canton?" Tony asked.

Sean hadn't had enough whiskey to make that a difficult question, but he stared at the bottle anyway. Kyle had go-out-for-dinner-or-drinks friends at work, but not come-stay-with-us friends. In fact, the only people in Canton Kyle knew well enough were— He looked up.

Tony nodded.

"Oh, that's great. So I suppose you're here to tell me how I fucked things up for your new best pal?"

"If I didn't think you'd enjoy the distraction, I would so kick your ass. Come to think of it, maybe that would help you get your head out of it."

The two of them could do some serious damage if he took Tony up on that. Sean grabbed his beer instead, decided the whiskey was better and knocked back another swallow. "I just made it easy for him. He was going to leave anyway. As soon as he got the nerve. You know Kyle and his OCD." Sean handed Tony the bottle.

"So you guys were what, a habit? A six-year, ignore-the-rest-of-the-world habit?" Tony tipped the bottle to his lips and passed it back.

The whiskey didn't even burn anymore, sliding along his throat with a pleasant warmth that spread through his gut. "I don't know what it was. Maybe I never did. What did we ever have in common anyway?"

Tony looked around the living room. "A lame old movie fetish?"

"That was always Kyle's thing." But Sean had grown to love them, watched them for himself as much as for Kyle and—shit.

Was Kyle going to take that Errol Flynn collection? Because in the early movies the guy kind of moved like Kyle and he'd miss it—him—the DVD's. He needed more whiskey.

Tony waggled his brows, lips parting, and Sean held up his hand, the bottle still in it.

"And don't say sex."

"Yeah, because awesome sex is such a trial in a relationship. What about that beach house you guys have been planning forever? I swear to God if I have to listen to the pros and cons of where to put the outdoor shower one more time..."

"See. Can't even agree on that."

"Jesus Christ, Sean. How about that look you got when you were going up to see him in Cleveland every weekend? Or watching you take care of each other for the last six years, so fucking easy you don't even know you do it? What about your lives? Don't you have six years of life in common?"

"I'm starting to wonder if I imagined it all."

"Imagined your lives? What the hell is in that whiskey?"

Tony grabbed it out of Sean's hand.

Tony could stay obtuse, but Sean knew what he meant. What if he'd just imagined the whole falling-in-love thing? That it was only a way to keep from being lonely, so he'd fooled himself into thinking that this was it. That Kyle was the one because everything about them together had been so easy, fit so right.

And look what happened the first time things got hard.

Tony put the bottle back on the table, but this time when Sean reached for it, Tony kept his hand on it. "Okay. I may grow tits for saying this but you know, maybe you two should talk? Like grown-ups instead of drama queens?"

"We have talked."

"About?"

About Brandt, about the publicity, about the fact that Kyle wanted everything to go back to the way it was before the shooting happened. The one fucking thing Sean could never give him. "He wants us to move."

"Might not be a bad idea. Wouldn't you like the chance to ditch some of this, be yourself again without everyone always looking at you and thinking about it?"

"I'm always going to think about it." Why the fuck was that so hard for everyone to understand? He was never going to be able to change it, never get there in time to save Nicole, and if something good didn't come out of it what the hell was he but a guy with a cane and a limp?

Tony looked away. "Sorry, buddy."

"It's not about the fucking pity. Don't try it." He rethought the wrestling match with Tony, to hell with the furniture. At least he wouldn't have to listen to this crap. "You want it to be all my fault? Fine. I changed and Kyle couldn't handle it so I pushed him away. He went. End of story."

"See, that's where you're fucked up. You didn't change. You're the same stubborn bastard you were when we met and you tried to tell me how to run the team."

Tony ignored Sean's gasp of protest and went on. "Even

slower around second now, but you're the same. You still think you know what's best for everybody. Fuck if they get a say. Did you ask him if he wanted to go?"

"He went, didn't he?"

"Christ, I don't know how either of us ever put up with you." Tony slammed to his feet.

Sean ignored the throbbing in his thigh and got on his feet to face him. "Oh, I've put up with a hell of a lot more from the both of you. Some of the shit you've pulled could have gotten me fired. And Kyle, Jesus, all I ever did was try to make him happy and the first time there's something more important, he gives up."

"So I guess you won't be missing much, then, huh? See you around."

It was just fucking typical that Tony would side with Kyle. Sean was done with it all. Just too goddamned tired of trying to deal with everybody's shit. He sank back on the couch as Tony headed for the hall.

When he heard the door click closed, he yelled, "You could at least have slammed the door, you pussy!"

The door swung back open and slammed shut.

ẞ

A week had passed since Tony had shocked Kyle with their first-ever lunch date. Two slices of pizza into it, Tony offered Kyle a place to live until he could sort things out. Tony's actual words were, "Until the stubborn bastard comes to his senses."

The more time passed, Kyle wasn't sure anyone was coming to his senses. If Kyle thought it would work, he'd have swallowed every last bit of his pride and begged to come home, apologized for overreacting, promised anything. But if nothing changed, they'd be right back to this point sooner or later and Kyle didn't think he could go through it again.

That one awkward phone call hadn't done much to

convince him that things would get better. Sean hadn't seemed all that interested in where Kyle was and had sounded relieved when Kyle said he couldn't talk.

Saturday, Kyle hid in the dining room with his laptop and listened to Jack murmuring, while the clearest words from Tony were *asshole, miserable* and Kyle's favorite *stupid fucking pride.* Jack went to work not long after that, and the sympathetic looks from both of his friends were making Kyle a little nuts. He couldn't keep living in limbo. Sooner or later, they were going to have to decide whether to sell the house or have one of them rework the mortgage. Half of Kyle's clothes were already in the closet of Jack's guest room, but he needed other stuff. He worked a lot on his computer, but he still wanted his drafting table.

That night he tried to tune out Jack and Tony's whispers, laughter and then the rhythmic thunk of the headboard. He had the pillow wrapped around his head so tightly he almost didn't hear his phone ring. He checked the time and the number. One a.m. and Sean.

"Hello?"

"Kyle?"

Sweet Mary, of course it's me, you called my cell. But Sean just sounded so hesitant, so unlike himself Kyle couldn't be angry. Probably another nightmare. "Yes"—not *papi* or *chulo* or *baby*, not anymore, but—"Sean, is everything okay?"

An embarrassed cough. "Fine. Just."

Kyle listened to him breathe. He wanted to be there, in their warm bed, pull Sean in tight and know they were both safe.

"Do you need something?"

Sean's breathing shifted, got tight and fast. "No, I'm sorry I woke you. I must have been sleep dialing or something."

"Like drunk dialing?"

"Yeah. I didn't— I'll call you tomorrow."

"Okay. Sean?"

But there was only silence on the line.

Sean didn't call on Sunday.

Monday at work, Kyle called Daniel about the mortgage and started looking for a place to store his stuff. Maybe when he came back from Detroit he'd know what he was going to do with his life.

Chapter Eighteen

Tony wasn't the most organized person in the world, but it wasn't like him to demand that Sean meet him somewhere and then flake. He was still trying to figure that out when he got home. Confusion kept him distracted enough that it wasn't until he shut the front door and took in the sight of the boxes that everything clicked: the white catering van out front that Kyle must have borrowed from Jack, Tony's manipulation to get him first out of the house and then back in time to watch Kyle pack.

Sean walked through the living room into the solarium. Empty. Kyle's drafting board would be the first thing he'd pack. So this really was it. And wasn't that what Sean had said he wanted?

He found Kyle in their bedroom, taping down a box.

Kyle turned around slowly. "I'm sorry. Tony said you had plans so I thought—"

"Yeah. I think Tony set us up."

The trace of a smile teased Kyle's mouth, no dimples, just the flash of a curve at the corners of his lips. His hands were in his back pockets, elbows at the sharpest angle to take up space at his sides. Kyle's nervous pose. Prepping for a presentation, walking into a new space, meeting Sean's parents, the press interviews.

Sean's gut shifted, the world shifted. Because now the pose he'd seen so many times was directed at him. That defensive, don't-hurt-me, back-off pose.

Sean hadn't been imagining their lives. He loved Kyle. Everything else was bullshit. *Thanks, Tony, you asshole.*

He wanted to reach for him, but couldn't. Not with Kyle standing like that. Like he didn't trust Sean not to hurt him.

He glanced down at the box labeled "Sweaters" in Kyle's neat block print. Always organized. Every box in the house was probably neatly packed and labeled. Sean looked up again. "Are you happy?" Almost a whisper, as if he didn't want to know the answer.

"What the fuck kind of question is that?"

"So why are we doing this?"

"Jesus, Mary and fucking Joseph, Sean, you threw me out. Remember?"

Sean winced. Kyle's curses rarely turned to blasphemy unless he was really angry or on the edge of orgasm. "I know. I'm sorry."

Kyle made a choking sound and sat on the bed. "Sorry?"

"Really sorry. I just—"

"Decided what was best?"

"No. Kyle." Sean forced his thigh to cooperate and got on his knees in front of Kyle. "Tell me you didn't think about leaving. Tell me things weren't going to shit." Sean rested his hands on Kyle's knees.

Kyle covered Sean's hands, but wouldn't meet his eyes. "All right. It was a mess. But I don't know what I was going to do, though, Sean. You can't just decide for me."

At last Kyle met his gaze and something came loose inside Sean. Everything he needed to see was there in Kyle's eyes. He still loved Sean.

"I know." Sean just needed to hear it. "Miss me?"

"Asshole." Kyle's hand cupped Sean's jaw.

Sean took the deep breath he'd been missing for weeks. Kyle's hand on his face, the affection in his voice, it was going to be okay. They could do this.

Kyle lifted him up with that hand on his jaw, and they fell

back on the bed. Kyle's lips curved in a smile as he dragged their mouths together. It wasn't just good—finding that connection again—it was better because it shut up the part of Sean that had been afraid he wouldn't ever feel like this again, wouldn't hear Kyle's breath quicken in his ear as he pressed their bodies together.

Kyle ground up into him, fingers vise-tight on his hips, and the next kiss had them both moaning.

Kyle's hands shoved at Sean's jeans. "Sean. God." His hand forced its way into the gap and grabbed Sean's ass in a bruising grip. "Need."

That word, in that desperate whine from Kyle's throat, was all Sean's body had been waiting for to go from yes to right-the-fuck-now. Ignoring the burn in his leg, he let his knees drop to either side of Kyle's hips and sat up. Unfastening his jeans, he reached for Kyle's fly. Kyle pulled him back down as soon as Sean freed his cock, grinding them together again, buttons and cloth and then finally skin dragging damp and hard.

Both Kyle's hands cupped Sean's ass now, dragging him up and down as their mouths tried to fit inside each other. Sean pulled away and kissed along Kyle's stubbled jaw to his ear. "What do you need, babe?"

"Want to fuck you. And then I want you to fuck me right over that goddamned box of sweaters. And then I want you to help me unpack and apologize again for being an idiot."

Sean could do all that.

He crawled up to reach into the drawer, fingers closing around the lube, knuckles brushing a box. Even as his brain told him it was the box of condoms they hadn't needed for years, he was already grabbing it too. Because it had been three weeks and if Kyle had slept with someone else, Sean didn't want to know, and he sure as hell wasn't going to ask him about it right now. This way, neither of them had to ask.

Kyle dragged Sean back, rolling him on his good side. This time Kyle held Sean's head and kissed him slowly, thoroughly, tongue flicking across his lips before thrusting into his mouth, and it was just heat and need, perfectly matched. The way it had always worked between them.

Kyle reached over Sean's shoulder and came back with the box of condoms. He sat up.

"What the hell is this?"

Sean sat up next to him. "Babe, I don't care if you did. I just didn't want to have to—"

"No, you just assumed—again—that you knew what was right and to hell with talking to me about it. So what, I can't go three weeks without fucking all four hundred gay guys in Canton? Or did you think I'd been going up to Cleveland after work? Or maybe you decided I've been in a threeway with Jack and Tony?"

"What I think is that you're overreacting—again. Not everything means the worst. I was trying to make things easier."

Kyle was on his feet and fastening his jeans so fast Sean could have blinked and missed it. "You keep right on fixing everything but us."

"What was this, a test? I would have studied. Or wait. I should have known. I always have to measure up for you."

"I never asked you to. I never asked you for anything but love and honesty."

"And when did I ever not give you that?"

"You've never lied to me. I believe you. God, I trusted you all those nights you spent with Brandt, even after I told you how I felt. But loving me doesn't mean that you always get to decide what's best for me."

Kyle was making Sean sound like an overbearing control freak. Like he beat him or something. "When have I ever kept you from doing what you wanted?"

"That's not what I'm saying. I'm talking about when what you decide affects us. And you don't ask me."

"You know why I had to do the publicity."

"I know why you think you had to. But you still put it ahead of us."

"Ahead of you, you mean. I'm sorry that for six months my world didn't revolve around you."

Kyle shut his eyes, hands closing into fists. "Fine."

"Is this where you do your Catholic martyr thing? Then admit the whole truth. You're the one who's changing the rules. I'm still fucking here." Sean drove his fist into the bed.

"Well, I'm not going to be. Young is sending me to Detroit to oversee the surveying and initial work on the mall. I leave in ten days."

Sean wanted to laugh but it wasn't funny and he couldn't make his lungs work right. "And I'm the one who makes decisions without talking to you?"

"You threw me out and told me it was over. I kind of thought that meant you weren't too interested in where I was going to be in a month." Kyle's hands relaxed and he picked up the box.

"If you leave now, Kyle, I am not coming after you. Not this time."

Kyle threw the box into the wall. The wall held. The box crumpled and split along a seam. Maybe Kyle had been right about being afraid of his temper.

After a long shaky breath, Kyle pulled his wallet from his pocket and took out a card. "Unless you think you're going to *decide* to throw all my stuff out, Jack will come get it tomorrow." He put the card on the dresser. "When you decide what you want to do about the house, call my lawyer." Sean hoped he never saw a look that nasty on Kyle's face again. "It's Daniel."

Though as Kyle turned and started down the stairs, Sean realized he might never see another look on Kyle's face at all. Were they really going to leave it like this? Six years and what? It all came down to boxes and selling the house? He pushed off the bed and pain shot down his leg, but he still made his way down the stairs without his cane.

One thing, one tiny moment.

In that split-second he'd turned and run toward the sound of the shots. Knowing how it was all going to go, the only thing he'd change about that second was that he'd have run faster.

The leaded glass in the solarium bent light so that at night it almost looked like it was raining outside. He could probably remember the physics formula for the dispersion if he thought about it. Kyle had just said the light in there was soft. He'd talked about the solarium nonstop when they were house-hunting. No matter how many other houses they looked at, Sean had known all along which one they'd end up in. He couldn't believe Kyle didn't know how much Sean did, how much he'd always done for him, given him. That Kyle could let the last six months matter more than all that—fuck.

He went into the solarium. As soon as the sun was gone it was always freezing. Sean didn't know how Kyle could stand to work there so late at night. The catering van hadn't yet moved from in front of the house.

Through the solarium glass, it still looked like it was raining, but when the van pulled away, the taillights didn't look soft at all.

Kyle had to sit for awhile before he could drive. He wasn't crying, wasn't even shaking, as long as he kept his hands tight on the steering wheel. And the only reason for that was how hard he was fighting the urge to go back into the house and find some way to hurt Sean. Not physically, but to find some way of breaking through that righteous shield he always had around him, his belief that no matter what the result, he knew what was best. Kyle had tried everything to get through to him and nothing worked.

The worst thing was, Sean was right again. Kyle wouldn't be so angry if Sean wasn't right. Maybe Kyle had changed the rules. But Sean had changed a whole lot more than that. Okay, Sean wouldn't ever be able to leave the shooting behind. But shouldn't he want to sometimes? Couldn't he try to make things work between them half as hard as he was trying to save the world? And of course the bastard had to be right about Kyle missing the attention. But Kyle had tried. He'd tried to be what Sean needed. Why the fuck was it all right for everyone else to rub his leg or get the door or help carry stuff and not Kyle?

There was one thing he hoped Sean didn't know. That the main reason he hadn't started the van yet was that he was scared. Heart-racing, teeth-clenched terrified that he would go back in and try anything to keep this from being the end, the moment when he had to drive away and remember how to live a life that didn't have Sean in it. But as frightening as that idea was, Kyle was even more afraid of staying, of watching things get worse and worse, until maybe he couldn't control his temper, and the box hit Sean instead of the wall. And in that second when Kyle was sure staying and settling for something less was worse than walking away, he started up the engine and put it in drive.

ß

Jack usually got home by eleven on a work night and waited for Tony to make it in around one. Kyle had tried to put the few boxes he'd taken out of the way, but it didn't mean they were out of sight. Kyle looked up from whatever crap he'd landed on when he turned on the TV at the sound of Jack at the door.

"Ah shit." That would be Jack seeing the boxes, Kyle guessed.

And then his dark head poking into the TV room. "Sorry."

"Me too."

"You okay?"

Kyle nodded.

Jack hesitated in the doorway for a minute. After three weeks, Kyle could time the routine. Jack took a shower, poured himself some wine and watched whatever reality shows he was DVRing. Sometimes having an executive chef picking the wine could compensate for having to endure the chef's hideous taste in television. Still it beat moping in his room, reading Circle Corp's latest request for design changes. They'd probably continue to demand minute changes all the way through construction. How long would he be stuck in Detroit, and exactly when did Canton feel so much like home?

Tony came in with the bottle and two glasses. "I'm still checking out the Southern Hemisphere. It's a Syrah-Bonardo from Argentina. Pretty good for what we're paying per case, which is about what a bottle of an Italian Pinot Noir costs."

Kyle didn't know much beyond Merlot and Shiraz and Pinot Noir, but the first sip was way too good for his mood. He took another. Jack didn't immediately grab the remote and start flicking through his list of shows. That probably meant talking. If it also meant more of the wine that tasted like he'd always thought summer should, he could deal with talking. But Jack didn't say anything, he just refilled Kyle's glass.

"Definitely order another case or four." Kyle toasted Jack.

"At seven dollars a glass, the owner's going to love me." Jack clinked glasses with him.

When Jack swung his sock-covered feet up on the coffee table, Kyle figured he wouldn't be overstepping guest privileges to follow suit, back sinking into the soft suede cushions as he slouched.

"Thank God you can appreciate wine. I get a little tired of trying to expand Tony's palate from beer."

Kyle poured his own refill, and put his feet back up, staring as he flexed his toes in his socks.

"Tony was right. You're a total lightweight," Jack said.

Kyle wasn't really buzzed, just looking for a distraction, but a man had to defend his honor. "I couldn't eat anything." And then he realized how pathetic he sounded.

"You want me to fix you something?"

"Nah, it might mess with the wine."

"I think I can figure out something to go with the wine. I'm a professional, after all." Jack went off to the kitchen and came back with a bag he tossed onto Kyle's lap.

"Doritos? You're all class, Jack."

"Tony's influence knows no limit." Jack sighed. "It's going to break his heart."

"That you found his stash of Doritos?"

"Yeah. That's absolutely the tragedy of the year," Jack said in a voice as dry as the white wine he'd poured for them last night. He let Kyle get through another glass of the summery-tasting red before asking, "What happened?"

"Fuck if I know."

"All right, then."

Kyle had known Jack about three years—through work—and never well until he hooked up with Tony. He hadn't even thought Tony and Jack would like each other, let alone end up moving in together, considering Jack was Brie and Syrah-whatever-the-fuck-this-wine-was and Tony was beer and chips all the way. But Sean had said he was sick of Tony's pointed comments about Sean and Kyle being joined at the hip and decided to fix them up. At their Fourth of July party, Sean had said, "Just watch." And damn if the asshole hadn't been right. Again.

Jack was hot—not that Tony wasn't—but they were so different. Kyle remembered Tony begging him to fix things with Sean because of Jack. Tony didn't have anything to worry about. Kyle had been around enough now to see Jack's eyes whenever he even thought about Tony. And suddenly he wanted to try to explain, maybe he'd even convince himself that he was doing the right thing.

"What's your favorite food?"

"You are seriously trashed, man."

Kyle waved that off. "So?"

"Okay, random. Uh, chocolate. Dark chocolate."

"So what if you found the best dark chocolate in the world, and it was so good and then they just stopped making it. And you could only get, what the hell is that shit, the substitute stuff for allergic people?"

"Carob? Kyle, you are so cut off. Do not hurl on my couch." Jack moved the bottle down to his end of the coffee table.

Didn't matter. Wasn't even a glassful left in it.

"Right. What if you could only get carob? Wouldn't you rather not eat it at all?"

Jack stared at him for awhile then scratched along his jaw. "I don't know. Carob might be better than nothing."

"Even after that really good dark chocolate?"

"Okay. You need to go to bed."

"Gonna tuck me in?"

"Save your drunk passes for my boyfriend. He's used to it. Can you walk?"

Kyle stood up. Everything was perfectly level. He wasn't even drunk. Just talkative. If he could just keep talking, maybe he'd talk himself back into somewhere where he got dark chocolate all the time. Or in his case, dulce de leche over ice cream. Or just off a spoon. Or on Sean's lips. Or—

"Stop." Jack's hand came over his mouth. It smelled like Doritos.

Had he said all that out loud?

"Yes. Christ on a cracker, you're a lightweight."

Kyle could see the perfect image of the glowing radiant risen Christ, standing on a saltine.

Jack's hand shifted from his mouth to his shoulder. "Okay." He pushed Kyle back onto the couch. "Sleep here. But if you puke, you clean it."

The suede was silky against his cheek, then Jack was lifting his head and shoving a blanket under it. The blanket was soft too. And fuzzy. And then Jack did pat his head. Lifted up his hair and let it drop. "I think I'd have to settle for carob. Sorry, Kyle."

ß

Kyle woke up with an infomercial stabbing him in the eye: Dance Hits of the Seventies. Exactly when had he died and gone to hell? He covered his eyes with his hands and rolled onto his back only to discover that in hell, your mouth gets stuffed with sand. He managed to get to some sort of a seated position and hell became the couch in Jack and Tony's TV room.

He crawled to his feet and made it to the kitchen where the stainless steel fridge dispensed antidotes to summery wine in the form of ice water.

"Aspirin's in the cabinet over the sink."

Kyle's heart tried to punch a hole through his chest.

"Jesus fuck." He made the sign of the cross in a whispered apology before turning to see Tony sitting in the breakfast nook, a little bluish in the light from the plasma TV. Kyle didn't know why he was surprised that Tony tapped a hand on the counter in time with the random riffs from Dance Hits of the Seventies as he slurped cereal from a bowl. But Kyle couldn't figure out how he hadn't heard him while he was getting water.

The adrenalin had pushed the headache back to bearable, but Kyle dug out some aspirin and took the stool next to Tony.

The smell of smoke on his clothes and hair made Kyle want to shift his suffering back to the couch.

"You don't smell too good either, dude."

"Sorry."

"Saw the boxes. Talked to Jack."

There wasn't much to say to that. And then there was, and it didn't come out of a bottle of red wine, and God knew how much Kyle had tried not to dump this on their friends, but suddenly he was pleading, "I tried, Tony, I really did. He's just so..."

"Sean?"

"Yeah." Kyle lowered his head onto his forearms. The crunching and slurping and the Dance Hits of the Seventies were still entirely too audible, but his head felt better.

It was that same insufferable rightness about Sean that had made Kyle fall in love with him. Sean had been so sure they could make it work. So sure that it overwhelmed every doubt Kyle had. And he'd never regretted giving in, letting that feeling finally make him feel safe. He loved to bitch about Sean being bossy, but he'd always admired Sean for not worrying over every single stupid decision.

"And isn't that what we love about him?" Tony said around

another mouthful. Kyle was glad he couldn't see anything but the marble countertop, because he was pretty sure as much cereal was falling back out of Tony's mouth as was going in. And when the fuck did Tony become telepathic?

"I don't hate him. It's not all his fault."

"Isn't that big of you?"

"All right. I'm so fucking pissed at him I could have thrown a punch, but I fucked up too. Shit. It was always so easy before."

"Sean does that."

"Yes, he does. I just..." And he might have kept from puking on the couch, but he couldn't seem to stop his sudden diarrhea of the mouth. "I can't see how we can ever get that back. As long as he keeps— I'm worried about him. He needs something and I swear I tried, but he won't fucking let me." The slurping stopped. "He—he gets headaches and nightmares and won't sleep. Maybe he'll let you. He fucking let Brandt help more than me."

"PR guy? You told me Sean didn't fuck around."

"He said he didn't. I believe him."

"Damn, PR dude is a fine piece of ass, man."

"Thanks a lot."

"C'mon, Kyle. You know me."

"I do. And it's something which I hope is working off some of my time in purgatory. You'll keep an eye on him?"

"Always do."

A week later, most of Kyle's life was in storage. His drafting table, a luggage set worth of clothes and a case of Argentinean Syrah-Bonardo—which Jack had given Kyle after he swore on his dick to drink it a glass at a time—were tucked into his Camry, heading west on the turnpike.

Chapter Nineteen

Sean had become fairly familiar with a variety of teleprompters, but the ones at the GLAAD awards were really cool. The words practically floated in the air, but didn't get in the way of the audience. He was just a guest presenter, but he got to give the award to a nice, supposedly straight actor for his role playing a gay character on TV. The guy gave Sean a one-armed hug and ad-libbed a quick bit about Sean's bravery, and after talking to him backstage, Sean decided that the actor was about as straight as a corkscrew. He tried to get Brandt's attention to see if he knew any good gossip, but Brandt spent most of the night on the phone, growing progressively more animated by the minute.

On the cab ride back to LaGuardia, Brandt said he was flying down to D.C. instead. The grin on his face was maniacal. "Don't forget to tape all the morning news shows on Monday."

"Why?"

"Let's just say someone from a very red state has decided to come out before he's dragged out, and based on my work with such a fine example of an American hero—that would be you—he wants me to handle the press for it." Brandt pulled Sean over to murmur in his ear. "A fucking U.S. Senator, Sean. This is the big dance."

"Which—"

"Have to wait until Monday. I owe it all to you, Sean."

Brandt's hand moved from Sean's shoulder to his face. Sean glanced up to catch the cabbie's eyes in the mirror, but they reflected more boredom than disgust. Too late anyway, he'd already let Brandt slide in close enough, and then Brandt was kissing him. And it felt good. Mouth open just enough for a first kiss, but lips moving, breath sweet with some kind of mint. Slow build of warmth in his gut, spreading down. Sean cupped his hand around the back of Brandt's neck. It wasn't cheating anymore, after all.

Brandt's lips were slick and soft. Despite having shaved before the award show, Brandt's jaw scraped against Sean's with a hint of fast-growing stubble. Sean changed the angle of his head and Brandt followed him, opening his mouth to Sean's tongue. Brandt's breaths came faster, deeper, the sound much harsher than Kyle would make. Sean dragged his mind back to the guy currently sliding a hand along the inside of Sean's thigh. He wasn't going to spend the rest of his life comparing guys to Kyle. A hot mouth and a hand inching toward his dick deserved his full attention.

Brandt moved his mouth to Sean's jaw and then to his neck and that got every bit of his now highly focused attention. "Been wantin' to do that since I met you." A low rough chuckle teased skin wet from Brandt's tongue. "Well, that and get your dick in my mouth."

Sean's suspicions about Brandt and his "Hey there" greetings had been correct. Pure Kentucky twang dragged extra syllables into every word. The vinyl seat creaked under them as Brandt shifted. Sean shot another glance at the cabbie. The guy was rolling his eyes and futzing with his radio. They went into a tunnel, and the cabbie gave an emphatic sigh.

The yellow bulbs in the tunnel splashed enough light to take Brandt's eyes from just a dark glitter back to their usual green, with the same I-got-you-figured assessing stare. His full lips twisted in a half-smile and his lids dropped halfway down as he gave a tiny shake of his head.

He pulled at Sean's shirt to drag him back close enough to murmur again in that almost musically accented scratchy voice. In addition to politics, Brandt could have done just fine in Nashville. "Shame you still ain't completely available." Brandt's fingers grazed Sean's balls, provoking a quick suck of air. "Still woulda blown you in a stall at the airport." His thumb ripped a line up Sean's cock. "Even gettin' half of you seems like a pretty good deal. But shit-damn, I've gotta get out at the Delta terminal." He raised his voice enough to get the cabbie's attention before he sat back in his corner.

Sean looked out of the windows. They were coming up on the airport now, traffic flowing fast this late at night.

As the cab stopped, Brandt handed the driver enough money for the full fare and tip. "Get your head sorted, Sean. Anything else comes up, you gimme a call."

ß

The farther west you went, Kyle decided, the crazier people got, because the zoning board of the Detroit suburb changed their mind about parking or sewage or drainage approximately once a week. Kyle would have thought they'd be happy about having a huge source of tax income parked in the middle of their county. The last notice, about concerns over traffic control at the entrance, the idiot head contractor gleefully passed onto Kyle at six o'clock on the first Friday in April.

An idiot in the black golf shirt with Piranello Contracting's logo embroidered on the right breast, smirking as he handed over the email printout. The idiot was also the youngest Piranello son, and just the sight of Kyle seemed to piss him off. Piranello the Youngest thought Kyle had been forced on him as a babysitter, and half the time Kyle thought the brat needed one. One entire holiday-free month on site, and they'd barely broken ground.

Kyle met the Piranello brat's smirk with a bored expression and took the email. The kid muttered, "See ya Monday," ending with a cough that sounded like an all-too-familiar two-syllable insult that started with an *f*, ended with a *t* and had *a-g-g-o* in the middle of it. Last week it had been "spic." Kyle looked forward to a week of "cocksucker" so he could respond with "In your dreams."

Extra work didn't really matter, since he didn't have much of a life beyond the muddy field and the Residence Inn. As he left the trailer at the site, he checked his cell. He'd had it on vibrate because his sister Sophie had taken to calling him every day to find out if he needed anything or if he'd given any more thought to moving home. He suspected she was looking for a convenient babysitter for her hell spawn. Compared to dealing with Piranello the Youngest, watching Ricky would be paradise. At first he'd wondered how she knew what had happened, but then realized she must have called the house.

He had two missed calls from a number he didn't recognize beyond the Canton/Akron area code, but no messages. For the first two weeks, he had entertained fantasies of Sean showing up, or at least calling. Now any fantasy involving Sean—at least the ones Kyle controlled consciously—had to do with enumerating every single one of Sean's faults to his face, with explicit detail and diagrams, possibly on a PowerPoint presentation.

Tony called almost every day, usually from the bar, with news for "Exile Island." Tony's idea of news was usually a dirty joke or whatever else rolled through his head. As screwed up as life had become, at least Kyle seemed to have acquired a good friend. Tony also sent daily emails with links to videos—either porn or of someone getting hurt in a spectacularly humiliating way. One day there was a link to the local newspaper and an article about how in September, McKinley High School's gym would be renamed the Sean Farnham Athletic Center. In the email, Tony typed an elaborate emoticon of an eye-roll. Kyle's laugh only lasted a breath.

Brandt had definitely been busy. Sean must be in heaven.

Kyle shut down his computer before he could start to wonder what else Brandt might be busy with these days.

At ten thirty, Kyle's cell buzzed and skittered on the desk, screen showing the same unknown number. He hesitated long enough for his hand to enjoy the massage and then pushed answer.

"Kyle."

Sean. Kyle sank into the closest chair.

"How's it going?"

Seven weeks and he got *how's it going*?

"Kyle?"

It sucks. I work with assholes. I hate Michigan. Why the fuck haven't you called me? I might poison Piranello's coffee. I miss you. Why the fuck haven't you called me? But if he started telling the truth, he didn't think he'd be able to stop. "Slowly."

"Same as always, huh?"

"What's up with the new number?"

Sean sounded embarrassed. "Forgot to pay the cell bill—three months in a row. Long story."

Actually, not so long. Kyle had handled all their bills online since Sean always forgot.

"Did you lose the account password?" He'd stopped the deposits into their joint account in February, but he knew there was enough money in there to cover a couple of months.

"No, just—forgot."

The longing hit Kyle so hard it stole his breath. Sean giving him that sorry-babe look from under his lashes, pulling him down onto the couch and offering increasingly bizarre penances until Kyle just laughed and said, "I'll fix it, you idiot." He tried to think of something to keep Sean on the phone. "How's the team doing?"

"Not good. Five and three, and we've got the toughest games coming up."

"Sorry." It really hadn't been much of a conversational opener. If he were home, Sean would have launched into a whole explanation of standings and all those three-letter statistics that Kyle couldn't keep straight, but Sean would be so into it Kyle could just watch him.

"So."

Here it was. Whatever he'd been calling about.

"The school board has this safety plan thing because of the

insurance and all, so I had to go to a couple of counseling sessions."

Thank God for safety plans. "Uh-huh." He had the feeling Sean wouldn't be too happy if he said, "About fucking time."

"Yeah. Gave me something to help me sleep. Haven't taken it yet."

Kyle wasn't surprised by Sean not taking the pills, only by the fact that Sean had even mentioned sleeping problems.

"So listen, the guy said that you and I had some unresolved issues and that I should probably call and resolve them."

Since they'd broken up, Kyle's hold on his temper wasn't what it used to be. "Wait. You called me because your *therapist* thinks you should resolve some issues with me. Well, this should take care of that for you." He turned the phone so that he could speak directly into the microphone. "Fuck. You."

And for the first time in his life, he deliberately hung up on someone. He turned off the phone—which had once again narrowly escaped being flung at yet another hotel room wall, maybe they could name a gym after it, too—and stuffed it in the bottom of his briefcase.

ß

Sean repeated the time and date and thanked the young paralegal before easing the phone back into its cradle. Motherfuckingcocksuc—nope. There wasn't anything in his repertoire equal to a situation this fucked.

He'd thought driving on I-90 had given him a curse for every occasion. But then he'd never been through a lawsuit before. Everyone he talked to, which lately seemed to consist of an ever-increasing number of union reps, paralegals and lawyers, demonstrated supreme nonchalance about the prospect of everything Sean had being put up stuffed into a piñata ready to spill on a wild swing from blind justice. Communication with union reps and lawyers progressed from phone calls and paper mail to physical meetings.

Although Vince Gerbino had settled for a hefty settlement from the school district, in the words of Sean's lawyer, Bonnie, he "continued to express a desire to mulct Sean personally for damages." What the hell kind of word was mulct? It sounded like something you scraped off your shoe. No wonder everyone hated lawyers. He'd rather have Gerbino spitting his psychosis at him directly than hiding behind a double screen of people paid to make you sound smart and polite.

When he opened his email, the familiar address stood out on the page as if it were there alone. The last communication had been Kyle's emphatic *fuck you*, so he wasn't expecting something as casual as an email. He'd expected a letter full of words like mulct and heretofore from Kyle's old fuck buddy Daniel, but what the letter would boil down to was "Now that it's as dead as disco, who gets the house?"

No subject. He opened it. One word. In bold, screen-filling font: taxes.

Maybe the body's ability to react to shock had a limited warranty and he had far exceeded normal wear and tear in the past year. He for sure was all out of variations to describe how fucking screwed up everything was. His stomach should have squeezed tight around the dread of yet one more piece of bullshit he'd have to deal with, but the sight of that one word from Kyle made his lips try to curl into a smile to match the tiny flicker of warmth under his skin.

He picked back up the phone and played with the speed dial numbers, alternatively tapping one and eight. Choosing Brandt's voice mail over the potential of Kyle hanging up on him again, he pressed eight firmly.

He told Brandt the time and date of the trial, and said that he'd really appreciate any help Brandt could offer. Brandt's new project, the junior senator from Colorado, was still making news, now with a newly minted book deal.

On the day before the trial, Brandt finally returned his call with apologies his flat speech didn't reflect. "The senator keeps me hopping. Scheduling's really tight, but I'm sure it will go fine. There's not much I can do with it anyway. Unless someone's dead or a celeb's going to jail, people tend to sleep through courtroom stuff as soon as they see it's not going to be like *Law & Order*."

Sean had always known that Brandt was using him; Brandt had made it perfectly clear from the start that he planned to get as much if not more than Sean out of their deal. But some form of idiocy had allowed him to think that they'd actually become friends.

And friends were something Sean had in short supply when his steps echoed on the marble stairs in the Stark County Courthouse on April twenty-eighth to hear the jury's decision. Tony checked in by phone to see how things were going, but his friendship with Tony didn't feel the same as it had before. Before Tony had let Kyle stay at his house, taken Kyle's side.

Tony had dutifully offered to hang out in the courthouse and wait while the jury came in, but Sean didn't see the point in Tony being there when they wouldn't be able to talk.

Bonnie stepped forward as Sean finished climbing to the second floor and paused to lean on his cane while the muscles settled down. Sharonda, the paralegal, followed close at her shiny black heels. The position and the similarities in their dress put Sean in mind of a mother and baby duck. Sean didn't know much about women's fashions—or even men's for that matter—but he thought if style points mattered, his team would definitely win. Bonnie in a black skirt and jacket with a pink shirt underneath, Sharonda in grey and red, everything crisp lines and confidence. The sight chipped a little off the boulder of tension sitting on his diaphragm.

The first time he'd been in the courtroom, the reverberations, the heavy weight of space had reminded him of a baseball stadium. Not the Jake, more like the Sky Dome with the lid closed, but after two weeks, the place didn't awe him anymore. He'd gotten used to the stand-up sit-down rituals and repetitive language, like Christmas Eve Mass with Kyle's family, minus the incense. And he'd even gotten used to Gerbino's hate-filled glare. It wasn't the burning itch that Sean usually associated with a stare, but more like an icy snowball slamming into the back of his neck.

As they waited for the jury to file in, he remembered Sharonda's sympathetic whisper on the first day. "It's a shame really. His wife left him just after Christmas. I think he's a little..." And her eyes had flicked to the left with a quick lift of her eyebrows.

Despite knowing that the union insurance company was handling the expenses, Sean was still the one sitting in the hard wooden chair, his numb ass on the line. They relived the shooting, experts back and forth on where the shooter was standing to deliver the bullet that caused the internal bleeding that cost Nicole her life. Each day of inactivity left Sean with as many aching muscles as the first day of soccer practice after a summer of loafing.

Judge in, jury in, up and down and then they were ready. At the edge of his vision, he caught Sharonda's reassuring smile. Bonnie had insisted that such a quick decision meant they would win.

Neither the smile nor Bonnie's confidence could get his pulse under one eighty. It throbbed in his ears, in his fingertips. He wiped his hands on his slacks as they stood for the decision.

The jury forewoman spoke. "We find for the respondent."

Bonnie was shaking his hand before Sean really processed the words. He was the respondent. So that meant he won. And all of it was over.

He shook Bonnie's hand and then Sharonda's, fighting the urge to just collapse back into the chair with relief.

"Filthy fucking faggot."

Sean's tenth-grade English teacher would have given Gerbino high marks for effective alliteration.

Sean turned. Gerbino's florid face was inches from his own. Gerbino shook off his lawyer's hand and his voice continued to rise above the growing murmur of concern bouncing off the wood-paneled walls.

"You're still going to pay. You took everything from me. I'll take everything from you."

The bailiff was between them now, his stern voice audible even over Gerbino's rant.

And it felt like someone cut the tendons in the back of Sean's knees. He'd experienced that knee-buckling sensation a few times in college when a high inside fastball went past his nose. But it wasn't the vitriol coming from Gerbino that had Sean gripping his cane for support. He'd been armored against heckling from Little League on. It wasn't even Gerbino's crazy eyes.

The knockdown pitch was what he realized as he heard Gerbino's last words. *I'll take everything from you.*

Everything that made Sean's life worth living was already gone. And Gerbino hadn't done it. Sean had. He'd driven it away with both hands on the wheel. It didn't matter about the house or the school or that fucking gym if Kyle wasn't there.

Another guard came up to him, and Sean was only too happy to be hustled from the courtroom. He was heading for his car and he was driving to Detroit. He was going to fix the mess he'd made.

He heard "It's not over," from Gerbino as he cleared the doors.

He wondered if that level of obsession was the way he'd looked to Kyle. To Tony. That he'd let one Tuesday in October control every single aspect of his life.

He thanked Bonnie again in the hall, and accepted a hug from Sharonda who thanked him for saving her cousin who had been in the hall next to Nicole. Sean hadn't known until that moment, but he didn't want to stay and rehash it. He just wanted to get to Detroit.

He took the steps as quickly as his leg would allow, zipped past the security guards on the doors and out into the April sunshine. He started down the courthouse steps and stopped, staring.

A dark green Camry turned the corner from Central onto Tuscarawas. He couldn't see the license plate but he knew it was Kyle. He'd been there. For Sean. And it was all far from over.

Chapter Twenty

Sean climbed back up the steps, but the car was gone. He fished his phone out and hit the speed dial for Tony.

"How'd it go, buddy?"

"Where is he?"

"What?"

"Did he stay with you last night?"

"Who?"

"Kyle."

"No. What the fuck's going on? I thought you were calling about the case, man."

"Oh. It's fine. It's all set. But did you know Kyle was coming?"

"No. Fucker should have come by and said hi. That's gratitude for you. If you find him, tell him to stop over so I don't have to pay to send his mail out there."

Sean had wondered where all Kyle's mail was. "He's not here."

"Dude. Sure you're okay? Because you're not really making sense. Did you wander over to drug court and get a contact high?"

Sean forced himself to take a deep breath and started back down the steps. "I won the case. I came outside and saw Kyle's car, but he drove off. So where is he?"

"As far as I know he's in Detroit. Or some shit suburb. South Lyon, like the football team, I guess. Residence Inn in

South Lyon."

"Thanks." Kyle must have left around five in the morning to get here. And if he wasn't staying with Tony, he was looking at eight hours round trip. That was pretty far from a *Fuck you.*

"So what are you going to do now?"

"I'm going to go out there and drag his ass home."

"Really? Any ideas about how that's going to go down?"

Sean hadn't really gotten that far, and fuck Tony for asking. "On the basis of all these years of friendship and how much you claim to love me, could you do me one simple favor?"

"Maybe."

"Don't call him and tell him I'm coming, okay?"

"'Fraid he won't be there?"

Actually, he was. He really hoped that a four-hour drive would give him time to work out what he was going to say. It'd be pretty anticlimactic to get there and learn that Kyle had gone into the city or whatever. He reached the sidewalk and peered down in the direction of the parking lot. "Can you just do that?"

"Not call? Okay. But try not to fuck this up. I hate watching soap operas."

"Because *Big Brother* is such superior entertainment."

He was going to hang up anyway. So when the screams started and he dropped the phone onto the cement, it accomplished the same thing.

"You can't get away with this. I can't let you. You killed my daughter." Gerbino stood in front of Sean. The guy's hand looked weird until Sean realized Gerbino was holding a gun.

And he was back there. Back to October. Dizzy adrenalin rush and the high-tight hammer of his heart.

This was nothing like that run down the hallway. That had been a blur. He had only flashes of memory from the time he started to run to the time he realized it was over.

But now, time froze.

There were ten seconds between each thick pulse in his throat, it took minutes for Gerbino to drag up his shaking hand

and point the gun at Sean, and in that hour as Sean stood and studied exactly how big the hole on the end of a pistol was when it was pointed at him, he had forever to consider what he was going to do.

No one else's life was at stake. Gerbino was aiming only at Sean. Every nerve screamed at him to move, but if he did, the people on the sidewalk around him, people who'd only been wallpaper a second ago, any of those people might die. There was a cop behind Gerbino. The cop would reach him in an instant, even though Sean couldn't seem to take his eyes away from the vibrating bore of that pistol. But an instant was all it took to squeeze a trigger and no matter how much Gerbino's hand shook, from a distance of four feet he was unlikely to miss. There was nothing to do but wait to feel the burn of a bullet spin into him.

Again.

Though maybe this time, he wouldn't be feeling it for long.

By the time the sound of the shot hit his ears, Sean knew he hadn't been hit. The cop had Gerbino's arm and the shot went up, a distant ping as it caught the marble overhang on the courthouse.

ß

Kyle knew Sean hadn't seen him slip into the back of the courtroom, and that was just the way Kyle wanted it. He still wasn't sure exactly what he thought he was doing here. Sean certainly hadn't asked him to come, and from the way Sean had acted before Kyle left, he doubted Sean would even want him here, no matter what decision the jury made.

When it was the right one, Kyle went back out to his car, feeling like an idiot. So maybe a part of him had thought Sean would feel him there, like that moment when Cary Grant knows Irene Dunne is there in that hotel at the beginning of *My Favorite Wife*. Life wasn't a movie, but Kyle had always felt that connection.

For Sean, it wasn't there anymore.

He thought about stopping over at Jack and Tony's on the way out of town, but they were in the opposite direction, and he knew the trip back to Detroit would feel that much longer if he didn't start right away.

As he merged onto Interstate 77, the local radio station had breaking news from the courthouse. Everyone was going to learn that their hero had been exonerated. Kyle didn't need to hear Sean's familiar speech about tolerance and safety—again, picture Brandt just behind him as he delivered it—again. Before the announcer could share his breaking news, Kyle switched the radio over to his I-Pod.

His current playlist—he could hear Sean labeling it "Emo Crap to Mope By"—took him all the way to the Michigan border.

Kyle went back into work, mostly to annoy Piranello the Youngest, but the long day caught up to him fast. Kyle's vision blurred with fatigue as he pulled into the Residence Inn lot, but it still picked out a dark blue Durango near the entrance. His stomach lurched every time he saw one, so he tried not to spend too much time roaming suburbia. He wondered how long that reaction would last.

The tie went as he slid the card into the key slot, the jacket as soon as he closed the door. A hot shower and then oblivion on the pillow-topped mattress, he promised himself as he unbuttoned his collar. But he'd only managed to put his briefcase next to the desk when there was a knock on his door.

Kyle didn't know why he opened the door without checking through the peephole. But he did and there was Sean.

The stomach-lurch at the sight of the Durango was nothing compared to the yo-yoing of his digestive organs now.

Sean moved as if to step across the threshold and then asked, "Can I come in?"

Kyle stepped aside. He swallowed, forcing his stomach back down in place with a load of spit. Sean was here. In room 118 of the Residence Inn. And it wasn't a dream, because Sean would have him bent over the back of the couch already if it was.

"I'd have been here sooner, but—" He shrugged and Kyle wondered if he was supposed to know what that meant.

Somehow he lojacked his voice and got it back in his throat. "Why? I mean—why are you here?" His eyes kept tracing the man in that wrinkled suit, tie long gone, the same one he'd worn to court.

Sean laughed, a quick cough of one, and looked around the room. His gaze fell on Kyle's drafting table.

Shit. Kyle couldn't very well leap across the room and fling himself over the blueprint.

Sean walked over and put a hand on the top of the board. "The beach house?"

Kyle bit his lip. "Yes."

"Our beach house?"

That didn't deserve an answer.

"Why did you keep it? Why are you still working on it?"

"I spent a lot of time on it."

Sean was coming back toward him, and as spacious as the two rooms of a Residence Inn were, it wasn't as if Kyle could hide behind the beige drapes.

"You could have ripped it up." Sean was right in front of him.

Kyle had started to half a dozen times, picturing the way it would feel coming apart in his hands. "Maybe I was going to sell it. It's a good design."

"Except for the outdoor shower."

The smile burst on Kyle's face before he could stop it. "Especially the outdoor shower."

Sean reached for him, hand sliding on the back of Kyle's neck. Kyle leaned back and watched Sean's eyes, pupils wide even in the lamplight, so wide there was only a thin dark ring of color. The way his eyes looked when Kyle was inside him. The way Sean had looked when he'd asked him to move in. The way he looked when he'd begged Kyle to get him out of the hospital.

"Kyle."

Sean pulled and Kyle started to go, felt himself slide back into the safety of Sean. The safety that had disappeared when Sean decided being a hero was more important than loving Kyle. He pulled back. Sean's hand dropped.

"I can't."

"Can't kiss me?"

"Just can't."

Sean stepped away and then turned back to face him. "You were there today."

Kyle felt like he'd been called on in Sean's class and he didn't know the right answer. He'd never expected that.

"Why?" Sean said when Kyle didn't say anything.

This was what it had been like in the beginning, Sean closing off every avenue of escape, forcing Kyle to believe in their future. It was the Sean he had missed. But as the breaking news from the courthouse clearly indicated, Sean still had other priorities.

"I felt like a drive."

And then it exploded, weeks of wondering if he was ever going to feel better, those fears and doubts rushing up his throat, and Kyle was yelling. "You don't get to do this again. You don't get to make me feel like this again. I can't."

Sean rolled his lips inside his teeth, and sat on the couch, cane between his knees. "I fucked up. I know that."

"Can I get the number of this therapist?"

"Don't. Please, Kyle. I'm really trying."

He was. And it was scary. This wasn't the Sean Kyle was used to, always sure of the outcome. Sean twirled the cane before he spoke again.

"I did lie to you."

Kyle sat next to him.

"Not about Brandt," Sean said quickly.

"I know that." And Kyle did. Sean wouldn't have done that.

"I lied every time I said I was fine. I wasn't. I haven't been since—since I got shot. And I don't just mean the nightmares and the headaches." He stopped twirling the cane.

Kyle shifted to face him.

"I kept thinking that I didn't do enough. Survivor's guilt or whatever they call it. But whatever it was I let it become the most important thing in my life. And that's where I fucked up."

Kyle's eyes burned. He couldn't say anything. Watching Sean like this was as painful as watching him in the hospital, but then Kyle'd known Sean would heal. Sean talking like this made Kyle want to do anything to shut him up.

"I don't want us to be over. And whatever that takes, if you still want to sell the house, move to Ontario, or Delaware, or wherever, I can do that. If you want me to talk to someone about the not-sleeping, I will." Sean swallowed so hard Kyle could watch it bob through his throat, almost see the shape of it in his chest.

The air in the room was too hot and dry to breathe. It burned inside Kyle's mouth as he tried to answer. "What about...?"

"The publicity? It's over. It's been over almost since you left. Brandt Sobell is now handling the PR of Paul Varoney, the junior senator from Colorado."

Kyle had seen that much of the news. Brandt must be busy.

Before Kyle could speak again, Sean said, "And the McKinley High School gym will now be named after Principal Frank Healey. I called the superintendent on my way over out here." Sean reached for him again, hand hovering before he let it drop back in his own lap. "I want my life back, Kyle. But I don't want mine to be without you."

"I can't promise I won't default to Defcon One all the time."

"You don't have to. I never needed you to change."

"I didn't ask you to either."

"I know."

"I guess we just had it too easy."

"Well, now we know. I don't think most people have to go

through a shooting. If we can handle this, we can handle anything."

Kyle wished he could remember their first kiss all those years ago. But drunk and in a dark corner of some party, he really couldn't remember anything except that from the first touch of Sean's lips he'd wanted more.

He was going to remember this one. Especially when he'd come so close to never having it again, never feeling the way Sean kissed him, holding Kyle's head in his hands as he swept into his mouth. Going to remember the way Sean's breath felt and tasted. A cold drink when you're dying of thirst, and you didn't know how desperate you were until the water hit your lips. Waking too early on a Saturday and knowing you can roll back under the covers, when all that warmth is all for you.

Sean kissed him full of the promise of better and better.

The groan ripped through Kyle's throat and into Sean's mouth. The kiss went from feeding a craving to starving it. Kyle needed every inch of their bodies together. Needed Sean to make that promise on his body. He pushed Sean's jacket off his shoulders and was pulling up his shirt while Sean's arms were still stuck in the sleeves.

Kyle didn't care as long as his fingers were finding skin. Warm skin. Sean's skin. He dropped down to lick at the patch of skin he'd exposed above Sean's belt. His hands shook as he worked the belt free, and then Sean's hands were there to help him.

"Hey. This place has a bed, right?" Sean asked.

"Yes it does. Pillow-top mattress, down pillows—"

"You had me at *uhn.*" Sean slid a hand over Kyle's thigh.

Kyle's phone went off.

"Since when do you have Poison as a ring tone?"

"It's Tony's."

"He has a special ring tone on your phone? And it's 'Talk Dirty To Me'?" Sean's voice cracked into a high register.

"I was bored."

Kyle rolled over the back of the couch and dug into his

briefcase.

"Do you really want to get that?" Sean asked.

"Just give me a second. You know how he is. He'll keep calling."

"I think it's time Jack and I worried about you two. Here let me show you how to put your phone on vibrate. You'll like it. Especially when it's in your pocket." Sean leered and reached over the couch for the phone in Kyle's hand.

Kyle swung out of reach and flipped the phone open. "Tony, can I call you back—"

"Is he there? Jesus fucking Christ. I've been freaking out." Tony was so loud Kyle had to move the receiver away from his ear.

"He's here."

"Oh thank God. The courthouse shooting was all over the news and he wasn't answering his cell and the cops wouldn't tell me anything."

Kyle's head filled with snowy white static.

"I hope they lock that bastard up for life. It's fucking Ohio not the Bronx. What the hell is in the water—" Tony's rant might have continued, but Kyle dropped the phone on the couch.

"I think it's for you."

Kyle walked over to the window and pressed his forehead against the cold glass. It quieted the static a little. Almost sunset, but still light enough outside to make his reflection faint.

Behind him he heard Sean say, "Remind me to cut off your balls with a rusty knife when I get home."

Then, "I'm fine. The cop was right there. Paperwork is done... No bail until a psychiatric evaluation... Look. I've got something more important than your drama-queen freak out to deal with. I'll be there with my knife tomorrow."

Sean came up behind him. Kyle didn't move as Sean wrapped his arms around his waist.

"Defcon One?" Sean asked.

"We have assumed crash positions. Gerbino?"

"He didn't like the decision. Came after me on the sidewalk out front."

"Were you ever going to tell me?"

Sean turned Kyle around to face him. "Absolutely. But it wasn't part of what I came here to say to you. So it didn't matter right now."

"You were shot at again." The cold from the window was starting to make him shiver.

"And I'm fine. Nothing broken. No holes. And I didn't tackle anyone or try to be a hero. I let the cop take care of it. It's over."

"I wish."

"Listen. I meant what I said. We'll sell the house. We'll move. I'll change my name."

"No. You don't have to run. And don't you dare quote *Casablanca* at me."

"I don't care how many times you run, I'll always come after you." Sean leaned down to press his forehead against Kyle's.

"I still want you to." Kyle wrapped his arms around Sean's waist. "We're both going to talk to that therapist."

"I have to anyway. One more mandated visit."

"So, if I were to run to the bedroom?"

"I'd come after you."

They couldn't wait. No slow kissing as they undressed each other, just clothes off and mouths fused as they hit the bed.

It had been so long, but the distance disappeared in the familiar scent of Sean's skin, in the taste of his mouth. They could take it slow and pretty tomorrow. Or later tonight. For now, "Need you. Fuck me, *chulo.*"

"Lube?"

"Drawer."

Sean reached in and came back with a half-empty bottle of Astroglide and a box of condoms. "Okay." He rolled on his side and put the box between them. His tone was as careful as it was in his interviews. "Not assuming. Talking. Asking. And it's okay. I don't care."

Kyle held the box so Sean could see it wasn't opened. "I planned to. I really did. I was going to fuck you right out of my head. But no. Not Daniel. Not anyone but my own right hand."

Sean bit his lip. "I lied again. I really did care. When Daniel answered that phone I wanted to fly to Cleveland and punch you both out."

Sean's jealousy gave Kyle the courage to ask. He held the box in front of Sean's face. "Brandt?"

Sean's eyes flickered left. Kyle couldn't breathe. Taking the box from Kyle's loose grip, Sean cupped his chin. "No. Kyle. Not like that. I'm not going to lie. Almost, okay? But no."

Sean kissed him again, and all that fear melted back into *yes, now, please.* They hadn't broken it too much. As much as Kyle wanted to believe he could forgive Sean if he'd slept with Brandt, he didn't know. Sean traced his spine with his fingers, and Kyle arched against him.

A press of Sean's hand turned Kyle face down into the mattress. He wanted to protest because he needed to see Sean's face when he slid home inside, but Sean was already pressing a finger into his ass, and Kyle was up on his knees to rock back into the sensation.

"I know what you want, babe."

"Now." Kyle didn't care that it had been months. He wanted it to burn. It should. Should be like a first time again.

Sean pressed the head of his cock against Kyle, but he didn't push in. He dragged Kyle's hand back, wrapping his fingers around Sean's dick.

"You do it. Put me inside you."

Sean's word pumped heat down Kyle's cock until the tip leaked. The silky heat under his fingers pulsed as he took a tighter grip. They went together, Kyle holding Sean back as he adjusted to that first tearing stretch. Kyle arched his back and dragged Sean forward, and just when he thought it was too much, his body opened and Sean sank all the way in. Kyle took his hand away, but Sean didn't move.

"C'mon," Kyle begged.

He felt Sean's smile against his shoulder as Sean scooped him up, lifting Kyle to drag him into his lap. Kyle's thighs dropped open over Sean's. He loved getting fucked like this. Flying, nothing keeping him grounded but Sean's cock in his ass and those strong arms on his chest.

And then he remembered why they couldn't fuck like this.

"Your leg."

"Hurts. But I feel so good holding you like this. I need to be able to touch you all over." Sean ran his hands down Kyle's chest, tongue wetting the back of his neck.

"I don't—"

"I promise you can play doctor after. Rub it all you want."

"That your fantasy?" Kyle ground the words out. Pressure was building inside him. If Sean didn't move soon, he'd have to do it himself.

"We can talk about that after I take a ruler to your ass with you bent over my desk."

Kyle's ass clenched as the image hit his brain, and Sean groaned.

"Okay."

Sean started moving. Hands, mouth, cock. Touching Kyle everywhere. Kyle's head dropped back onto Sean's shoulder and rode the waves pumping heat from inside his ass to his dick. Sean's fingers pinched hard on both nipples as he started driving hard.

Kyle didn't care if this was a blink-and-you-miss-it round. He'd make it up to Sean. "Gonna come." He fisted his dick.

"Do it." Sean held him tight as he slammed them together, his teeth and mouth on the back of Kyle's neck.

Kyle shut his eyes as it broke loose inside him, pounding hard in his chest and throat and behind his lids until it poured out through his dick, body clamping down around Sean over and over until Sean bit harder and came.

When the phone woke them up, the rest of the lube was gone and Kyle's watch said it was ten o'clock. Sean held onto Kyle's waist as Kyle leaned over to pick up the phone. Probably that little prick Piranello.

"Kyle?" He might have recognized the voice if he weren't so fucked out and uninterested in anything but Sean's mouth on his shoulder.

"Yes?"

"It's Brandt."

He must have tensed because Sean lifted his head. "What?" he whispered.

Kyle covered the receiver. "Brandt."

Sean held out his hand, but Kyle shook his head. Smiling, Sean rolled away.

"Yes?" Kyle said into the phone.

"I'm really sorry to bother you, but I haven't been able to find Sean anywhere. After what happened yesterday, I've been worried."

"Really?"

"Didn't you hear about it?"

"How did you get this number?"

"I called your firm. So do you have any idea where he might be? The school said he took an emergency leave. I'm afraid I've gotten his parents upset. And that guy Tony? He wasn't very helpful."

Kyle covered the mouthpiece again. "You didn't call your mother?"

"I was busy."

"You are in such deep shit."

Kyle got back on the phone. "What did you need him for?"

"I really need to talk to him. If you have any idea where he might have gone..."

"Oh I do. At the moment, he's sucking my cock."

Sean burst out laughing behind him. Kyle flopped back down next to him. He couldn't hear Brandt's answer over the laughing.

Kyle sighed. “Well, that was a mood-killer. *Para ti, papi chulo.*”

Sean took the phone and put it between them on the pillow.

Kyle listened to Brandt’s, “When—I thought—I’m sorry,” sputters.

“So what did you need?” Sean said.

“Well, Senator Varoney feels that given recent events, he’d like a photo op with you.”

“Would he?”

Kyle was smiling. He already knew Sean’s answer.

“You know, I’m afraid that’s not going to work for me. Scheduling’s really tight.”

“The principal said you took a leave.”

“But not for that. Good luck with the senator, Brandt.”

Sean passed back the phone and Kyle hung it up.

“You really took a leave? In the middle of baseball season?”

Sean shrugged. “The therapist can write it all up.”

“I don’t want you to miss the season.”

“So when are you coming home?”

Home.

“To Canton?”

“Wherever you want.”

“Canton. I have to see what happens when Tony tells Jack he wants kids.”

“He does? What the hell? Why didn’t he tell me?” Sean sat up. “Are you making that shit up?”

Kyle pulled him back down and held Sean’s face between his hands. He needed to watch his eyes. “I love you.”

Even in the morning light, Sean’s eyes held that intent focus, wide pupil forcing the color to the edge, turning it dark blue. “And I’ll love you better.”

About the Author

K. A. Mitchell discovered the magic of writing at an early age when she learned that a carefully crayoned note of apology sent to the kitchen in a toy truck would earn her a reprieve from banishment to her room. Her career as a spin control artist was cut short when her family moved to a two-story house, and her trucks would not roll safely down the stairs. Around the same time, she decided that Chip and Ken made a much cuter couple than Ken and Barbie and was perplexed when invitations to play Barbie dropped off. An unnamed number of years later, she's happy to find other readers and writers who like to play in her world.

To learn more about K. A. Mitchell, please visit www.kamitchell.com. Send an email to K. A. Mitchell at authorKAMitchell@gmail.com.

High-powered stock trader. Simple handyman.
Can they find common ground?

Handyman

© 2008 Claire Thompson

Will Spencer is a player with a reputation for using and discarding lovers as easily as he earns big money on Wall Street. Handsome, sexy and openly gay, he's used to having whatever—and whoever—he wants at the snap of his fingers.

And what he wants now is his new handyman, Jack Crawford. But Jack is skittish. One lingering touch, one stolen kiss could send the older man into full retreat. Where Will might have quickly moved on to a more ready-and-willing partner, he unexpectedly finds himself wanting to go slow. With just a little coaxing, he's sure he can show Jack how good it could be between them.

Jack, a recent widower, never thought of himself as gay. Frightened years ago by an erotic encounter with his best friend, he focused firmly on his marriage. Now that his bed is empty, however, those deep sexual longings are rising dangerously close to the surface.

Their connection is deep, instant, and one that Jack tries to ignore. Yet friendship grows into an erotic journey that must cross a divide of different generations, backgrounds and worlds.

The prize is the one thing neither is sure he can handle—true love.

Warning: Hot, delicious male/male erotic romance. Danger: Explicit m/m sex.

LaVergne, TN USA
10 September 2009

157491LV00006B/3/P